Trevor

His Story

PUBLISHER'S NOTE

This is a work of fiction. Names, characters, places, and incidents
either are the product of the author's imagination or are used
fictitiously, and any resemblance to actual persons, living or dead,
business establishments, events, or locales is entirely coincidental.

Printed in the United States of America

ISBN-13: 978-0-98840-830-2
ISBN-10: 0-98840-830-9

Trevor

His Story

by Connie and James St. Leger

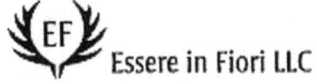

Essere in Fiori LLC

Table of Contents

Chapter 1 - Through to MacFardens..1

Chapter 2 - The Loss of my Life 11

Chapter 3 - The New Life..21

Chapter 4 - Up Island Park Way 25

Chapter 5 - Gettin' There 41

Chapter 6 - The Game...49

Chapter 7 - Another Member of the Fraternity 57

Chapter 8 - More Useless Chatter 63

Chapter 9 - Buzzy..67

Chapter 10 - My New Life Begins 73

Chapter 11 - Portage...77

Chapter 12 - And Thus We Come to the Armored Car Robbery......85

Chapter 13 - Through the Grating 93

Chapter 14 - Armored Car Guys Back to the Car 97

Chapter 15 - The Triad – A Second Encounter...........................103

Chapter 16 - Through the Grating Again......................................107

Chapter 17 - Bill and I Ponder the Armored Car Incident............113

Chapter 18 - The Broken Tooth Event............................117

Chapter 19 - The Three Investigators 123

Chapter 20 - The Ladies..127

Chapter 21 - 'Manda and Me 131

Chapter 22 - The Rope Bridge 145

Chapter 23 - A Church Project 155

Chapter 24 - An Entry..157

Chapter 25 - The Back Stairs 165

Chapter 26 - Not Us 173

Chapter 27 - The Triad – A Third Encounter...................177

Chapter 28 - That Guy O'Hara 185

Chapter 29 - Spying at the Dance 191

Chapter 30 - The Califer Housekeeper 197

Chapter 31 - A Big Boat on the Horizon 203

Chapter 32 - Old Folks..207

Chapter 33 - Stage Set..213

Chapter 34 - New Face in Town..................................223

Chapter 35 - George, The Dick, and Angel 233

Chapter 36 - More of The Dick Affair................................235

Chapter 37 - George and The Dick................................237

Chapter 38 - A Field Ripe for the Corrector................241

Chapter 39 - The Dick................................245

Chapter 40 - I Talk to Marty................................253

Chapter 41 - Mandy and Me Check the Times................263

Chapter 42 - Did It Work? 267

Chapter 43 - God's Ground Agent 271

Chapter 44 - Skip Day................................275

Chapter 45 - Did it Work or Not?................................277

Chapter 46 - The Best Forbidden Kisses in the World 291

Chapter 47 - The Lure of The Hut 295

Chapter 48 - Out and Away................................305

Chapter 49 - Over Between Us 313

Chapter 50 - The Investigation's Aftermath................315

Chapter 51 - The Provocateur 321

Chapter 52 - To Get Things to Jell................................323

Chapter 53 - She Needed Me 327

Chapter 54 - Town's Gettin' Worked Up..335

Chapter 55 - The Girl from Frisco 337

Chapter 56 - Thus it Goes...357

Chapter 57 - B&B 375

Chapter 1
Through to MacFardens

"My God that's good coffee."

"So what's you come over here for? Just saw you last weekend at the dance. What's up?"

"Guess I'm looking for advice."

Barnaby looked at me a moment and snickered. "Took a long enough to get here. I been watching you and Betty for a good while now, and wondering how long you'd be able to stick together. I'm not surprised. By the way, advice used to be free. Now I charge."

My turn to snicker. "That obvious, huh? Wish you'd said something."

"Ah can't tell some man in love ta knock it off. You know that. So yer really breaking up?"

I nodded. "Not much choice I guess. She's already got another man lined-up."

Barnaby tilted his head. "Yep. That's the way it goes. You know who it is?"

"Pretty much. I got suspicious so been keeping my eyes open."

"Trevor, you jerk. You mean you been out spying on her."

I nodded.

"So?" Then he interrupted himself. "Come on. Come with me. I told Bill and Angelica that I'd give 'em a hand cleaning up the old barn. Why don't you come with me, we can talk on the way. It's about an hour's drive so we'll straighten you right out 'fore we get there. Come on." And he was up, putting his coffee cup in the sink and standing at the door, gesturing. He yelled his intentions out the door to his live-at-home-oldest-daughter working in her garden, gestured again to me to come along and we were off.

The road ran a goodly distance alongside a great field of short, scrawny grass and a few seeding-in white pines. The big field, bordered by a ridiculous, worn-out, scrawny hedge row with a deep ditch roadside, ran on and on till it petered out to a solid bit of ground which was the way in. So what do we see? Way off, at the far end, there seemed to be a column of low smoke hanging in the sky. Turned out to be a grass fire, not burning well, the rain last night must-a damped down the growth enough. A fire struggling to get a healthy start. A car drove off as we approached, suspicious, but the fire was more important right then and we stopped. Barnaby had a couple of old brooms rattling in the back of the pick-up. He shoved one in my hands and said, "You know what to do."

"Yeah, well sort of," he watched the low flames mostly burning in one place reluctant to get on with the business of burning up the world.

"We'll sweep any tinder back onto the flames. They ain't too big. Go along this edge and sweep the fire back on itself. With no tinder it'll probably die out, but keep yer eye on it. Go back if ya have to, sweep back so there's nothing to burn. Don't burn up my broom. I'll get down to the other end. Ain't no wind. We might be able to work it back and cut its progress. Save the MacFarden's woods. Angelica will be here, she watches for fires. Her hired man'll come too, probably. We'll stop this fire 'fore it gets to them trees. If the wind comes up, well we'll do our best. Sorry. Ain't much of a greeting to ya, but we'll talk more when we get this done. Gotta get over t'other side. Stay behind it if it gets bigger. Brush it in on itself."

There was a whoosh, and both turned to see one of the young pines totally in fire. The low stuff had ignited it, just a young tree getting started in the field and the low flames got to it. Now gone like a torch.

Barney was gone, his pick-up rushing toward the other side of the fire, probably as big as a city block by now and spending all its energy trying to get a good start. I wondered about that car that had gone off when we came. Might be arsonists. How else would one of these get started? And why a fire? And why on MacFarden's land?

Basically it took the rest of the afternoon but we squeezed the fire in toward itself and finally looked at each other and nodded. "Well, it's over."

"Wonder why it started?"

"What about that car that sped off when we got here?"

"Could be, but why set this field on fire? For what purpose is a scrub fire?"

"Make trouble for someone? Maybe distract us from something."

"I don't remember ever seeing a car like that around here. Do you?"

"Toyota? No."

"Kind of expensive for these parts."

"Yeah. Let's head on."

Driving quietly, locked in our own thoughts, Barnaby turned to me. "I bet you're right. Cause a little trouble but really to distract us. Wonder why?"

"Distract us from what? We're about the two dullest persons around."

The road wound its way up the slope, then burst from the trees at the top of the ridge into the open. It looked out over the tree tops of the lower ground. Green, dark green, light green. We could see the wind working the trees, looking out over the long, slow swell of the terrain to another ridge maybe four miles off, a green slope way off. Ten minutes of slow driving. The road okay but rough, dirt and an occasional bedrock surface. We wound around a small knoll amid the base rock where up on top perched a squat house of stone and wood, front designated by a porch like on my cabin back home. It ran the length of the house, maybe fifty, sixty feet, and a bunch of chairs on it, an old woman looking out at us as we got out of the pick-up. We greeted back and forth, introductions and such, and then we settled down with her and looked off over the lower ground's forests. I noted the tip of the lake just showing way off there, just the tip, the main body hidden by the forest as I looked at it from this not too high point of view.

A girl, about fifteen, came out with coffee all around.

The old lady jerked her head toward the girl. "She's getting married Saturday."

Barnaby looked the young one over. "Pregnant?" he said.

The old lady nodded. "I'm taking care of her for a bit."

"Start young up this way, don't they." Barnaby said.

The old lady nodded. Then said, "Tell him who the father is, Abigail."

The young one, drinking coffee, shook her head and looked off meeting no one's eyes.

The old lady snorted. "She won't tell. It's some big secret. When she gets the doctor's bill she'll think again. It cost plenty these days. She'll have the kid, that being her part. The father ought to do his part having done his already (she gave a wink to us). Let him pay the bills, I say."

"Where's Angelica?" asked Barnaby.

"Out gathering firewood. It'll get cold up here in winter. But fer the view we should have built down at the foot of the hill in the woods where it wouldn't be so cold."

"There was a fire down there in the big field as we was coming up. You see it?"

"Oh yeah. Not much smoke but we caught sight of it. I think she may have gone down there to stop it. Can't say. You see her?"

Barnaby shook his head.

"She may have gone to round up the hired man. He went off to cut some cordwood. You see 'em?"

Barnaby shook his head then a sideways glance at me. "Ain't too much to talk about out here. Folks talk cordwood to fill up the day."

I nodded, thinking back to Betty and my own problems. Leastwise, I thought, you can deal with a grass fire easier than with Betty. I lost the rest of our conversation looking to the lake way off there, thinking how it split the distance from the house to the ocean. That bunch of dead-end communities added visual interest in between, where the land leveled out. Looking off the end of the porch you could see that dark slit that marked the river's path through the forest, and out to the ocean beyond, going through the farmland. The towns out that way were pretty much isolated from the rest of the world, almost. No big cities around so, well, people made jokes about 'em, treating them as backward, old colonial types.

Barnaby interrupted my thoughts. He'd been watching a hawk or eagle soaring out over the trees. "Airplanes ever come bother you here?" he asked of the old lady.

"Once in a while. Once in a while one'll come and circle us and go off some other way. Why they do that? Know?"

I answered. "I guess they're on some training flight outta some flight school. You're prominent on this hill top, kinda like a pylon, a place to turn at. So they come out here and turn and go off. All part of the game of getting a license." I looked over my shoulder, the wind hitting me in my face as I did it. Coming from the east, I thought to myself. "Gonna rain."

"What makes you think that?"

"Simple enough. It's not the way the wind usually blows. Usually comes from west or off to the side of west. This is from the east, the opposite direction. Not usual; so I guess it'll rain."

"That don't seem too scientific ta me. There has to be a reason, you know. 'Cording to the scientists there's a reason to everything, even if you don't know it." Barnaby looked around at the two women, neither looked too energetic, so much for good conversation. He shrugged and looked at me, "Tell me about it."

I launched off, "No matter what direction the wind is coming from if you put yer back to it and hold out yer left hand, it is then pointing to the center of the low pressure system. Since the wind goes around the center in a big counter clockwise swirl you can get an idea of how long the storm'll last and all that."

"Huh?"

"Well if you're back is to the east the center is dead south and is probably moving eastward The general movement of storms is generally easterly in direction, coming from the west, that is. So the rain'll stop when the center is moved way off east. It's still circling around counter clockwise, meaning that soon the rain'll come from the north or at least the winds will, and that means the center is moving away from you eastward and the storm will probably be over gradually. Might take a day or two or three.

"As far as today goes, we must be at the top of the circle, winds behind us, and that's east. They'll bring rain. When the wind gets more from the north the center has moved farther east and maybe a little south, still moving eastward constantly. It's that big circulation, counter clockwise in a low pressure system, and low pressure systems generally are full of rain. And with the center constantly moving east you get winds changin' direction in hours or days. Depends on how big the system is. It's tricky thinking about it."

Barnaby scoffed. "Maybe. Why say it's low pressure? Could be high."

"That's true. But its low and I'll tell you why I think that. I'm not a meteorologist but I could see the clouds coming yesterday, the day before, slowly the sky got darker and that would be a low pressure system in my eyes. A high would have been a few fair weather fluffies, and then a front. High winds, like thunder clouds and rain and all that, hard and fast, and be gone in half a day probably. Maybe a few hours".

"Well ain't you the smarty pants though." Barnaby nodded, sipping the coffee and looking at the view and the old lady and her new charge, weather dismissed and moving ahead to winter and how these folks would make out as fall came and winter set in. Cooped up here might make for harsh words and if they got snowed-in the old one might be doing a midwife's work. "When's the kid due?"

The old lady looked at the kid. "Tell him."

The girl said nothing, continued ignoring us. The old lady filled in. "She says she don't know. I guess they been at it so long it gets hard to set a date." I watched Barnaby make a face. I knew Barnaby had been a medic in the war so probably had some know-how on women and pregnancy. How could a girl be so unaware of what her body was doing? It must be the girl was just being cantankerous.

I could feel it coming. Barnaby swung his head to me and said, "So let's finish that conversation we started back in the car before the fire."

"Later."

The old lady got up. "I'll see to Angelica. Abigail here'll get you more coffee." She took the girl and they were gone."

Barnaby spoke, "Knows we want a talk." And that was it. The two of us sitting there alone, sipping the coffee and kind-a relaxing after the afternoon of fighting the fire. Angelica and her hired man went down there after about an hour and checked to make sure the fire was out and then went on about their business. Now Barnaby asks about what happened in my life that I wanted to talk about, or get advice on, and that's what I liked about Barnaby, always straight out. Made a guy almost cry with sympathy.

Barnaby finished up with: "You told me you was suspicious and you were gonna spy on her. How'd ya do it? You subtle or just naturally blunder into things?"

We'd been sitting there awhile, looking out at the tip of the lake showing, probably three miles off. I knew the lake, had canoed it several times. There was a cabin there, stocked with stuff people brought in and left for anyone's use. It was open to anyone, a contribution by out-of-door types to help each other out. It was built by the local outdoor club from down by the village; the one by the estuary.

I looked off that way, thinking all those things and relaxing after the good workout fighting the fire; and Barnaby, good friend, has to remind me of my troubles, dad-rat-it. So now my peace has to go and the misery re-enter my mind.

Being tired from good work and all relaxed of course I started talking away, more to myself than anyone who happened to be about, speeding up a little as I went on, telling more of the story than I had planned. Oh well. Quite excited with myself and then the shock when I realized I was talking out loud, letting my unhappiness come out. The psychologist types would say that was good, and get a hundred bucks or two to tell them my tale, but with this here Barnaby-type therapy it was free despite him saying he was charging for advice now. So I told him, and now that I realized I was doing it, told on, the whole miserable thing. On and on. I was almost ashamed to think this was me telling, but why not? It's good for one to unload all that crap. The psychologists say so.

Chapter 2
The Loss of my Life

"Like I was saying, she and this guy with the golden mustache were dancing some waltz and the look on Betty's face was an open book, some type of romance novel for sure. It was just a moment, but it was there. Sheer pleasure and admiration. I can't dance a waltz worth shit. This man evidently could, so I watched. They did make a fantastic couple. A few others were watchin', too. They made a great dance team and Betty wouldn't even admit they'd been dancing when I tried to talk to her about it, nor about him. So find out who he was and where he'd come from. Like I said, not a word about him from her. Something was up, that was fer sure. I started to pay attention. No more letting life run along on its slow course thinking everything was fine.

I got with it and lordy, I found out too much. They were 'seeing' each other, maybe for months, and I'd had not a breath of air about it. And more over she had signed up and paid her money and was to go off to some dance camp on a lake about thirty miles from home, and insisted! Wouldn't listen to me trying to say to drop it. She insisted on going. So now I knew why.

Take action!

Hell, what's this all about anyway? I'm old and gone, in a sense. And now with my wife leaving me, I'm all alone. Not good for an old codger like me. They say you'll die sooner if you're all alone, and no one wants to die ahead of schedule. My children come and gone, so I'll be alone, but it's not a good set up. It's not that I don't have alternatives, though. My step daughter up in Portage, name of Sara, married to Marty, she's the closest. I could go visit her till I get over this spell that keeps eating at me.

But that's not exactly what I want. I'd rather be married to Betty but she's on this new course and sure acts like she wants done with me and off for a merry life with this new guy. Being the ole man-of-action, I pull out all stops. Go back in the wastepaper basket and come up with the flyer for this dance camp and get the dates, put that together with Betty's departure time with a couple of other girlfriends (for cover, I was sure). Then I sat down in the rocker and thought and thought about what to do about this gigantic tryst with this new guy which (per usual) ended up in me fantasizing about what might be going on. Not 'might be going on', what *was* going on. Decided to go down there and see for myself, but I must not be seen. This is a clandestine activity, spying on my wife. So decision made, I high tailed it down that way.

I checked the map, drove there, skirting the direct route to the lake on which the camp was situated, and explored all around the adjacent roads coming finally to this lake where the dance camp was. This lake was like an egg with a broad tail that gradually diminished as it worked its way a mile into the woods. The dance camp was at the apex of the tail and body. I went around to the far side of the lake with my field glasses and pack, exploring the section across from the camp. Where I was, there were skinny trees and heavy underbrush, good cover, and it put me about maybe 600 feet from the other side where the camp spread out its dozen buildings, its volley ball field, the swimming area and so on. It was an ideal spot to watch from, plus well concealed by a drop in the ground behind the shore line. I parked the tent out of the way, unsuspected, perfect, and ready to watch. Far to the right I could see where the entrance road came in. Cars parked there. There was no one on this side and swimmers confined by a floating rope to their own side. A path on this side, but apparently little used for those people stayed over there, dancing, and doing dance-workshops or parties night and day. I was free to observe to my heart's content.

Me, the big secret agent, spying on my wife to see what she's up to, her and that golden mustached wife-stealer. Me, the under-cover cop, doing secret agent stuff from my observation spot across from the camp, Me and my binoculars.

I watched the camp and moved my stuff twice until I figured I had the best observation post ever. It was a small copse of trees on this side dead across the lake, near the biggish dance hall and within watching distance of the beginning of the train of little sleeping houses for the participants. So now settle in and watch. Some see me, some don't; but not close enough for identification. I don't want to be seen, but you have to accept the odds that I wouldn't get caught at what I was doing while all the time swearing and cursing myself for even caring for her, still so in a tizzy over her, losing my wife to some other guy, and trying to analyze myself and make a promise to out-love him from now on and whatever else it was that happened to me in this mess. I lay all day beneath that thicket and watched, and thought about the whole mess. Stupid me, as I see it now. For all I can tell no one calls for her to come out and sneak off into the woods and fields and play, and court and mate. Do they? Would they? It wasn't happening that I could tell, but I wanted to find out, trusting no one to tell me the truth. So that's the kernel of the story that I tell Barnaby. Suspicion, the execution of a tryst, unfaithfulness. This is my own misery and the desire to see for myself and all the while I know that Betty's in there somewhere having fun with old dance friends and that cursed man she had to be with. So I watch expecting to see the baker sneak from the kitchen cabin to kiss and whisper and all that courting business but no baker shows. On the second day I wonder where I got the idea that this boyfriend fella was a baker, and being as that wasn't proving out, I open my mind and wait and with me still not a clue as to who this guy was.

Like I said earlier, better to not know, but it's hard to take your own advice.

I said to Barnaby, "I'll tell you how I got wind of this. It's so simple, but I suppose typical. You know. You see someone talking with your wife and it's meaningless, but every once in a while there's a nugget of 'something' that sets off the old warning bells. I may have seen him before, a long, long time ago. I never knew his name, but sensed there was, or had been, something between them. It was like that. Now listen, this is how I'd write it up if I had to make up, say, a disposition for a lawyer, part of the divorce proceedings. It goes like this. Listen."

"I returned my empty plate and continued on to another hallway to return to the dance hall and must have come to a brief stop, for there ahead, through another doorway giving into another hallway where the settee was, sat a woman in a red skirt, black top, red kerchief: my wife. Crouching at her feet was a young man, talking. She had a half smile on her face, almost a nod, maybe replying. Surprised to have found them, I hesitated. Embarrassed, I quickly moved on. They hadn't meant to be seen, my wife and the old boyfriend. In the dance hall the music was loud and invigorating, some line dance which I knew, so I slipped in between two dancers, oblivious to them for I was back years in my head while I danced on automatic. Words about her past life of which I knew so little came up, and this fellow's face appeared, how others in the dance community had thought she and he had been "a pair". I had been jealous but never let on, and now here they were having a tete-a-tete again. I danced on, trying to sort the thoughts in my head and the old mantra emerged.

Let no ancient jealously show.

Be your own pleasant, friendly self.

Would that gentle, non-threatening way work again, or was it too bland and too late?

Life had gone on and that old feeling between me and Betty had dissipated with time, as with many couples. Would she go off with this new temptation now, the dance activity covering a ten or fifteen minute escape to be alone together, to chat of old times (if there were old times between them) with a hand on the arm or on the waist and words of long ago whispered, a kiss, the plans for a tryst, comparison of times, days, distances to cover to be together for a coffee, an ice cream, plans for another day together, maybe more time; "Could you meet me, say after choir practice? Get home late?"

"Yes, possibly. Usually he is asleep when I come home. We could. Where?"

"Leave the church and go the other way, toward my place."

"Your place? But your wife. We can't."

"She's a nurse, remember? Currently on night shift. She won't be home. No one will know. Do it please, for me, for us, it's been so long." His hand moved up her back, drawing her towards him.

"We can't. We shouldn't. You know that. It's so common."

"No, not common. It's us, remember? It's the us of ten years ago. We must. This fifteen minutes every week is so short. Please. Oh, we must." His lips were covering her forehead, her nose, her cute, pointy nose that he had always kissed. She stirred suddenly, head up slightly, tightly in his arms. His hands and arms moving hers lightly to his left, her bosom against him, he into a slow chest movement, pulling her against him, feeling the breast of this woman.

He was pleading and she could feel the rise of desire, her voice without words, intimacy, only the almost whisper, the faintest of moans, desire of body in sound. Faint, sound, for they mustn't. She pulled away, half turned, remembering her mother's once words of how the woman was in command, set the pace of love. Yes, the man would plead, struggle for command, arms like an octopus, enveloping, his whole body calling for satisfaction in her, but the woman set the pace, at least in civilized societies. In less than civilized it was raw power and he would win, but in the long run a woman's persistence would set her to win.

She flung herself away, the outside door swung open and she was on her feet moving past the front of the house toward her own car, hearing his door opening and his words coming after her. At her car she swung back to him, hand raised in a 'stop' and the words, "Yes. Call me." Then she was in, motor on, and leaving. Driving, and realizing that she was going too far and appalled at her words: 'Yes. Call me.' Appalled. What am I doing? An Affair? NO! Even if I still loved him it makes up into all sorts of problems. That was the way between Charles and Darlene and it's not going to go that way with me. So be it. She drove another hundred feet and it came to mind that she and Trevor, her husband, had come together in the one car to this dance. She had to turn and go back for him, after all they were still married.

I was studying Barnaby's face, he was lost in thought it looked like. 'Anyway, that's what I imagined it must have gone like."

Barnaby looked like he was still thinking it through, so I continued. "It was obvious to me (I think I'm so smart) that neither of them lovers got anywhere near each other since that time, but then they could have been extremely careful. Not a word passed between them that I ever saw which is sort-of a dead giveaway. Them behaving like they had not even met, and of course that wasn't true. Anyway, I guess it had been one of those things that just popped up in their lives. A man and a woman, that something there between the two, a look, maybe a string of words, something sparked an interest and they liked what they saw all over again. Then getting together to talk and it gets deeper and so it gets a little momentum and then a rush of desire. But I didn't think it had happened between them yet.

"So I finally meet this guy she was dancing with that set this all off."

Barnaby looked up at me, face changing. "Tell me."

"I'd heard once, picked it up somehow, that he was a flyer, so a little glamor in him that I didn't have, don't have".

In the single engine seaplane, looking ahead, he ran his index finger through his little blond mustache, thinking, studying the lake, the terrain, planning his landing. The lake was a shiny mirror in the dark green of the forest, and he began the set up for a water landing. He looked carefully, seeking ripples or waves on the surface, a sign of wind in the trees, the clouds ahead, higher up, fluffy white things drifting in the wind. There was probably a light wind at the surface, an easy landing right down the lake and into the broad inlet where the lake extended into the forest. She'd hear the plane, see it when she looked about, she'd know he was coming. Would she admit him as a friend to all the others there at the dance camp? Would she ignore him, planning to meet him later on, maybe after dark? Would she meet him with a collection of her new friends or come alone? He should stay near the plane to protect it from the hands of the curious.

He was at 500 feet, a good altitude to study the layout of the lake, where the shoals and bars were, big rocks below the surface could more easily be spotted from this altitude. All that ground-terrain business at the surface and below that one had to be aware of, lest one bite the light covering that was the seaplane hull.

It looked good. He cut power some, checked that the gear was up, the flaps down, carb heat on, check controls, look at the lake again now seeming to move rearward as the plane sped ahead. Attitude, altitude, and airspeed all looked good. He looked around three hundred sixty degrees for other air traffic. None.

Coming over the trees now, he looked to the water close below. Getting antsy, he wanted to slow the descent, but it was not time to touch down yet. Wait. Wait. Now he began to level the plane, changing from a very slightly forward-down attitude to level, the water probably twenty feet below, headed into the gentle breeze, slowing more. Good. Almost to the surface, he held it steady. Hiss-s-s-s-s. the sound of water grazed the hull. Good. Down. Stick back slightly, nose very slightly up and the plane coasting, slowly. Stick full back. Nose full

up, the plane stopped fast, nose bobbing, and settled to level. He
powered up and taxied slowly ahead toward that sandy stretch beyond
the big rock that was the outer limit of the swimming beach of the
dance-camp.

He scanned the shore, the dock, and the cabins and assembly hall
looking for her.

"I watched this seaplane land on the lake and taxi over toward the swimming area of the camp, shut down, drift, and up pops the canopy and this big, blondish guy stands up in the cockpit and takes a paddle and starts leisurely paddling the big plane to the beach. He starts tying it down and all that stuff they who own airplanes do before they walk away. A small group collected to look at it and suddenly there's Betty running down to the beach and up to this guy and they stand there together, talking, then the two walk off toward the assembly hall and, well, that's it. Him and her. Not me and her. I stuck around a couple more days, saw them through the glasses occasionally, walking arm in arm like folks who are close do. It was useless watching them. I packed up and went home. Found a letter waiting in the mail from her lawyer. Didn't know she had one, but I guess it's for real, it's over."

Barnaby was staring at me, rather hugging the cup of coffee as if warming his hands. "Well, my friend, it sounds like you pretty well figured it all out."

I started arguing with him about that and telling him it wasn't over and I was still alive, me, in my eighties, but still kicking. But he put up his hand.

"Cut it out, Trevor. It sounds all over to me. You can talk on all you want, but unless she has a sympathetic streak for you, she's hooking up with this other guy. Face it. It's over, or damned close to it. You want to spend some money? Have a shrink tell you? It's over buddy." He searched in his pocket, drew out a set of keys, subtracted one, and tossed it to me. "There's the key to my camp up on the edge of Hathaway Mountain off Route 9 where the view ends. There's a tree with a red band on it at the entrance road. It's a marker for my camp. The road in isn't too hot, but it keeps out the idle curious. Go up there and stay awhile. However long you want. Get over it up there. Look out at the view, chop some firewood. You need a change so cut away."

Well now, I thought. I suppose I could. Get me out of familiar surroundings and into a new world, so to speak. I suppose he's right and so why not? All this spying is too bothersome, and what's the point? If she don't like me, well-l-l, that's the way it goes. She don't want me, so why fight it, worry and be tense and upset and trying too hard to keep her. She don't got no interest in me any longer. Let her go. I felt almost like crying over this horrid mess I've made out of my life, and maybe hers, too. Maybe she'll be happier with this blond, airplane flying bastard and can rise to new heights, like she muttered about just a little too often.

So adios, Betty, and good luck. I looked over at Barnaby, and reached for the key.

Chapter 3
The New Life

It seemed pretty good, using Barnaby's place up on the mountain side. It came with a five mile drive into town and a temporary job at the post office that turned out to go on and on. "Temporary" was just a label apparently. The Postmaster was keeping the job open for one of his relatives when they needed it and would dump me when this happened, but for the time being the job went on as if there was no end.

No wife. No girlfriend. I was building a boat: a twenty footer, taking my time, for something to do. Folks around think it's a lark and laugh at me, building a boat way up on top of the mountain, as they say. Ask if I've got a Noah-complex and need to lay in a couple of each kind of animal yet. Maybe I do. Despite all that, I'm doing okay, staying healthy. Ole Barnaby certainly had laid in a good bunch of books so I read a lot. I suppose I'm getting smarter for all that.

I said I had no wife, but that isn't exactly true. There is this woman that discovered me, Magdalene by name. She comes by and stays sometimes months at a time and it's good to have the company for a change, so she's always welcome but we don't make nothing permanent of it. She's got something going in Albany, I think, for she talks about it and the social intertwined problems with some sort of business down there and scoffs about this and that and eventually disappears, you know. A space of time goes by and she's back again, all refreshed.

Let me tell you about Barnaby's place up here. It's pretty much like what I had in mind when I was in the army, something from my dreams that I was going to build when I was discharged.

It is way up on the side of the mountain and the porch faces out to the far river valley, a dark bluish green in the haze; and beyond that it is a lighter haze of pale blue, bespeaking the real far distance, fifteen miles, maybe twenty, away. A rather big one room shack, you would say, thirty feet square sitting there at the place where the level mountain top comes to an end and the life of an open bedrock face begins. It probably got cleaned of forest and soil ten or twenty thousand years ago by a glacier and stands looking like a cliff from the distance; a steep slope drops down several hundred feet to the forest covered tallis below. It gives a great view. The forest cover below looks to be sloping away in ridges and shallow valleys with the remnants of a hundred years gone to farms, country roads and those beautiful green and tan fields.

Farther off is the river. It doesn't show, being hidden down in its valley. They tell me that it was once close up under this escarpment, but now is moved well off, the way a river carves and meanders. It probably started as an old fault crack in the earth's geologic history and keeps working at moving all the soil away to the ocean. This area beneath the escarpment used to be one big lake way back thousands of years ago, but old man river, helped by some upheaval, changed its course again and again. Great big geologic events that never end, and I'm the lucky resident up top of the bare rock edge of this tectonic plate to enjoy one little moment in its millions of years of existence.

But I mean it: a big geologic experience for the earth happens and little me is here for only a few years enjoying one moment of it. Most people don't even realize their part of such an experience. So what have I got here besides being part of this slowly changing earth?

I have a big one room shack with a kitchen at one side; and a bunk bed opposite. The lower bunk is a disheveled swirl of blankets and sheets, the bed not made yet. The middle of the room is furnished with a table and chairs, several others about, book cases on one wall, an iron woodstove and a galvanized stove pipe. Home. No wife. Alone. Lonely but fitting after the closeness of military combat-living, now done, and discharged to this for compensation, thanks to Barnaby's make-up which is close enough to mine to make a pleasant match for me now that Betty is gone. Seventy acres bought with discharge pay, cabin built with his own hands and okay. Back then it was college in the fall for Barnaby as it would've been for me if all had gone unchanged, if I'd been the one to have bought it. A life more or less haphazardly planned, as done by so many. Waiting. Sitting on the porch and studying the distance through the haze. A pipe and Mixture 79 on the tiny table next to the chair. They say not to smoke, but what the hell.

Girls? Why? What for? Magdalene suffices. Something it took me a lifetime to learn.

So I live here and have the job in town, a quiet sort of life. Waiting for the Grim Reaper, I suppose.

And as so often happens, things seem to be sliding along alright when something pops up that changes it.

Chapter 4
Up Island Park Way

Now all that cheery talk about the grass fire and McFardens is interesting and lets you know about me somewhat, but the real story picks up here.

Barnaby got a letter from someplace in Maine two weeks ago and he was still thinking it over. Some kind of trouble up there, or something going on that they needed a trusted hand for, fer only a few days, maybe a couple of weeks, expenses paid. "Need you", the letter had said.

Barnaby wants someone up there with him that he can trust. So he stayed over last night, we chatted a good bit, and drank some whiskey before he said I should come along with him. Do it, just for the change.

We started slowly on this trip. First went over to the Cove near where I used to build boats and walked down to the wharf near the breakwater. I hadn't said I'd go along with him, not being sure what it was all about, but I was inclined, still hadn't said yet, kind-a waiting to hear more of the particulars.

"So they say there's trouble up in Maine, huh? Think we ought to go up there and look into it, huh?" That was me talking, feeling out the situation wishing to hell he'd just get to the core of the apple, so to speak.

He was sitting on the log, the big log that had been part of the derrick business when the coal barges came in. He scuffed the cinders underfoot, cinders marked with bits of broken glass. He was sort of looking out over the little harbor but watching me out of the corner of his eye, slouched down some as he sat there.

Last night I'd sort of agreed to go along and help out, whatever he needed, and here he was asking about it again. He wanted a hard and fast agreement so he'd know he had a strong helper; devoted, you might say, and I guess I'd been slack in my "yes", still thinking it over sub-consciously.

I kept staring across to the breakwater and along the other side, thinking of women, the rich ones that came down to the little harbor summers and sit on blankets up there at the head of the water where the sandy spot made a beach of sorts if you didn't mind a few sea shells and skate eggs and sea weed bits about; and especially thinking about the one that came last summer with the boy. Couldn't have been over thirteen, either of them, or maybe seventeen. They'd lay, she and that boyfriend about her age, up on the top of the breakwater where there's a few stone blocks that had gotten dislodged in some storm and made a sort of low cubby hole. He'd lay on top of her and every once in a while lift up and cast a good glance around, then duck down to continue his love making. Thought no one could see 'em, 'ceptin' him bouncing up and down to look around, but they was up there going at it. Half an hour or so some days but more like an hour or two, depending. And then after, showing up along the sea side of the breakwater, round the end and walking so innocent-like over toward the end of the breakwater and the beach and in for a refreshing swim. They were summer people that rented some camp farther along the shore.

Barnaby was scuffing his feet and waiting for some talk about this business up in Maine. Well, he needed to decide what to tell me.

"It's woman trouble up there, somehow."

I kept looking over the breakwater, thinking about those two lovers, about Barnaby and whatever his problem was and how Maine got in it, but without more information it was useless thinking. Thinking without info doesn't solve any big problems. So I dumped my mind of women and men and thought about Maine: the distance, the cost by car. We could sail up part way. Maybe MacFarden could pick us up. Meet the boat and give us a ride. Work and help out and so on, get a ride back somehow. Would make a tough trip back by boat, the wind would most likely be against us, generally speaking. Head on home and pick up our own lives again.

I don't know what made Barnaby so slow to get to the point of all this, the rest of the story which he didn't talk about last night, accommodations, food, what the job really was; but I was willing to wait him out today. Too much whiskey last night and not enough sleep.

"Yeah, Barnaby, I suppose we ought to go up there and see what we can do."

Then there came the mess of talking, half-finished sentences and half-finished ideas, and finally he and I decided to give this a hard try. We are to sail up the shoreline to Maine where the coast swings more toward the east. Finally, a clear decision. We head back to the camp for a good night's rest and then off for a helluva long small sailboat ride. Actually I didn't care too much about going up there to help some poor sucker that had got himself in trouble, but Barnaby is a good fellow and so I could give him a week or so; beside, wherever he was going to do this good deed sounded somewhere near where my step-daughter lived so I could go over and visit her, maybe even stay with her a few weeks, if she and her husband were agreeable. So off I'll go with him. Barnaby is a good man in all general ways, but not much of a sailor, so that's probably why he called on me. Barnaby, like lots of basically good fellows, ain't rich, so we do it the cheapest way. I do things efficiently and inexpensively when possible, and it's cheap to sail 'cause the wind's free, leastwise, today it's still free. Those government people inside the beltway'll figure out some way to charge for it someday, like they did windmills in the middle ages. So we sail halfway to save some dough and then get a ride. Barnaby's got the basic idea all worked out and it sounds workable to me.

But it does sound stupid, doesn't it? Us going all the way to Maine and sailing the first half of the way in some little fourteen foot dingy with a rag sail. Real smart; but hey, we're men and so do things different just for the sheer fun of it.

Well now, my fourteen-footer was off up Island Park way where the chap I'd loaned it too had left it, so we had to go all the way up there, twenty or thirty or so miles to pick it up. Outfitted like going on a backpack trip, we set off toward Island Park which we never would have found except for some disconcerting distant noise. When we misplaced the map we were out of luck. Of course I thought it was Barnaby who lost it, and he thought it was me. So we went on memory alone neither being willing to admit one of us had fouled up. We ran the afternoon out, not finding Island Park and replenished the gas and were on the road again. Did a pit stop somewhere along the way, and out there in the pucker brush, alone for a moment and no auto engine noise to distract us, heard some tremendous pounding sounds. Constant, ascending some, descending, but very prominent in the presumed quiet. Same sounds we'd heard before, sort of, but one helluva lot louder.

"What the hell is that noise?"

"Sounds like some factory at work, big engines or whatever."

"I don't know but it sure is loud and powerful sounding."

"Well, when we get there we can ask them what's up. They'll know. Maybe some new factory went up since we came out here last. It's been three years. It could be factory noise."

On we drove. About twenty minutes, another stop out of curiosity. Barnaby wanted to know why we were stopping.

The noise was still there. We looked at each other, raised our eyebrows and were underway again. Now, tuned to it, we could even hear it above the car sounds.

We pulled up to the top of what I recognized as a lateral or terminal moraine. The ridge road was only maybe fifty feet above the general terrain and swung along the top for about five miles so we had a good long chance to identify the source of that noise. Course it was almost dark by then, but there was enough light even though the sky was partly overcast to see that it was the surf. The surf pounding the shore like there was no tomorrow. We could just make out huge waves swelling up and advancing, crashing into the shore with great force. Some storm had created it, and on that we were in agreement. It was big, and raising one helluva matching noise. That was what we'd been hearing as we'd driven well behind the shoreline for the last hour. Not too smart of us to fail to recognize it.

It made me uneasy, thinking about sailing in that kind-a sea, and made Barnaby uneasy too, and each of us asked ourselves if we should reconsider. Barnaby kept listening and watching and looking at me, waiting for me to say we should skip this trip completely and actually spend money, but hell man, once I made up my mind, I get convinced we could do it and it'd be one damned exciting trip. Smart huh? Not really.

My fourteen-footer was at this house in this place called Island Park situated along an estuary on the inland side of the hill. The moraine protected it from the sea and sea wind, and I looked at it wondering how many decades it'd been protected from the surf and how we'd fare if we lived there. Island Park was a few dilapidated shacks, and one real house with a rickety boardwalk to a dock with a cluster of boats. The area was poor as church mice. My fourteen-footer was there okay, parked in this back water behind the moraine, and needed to be refreshed and broken parts fixed before we set out.

Well, we were okay protected behind the long, low, skinny, moraine, but on the sea side the wind was at thirty, maybe more. The sea was throwing salt spray which dissolved into a mist, so 'twas tough to go stand by the sea on the beach. A boat would have a tough time being launched from the beach; it would never make it just as coming in on one of those huge combers would probably smash itself on the shore. The surf would just pick up a small boat like ours and crash it down on the beach. Smash it all to hell.

We went into the house and they were all there, glad to see us, feeling our support going out to them and all that. They were pretty poor, but nice folk. So we were there a bunch of days, and it's funny. Although the surf kept pouring on, after a few hours you'd get used to it. Not hear it, think it was over until you stepped out for something, then you'd remember, hearing all that pounding all over again. And sometimes you'd feel it pound, some extra big wave or something, and it'd hit the shore line and the vibration would come through the moraine and shake you and you'd know that was a big one.

This fella, Skipper Dan, who kept Island Park had a couple-a kids: a boy and a girl. The girl, at twenty-two, is still living at home. The son is running an exercise place in Concord, NH. He was in the army, in Afghanistan, and was in a Humvee which ran over a mine and they were all blown up. He was burned from neck to ankle in his back, and had an upper arm badly broken in two places. They put two bolts in it with a steel bar finally, and saved the arm, otherwise it would have been amputated. It was a surprise to hear what folks in these little out of the way spots, as any people, have in their background. I was curious about his kid working up there in Concord and asked more about it but Skipper Dan, he didn't have any more to say. He groused about the war some, but that was it.

"No, I don't blame anyone," he'd say. "You sign up for the military and have to assume you're headed for an early grave. That's what it's all about. You know, shootin' and killing and all," he'd continue.

"No point in blaming anyone, it fer our war."

He kept coming back to that statement, like trying to convince himself, which was okay. He got to one thing that really interested me though: his knowledge of the history of that part of the world. He said, "Afghanistan. You know every nation that has invaded Afghanistan has been defeated, eventually. It was the British at the beginning, sometime in the early or mid-eighteen hundreds, then again later in that century. Something like three times they tried themselves out against those Afghans. Then the Russians were defeated in the twentieth century, around nineteen seventies, and then later on us, good ole peace loving US of A." He shrugged and fell silent.

What can ah say to that? He almost gave up his son for it, so had a right to his opinion. "So the kid's okay?" I said.

"Yeah. seems happy, doin' ok."

"Well that's good." And then he started in again, just as if it was him that had gotten blown up. Telling the story again in more detail so I knew he was more affected than he let on. It was his only son, after all.

He shrugged his head again. "He was in a Humdee, going someplace and went over a land mine, one of their home-made ones, maybe. So it goes boom and they go over all fire and that. He got burned up his back and his upper left arm was busted in two places. He told me it was touch and go, the fix, that is. The burns they fixed OK, but the arm was in tough shape. They put a piece of steel in it and put a couple of big bolts through into the bone each end, and there he was, not good as new but working fine, so they did a good job and saved the arm. It hurts him up by the shoulder sometimes, but that's minor. He's alive, got all his parts and, well, life goes on. Got himself a girl up there, he writes. Never seen her, myself, but says he'll bring her along when he comes down for some fishing or something."

I stared at him, I know I did, but wasn't aware of it. His kid was blown up, and never a word about it. You take what life offers and move on, I guess.

So we had some chow and put up there fer a bunch of nights and give the fourteen-footer a going over and ready 'er for the trip.

You think it's funny, huh? Me and Barnaby going to Maine by boat, sailboat to boot? Well, it's understandable if you think about it. Barnaby don't want to row all the way to Maine, nor do I, but I wouldn't say anything. Didn't want him to think I'd share the rowing. Ha-ha. That's a joke of course. But seriously we will go by sailboat. The wind'd do all the work. I was thinking of my fourteen-footer but considering those waves, well, I don't know. Mulling it over aloud, over breakfast coffee, a'sudden I heard Skipper Dan, who was Mr. Island Park, say he'd loan us his Twenty-Two, a bigger sailboat with a small cuddy and some old engine he called its "inboard", a dirty weak-looking old thing. Hindsight later on said, "Don't depend on it". But right now a boat with an auxiliary sounded good ta me. Barnaby, sometimes the skeptic, crinkled up his nose. "Needs to be big enough to sleep two." Thus we borrowed this boat from good old Dan, he getting uncomfortable with his knees and legs in general and hasn't had that boat out once since putting it in last May. He refused to go along as second officer aboard so we had the boat all to ourselves for the rest of the summer at no charge which was a good deal.

It was moored almost up at the end of the little spot of harbor over to the end of the inside, next to it a positively ugly single-masted vessel about thirty-two feet long. Ugly as sin and moored as it was, the thing had a tendency to swing and sail wildly at the end of its mooring line 'cause the wind gets up'. Its bowsprit had a tendency to crash into the boats moored beside, and Dan's little sloop was a target, not by design but simply because it was moored there next to this thing whose bowsprit caught the window of the motor-sailer on the far side and punched through. The owners had words. Not surprising as that bit of harbor is full of local as well as "foreign" boats that make it over here from the big river and harbor where they're really full-a boats. All sorts of nar-do-well sailors come by and the harbor's full of complainers. That ugly thing made a swing our way and came close to nicking our mast. Dan's being smaller and low down to the water got a complete miss on that as well as all subsequent flirtatious advances so we were free of later-on payments for damage to "a vessel in the course of its assigned duty for which we were responsible," or something like that. We ignored all that and started ferrying out supplies for our trip. When done the next day, we'd leave.

So the next day we were out before eight stowing provisions, ferrying them out in the skiff.

"We aren't taking this skiff?"

"Don't know as there's a need, being as we can run ashore in this twenty-two just as easy as in the skiff. Just as easy. What'da you think?"

"Take it. We can sell it for food if we get desperate."

So now we got a twenty-two foot sailer with one mast, jib, and a spinnaker, and towing my skiff. What a ridiculous caravan, but this was Barnaby's expedition and I was just the sailing master, so him the leader and we do it his way.

Long about then Mrs. Johnson comes by, looking us over as she walked up. She was on the foot bridge and looked down at us. She kicked a clot of asphalt and it landed with a kerplunk on the cabin top and the expedition leader started chewing away at me for marring the finish 'till he heard Mrs. Johnson ask where we was off to. "Whales in the south Pacific?" she asked, him looking up surprised to see her there.

All four of us laughed and Skipper Dan explained. "Off to Clute's place."

She looked skeptical. "What, way up there in the mountains? They got a deep water creek running uphill to their place?"

Skipper said, "Don't know. Never been there by water. It'll be an experience in meeting the unknown."

"That's certainly true. I think that up by Portage you can run a shallow draft in as far as the lake, but beyond a few miles it gets into white water. I wouldn't be surprised if the run of water might do the same at Clute's place." She grinned. "Enjoy yourselves." She had a nice smile. "Well boys, have a good trip wherever you end up. Say hello to 'Manda Cunningham when you see her, if you get as far as Portage. Tell her the invite down is still open." And with that she was off.

And we were off, too, in about twenty minutes before she came back with her groceries. Barnaby, the expedition leader, rowed us out of the little harbor, about a quarter mile and then in the river channel. I, the sailing master, hoisted the mains'l and took the helm. Our first stop was seventeen miles north, more or less, a little island with a white tower on one end with white light blinking. We'd been up there four or five times in the past so it was like sailing over home territory. We puttered along about two hours and the home port was disappearing astern and us picking up a dot on the horizon that had to be the island. A good stern breeze picked up some around noon and about three died pretty much, us just ghosting along with barely steerage way.

We got there, dropped the hook among the rocks, enjoyed sandwiches an' drink and got into the two sleeping bags one each side the centerboard trunk and fell asleep. Yep, Skipper Dan's twenty-two was a center-boarder, and as uncomfortable as hell laying on the plain board bottom. One day out.

So the next day we are putting up in South Portland, tying up for the night, so to speak. The boat on the shore, tent and gear next to the boat, we should be more comfortable. The night warm, insect sounds around, dark now that the sun had finally gotten put to bed for the night, and a tiny light from the Primus, sputtering away with the kettle of some one-dish meal Barnaby had put together, usually his old stand-by: the Spam meal. Tasty, but generally too much oil, which no amount of talking would cause him to readjust. We had energy for several nights all wrapped up in this one meal. We'd lay awake, sometimes talking, mostly pretending sleep just to avoid the talking, all the same old stories seen tonight from a new perspective. So here we are like a pair of Indians on the shore, cross-legged in front of the Primus with its kettle of supper preparing itself by a good warm boil and occasional stir, and what should come to pass but a car, headlights on the road above the slope casting out and enveloping the twenty-two footer in its light. It's a pretty little boat with white sides and varnished bright work, and should be out swinging at its anchor.

The lights go off and presently the sounds of shoes on sand coming our way now. How can they miss us with this loud sputter of the Primus and its miniature bluish light interlaced with a burst of orange from time to time? Neither of us said anything, awaiting the unexpected, perhaps an angry, "Get out", or some curious soul wanting someone to talk to. So we were surprised to hear a woman's voice.

"Hi fellows. What's going on?"

Barnaby, ever interested in people, especially women-type people, answered. "You the police or beach patrol?" This was his private joke harking back to the World War II times when there were beach patrols to protect the USA from German spies, saboteurs and such, coming ashore from submarines to reek havoc.

She came around in front of us, a usual looking female in this darkness. A Primus don't throw much light.

"Sorry, no beach or fuzz patrol. No such thing. Sue and I are on our way to a party and saw the boat late this afternoon. You two from that one?" She had a pleasant voice.

And thus a conversation ensued between Barnaby and this new friend of his, who had a partner up in the car on the roadside and more cautious than this curious, aggressive one. I suppose she was aggressive, if I were a woman I'd not go down to a couple of strange men on the beach.

I stirred the food and they went on talking, she skittering around left and right. She was dressed up pretty: dark skirt, stockings, and a light colored blouse Presently I heard Barnaby invite her and her friend down for a bite. Apparently she had accepted for the two of them for she disappeared up the slope of long grass and where upon the other one came down, somewhat invisible in that she was dressed much as the first one. Dressed too well for a night on the beach; but it wasn't any beach supper they were out for but a couple of sailboat bums to come to the party with them and, "We'll bring you back here when you've had enough." And so on.

Barnaby being the younger and more attractive of the two of us, accepted for us while they were tentatively testing the stuff from the pot. He gave 'em three spoonsful on two paper plates and they picked at it, pronouncing it "tastes real good", but we had to come with them to flesh out the party, as she said.

So ok, we went to the party. It was at a house way along the beach in a sort of village cluster. All lit up like Christmas you couldn't miss the party where about twenty young souls were talking, some dancing or tryin' to, and munching off a table laden with little sandwiches and goodies and bottles of drink and that sort of thing. Barny was off, mixing in with the first talker 'fore I knew it, and I stood looking them all over. Any drugs? Not that I could see. Everyone was lively and talky but nothing out of line that I could see. It was a rather normal bunch of men and women. Some married, apparently, others singles or pairs. There was a fireplace with a fire and rugs to sit on, chairs and such, and a big porch out back on the water side, with a few couples and a group of five having some sort of low-key argument about global warming and erosion and insecticides. One woman with a couple of young ones on her tummy stretched out on a rug talking and playing with her brood and running a conversation with a very pregnant woman on a settee. Another couple was holding hands on an adjacent couch. The whole thing very ordinary and 'safe' I guess you'd say. After a bit we became a set piece of two whom everyone was interested in because we were strangers that had sailed in. Interest in us broke off when one of the women claimed she was hot and was going in swimming. She took off her blouse and was walking to the beach followed by some man. Everyone kind of broke off and went either to the beach or the porch out back to watch. From what I could see no one was going in, just watching her strip off her slacks and walking to the water in her underclothes. Someone said she was a nut to go out in the ocean at night for no one would ever find her if something went wrong, but she was out there and nobody did anything about safety except watch and talk. According to Barny she came in, stripped off the wet underclothes and dressed in the dry clothes flung off earlier. I guess some of them watched. I was inside doing rum and coke so didn't see 'cept when she came in. Her long wet hair stained her blouse with water making it stick to her curves somewhat and the men and women watched that from time to time. I was talking to a couple of men interested in the twenty-two footer and getting its vital statistics and stories about it and so on, so didn't see her but once. Barny's evening girlfriend drove us back to the boat and I left them to figure out how to say goodnight and went along. I guess he got in because he was there in his sleeping bag when I woke up in the morning. During breakfast all he wanted to talk about was sticking around here for the rest of the weekend, maybe, and what did I think of that? Not much, was my answer. I wanted to get up to Clute's.

Chapter 5
Gettin' There

We sailed on, got a bit of weather up beyond Portland a ways and later by Owl's Head but got on up there okay. In his head Barnaby was still back with her every once in a while, talking about her and so on. Some guys just seem to get fixated on one girl more than others no matter how they happen to be. Just seem to follow them through life, but then I suppose that's what life is all about; you know, go forth and multiply.

We got up to Twelth Port finally, sailed and rowed a little ways up the river to that dilapidated farmhouse and put ashore, up with the tent and a good meal of that 'Edmonds Col' dish Barnaby was such a candidate for and a call up to Clute's on the cell phone. He got 'em and they said they'd be down in the morning, so we headed off to bed.

And who should come to pick us up? Not MacFarden, but that young girl, and in a Toyota. Maybe fourteen or seventeen I think, as I looks over at her, then remembering how the old lady said 'fifteen'. Saw her at the old lady's place several months ago. This is the one the old lady said was pregnant. She looks it now. A nice looking bulge at her tummy. Kinda cute. Somebody sure does have trust in her to let her take their car. Oh, well, they know what they're doing. The folks up this way, all agriculture and business, tied to the land or shore, have their kids grow up a little faster than down home way. Down home the kids drive around and some smoke and they drink, and they go to games and swim parties and titillate each other with tales of going to college next year, or this, or that, and go dancing and to movies, and each other's houses and talk and giggle, that's the girls, of course, making vague plans out loud and exciting each other over some heart throb. Up here some do that, the richer ones, but those with no prospects, their parents can give 'em none, they get down to making a living wage and disappear from the limelight, like that girl there driving. Pregnant, the old lady had said, and she sure is. She's looking at good ole Barnaby, all of fifty-five, pretty strongly. And look at him, studying her up and down like she was a new person to him. Known her as long as me, I'd say. A few months, maybe six or so. I never even remembered her name 'til lately. Abigail.

So like I said, it surprised me that she showed up for us. I thought she'd be down at MacFarden's place with the old lady and Angelica waiting for the baby but here she was, tummy crowding the steering wheel. I said nothing, for the truth would come out after a while, whoever the father was and that sort of prying into someone else's life. She was a little disgruntled and touchy so we didn't talk much on the way, thirty-five miles to Clute's place. We got there just after noon, our destination, the place where there was some kind of trouble that Barnaby was going to inject himself into and straighten out, and I was his back-up.

I stood out there by the car and watched Barnaby go rushing up to the house, it was up a bit above the turn-around. He missed Mrs. Clute's entrance for she came from around the side. She'd had her baby two or three months ago and looked pretty good. Long hair down over her shoulders and bosom twice its size from since fall (Barnaby told me).She had a good figure and she smiled while looking around. She walked down the slope, still searching with those eyes. I could hear it in my head, her voice asking, "Barnaby? Barny? Where are you? Barny?"

There he was. Barnaby coming around the house from where'd she been. He saw the three of us all collected together and stopped, leaned against the wall of the house, sizing up the situation. Mrs. Clute, Betsy, hadn't seen him so was greeting me and trying to figure out where Barnaby was I suppose. And now the pregnant Abigail was going up onto the porch and out of sight and there was this biggish guy coming towards us. MacFarden, I figured, wondering about him. He live here, too? Clute's were Barnaby's people so although he'd told me all about 'em, I knew I'd find out more soon. Was he the guy that was supposed to live here, called "Sarge"? Sarge Clute? What about that Angelica MacFarden, the wife back there? Not married up here 'cause he was married to Angelica back there, I wondered, but I'd find out. Strange folkways up here. Not that it mattered to me, but Barnaby, he was a different case. He was friends with them for a long time. This Betsy Clute had drifted off a bit and now came strutting up again, gave me a kiss, her arms swinging way out and around and coming to rest on my shoulders and drawing close for a greeting kiss. She backed off, still holding my hands in hers and looking at me.

"So you're Trevor, the one whose wife took off with another guy. Barnaby told me. Despite all, you're looking good so I guess 'difficulties' is yer middle name. Yes sir, you look good. Now how's life been since then?"

That smile on her face! Knowing I was single now and no prospects. Probably wondering how she could get me fixed up being here in the wilderness with only backwoods women as big as grizzlies for candidates. The man, MacFarden (or was he Sarge Clute?) Stood beside her and we looked each other over, more or less, as if new to each other, which we were. "I'm a letter writer," she replied to no one in particular, "So I knew about you. Barny wrote back giving me the local news from down your way." She went on talking about Barny, as much as she wanted to tell.

This MacFarden fellow started. He was facing the house so saw Barny get into motion. His frown was real. I don't wonder. Barny was a running down the path and shouting all kinds of greetings at her, words of greeting and enthusiasm at seeing her, ignoring MacFarden totally. He didn't see MacFarden-Clute in his excitement. I tried to make big, pointing gestures to Barnaby but it didn't take 'til he was on site and grabbing for Betsy and it brought him to stop, staring at Betsy and to this big bruiser of a man. He got out of it with a bow of the head to her and words of greeting and all the time standing there staring at the man and back to her.

MacFarden put his hand out and Barnaby got out of orbit finally and said, "Betsy" and shook hands with MacFarden. "Hi. I think you must be MacFarden. I heard 'bout you through Sarge here. Where is he, by the way? Nice to meet you. Hope we can be of help to you." He pasted on a smile.

"You men had anything to eat?" Betsy looked the three of us over. MacFarden was still standing by the Toyota. "Come up to the house. There's leftovers enough for an army, we thought you'd be here about eleven. Come on." She took Barny's arm and started off, him falling in step beside her. I heard MacFarden's voice behind me. "Which one're you?"

I half turned, hesitated, and fell into step with him "I'm Trevor. You must be MacFarden."

"Me?"He rather laughed. "MacFarden? Not me, mate; but they do call me that only with MacFarden tacked on: I am MacFarden's hired man. Once in a while I get called that around here but it ain't my name. I'm Terry Blanford. Sarge Clute, Betsy's husband, left about three weeks ago, a job on a tanker awaiting him in Portland. He'll be back in a month or two. He said I should come down and give her a hand 'til he gets back. I weren't doing nothing else so why not? Mostly I watch the baby and that Abigail girl, the pregnant one. She brought me up here two days ago, then got sent off to collect you two up the inlet a-ways. I don't know why they let her drive, that Toyota's expensive and she don't have no license. But we didn't get caught. Ain't too much law out this far."

That explained how she'd gotten here, and him too, and straightened out this MacFarden-Clute bunch of people and names. It wasn't as unusual as I had started to think.

"Actually Blanford ain't my name neither. I did a little time and they got the record's screwed up so I ended up Blanford. My real name's January, something my ma picked up, but mostly I'm called Jan. January Fargo. Jan Fargo. You're one of the guy's that fought that little grass fire down there, ain't ya? We came in late for that. You'd already left."

We fell to chatting, this Jan Fargo, MacFarden's hired man, and somehow the subject of Sarge on the tanker came up. "He didn't always work on a tanker. He used to work in the city. Commuted to the same company that Barnaby worked at. Never saw each other at work, though. The Barnaby fella, pretty nice guy."

I was puzzled so I asked about Sarge and Betsy. Jan laughed. "Betsy and Bernard were married. Sarge was always a friend. Well, sort of."

Then he got confidential, leaned closer and said, "Bernard and her didn't do so well; married a couple of years, maybe even five. He came home one day and, well, listen. He drove in, mid-afternoon, little earlier than usual, something about his work finishing early for a change. Drove in, parked, up the hill to the house and went in the back door. There was no noise about. Walked into the next room, some sounds out on the porch, through the next room and there in front of him, on the couch on the porch were Betsy and Sarge. Her big white thigh pretty much hid Sarge's hips and her arm was around him hugging him to her. He was over her, propped up on his arms and his head over to the side of her face, her eyes closed. Heavy breathing and a steady gentle undulation of him up and down.

"Bernard went berzerk. He grabbed the floor lamp that was by his side at the doorway and swung it at the two. Hit Sarge over the back and, cheap thing that it was, it bent with some metal rending noise, which combined with his yell sounded like a bull ring in Mexico. Sarge was up, looking, grabbing himself and his pants at his knees and trying to get up and off, she was grabbing her skirt and yanking it to cover herself, rolling at the same time to free herself of Sarge. The deed was done. Sarge tried to run to the door but Bernard took another swing, Betsy calling 'It's not what you think and all that.' And of course it was. Sarge stumbled on his knees but the lamp stand caught him aside the head, and badly sliced his ear, a memento he carries for the rest of his life. Sarge is bigger than Bernard by half, but caught as he was in the wrong, he was seized by the morality of a lifetime and tried to make it to the door in the face of this little pipsqueak. He stumbled down the porch steps, missing some and falling and the lampstand coming down on top of him, thrown, and he was up and down the walk flying with clothes half up. Bernard dragged Betsy from the couch by the arm and shoved her off to fall on the floor by the porch easy chair her making sounds of, 'No it wasn't what you think,' and calling for him to stop. Little good that did. He went at her anyway and shoved her down and kicked her on the hip and then threw a folding chair at her. She was through the door and into the bedroom and the door slamming shut on him. He pretty much in six seconds broke the door handle trying to get in which left him in a greater rage. He smashed it on the dining table and slammed it at the door like a baseball bat, then he went to the kitchen and grabbed the edge of the sink and stood there, panting with rage. He remembered Sarge out front so he headed out the back door and around the house, but Sarge was out of sight down the hill. 'To hell with him.' He stood, yelling obscenities and threats at the bedroom window where she was, and got calmed down and then stalked into the house."

So that was Bernard and Betsy.

"They got a divorce and later on, a year or so, she married Sarge who had divorced his wife. Betsy had the baby, a girl, a while later, like eight or seven months, which spoke to about when she had been conceived. Don't know what happened to Bernard. Sarge is the big husband around here now."

The place had been filling up with other folks coming in while we talked so I fell quiet, wondering about all I'd heard and kind-a wondering what this Sarge fellow looked like. I'd meet him sometime when he wasn't out on some tanker.

Chapter 6
The Game

I looked around curious about all these people and this place. I wanted to get on to Sara, my step-daughter, but Barnaby was heavily involved with these folks, and after all there was no pressing need to get to Sara. I could sit here and listen and learn about this section of people. So sit, pretend I'm focusing on the group as a whole but really listening to the two on my right, Jan Fargo and that guy that came in a little ago, name of Bob. Wife left him apparently. Is this a pattern? Seems like all the wives, all over, are leaving their husbands for some cause or other. Except right here in this room all these folk seem in accord. I thought: so be it.

So I sit here a bit, more or less cogitating on the accord of husband and wife and the perfect marriage and the understood rules of marriage a la 1890 (supposedly no monkeying around during that era), when a movement by Betsy caught my microscopic eye. I studied her, wondering if Betsy would be sleeping with Barnaby. I don't know why that popped into my head then, but it did. It would explain why he wanted to get up here when I couldn't see any sensible reason he might have. It would be like him. Her husband being away a lot maybe she felt a bodily need that someone like Barnaby, affable and energetic, could satiate. Take him. He was free. His wife had been wiped out in an auto accident years ago. Maybe he felt a need and this Betsy woman was a healthy, good looking broad. They could never stay together 'cause Sarge was the faithful husband, always coming back to her from the tankers he worked on.

Still, elements of it weren't my idea of the perfect relationship, but then I was too old to keep up with young folks these days.

Jan Fargo's deep voice barged in on the general conversation. "Hey now, quiet! Listen up." He talked about a job to do over by the river. Long winded he was, and put in his personal philosophy and the desires of society. All that took a while.

"There is some kind of murder over there, I think –."

"Don't you know?"

"Information is sparse from there, like it always is."

"You hear it on the radio?"

"That town never gets on ta the radio. Too small, too remote."

"Too unimportant."

"Besides, they run their own show over there. It's got lots of queer ways."

"State don't want ta bother."

I wondered, is this the place Sara, my step-daughter, lives?

"Well it's alone over there and no one gets there. Nothing to go for. No tourists."

"We still talking 'bout Portage?" That's it, I thought. That's where she lives.

"Course. Where else?"

"There weren't no murder. Probably someone misunderstood. They're over there getting ready fer the game."

Someone else spoke up, "Maybe there weren't no murder this time but there will be someday. That bunch of people out there are so ignorant."

"They ain't ignorant," another spoke up. Here we go, I thought, into another discussion, one tangent after another.

"They're just plain out-of-it. Don't know what's going on in the outside world and just live along in their own way. Only things from outside that happen there are the Wells Fargo money truck coming to change money at that little bank and a tank truck to deliver oil. Isolated and wrapped up in their own little problems, which don't amount to a hill of beans!" he added. He'd gotten standing up to deliver his little soliloquy and now sat down abruptly. There was a modicum of clapping and a few off-color remarks directed at him.

The main topic got picked up again by one of the men across the room just as if there had been no interruption. "Not that stupid kid's game." It was a fella named Spencer talking.

"Hell man. It's community wide."

Laughter. "I'll say. The whole town gets in it."

"It's dumb."

"Hey you there. Trevor?" It was Barnaby. "You got a daughter up there. You know anything about it?"

"Can't say as I do," I said. "I don't know what you're talking about."

Spencer spat on the floor. Actually here in someone's house he spat on the floor! My God what kind of people are these? Well, I kept quiet and listened. Obviously Spencer didn't go much for my answer. He was a man who wanted answers, not "I-don't knows".

"Fer Christ's sake, Spencer. What the hell you doing?" It was Barnaby - him taking over for Sarge since he wasn't here? I wondered. He is wrapped up in Betsy, isn't he. Being her spokesman. The women here had gathered separately on the far side of this big room, casting glances over at the men from time to time and certainly listening. The men were pretty noisy as a fact.

Spencer looked sour. "Anyone who goes over there for that must be a moron running about on a half cylinder. I say stay here and enjoy life. Couple good-looking broads here, and I bet Cindy could round up a couple of more."

"Like Abigail?"

"Hell no. Gimme a cloth and I'll get this spit off the floor. Sorry about that. I just couldn't stand another day talking about playing that crazy game."

"But it's fun."

Spencer gave a snort.

I leaned over to Jan Fargo. "What are we talking about now? What is it that's going on over at Portage?" He whispered to me, the plus and minuses of going to Portage for whatever it was.

"It's a version of the boy scout game that they used to play at boy scout camp, only it's the whole crazy town that plays. 'Steal the flag' is the name, only it has gotten big enough for adults."

I crinkled my nose and was close to laughter.

"Don't laugh at it. The town folk play one side and all those that live in the town outskirts and countryside play the other team. You know how it works? I'll tell you. Listen."

I remembered. Who would forget? But it was a kid's game.

"There are two teams and a border is set up between them. Each team has a flag set up somewhere and the idea is to cross the border between teams and reach the other team's flag without getting caught and carry the captured flag to your side. You win. If you get tagged on the other team's territory and are caught, that is, one of the defenders gets two hands on you, you have to go to jail and are out of play until released by someone on your side tagging you, then you can join your team again and play. There's not supposed to be any violence, but of course some men, or even women, can get excited and carry on strongly. There's supposed to be a referee to insure the rules and no violence but some folks get over excited."

"You for real? That's really it?"

"Oh yeah. A big event. It's coming up soon and everyone looks forward to it. It is fun." Jan Fargo was looking at me intently, definitely hoping I really did understand and might join in voluntarily.

"I can't do that," I whispered back. "I can't run any more. Haven't run probably in four years. My knees are really bad. I couldn't play something like that."

"Of course you could. There's some job you could do. Perhaps be a lookout and call out when one of the other team crosses over the border and tries to steal our flag. They carry it back without getting caught and win. We don't want 'em to win."

"Spencer is right. It sounds stupid."

"Naw. Everyone has fun. Whoever wins gets the prize to split with the whole team."

"Which is —."

He rather looked around surreptitiously, then. "There's a big pot of money, and the losers pay for a great meal at Portland or Bangor, depends. Sometimes folks get carried away. He lowered his voice again. Now listen to this. Five years or so back it was supposed to be played naked. Naked 'Steal the Flag'."

I snickered a little too loudly and a couple of the guys looked over at us.

We whispered more quietly.

"Don't laugh. They all really tried it. 'Naked Steal the flag'."

I did. I couldn't contain it and laughed out loud. We got a few shushes from one or two because they were in such an important discussion. I didn't know what it was about, paid no attention. This business Jan was telling me was so utterly foolish, yet far more interesting.

"They really did?" I asked, having gotten laughter under control.

"Oh yeah."

"Men and women too?"

He nodded.

"They still do that?"

"Oh no. No."

I was through laughing and beginning to think. It wasn't without antecedents. I took Jan's arm and drew him close. Whispered, "You know anything about ancient history?"

As expected, he shook his head. "Listen. Back in Roman times fighting was common without clothes on. It happened in England. You know where England is?"

He nodded, looked annoyed. "Of course. I'm not a dummy,. Fer Christ's sakes, what do you think I am?"

"Ok," says I. "Listen. When the Romans invaded England the tribes that lived there fought them. It was all bows and arrows and swords and all that. But they fought the Roman invaders the way they always had fought, naked. No clothes. So these people playing 'Naked Steal the Flag' weren't inventing something new, they're just out of sync with time. Should have been a couple of thousand years earlier."

He curled a lip. "You're kidding."

"No. Naked. But they did paint their bodies blue."

"Blue? Why blue?"

"Quien sabe? Who knows."

He rolled his eyebrows, looked off a moment and ignored history, went off on his story about 'Naked Steal the Flag'.

"The women by and large fought it. There was a set of older men who were supposed to disrobe anyone who didn't cooperate. Unpopular they were, but they weren't too effective, being as parts of them were really old and didn't work well and they were slow. The women out ran and hid out in several houses, doors locked, couldn't be gotten into the game. Besides, being barefoot bothered a lot of people, so both men and women couldn't catch each other well. Barefoot is hard when you're not used to it. It was unanimously voted never to do that again. There was one couple got divorced, they say, because of the game. But there's no proof of it; but then Portage is far off and isolated pretty much so they do unusual things there from time to time."

"That's weird," I commented, thinking: My step-daughter is in on this kind of stuff?

"Unusual. Sometimes people talk about it, behind closed doors, of course. They're beginning to forget about it, but there were lots of funny incidents and people remember and laugh."

"Were you there?"

"No. It was a year or so before I got work up this way. People just remark about it so I kind-a got the picture."

I laughed again. "I can't believe it."

"Don't mention it, but it's no worse than painting yourself blue. That can't be true, but anyway in real life there in Portage generally people are opposed to it and don't like the story to get out. So keep yer mouth shut. It's dead and gone. But the game is still played, with clothes, naturally. And it is a Sunday. Starts about nine and ends mid to late afternoon when everyone is pretty tired out."

I looked at him and around at the group thinking about this queer turn of events. Putting ancient England aside, it made me think of famous old oil paintings of Italy and Grecian and Roman days - paintings of gods and others often naked in silvan scenes. I kept my face straight but inside I had to chuckle at the ridiculousness of man. If there was a possibility in anything, someone sure would give it a try. It's the nature of mankind. But I had to think it sounds more like high schoolers or collegers exploring nakedness or sex in some fashion or other, not a whole town of average people. I shook my head and tuned in to what the group was talking about. The game, naturally.

It was interesting, but not that interesting. I was wondering about that Bob-guy that had come in late. I switched chairs over next to him and said, "I lost my wife a couple of months ago to some guy with better looks and more dinero. Someone told me you lost your wife. What happened in your house, or shouldn't I ask?"

He looked me over a minute or so, turned away, then back and said, "I don't mind. It's a fact of life. My life. I tell you my tale and you tell me yours and we'll try and figure out what we did wrong, okay?"

I agreed and he started in.

Chapter 7
Another Member of the Fraternity

"I live" Bob hesitated "or lived, now with her gone I don't know what I'll end up doing, on the upside of a hill over towards Ellsworth way. Pretty view from up there. I'm an artist, do black and white's and some painting, and make a living selling my work to tourists going by on the highway. It's a living, but not by much, I tell ya."

He was off, I could tell, staring into space and talking. His voice cracking every once in a while as he told his tale. His wife had taken form and solidity in his mind as he spoke in that soft manner he had.

"Up there at home, though, it's real pretty looking out over the land. The cap of foliage at the top of the trees makes the trunks seem so thin in comparison, and the tall triangles of evergreens go up and up. This great mask of forest covers the earth, hiding and smoothing out all her imperfections. Off in the distance the haze cuts the detail of hill and valley, and it is just beautiful. I'm an artist. I appreciate that beauty. This day is warm. Comfortable without a sweater. It was only nine-thirty in the morning and I had the whole day ahead of me. Do I go to town, or stay and work on that big 20x30 oil I'd gotten started on? Life was beginning to empty itself of things that had-to-be-done. What would I do with myself?"

He's lonesome, I guess.

He looked at me a brief moment and then continued with his story.

"Cinderella, that's what I call her, it is her name anyway, is gone a week now, off to mama's house in Pennsylvania.

Maybe to come back in a week or two, maybe not. Maybe stay there for a long time, tired of a man and his critiques of life in general, tired of the government, the bankers, her and the baby, the foreign situation, the little government allotment in thanks for my bummed leg in the war. Tired of my drawings which aren't good enough. No one wants black and whites nowadays. Tired of the little money coming in. Our garden was a shambles. The big rain and wind had washed the meager depth of soil off the bedrock and so went the bonanza of eatables. The cell phone has rung once since she's been gone, a short phone call filled with long silences the same day she left. A query about how I was, maybe a chance to beg her back, but I was monosyllabic."

He used that word 'monosyllabic'. A big word for a guy eeking out a living in the wilderness with little stimulation coming his way, but certainly not dull by any standards. Maybe his big mistake was moving out there.

He told of how he yearned to hear her voice, or the tiny voice of the little girl. He remembered watching his wife standing there on the edge of the cliff, seeing her body through the thin fabric of her dress. The memory stirred him and he shifted in the rocker.

"Sittin' here creating wishes isn't doin' me no good. I should get up and do something, so I think. Now without her I could go over and check on Clute's. She didn't like my journeys over there, over here, actually." He looked around at everyone, no one paying any attention to us. "I would stay too long sometimes, overnight, and she was suspicious of the women here and what they all concocted to do. It didn't reek of honest doings. Well, so much for Cinderella's thoughts. I could come here, see what they had for doings.

It was always interesting. Like they have half a boat built here, (he looked at me intensely for a moment) way the hell up in these mountains, that they are going to haul to the ocean or Great Lakes and have a sail. Half a sail. Two years ago when it was nothing but a helluva big keel timber, it was across to Spain. Cinderella didn't care for their ways over here. She just didn't trust this place. She'd spotted me one time studying the thrust of Betsy Clute's blouse like any man would do. Hell, I'm an artist and she looked like a good subject. (He smiled and gave me a nod). Men are big on women's breasts and who would escape noticing? In fact old Benjamin told her that one time, referring to me. 'It's a natural for him,' he told her. 'He's an artist, isn't he?' She told me he said that. Also said he praised my black and white's, but she knew she was being warned that her man was susceptible to that teen-aged girl over here so as she saw it she was just protecting her interests: me, from wandering. Well, it wouldn't have happened. That was one thing, but you couldn't stop a man from looking, and that teen-aged girl liked to be looked at, that was apparent in the way she dressed and moved, so my Cinderella thought it'd be better for me to be away from here. I guess she was right because look at that girl now, pregnant. Right? Plus being a road-side artist gave me too much freedom. She wanted me to get a regular job and be out of circulation, so to speak, but like I told her, I wasn't ready to drop into the usual capitalist pattern of a job eight to five, five days a week and disappear into the great vat of American workers. My little stall on the road-side touched tourists ok, but sales are slow, and black and whites and paintings don't supply us with the cloth for dresses, or the money for college in fifteen years for the kid. I need a real job. So Cinderella proved her point. She is off to Pennsylvania to Mama and a make-over of her life. "I'll come back if you send for me," was her last words. Who knows? Her mother might send her back anyway.

"So anyway, after another three-quarters of an hour of looking out over the treetops and thinking, I closed the door, a last look across the view, and into the pick-up and come here. To hell with Cinderella's feelings about Clute's. At least I'd have someone to talk with to break that spat of loneliness. I drove into the parking place at the foot of the little hill and came on up, and guess what, that partner of yers, Barny, was there at the top of the climb, looking over the porch rail at me and he says, 'So here is the great wood chopper.' He saw me chopping wood one time. So out back they got a pile of light logs they've been pulling out of the woods. He's quite a guy, that Barny, he's persuasive. 'Why don't you build up an appetite out there for a bit and we'll have lunch soon. Give it a shot,' he says, and goes inside.

"Thus to the logs. Some cut into cord wood, others not. The chunks needed splitting for the stove. Someone had been chopping wood and stacking it across the back yard as a sort of wind break so I gathered up an ax and started in. Stopped for a rest and here I am talking to you. That's my story. Here for the duration."

He smiled at me; threw a hand up in a frustration at the future, at Cinderella his wife, and wanted my story so I gave him my 'ready-for-the-public' version of the duplicity of my wife and her behind the scenes boyfriend, their dance partnership, his airplane and that envelop that had arrived from her which I hadn't opened. A lawyer's announcement of our break-up. Whatever. He enjoyed my story, and shook his head and laughed, marveling at our connections.

We tuned out attention to the 'Clute's Gathering', which was what Bob called it. They were all there at the table and others like us spilling into chairs around the room, a sort of council of war. What now with these always 'up-to-something-Clute's' according to my new friend. Everyone was sitting there sipping coffee and all talking more or less at once. He got a cup, tilted the big thirty-cup urn put on every morning, some real cream, a spot of sugar and he was next to that one called "Jan", or was it "Mango"? Jan stuck out his hand to Bob and pronounced his name.

"Not 'Mango', Fargo. Jan Fargo," the man corrected and smiled. "I remember you from before," and after hesitating continued. "They tell me yer missus is gone home."

"Wow. Bad news travels fast, doesn't it. I never even got into the house to tell 'em myself" He answered. "Not to my home. Hers. Back to her mother, couldn't hack life with a true artist."

A slight laugh. "Who's got the kid? Didn't you have a kid with you when I saw you before?"

"Hers. Gone with her. She took the live stock with her, too, the kid and that cat."

Jan Fargo nodded. "True to form." He hesitated, then swung his pointing finger at Barnaby and me. "You know these two? They're up from the coast."

Bob said, "Um-m, yes. Well, that one there is Barnaby, Who's the other?" Meaning me. I'd never given him my name.

"He's called Trevor something. Don't know his last name. A friend of Barny's. They sailed up here from down Cape Ann way. Imagine that? A long way. I heard his story a night ago. He also lost his wife. Some guy stole her away."

"I heard it. He just told me. What's he doing here?"

"Just a companion to Barny. Heading on out to Portage. He's got a step-daughter out there to see."

I watched him turn close to Jan Fargo and say, "What happened to the so-called Sarge Clute, the great sailor?"

"Still out on the briney deep."

"That tanker took him and he's still out there somewhere?"

"I guess so."

Someone at the table got too loud and the others stopped their conversations and paid attention. So we did, too.

Chapter 8
More Useless Chatter

This big fellow with the belly was talking. "So we're getting on down there. Now look at this angle. We got the boys up from the coast, so there's some help there, and we got Sarge here, too. He'll be back in time. So there's a chance that we could out number 'em. That's good in our favor. Now they'll be surprised at us showing up so won't all be together, meaning that they'll be surprised, that is weak, and scattered, not together, so we should be able to overpower 'em. Now that's good. Now here's what I got in mind. We don't have ta come out the way we go in, we could go out the old covered bridge." (Mumbling among the assembled.) "We was planning on out over the concrete bridge on 103, making it a long run to get to it, being there before they get it together and stop us there." (More mumbling.) "The bridge is under repair, you men know that. And with only one lane open, we could block that or they could. There's equipment parked around that job and if just one rolled down the hill onto the bridge we'd be locked in. Not good. We talked of using the covered bridge but it has those old heavy gates at the near end. Just one of their men there, phoned in and standing guard, could get those things closed and bolted and we'd be stopped. We even talked about sending one of our guys there and doing that very thing so they can't escape, but discarded it 'cause it's too far out, and one man with a BB gun could frighten off whoever's there. And why bother? It's just a game. And don't forget we got Sarge now. He could be down there by the Ambrose road and get there plenty early and stand guard. Frighten any guards they send out. Keep the highway bridge open. We do the job, win our part, and instead of heading out like they expect, on the regular road, duck off east and go over the rope bridge. We'd be away and gone and they'd never get the flag back, exactly what they expect to do when we get to the 103 bridge, what they'd expect. Bottle us up there on the one lane thing and we're caught. Can't get away and they get the flag back. So we go out the rope bridge and that's it. What'd'ya think? We win."

"We could have Sarge close and gate it after we're gone. They couldn't chase us then. We'd be home free." one of the others said, and slapped the table and laughed in glee.

"The stakes."

"It's a big game of 'Steal the Flag', done between two communities. The rope bridge is over a rough canyon full of rushing water and impassible. There is no crossing but for that bridge, the covered bridge, and the one on 103."

Someone else put in "Now this year the gang in town is big, rough, and scattered about the village, and the flag is there with an envelope attached and in the envelop is a thousand dollar bill to 'sweeten' the stakes for the flag."

"Big men play little boy games," I whispered to Jan.

He retorted with, "Just like men, say the women, mostly foolish."

"They make a real day of it, you know, hot dogs and potato salad and beer, all that sort of thing?" I asked Jan Fargo, or January, as he every once in a while liked to be called.

"Oh-h-h yeah." He said it with a rather lilting up and down voice.

"It's the Full Catastrophe, as someone once said as he laughed. It costs a helluva lot of money. All the foods along during the day, and lots of it, and the big banquet at the end, it costs plenty."

"They all chip in?"

"No-o-o. There's a rich guy out there, he funds the whole shebang. Leastwise that's the going belief. That's why folks participate. You couldn't get all those na'ar-do-wells to do anything as athletic as that otherwise. Even a lot of the women participate. It is fun, you know. It's a ball. Ya gotta do it. You will won't you?"

So I found out that this Silas fellow was behind it. He was rich, into investments and such. He spent mornings on the computer making money. He was tall and fat and his feet went out to the side thirty degrees when he walked, slow and flat-footed and a stride like he had stones in his shoes, and dressed like he was poor as a stovepipe. Moth-eaten suit, always dirty with food stains on the front and from time to time down his chin out of the corner of his mouth like old men do, not aware that they drool when they eat and being old and unaware, they don't use a napkin. Teen-aged girls make fun of him behind his back, but he's rich and getting richer. Melissa, the divorced woman from Bert plays up to him, hoping to latch on to that money, but he's immune. Likes her attention but that's all."

"No luck there, Melissa," he added.

Silas Vanderstein. Jewish. He's called by the locals 'B&B'. Claimed his daddy died in a Nazi concentration camp. Says he was born in the late thirties, his mom carried him off when he was ten or eight or six, he never has the same birthday year. One of the boys swore he would sneak into his office someday and check his IRS records and find out when he really was born, but hasn't done it yet.

There has to be a referee. They pick Jason Brown, as solid a drinker as there ever was. The proverbial Pay Day Drinker and what's left to the missus, a thin, worn out woman with bad legs and a cough. It was said he used to beat her regularly but she nursed him when he was sick that time and he's thought better of the beatings since, so she's fairly better off, in a sense.

Jan Fargo looked at me. I could see he was getting ready to tell me a secret, or a near equivalent, so leaned closer.

"It's the dumbest thing these men have ever done is the general feeling amongst the ordinary church-going folk in town. Portage, that is. It used to be a big secret, this game the men played; but being as these men, almost to a man, always told their tales out of school, just like men, it's come to be a well known exercise. Leastwise that's what I call it. So all Portage knows about it and pretty much everybody gets involved one way or another, and there's laughter about it. It's just a fun exercise for grown-ups, but nowadays the kids get into it one way or another.

You gotta do it. It's fun."

Chapter 9
Buzzy

Barnaby had sauntered over followed by another of the men. He had on a T-shirt with the word "BUZZY" on it, front and back. I recognized him as the one they had said could give us a ride up to Portage.

"Why's it so God damned far, anyway?" Barnaby said, talking to no one in particular. .

Jan answered authoritatively. "It's the way things are. It's geography. It's in an out of the way spot, too. Portage almost doesn't exist."

"It wouldn't hurt for it to drop out of existence," that was this Buzzy fellow chiming in trying to make joke, I figured. Jan looked annoyed at him.

Bob looked at him. "What kind of answer is that, anyway? Portage is just lucky it still exists."

"So are we, so we can have 'The Game'." Jan was really a proponent of 'The Game', no question.

Buzzy interrupted our great discussion. "Tain't worth fusing about. Like he says, it's too far off from us. It's not good for our mental health to be playing kid's games."

"Come on, Buzzy. It's just a long way off and you can get there on foot, by car, or canoe. Probably by parachute, too, and break yer god damn neck, thank you. Try it." Proponent Jan Fargo sounded like he'd defend it to the death.

Barnaby said, "Well, it's not much of a distance if you go by canoe. It's maybe a two day trip and almost straight. The halfway point is at the lake. You go down the river out of the gorge and you're at the lake. There's even a cabin there that folks can stay overnight in. Then the next day you're there. Maybe twenty-five, thirty miles total. Go in from the seashore and it's an easy canoe. Done it once." Buzzy was whining something about it but I couldn't understand.

Barnaby gave me "the look" and I knew it was to remind me this was the taxi driver that was going to take us to Portage.

Bob whispered in my ear that no one liked Buzzy, he added not to pay him any attention because he told stupid lies to people to entertain himself and didn't help anyone. He had a cursed, stupid, dumb streak and pretended to have this brilliant brain. It was really a dull, screwed up mind. I didn't think he was going to stop with this man's ways and manners, he had so many unusual ones, but he did and I thought I suppose an artist has lots of time to analyze one's characteristics.

I apparently missed something for Jan was up and snarling, "Now come on you ignorant turd. What's the truth. Don't give us that nonsense."

Buzzy started to say something about the glaciers but got busted on the side of the head by Jan's fist. When he turned to look at Jan he said, "What was that for?" and found a poke in the nose awaiting him. He didn't say a word, just got a rag from somewhere and gently touched his nose. It started running red.

Jan said "If I knew you'd be so asinine we'd never have let you come to this meeting. Now tell us the truth about the glaciers, and remember I've read up on Portage and the glacial lake and the gorge and all that stuff. Now give it to us straight."

Buzzy started, "Now you wait a goddamned minute, you – "

Another fist in the head.

"Cut it out. Okay, okay. It's true, it was the glacier and this tectonic plate."

"Keep talking."

So then Buzzy told about the tectonic plate that lifted here millions of years ago and the land between it and the ocean became the coastal plain. A giant lake filled up this part and the water cut its way out as the land rose gradually, the tectonic plate, that is, and the gorge where the water ran got deeper and so on.

"The town got started because it was such a job hauling a canoe of supplies up the gorge, or else hiking up with the stuff on your back, and that's what happened until finally some guy back in the eighteen hundreds hacked a road through the forest, but the terrain was unfriendly."

"Careful." This from Barnaby, keeping Buzzy on the truth and not some fancy made-up story.

"Yeah. So the terrain was post-glacial and full or rocks and twists and turns that the river had dug in the tens of thousands of years as it followed the least resistance in the ground. So now that road, following the easiest way, winds way up north, then south and loops and so on. It's like ninety or a hundred miles."

"No one gives a shit," muttered Barnaby. "The country's useless and no good, worth nothing. Just glacial till like the glacier came and went and came and went and left a disgusting layer of till, layer after layer."

"That's right," shouted Buzzy. "That's exactly what they say happened, but how they know I have no idea. And you didn't have to poke me in the eye."

"It wasn't your eye. It was your nose. Don't you know your nose from your eye?"

"Yeah, yeah, my nose." And he continued talking, "The road was no beauty, although they say that the tourists who venture up this far say it's a beautiful sylvan example of the primitive environment and so on. Baloney, says I. It's just a long boring trip seeing all these trees."

It was obvious that he couldn't stop talking. Even with the handkerchief at his nose.

Then he asked, "You guys really did sail all the way up here? Why didn't you go the rest of the way, you know, all the way up to the mouth of the river?"

"We heard there was a road and we were tired of sailing." Barnaby said.

I said nothing. The fact that we'd had a massive argument about it and had this little falling out wasn't any of his business. I wasn't sure about this Buzzy chap. His info about the glacier and that geology business sounded accurate, but these folks certainly didn't seem to like him. 'Course he butted in whenever he wanted and that was annoying and impolite.

"So you guys stopped your sailing way down there at Twelfth Port and hired a car this far?"

"No," I said. "We got a ride up here to Clute's and we figured we'd hire you to take us on to Portage. Heard you did a taxi service."

He sounded funny when he talked. Holding that cloth to his nose made him nasal sounding. "There's gonna be trouble at Portage in a week or so. The Game's beginning. Now this game is a tradition there and we, well you outsiders could get hurt."

"We're here at Clute's down the coast a bit from Portage and it doesn't sound like we'll have any trouble."

"Ok. No trouble. We're sending a bunch up to play the game this year, just like last. I'll ride you guys up there. It's like seventy-three miles. Figure you'll lose a day getting there."

Barnaby nodded. "We're ready to go. All briefed about the game and gave 'em a donation to help our team get up there."

"Really. Well, By Christ. Just you two?" Buzzy dabbed at his nose. "Whenever yer ready."

"There's more coming along on their own. We'll win. You just watch."

Believe it or not, Buzzy was at Clute's for us at dawn and by late afternoon he let us off in the center of town. Barnaby gave him forty bucks and he was off for the trip back. Barnaby turned to me and we did our good-byes as I started walking toward the rise where Sara and Marty lived.

Chapter 10
My New Life Begins

Well, Sara accepted me, I thought she would, and Marty did, too. I guess they were bored, particularly at meals having had no one different to talk to over the eight years they've been married; and with no children either, I might add. Strange about that, a young couple like them and no kids. But anyway, I felt that I should contribute some to the family coffers so when Marty mentioned that Bill was advertising for an assistant at his garage, I perked up my ears. Wandered down to the *Empty Plate*, a neat small restaurant with some booths and eight tables, for a cup of Java and then on over two blocks to Bill's Garage. He fixed all kinds of cars and trucks and farm machinery, even sometimes doing house calls when the machine was too big to get to his garage in town. So now here I am working half days and I'm learning a new skill: car fixing. I know nothing about it and Bill says he's not much better. Cars these days are too electronic in all sorts of ways so it's a new world. I thought I was getting into a world that life had left behind coming up here to Portage, fixing model A's and cars of the Great Depression. Well, it's okay, we do fix up-to-date modern cars, and if I can't do it, we suggest some place in Ellsworth or Bangor and a flat bed will come and haul the car to the city for fixing. Bill's an easy going guy so it's pleasant work, only half a day, but it helps Sara and Marty out. I usually get in to Bill's about ten in the morning and leave generally around two. I cover the garage and gas pump component while Bill's off for lunch. He likes martinis and although I tell him what my other daughter says, namely liquor will eat up yer liver and a few other organs and you'll die, he don't pay attention and says, "I'm gonna die anyway, you know that." So I don't push the idea of teetotaling on him.

So you know what I do? Well, Marty and Sara are up at six, so I am too, and then after breakfast and Marty has left, Sara and I have another cup of coffee, chat a bit before I head into town, such as it is, only about two thousand people if that. Walk into town and stop at the *Empty Plate*. It's on the main drag, comfortable little place, low key. Come in and have a cup, sit and chat, which I do until it's time to get on to Bill's Garage. Saw a nice looking woman in there three weeks ago getting on into her middle ages, well put together, friendly to the locals, seems to know everyone and occasionally some other woman or two with her like they were departing some sort of church committee meeting or somethin'. We ain't been introduced so don't talk but she seems a nice woman that I could stand to know better.

Last week I saw her there again and later asked Sara who she was. She didn't know but toward supper she repeated my description of the woman to me, accurately too, and said it might be 'Manda Cunningham who lived down the road at the foot of the hill. Sara looked at me and smiled one of those woman's smiles that says she knew what's going on inside my head.

I said Bill's an easy going guy, and he is, but I wonder about people and how they bring up their kids. Now Sara and Marty ain't got no kids, so they're exempted from this discussion, but Bill, who runs Bill's Garage is a puzzle to me.

We were working on the engine in the shed, the two of us. Bill doing the work 'cause he knew engines and I was the gofer, watching and trying to help and asking questions and getting answers of a sort. There was car noise out in the street, of course, and we'd look up occasionally, then one moment there was a girl's voice, "See, ya, dad." We looked up.

I saw a girl in the usual scruffy outfit maybe in her early twenties with a huge back pack going by the open door of the shed, and heard Bill's voice say, "So long, Amy," and then to me as he continued working, "My daughter. My second daughter. On her way back to school."

"Where's she going?" I was generally puzzled. No car? No transport? I could feel my nose crinkling up in puzzlement.

"On her way back to school. College. Hitchhiking."

I couldn't believe my ears. Hitchhiking? A girl? And her father lets it go by like nothing.

She never came back, so I assumed she'd gotten a ride. Apparently she did this all the time. And her dad let her! I'd have been concerned that something would happen to her.

I watched and listened, but there was little information over time, and certainly I had concluded that Bill's approach to his children was different from mine. He had another, older daughter of whom he said one time that he was taking to Cancun with him on a vacation trip, not his wife, not the other children (there was also a boy). Just this one, named "Jeanie" was going.

"She's easy going, and pleasant, doesn't complain, more amiable than the other, who's always off in her own world, I guess. Jeanie can let things slide by without complaint and is helpful and more interested in what's around. Better company".

Bill, Amy, Jeanie. I was thinking about them while sittin' at the table in the *Empty Plate* and looked up from my coffee and there was that woman that Sara called 'Manda Cunningham looking at me. Gosh!

Chapter 11
Portage

So now I've lived a bit with Sara and Marty and got myself a fair assessment of this town called Portage. Small town, but an economic center for a big dead area. "Dead" isn't a polite term so I should say instead it's in the doldrums. It's poor and there are few jobs. Mostly trees and subsistence agriculture, so the people constitute a mix, 'cause people with computers are moving in and working from home, there are a few retirees, and some people with far-away jobs hang their hats here. Like that George Cunningham, a consultant, and 'Manda Cunningham's husband. And there's the political wing, the ones who in or out of office seem to run things – like the town. An', you know, some are hayseeds and some are smart as whips, and some have ideas of their own that they can carry out here, no interference. People don't give a hoot, mostly. Now take B&B, for instance.

Now ya'll pay attention. I'm gonna tell about this big, self-important ball 'o fat called B&B.

Big and Burley was his nickname (never spoken if he was present) and big and burley he was, and he smoked a big Winston Churchill cigar constantly. When one burned down or out, he'd chew it. He had bad breath but women, for some incomprehensible reason, seemed to love him. His real name was Bertram Bennett III (nee Silas Vanderstein) and although no one knew for sure, the general consensus was he was rich. He dressed frequently like a pig, other times like a southern planter. No telling which outfit or persona would appear, but whichever, it lasted the whole day and into the night, nor was there any way to tell which persona was the real man. If it was a dance night at the Owego Hall out on route 103, he always sat and watched the dancers and the band and chatted with those about. He had a special group that in some ways seemed a creation of his own personality, in all fact, an extension of himself. I would almost be inclined to say that if he were suddenly to erupt into a puff of smoke, he and all his friends would evaporate at the same time. A chunk of the Earth erased. The Earth would wobble in its orbit until readjusted.

Yes, he had this core group of friends, but he mixed with everyone, and when it was time to go home he always took Bernice with him. Whatever happened between them no one really knew for sure. If he didn't move to her at the end of the evening, she'd wait and he'd come and get her. Bernice was a senior in high school. She did pretty well according to her teachers and had no known boyfriends of her own age or social set although she had lots of friends. I noticed that he started taking her home despite whoever she danced, sat, or talked with during the evening. Now about two years ago, so I'm told, she was just a sophomore in high school then, he gave her a ride home one night when she was there. It was the first time he'd ever given her a ride, but apparently, or so it looked, she was to go home with a bunch of girls that she'd come with. They went off without her and she was standing softly sobbing out among the trees where cars were parked. Leastwise that's what Henry told us when suddenly he appeared. I was talking with that French-Canadian gentleman that plays the bull fiddle and asking about that tall, well-built young woman named Bernice. Trying to get myself oriented to the community I guess you'd say. We'd just gotten to chatting about her and here is this Henry kid, listening, then butting into the conversation and telling us about her. Henry said Bernice had been left behind and was out there by that big pine, looking forlorn in the dark, and crying. "I think they forgot her," he said. Anyway he claimed he was there and trying to help so went up to B&B and told him.

"So what am I supposed to do?" B&B presumably said, rather annoyed.

This Henry must have a good memory because he then supposedly said to B&B, "Well you're older. I thought you'd like to know. Maybe give her some help." Him telling, talking to B&B like that is a first in the world of stupidity, I'd think, but then he was young, still is actually, so you have to forgive him a bit. So here I am, an old codger, listening to this kid tell us about something a year or two ago, something he had never forgotten and probably never thanked by either B&B nor the girl for his help.

The bull fiddle player asked him if he always interrupted adults in conversations and he rather gave some sort of late-teen jargon, a little embarrassed, but then he burst out with: "But they're doing it again, right now, B&B is out there in the grove talking to her. Ain't gonna do anything about it."

The bull fiddler replied, "He's been riding her home for two years. It's none of our business."

"Well come look. It's not right."

So the three of us now went to the exit and peered out. We closed the door and looked into the dark, then walked about a hundred feet toward that big pine and saw two silhouettes in the dark against the one yard light. We could hear voices, but not what they said. The girl, whose head moved up as we stood there, was looking at this big body shape who had to be Big and Burley. B&B was headed for his Cadillac, and the other shadow moved right along behind. He opened her door, she got in, and then he moved around to the other side and he got in. We could hear the crash as the door closed. And they sat there. Talking, I suppose.

I heard Henry muttering about it. "So that's how it happened?" I asked him, trying to be polite to this Peeping Tom who had kept his desire alive for two years thus far.

"It's always this way," he said.

I felt sorry for him and was going to say something of a counseling nature to him when the bull fiddler whispered a little loudly, "Well forget about it, forget her, she's made a choice and her folks probably support it or she wouldn't still be seeing him. Run along before you do something stupid. Now get."

So I imagine this Bernice girl was B&B's girl, had been a long time and still was. She'd grow up and go to college and meet someone else and drift out of sight, and even this kid would forget her. That's the way life is.

So we're standing there by the big pine watching that Cadillac and here's this kid again with his dumb questions.

"Do you think he takes her directly home?" He was fishing for information.

"I don't know."

"Do you think they stop some place on the way?"

"I don't know."

"Where would they go? Park some place and kiss?"

"I don't know." B&B wasn't all that old, maybe in his mid-forties, maybe even in his mid-fifties; and she was, hell, only a high school girl. She had a mom and dad so couldn't be deprived or something like that. And there was never any word from her mom or dad. Who knows, maybe they wanted her with B&B so's she'd have a protector 'till she got older and knew the world and could marry well.

So Henry goes on, "I tried to ask her out for a date. Go down to Skowhegan to a movie on a Wednesday. You know what she said?"

"I don't know." That was the conversation between Henry and me and the bull fiddle player about two weeks ago.

Then it seemed I wasn't the only one he'd asked about Bernice for he continued, "Well she didn't think her mom and dad would like that. That's all she said. What do you think of that?"

"I don't know." I didn't know the 'she' in his chatter but I wasn't listening particularly well anyway. Didn't make no difference no matter what.

"I guess I'll not ask her again. I think that B&B has her all tied up with him. Isn't he a little old for her? That's what my dad said. But all he did was shrug, as if it weren't important. What'd ya think-a that?"

"I don't know."

Later on, another Saturday dance and I saw Henry dancing a lot with one of the other girls at the dance so guessed he'd pretty much figured it out himself, still he came up to me the Sunday after the dance, first time I've talked to him in a long bit of time, so what does he talk about? You guessed it. Bernice. I've gotten to hate that name even if everyone looks at her and thinks she's a beauty. Tall, voluptuous, and I mean voluptuous, and that's what he wanted to talk about. Voluptuousness.

"Do you think she pads her bras?"

I laughed. That's what he wanted to talk about. Well, of course I answered truthfully, "I don't know." And that was the truth. I hadn't been watching like he did, or so I think. So I began casting her a glance every now and then. I couldn't tell. Never could. Always thought there were more important things in life to study than how women attract men. Well, he was attracted I guess. Good thing B&B didn't know or there'd have been some young lad getting a beating when he least expected it. The underground word was that B&B had his buddies do that sort of thing.

Of course one of the current fashions of women is to wear tight fitting clothes, has been for a while, maybe two or three years, the fashions finally get up this way. And she was decked out, looking real nice, as always. Yep. They say she was stacked, to use the old-fashioned term, and she was. A pleasure for a young man to look upon, I'd say. As for me, yeah, a picture worth taking, but that B&B was quiet but a tough one and he was still giving her rides home. Persistent fellow, and dangerous, I think, despite his quiet and oh so proper and gentle talk. All a pretense. Stay clear of that.

So that B&B is a sample of the power elite here in Portage as I see it. So that's somethin' to keep in mind, and the fact is I think he's behind that fiasco at the Steal the Flag game. Not a fiasco so much as a very clever disguise of a major robbery. And the so-called accident that left poor Jeremy with a broken leg and internal injuries.

So do I think she pads her bras? I hope not. Shame to look on a beautiful woman and know she's all false. So next time Henry asks it'll be "of course not." and he'll want to know how I know, then what do I say? He shouldn't still be thinking and dreaming about her anyway.

Now you may be wondering how I got into this discussion with Henry and probably you noted the time frame running a year and a half ago to today, well that's all fact. So I was telling you being up at Clute's and helping out Barnaby and the fire and our trip up the coast to get here for whatever help they had needed, which I never did figure out because it was Barnaby's effort and I just went along. Old guys like me need stimulation or we slowly solidify and topple over dead, so I got stimulated, and Henry and his worries about that girl were stimulating, after a fashion. Anyway that was a bit ago and so I got to my step-daughter's place and stayed with them, helped out around the place some, Marty, her husband, was a carpenter and away during the day and I filled in at Bill's and did little household chores to earn my keep.

Well anyway, it was a place to be and watch things going on. But you know, that talk back then over at Clute's place was interesting because they mentioned the murder that hadn't occurred yet, and even this B&B stuff, and a robbery and soon. Well, so that brings me up to date and here and now, all those things take that long to come together and you'd never expect it, mostly because people don't remember all those little 'suggestions' about what's to happen. But I remember. That's why I mention all that again, to refresh my memory and come up to speed with the slow pace of things around Portage, 'cause things do happen, and if you can remember back, you can see hints about it. Like foretelling the future, but the time frame is so long between "hints" that people don't remember, make no connection, like they say these days, people don't connect the dots.

You know, when you put it together, it just proves the saying: "the mills of the gods grind slowly, but grind exceedingly fine", because that's pretty much what finally happened here in little isolated Portage while I was living there. Of course I moved on, but that was after it had all transpired. Sara was pregnant (we think) and 'Manda had settled herself about her marriage and there was no problem over the murder and all that business was done and, well, what do you do? Head on out.

It was fun in a way, dangerous and the murder and who had to pay for it, for the non-murder, actually, with all the town caught up in the thing.

It 'Was-a-Time', I'd say. The kind of stuff that should make a Great Myth, like King Arthur and all that. We'd have to include B&B and Bernice. There was 'Manda who I'd just about marry if she'd given me the chance. The 'chance' meaning if she'd get over the husband who was always out consulting, and of course Sara and Marty, and maybe the baby although we'll have to wait a bit to see that one, and maybe include Jeff in that. Nice to know who's baby it is, I guess, although it doesn't really matter in the short turn. Other folks, nameless to us, might not like that, they want the final tale.

We must include The Great Robbery, and those poor bewildered armored car cops, that detective they called 'The Dick', and George, naturally. The ladies at the church, and a whole bunch of minor characters. What a bunch. What a myth that would make.

Chapter 12
And Thus We Come to the Armored Car Robbery

I was thinking about that Myth business. All kinds of guys got caught up in it. Amazing. And me too, I was part of that great mess, I mean myth. Everything didn't happen with me in it, but being old, and wise, or so they thought, I heard about it one way or another, and here's what happened and to who, or is it to whom?

Oh, that being the case, and me being advised of what happened and to and by whom, I hear about the armored car robbery. Can you believe that? It was the armored car man who told me. I shouldn't mention his name because he thinks the authorities are still nose-to-the-grindstone to find out what really happened, but here's what he told me that night, us two sitting in the corner booth at the *Miss Tracy*. It was sort of funny, but so typical of things happening up here. That, of course, was before I left - all that robbery and later the so-called murder.

Let me tell you about the robbery, probably the most interesting story.

There was Jeremy, the village half-wit, and the armored car guys: the fat one who lost the key, and two others. From town there was Abraham (Abby) Black, nefarious helper to B&B. There was Sam Bernideed, another of his henchmen. They were involved alright.

The armored car comes once a week. This time it ran amuck of the 'Steal the Flag' game. Men running here and there, crossing streets all of a sudden and running in herds down streets, yelling and hollering, and someone had fireworks so there was noise and confusion all over. Sam Bernideed got into the UCC church and started ringing the bell. Might have been deliberate since it rang twice, or four times, or seven, and never in the same order so I think they were signals, but that dad-ratted bell ringing every once in a while made pandemonium seem real. And it was. It was quite a day. The armored car did its money pickup and was off on its way, but one of the men from up this way had short circuited a semi-truck parked down by the station and drove it about a half mile up the road and parked cross-wise on the 103 bridge and blocked escape from town. So the armored car ran up to this and realized it was trapped unless they went out the gorge road where the covered bridge was, which they did. But the covered bridge is rickety and the left side (left, remember your old Latin class, left is translated as sinister, or something like that), and it was. The sinister side (left) cracked with a bang and the rear left wheel went into the resulting hole where the underpinnings of the bridge on that side had let go. Down in the hole it went, and it's heavy, and it stayed there. Weren't going nowhere, that was fer sure.

They called their headquarters on the radio or cell phone or whatever they had, and the bosses were angry. Sometime later a big wrecker came and lifted the armored car free. The wrecker had to back onto the bridge causing the underpinings to crack once, twice, three times and they had a seething, small earthquake of soil and rock that supported it. It gave a deep, whooshing sound and the armored car slid down over the parapet toward the surging stream below. The wrecker was tangled in the broken bridge and just managed to get itself hauled up on the good section of road. They radioed or telephoned some other outfit who came the next day with a crane to lift the car free, but no one had seemed to mention that it was a covered bridge and the top of the covered bridge was in the way of the crane dropping a hook and line down to lift out the car. So having been there one night, it stayed a second.

What about the three cops, the crew inside this car sitting intact but at an angle and sworn to protect the money? Too hot, too dangerous, it might slip in the hole and who knows, fall to the bottom of the gorge, so they abandoned the car. They walked into town to get something to eat. It was about a three mile walk, and a hot day, a discouraging day, and they weren't equipped to walk three miles. They weren't in trim, that is to say they were armored car cops, a sedentary job fraught with occasional moments of brandishing the pistol, more to impress the ladies and children. So they took frequent rests. Take Steer for example, the cop with the frightening nickname. He'd grown somewhat overweight, actually a lot of overweight, and he'd gotten a special permit to wear suspenders on the job. At mile one Steer sat on a rock until his companions lost patience. He relieved himself behind the bushes and rejoined them on the trek to town. Diabetic, it was a tough walk and he never noticed that when in the bushes with his pants down his wallet had slipped somewhat, not out, but high in the rear pocket and subject to tumbling out should it become displaced with the roll of buttocks as they worked left and right to support the steps his stocky legs took to propel him after his companions.

It fell out somewhere along the way.

Three kids, honest lads, found it when they went out that way for whatever reason kids do things. They must have been sick of trying to figure out the Steal the Flag strategy of the two teams. Some kids played, some watched and cheered or laughed. These three went off for a bike ride. Slow and grumbling, they argued Samuel into splitting the *Butterfingers* bar into three so they could all enjoy it. Distracted or not by candy, one of them saw the billfold, and being honest kids they picked it up before running into old Jeremy, a somewhat friend of B&B. Jeremy, runner-up for the stupidest numskull in town, was as honest as the day is long, took it, said he'd get it to the newspaper so they could put in a notice about lost wallets and how people should be more careful, took the bills out of the wallet as reward for returning the wallet to someone responsible for such things and went along his way.

B&B, being a big bruiser of a man, had been stationed as lookout in the UCC Church tower where with his cell phone he reported the doings of the opposing team, several members forming a diversion toward the drugstore while the rest were out somewhere else. Jeremy saw him up there in the cupola window and called up to him, the secret watcher that no one knew was up there, pointing out to him what he had found and holding it up for B&B to assess.

B&B imagined money somebody lost. He called Jeremy up and ten minutes later Jeremy, overjoyed at being in the cupola with his idol gave him the wallet to assess, find the owner, return it, all that. "No, there weren't no money in it when it was turned over to me. Whoever found it first must have helped themselves. People just ain't trustworthy these days" thus spoke Jeremy.

"By gum, there ain't a single buck in this thing. Where'd you say you found it, out in the road east of town? Christ. It's a crying shame people can't be honest."

Jeremy was almost of an honest persuasion and told B&B that he hadn't found it, it was a bunch of kids. He felt like crying.

B&B nodded, patted Jeremy's thigh. "It's alright. Can't trust kids these days. We'll check the rest of it and see if we can find whose it is."

Lots of papers, a metal key, some change. Papers referred to the official cop and the company and so on.

"See anything?" said Jeremy, watching his idol look out over the village and stare and stare, holding the official cop's license (with photograph) and silver key. He remembered looking out below, into the square, where three dusty policemen had appeared, working their now slow walk toward the police station, stopping for a cup of coffee and a good sit down, maybe a late lunch at the *Empty Plate* lunch room half a block on, then on to the police station.

"See anything?" asked Jeremy, watching his idol stare into space.

B&B waited a minute more then gave a note to Jeremy and told him to find Abraham Black. The game had been on since early morning, and no winner yet, but, "I bet Abby is in the *Miss Tracy*. Try there first. Hey wait. You got any money?" B&B didn't want Jeremy going in the bar if he had money."

Jeremy swallowed and looked at his idol, and then lied. "Naw. I ain't got none."

That B&B is sure one smart man, thought Jeremy as he looked in the bar and saw Abraham Black with two friends sipping a cool one before going out to steal the opposition's flag.

Abraham and B&B, best friends, drove out to the bridge. Abby, thin and lithe, slunk along the bridge structure and tried the key in the side door of the topsy-turvy armored car. It opened.

Taking only enough for a nice weekend, then a new winter coat for Bernice, then a hefty metal box for Abby's wife's Christmas fund, then a bag of mixed bills for the church for letting his team use the cupola, three bags of mixed coins were cached in the woods by the bridge, eight boxes of mixed money stuff was carried a hundred fifty feet along the road and tucked under a culvert overhang. In a moment of altruistic glee, they locked the armored car up and with one bag extra to hide under their team's flagpole, so's whether they won or lost they could have a termination party when the game was over. And joy of joys, now for a beer to finish off the venture.

They sipped their beer quietly, ignoring three blue uniformed men having one at the booth in the corner. The empty mind is the workshop of the devil and an additional idea began to percolate in the minds of Portage's two. They left the *Miss Tracy* and returned to the armored car to find the wrecker there and officials on the other side of the river, gathered there because the regular road was blocked by some semi-truck and wondering where their crew had gone. The car was still locked so everything was alright. Abby and B&B yelled excuses and made complaints about the broken bridge to the officials and workmen on the other side and departed, only to return at 2am when the guard the company officials had left for "security" (just in case) was asleep at his post: a campfire, sleeping bag and bottle of Seagrams.

B&B and Abby had a wheelbarrow and walked seventy pounds of coin and paper a quarter mile down the road to the car. It was quick effort because there was a celebratory dance on and B&B had to pick up his high school girl. Moving the coin, Abby got sweaty and got out his handkerchief not realizing he'd pulled out the key also, and dropped it. He wiped his sweaty face and neck and they headed out to the celebratory dance.

Chapter 13
Through the Grating

You know how the old fashioned ventilation system used to be? There would be a heater furnace on the main floor, and there'd be a hole with a grate over it cut in the ceiling so that the hot air from below could go up through the grate and heat the second floor room. A grate like that is what I had in my upstairs bedroom in Sara's house. I could hear, even look through and see what was going on in the kitchen below. Voices below caught my attention; Sara, and Marty's helper Jeff who had come in with a pitcher for water.

Marty has a construction business, and he and Jeff are working on a three story office building at the edge of Portage where the chasm cuts next to the town. They have other work too, one of the jobs is fixing up the corner of his house, so it is not unusual to see Jeff around. Except on this one day they are working on the corner reconstruction and when Jeff comes in for water Sara is at the sink, doing something for lunch probably. She steps aside slightly so that he can fill the small pitcher, but not too much, and he brushes against her. A tiny noise from her, and he makes a playful press against her as she stands there, and she presses back. He looks at her and smiles and winks. He half turns with his arm out and she slides into it. The water runs over the pitcher and into the sink and down. She reaches around past him and turns off the water. He has her outstretched arm in his and turning slightly, she's in his arms. A couple of young pups foolin' around. He leaves the pitcher in the sink and manages a slow careful turn and their bodies lock.

They kiss and he reaches around to fiddle with her bra. Trouble for me is I hate sneak-watching on other folk. And me at the grating can't help but watch and listen. I was drawn and couldn't stop myself. Lordy, lordy, lordy.

"Are you having trouble or something?" says Sara with a smile. He presses against her and his hand moves from her back and then down, "Yes, I think I am."

"Poor boy. Can't unfasten the lady's bra? She said over his shoulder.

"I know. Let me try again." His hand moved to fiddle with it, knowing he can't undo it with one hand and moving to free the other hand to help.

She takes a deep breath, and now her breasts were pressing against him. "You must practice."

"It's too tight." he says.

"Poor boy." she exhales slowly, letting her chest collapse and feeling him working on the straps. It feels good and their lips meet again, and her reply continues, "I guess you'll just have to come by next time before I get fully dressed," and as if remembering who she is, she continues, "But you shouldn't."

He is lifting her blouse from within the slacks she is wearing, his lips on hers again. The kiss lingers, his hands have the blouse high, almost to her shoulders, bra exposed. He looks over her back at it, guides his fingers and the clasps with the three hooks fall loose. The pleasant sensations overcome her and she exhales a quiet, soothing exclamation, pressing close to him, and he is forced to hold her. His words penetrate my mind, "don't you dare wear all these clothes the next time I come by." Gracious! I am thinking.

"Yes master, as you wish."

His hands move down her sides over her hips.

"Oh, Marty is coming" and she turns and pulls away.

He grabs the water pitcher and starts toward the door, and she heads up the stairs toward the bedroom, pulling her blouse down around her.

Marty and Jeff are at the door facing each other; Jeff going out and Marty on his way in with a suspicious look on his face.

"What's holding you up?"

He brandishes the pitcher. "Stuff in the sink, wouldn't fit against the dishes there. All set now. Last dishes cleaned out. Got it."

Marty is turning to go back out, "I got that two by six up inside the edge. It's ready to nail if you can push it up about a foot and hold it." They get into the job ahead but Jeff's mind is on the woman, another man's wife.

Later, at one point during the lunch conversation Sara says pointedly to Jeff, "That must never happen again." Marty is busy eating and participating in the conversation but the sentence fits so well that he misses its intent, while Jeff sees her eyes fastened on his and knows all too well what she means. His eyebrows lift, drop, and he swallows.

And on the ride home he thinks of her words. This business with her could be curtains for a friendship. She is right. No more. Never again. Just stay clear. It's like my dad said once, stay away from foreign entanglements.

Now that all may seem a little farfetched, but it's what happened and I know, jolly well know, that neither of them, or even neither of the three, knew I was up there plastered to the grate and watching. Of course I filled in a few bits and pieces to smooth out this meeting between two people. That's what makes gossip good. Whosoever started it fills in the gaps. But I have no intention of using this as gossip. It's private between them. I just watch and wonder at mankind and how different people handle things. So naturally when I went down for lunch I said nothing, and I, unlike good husband Marty, didn't miss that little remark Sara made to Jeff. He ain't married, but she is, and that's the problem for them. For me, the problem is whether I should be a good buddy and inform her husband, or sit tight and keep clear of it.

But the fact is about people, or so I think I notice, is that even happily married folks break off for a little temporary tryst with someone else, just a little side dish, you might say. It is all forgotten and generally doesn't happen again. Leastwise that's what I think.

That's my step-daughter. So what comes next for this little triad?

Chapter 14
Armored Car Guys Back to the Car

The armored car cops got to Portage after the three mile walk and went directly into the *Empty Plate* and sat, relieved that they'd made it and in no way looking forward to the walk back. They sat enjoying coffee, a roll, and chatting with the waitress. It had been a long, mostly silent walk with the fat cop trailing and eventually falling well behind. The truck was stuck in that hole, they'd reported it to HQ and had about four hours to kill before help arrived. The occasional bunch of men running about the main street playing Steal the Flag was interesting to watch, but it was the only entertainment and after an hour or so it was time to head on back. They walked and daydreamed or whatever men do when out of conversation.

They arrived back at the car in a straggling group of three. Fats was well behind because not surprisingly the soles of his feet hurt. Walking wasn't his thing. They figured on going into the armored car and getting on the intercom to HQ and getting a status report. But the truck, which is what they called the armored car, was locked. There was only one key among them (company rules) and they were out of luck. "Where is the screwing key?" asked Cop #1.

"Who gives a shit," announced cop #2.

"Shouldn't there be a spare hidden somewhere on the vehicle?" asks cop #1.

"Ain't never seen one yet," announced cop #2.

"Well, fer Christ's sake. Look around on and under. Let's get out of here."

"We ain't going no place 'till we get inside. Then I'll try backing out, or forward. Whatever the hell does the job."

They looked, careful to keep clear of the broken bridge where the truck was in full to its right axle.

"Ain't finding nothing." said Cop# 2.

"I'll get in and give it a shot. He moved as if to pull open the side door. To hell with the smashed deck of the bridge and the over two foot wide hole in which the wheel laid. He went through his pants, searching with fingers, finding nothing.

"You ain't going no place 'till we get the door open, and that means we need a key. Translate that as one key missing. You got it, Fats?"

Fats shook his head. "No".

"Well look around. Maybe someone dropped it. You, Fats, you were the last to see the mess. Where's it?"

"I ain't got it. Never had it."

"Bull shit. You locked it. Where's the key?"

"I gave it to you."

"Bull balls on that. You didn't give it to me."

"I did. Look."

"Someone could have dropped it," said #2. "Let's look around." He never liked it the way #1 always argued.

"I don't like the way you're looking around. You'll never find it that way."

"Screw you. I ain't got it."

He looked at the two. "I'll take a putter around. See if one of you jerks dropped it about. If it's not one thing, it's another." He started at the front, worked along the side, looking left and right and thinking every once in a while what an unpleasant trip, hearing the two others arguing and every once in while yelling suggestions at him. "Farther out, do a zigzag pattern. Look alive." Internally he was in a bedlam of confusion. He'd had the key when he locked up, and had it for at least a mile because walking was so fucking painful and he'd held the key, wondering if he should carry it in his mouth like the old timers carried a stone in their mouth when crossing the Gobi or some of the deserts in the American west, carrying it so's the saliva would stay and keep his mouth wet feeling, instead of that terrible dryness. But had he? He really didn't think so, carried it in his mouth for a time but spit it out and went on.

Had he spit it out? Really? He could have and forgotten it and now it was somewhere along the road, on top, hopefully, where he'd see it. He'd better find it. They'd logged his name as being with the key. Or was it logged? He'd get in and find the log and see if it was him.

The spark ahead brought him up short. A spark? A sparkle? Sparkle of an armored car key on the road, shining in the sun from just the right angle.

That was it! He bent his beer belly and reached, stretched so he wouldn't have to take another lazy step, and it was hard to stop when your foot and knee are sore. He had it and straightened up, looked back, hardly around the corner of the truck. Leastwise they hadn't seen him pick it up. He'd be blamed again and then what? No job.

At the armored car, he looked all around the outside, probably one hell of a better look than before when he'd looked for it. Made it look like he was serious now. He'd dropped it and was responsible. He'd had it and it was his fault. Least no one else had found it and robbed them when they were in town, it was against the rules to leave the truck unattended, but then, what the hell, the townies were all over town and country playing that fool game. He walked around the car, avoiding the hole unlike Cop #1 who practically jumped in it.

Alone, he popped the key next to a bit of bridge wood that had popped off from the accident. He went on around and stopped in front of the two. He shook his shoulders, "Didn't see it nowhere."

"What'd you do with it? You had it."

"Not true. I think you did. I was already out when you left the truck."

"That's a lot of bull. You left last."

"Not me. You did. Ain't that right now, #2?"

"Hell, how would I know. One of you left last, that's all I know. I weren't watching you. I had better things to do."

"What was that?"

"Stare at that wheel and figure how to get it out."

"You are one asinine cop if I ever saw one. I'm thinking you were the last one out."

"You're nuts."

"I'll look around." #1 moved out around the car, avoiding the rickety looking guard rail but looking up at the covered bridges roof to see if it'd fall on him or not, and then at the ground and walking slow, cursing his two companions. He stopped and looked back as something sparkled in that spot of sunlight. He saw the key and touched it with his foot and it moved an inch. Jesus, there it was. He stared at it for a minute or two, heard them back there arguing, and thought a long minute, left it and walked back and said, "I didn't see nothing. You take a look,. Which one of you guys left last, anyway, you ass holes."

They both pointed at each other, then him. He snarled, kicked a stone at them and sat down on the heavy horizontal structure at the side. "One of you guys look around everywhere, you numb skulls."

#2 went off wandering slow and letting his head wag side to side, apparently looking. When he was out of sight and around the other side he yelped "I found it, it was under a chunk of this rotten wood, right near the deck and I saw it. You see it #1?"

"Me? No, I didn't see it. How come you did? I just looked there and didn't see nothing. You must-a dropped it if you saw it."

"I didn't drop it. I never had it."

"You did. You got out last and went around there to take a leak."

"Yeah, I did that. But I didn't have no key and I didn't leave last."

"Course you did."

"No way. Not me."

They went on arguing, yelling, accusing. Fats argued with one, then the other, and back again.

Chapter 15
The Triad – A Second Encounter

They were working up at the house again the other day, Marty and his aide, Jeff. I just happened to come up the hill mid-afternoon from the garage when their work day was also ending, both men out of sight and Sara out front by the cars doing something in one of her gardens. No one saw me coming into the yard so when Jeff came from the back of the house and saw her, I had that rare chance to observe movement in the most primitive of situations. I watched him see her and come alert, so much like a wild animal, the same manner of the hunting animal coming alert to some bit of game. His head went up slightly and the whole body tensed then slunk toward her, steadily and quietly, moving gracefully. His whole being at attention to its target. She somehow sensed his presence and came alive, and raised up from her flowers directing her attention to this approaching creature. She stood tall and straight, almost as if privately posturing to him; then moved simultaneously and equally gracefully to him. Their lips touched, and it was done, each moving apart as if just friends with a typical good-bye familiarity. And thus it was interpreted.

But this is not forgotten. Me thinks that next time, no goodbye kiss. Thus it should end before there is no turning back.

So with this I had fallen into a little village scene. I decided not to interfere with other people's business so could rest back to just watch mankind walk by, as in that old poem about living by the side of the road and watching the races of man go by, a little something to occupy myself.

Maybe someday write a little treatise about this 'eternal triangle', as it is sometimes called. I watched, enthralled, as my mind ascended to a higher plane, not simply this one couple, but to the many couples in a community where those ranks have so multiplied. This act, so common, and thus the race of man multiplies. So this little town called Portage is no doubt a microcosm of humankind and here I am becoming acquainted with folks and their ways, no different from anywhere else I suppose.

A few weeks ago I had started part time at the motor garage so was in the center of this little burg and, well, you see and hear things. What's new in this world? Not much.

Marty and one of his construction teams was working mid-town on the roof of this rich guy's house a few doors down from the garage, so when lunch time came Garage-Bill and I walk a few paces and join them all, a kind of male get-together out front with Marty and the crew who'd been working on the highrise. We sat outside on those two street benches eating and sipping from thermoses. We happen to look right along the street and see Bernice coming our way. A tall girl, nice figure and in no way concealed by today's standard of dress, going somewhere, her walk purposeful. I was reminded of Sara, Marty, and Jeff.

We watched her go by, apparently not realizing a couple of benches of construction workers were there, tongues hanging out, watching every cell of her body as she moved. One of the workers spoke, "That there's a nice looking woman with friends but no boyfriend, ain't she a looker?"

One of the guys started talking and laughing and noted how that was a pretty reasonable thumb nail sketch of a nice looking broad, in case no one had seen her before. The guys next to him were watching her go, men do that, and one asked who she was and then another saying "Bernice Smith or something like that."

"Not a bad looking babe."

The other nodding, "True, true. Look, but don't touch."

"Pfft. Why's that? She married or something?"

"Don't think so. Goes to all the dances and all that high school stuff, the games, school plays. She's only in high school."

"I think I'll go back to school when this job runs out."

"Sure." A skeptical tone.

"Yeah, why not?"

"Stay away from her, B&B always takes her home."

"B&B? Who's he?"

"He's one of the town leaders, an older guy. You've seen him around. That big fella, fat, tall, glasses, drives a big yellow Cadillac."

"Oh him."

"He takes her home from dances?"

"Uh-huh. Him."

"What's the matter with high school boys anyway? Nice girl like her and B&B? What's they do that they don't measure up?"

"He takes her home. It's been going on for a few years. Stay clear. No one messes with B&B. No one messes with his girl."

"So I guess I won't go back to school," the other young man said.

We were still looking after Bernice walking down the street and thinking of B&B and Bernice, wondering about them. So that's the way life goes here in the small towns. I suppose things, couples, like that occur everywhere. I started thinking of Sara, but of course Sara is older. She knows what it's all about as my dad told me once years ago. And here I am old as the hills an' these young fellows don't give me a second look in matters like that, yet I've been through it all and smart enough to know what's happening. So here I am sitting here eating lunch with these guys and I look past Marty over at Jeff. I remembered the sink and how he'd brushed against Sara, deliberately, and how she had brushed back. Then kissing good-bye the other night. But they'd stopped, and it should stay that way.

Jeff was looking down the street like the others, watching the girl and thinking about her or maybe Sara. Jeff's smarter than I might have been in the same position years ago, though. Thinking about all this stuff, listening to these guys seems to have brought it to my mind again after months of bachelor solitude. I had to snicker at myself and shake my head. I need to get out and meet more people. They talked about the dances on Saturday. I should go every week.

And I did it, went to the weekend dance on Saturday night. Not bad. Three square dances then three what they called 'round dances', that is waltzes, fox trots, polkas, schottisches, mixers, line dances from eastern Europe like Greece, Bulgaria, Hungary and so on. There was some instruction by several people for certain dances as if they were trying to extend the knowledge of all these different dance types so it was interesting and mind bending. Yes, sir!

Chapter 16
Through the Grating Again

Yes, the dance was totally a fun-experience, both the older dances that have been done for years and the new dances that were taught were mind bending, but not as mind bending as what I saw down through the grating in my room Monday morning.

Bill didn't need me Monday so I was sleeping in. I should have been up and about, but was laying there thinking about the weekend dance and the people there. Several nice looking women there at or near my age, so all was not lost. Yes, it is true. Even old guys like me find the other sex a fascination. So there I was laying there thinking it all over and wondering what comes next when noises came from the kitchen below. I was there at the grate in a jiffy, watching and listening. The worse kind of things was going on down there in my opinion. It was Jeff and Sara again. Can you believe that?

She brushes against him, and he brushes back. He hadn't really looked at her this morning. It was deliberate. He didn't want those desires, foolish desires, to start up again. At least that was my feeling on his behalf. It was unwise. Her husband was his friend as well as employer. So as needs for talk came along, he saw to it that he was tying his shoe, looking for a tool, gazing off. He never looked at her, but pretended to by facing her with his eyes elsewhere. Maybe she noticed, maybe not, it didn't matter to him. In fact, maybe she would get the idea and lay off. He wasn't sure she had the same feelings any longer. She was by the sink, doing something at the cutting board, a small pile of red things, probably peppers, in front of her. So he looked at her, her attention on the work and not watching him. He was free to study her and he did.

He leaned on the doorway and spoke her name.

"Sara."

I feel almost embarrassed spying on them like this.

She looked to the doorway. "I thought I heard you coming. How goes it on this fine day?" Her eyebrows were up in the question and she turned to face him, putting the knife down, breathing and smiling. It was a slow breath, her chest inflating and the outline of her bra seen beneath the tight, white cotton fabric of her blouse. She moved toward him slowly, her head slightly leaning to the right, and smiled.

"I haven't seen you today, yet. How are you?" And her posture as she moved asked for a kiss.

She was against him, her arms over his shoulders, and around his neck, her body closing onto him. Her stomach, and hips moved closer, her lips at his cheek, moving toward his lips.

Some minutes later, it seemed, she slid her right side free and rotated some, "Good morning," she said and smiled. "It's been awhile. Nice to see you again." Her mouth open, her eyes spoke silently. "I've waited for you, where have you been? Come in here and sit with me." Now her hand was leading him to the table and she pulled the chair out as she passed and gestured to sit. She moved past him to the stove to get coffee. "Sit. Tell me what's going on now with the job. Where've you been?"

He was still speechless. The kiss was real and more than just a memory not about to disappear. The resolution to stay away from her, to not look at her was over. She was here, and friendly. Was she wanting him as he wanted her? Standing next to his chair, her arm was on his shoulder while the other poured the coffee. His arm moved down, holding her leg, drawing her to him tightly and she reached and pressed his head against her bosom.

She moved away to the stove and replaced the coffee pot, resting across from him and saying just as if nothing had happened, "I haven't seen you in weeks. Tell me, what have you been doing?"

As for me, I pulled away from the grate, and quietly as possible slid back to my bed and laid down quietly so they wouldn't hear and know I was up here. I had to get away from the grate. I was getting bored. It's just so boring watching two others making love, or being in some stage of such a private endeavor between two people.

Somehow, later that day or maybe the next I ran into him and we talked. He realized I'd seen them carrying on and we talked about it. He is betaken by her, as people a hundred years ago (almost my age) would have said. No question, and wanted to talk about it. He filled me in on what I'd seen, although he didn't realize it. Knowing how these things go on until the little affair breaks somehow, I didn't want Sara or Marty to be hurt by what was developing, so not telling how much I'd seen of their little 'doings', I tried to get Jeff to realize what he was doing, and stop this affair.

Yet another day comes and Jeff is sent back to the house to get three roof jacks. And he says to himself, "I will not go in. I will stay clear. Not even look around. Just get in for the jacks and out into the truck and away before she even knows I'm here. That's how it has to be."

And he smiled. "That's the way it is supposed to be, and I will do it that way, but I really want her to see me and come out and stand and talk. Maybe a coffee and her strutting around, knowing I respond to her, her body, her chatter, her smile, the way she moves, knowing how I feel."

She was in the yard sanding the canoe, prepping it for paint, and when she heard him, she looked up. Looked from the driver to the empty seat next to him despite the glare, almost hiding the interior, but she saw enough and when the truck stopped and the dust settled, she walked toward the vehicle, moving to her left, coming to the passenger side, opening the door and crawling up into the cab and sliding into his waiting arms. A long, satisfying kiss and his free arm going around her back, at the bra strap, feeling it go loose as she exhaled, feeling the clasps separate and the bra hang open inside her blouse. Lifting her shirt tail from the belt and slacks, knowing she was pulling her stomach in to let the blouse slip up easier. His hand sliding around to her stomach, and up. How did I become so skilled at this, he asked himself and skipped the answer for her lips and his were at it again. She slithered around and facing him, worked on his shirt buttons as they talked words of greeting and explanations as to why he was here and had to return to the job immediately. They whispered each other's names, and snuggled tighter, his hands working her over and she inside his work shirt, it up almost over his shoulders as she pressed against his bare chest and emitted sounds of pleasure and satisfaction and desire.

Looking past her as they kept the hug going, he saw the dog, once asleep under the sawhorses, lift its head and peer dead ahead but not at the truck, at something else beyond but in line.

A warning, and he heeded, moving her away from his chest and looking in the mirrors, nothing seen; but now he heard truck noise, the whine as the driver shifted gears to come up the slope. It was a steep hill and stony where the once-in-awhile rain gouged away dirt and let the bits of rock remain. Stones that skidded away as the wheels lost traction and the driver punched the accelerator harder.

She was back into her blouse and he fastening his shirt as he looked rearwards. Not one of the company trucks. Who?

It was out of sight where the driveway swung around the hairpin turn in front of the house and she was out and at the canoe, looking around to see who it was. It appeared up the tight turn at the other end and came to a stop next to him.

It was Marty. Oh Christ, Jeff thought. Another half hour lost getting the talk out of him, and what's he doing up here this time of day. He got out and walked around to Marty's cab. Window down, they shook hands and greeted, mostly looking at each other and wondering what the other guy was doing here. He explained the need for the roof jacks and Marty asked where the rest of the crew was today. Sara walked up, Marty noticing the sanding dust on her shirt, and gave Jeff a curious glance. Not the ordinary curious glance but the deep curious glance. The talk went on, now the three of them passing the time of day and he got a chance to look at himself. His shirt had traces of sanding dust on it. Uh-oh. But Marty didn't say a word. They walked on to the shed and got the roof jacks and he was splitting to head on back to the job as Marty and Sara walked over to check out her work on the canoe. The last he heard it was Marty approving her work and offering to let her do the sanding job on the finish work of the high rise office building they were working on by the gorge at the edge of town and her laughter and, "No-thanks, this is enough," from her.

Chapter 17
Bill and I Ponder the Armored Car Incident

Me and Bill sitting out front of the garage one lazy morning. Not much work.

"You know, I think all these strangers hanging around town lately are government agents."

"Why?"

"Plumbing for the money."

"Probably right. Looking to see what type of guy gets into an armored car and makes the money disappear without a trace. Had to be an inside job, wouldn't you think so?"

"I suppose. They must have some way of tracing it, wouldn't you think?"

"Nobody in town lost a cent, it was money the bank was sending out. Only the bank lost money."

"And they didn't lose it. It was the armored car company. That big trading bank that does all that money business."

"And of course they were insured by the government, the FDIC or something like that. Big government organization that insures all the money in banks."

"So it was the government that makes up the difference. That means the taxes we pay. All the money's covered by some money outfit in the government, something like that. We pay our taxes and some of it goes to that outfit and they pay off the armored car company 'cause they're insured with the government. So we're really paying it. Makes government more expensive, and we pay fer that."

"Well, it keeps the wheels turning, anyway."

"BUT IT'S OUR MONEY"

"So don't get all heated up by it. It's just money."

"But I pay all that. I worked for that money. I can't afford that. I could use that money someplace at home."

"Well, so what. It ain't mor'n a few cents of yer money. Everyone in the good old U S of A pays in. So it's only a couple of yer cents. Don't get yer liver up over it."

"What about that scruffy looking guy looking for work around here. He wants a job with engines, like in a garage fixing cars. Where'd he come from?. I think he's one of them, too. Trying to find the money and who engineered that heist. Just another agent only in five day old clothes."

"Could be. So what do we do about it?"

He sat awhile, running that stick around in the sand before his feet and finally looked up with a laugh. "I'd just as soon find out myself, and get a slice of the take."

"Wouldn't we all. They say it was like a quarter million. Do you believe that?"

He spat at the center of the circles in the sand, all concentric circles around a broken bottle top laying there, like all this dumb town. "Not really. This town ain't never had a millions bucks or even a half million. Something like fifty thousand would be it, especially if that armored car only comes once a month. That's what I think."

"Anyone who took it, and someone had to or else it was a concocted deal just to put the town on the map, whoever did it, ain't used it yet, and if they're smart they won't. Sit on it ten years then use it little by little."

He looked up at me. "Maybe you and I ought to go out and browse around in the woods and maybe down the canyon and see if we can come up with something. You know, find it."

"Every agent in town and a whole lot more have been slipping around after dark looking and have found nothing, why would we find it?"

"Luck of the Irish."

"You ain't Irish and neither am I. We won't find it."

Chapter 18
The Broken Tooth Event

I was sitting on the porch watching a couple of hawks soaring around down by the river when the pickup came in. Marty and his wife'd gone out just after breakfast and were now back. Both pretty straight faced looking, uncommon for her as she usually moved around fast and chats with all and generally has a good time. She's a very positive woman, my step-daughter Sara. I couldn't see Marty in the driver's seat as the reflection on the windshield at this angle hid him pretty much, just a kind-of bright flash on it. There was a big, long toot from the horn and I heard words but couldn't distinguish them. He got out and went around to her side of the cab and opened the door but she didn't get down. He stood there and yelled for Jeff. He had a good voice, could have heard him in Santa Fe if'n we were a few thousand miles closer, but hell, Santa Fe's diagonally across the map from Maine, so he had a big, booming voice today.

Jeff had come in sometime to get some supplies for the job and I'd forgotten he was somewhere around and obviously hadn't taken my advice very well. Jeff came from around back and waved to Marty and walked toward the truck, saying things, words of greeting I suppose. Marty stopped talking. He looked sort-a like he was seething to me. His one hand that I could see was clenching and unclenching his fist. Sara up there in the cab looked serious and was not getting out, which isn't like her, usually she'd be down and walking up here.

Jeff was there, still saying something, and Marty standing there moved a step closer and I saw that fist all made up and like lightning it came up and got Jeff in the stomach and he immediately doubled over. Then the other fist caught him somewhere in the face and he went down, crumpled at Marty's feet, getting a kick in the side. He rolled away, sounds of pain coming out of him. Sara, aghast, moved down from the door of the truck and stood looking alternately at the figure on the ground and her husband. I was up and running down there in time to hear Marty snarling out, "Don't you ever come around my place again. My wife don't want none of you and neither do I. Next time both of you get it. You and your so called cute little girl-friend. She'll get it too, understand? Even if she is my wife."

The cute little girl-friend was a few steps away from the truck cab and holding a fist in front of her face. Frightened at what was going on, I suppose, chewing her knuckles.

Marty half turned toward her and yelled, "You get the fuck back in and stay there." She was back in the cab in a flash, as she hadn't really more than started out.

Jeff rolled a little and twisted here and there and looked up at Marty, squinting, holding his gut, asking, "What's that all about?" He was trying to get to his feet, wary too, looking carefully at Marty and past to the woman and back.

I was there staring at the three, wondering what was up and what should I do? Well, I knew what was up. It was the show down over whose girl she was.

Marty settled that for me, if I'd had any doubts. He was looking at me. "You see that dog-dung around here again, you tell him to stay away from my spread. UNDERSTAND?"

Me, acting dumb, asked, "What's going on?"

"That prick's trying to horn in on my wife. I see him around here again and I'll whip his nuts off."

Suddenly he was at me, scaring the life outta me. Had my shirt front and twisting it into a knot and pulling me up to him. "Tell him to stay away from another man's wife. GOT IT?"

Dumb me, I said, "Who's doing that? Not me, for heaven's sake. And Jeff? Why you punching him, that ain't-"

Jeff had his balance and was standing, facing Marty six feet off and trying to say something. A trace of blood came and he stepped back, sort of losing his balance for a moment. His face was screwed up a bit like he hurt somewhere. One hand was on his side and I guessed that was it until, while Marty was getting back into his truck, Jeff ran the back of his left hand over his lower face and the back of it came away red and juicy. Then he bent his head and exhaled catching the stuff in his other hand and he stood, staring at me and the truck and the girl in the window, straight faced now, then holding her head in her hands and crouching down below the window level. They drove off. I had no idea where they were going. It was their house here, but I guess Marty had had enough of it for the moment, attacking Jeff like he did. Of course, what was Jeff doing here at Marty and Sara's anyway? 'Course I knew. I wasn't that dumb. Putting on a dumb act hangs with a person for a bit.

I took Jeff by the shoulders and started walking him to the house.

Inside I started wiping his face with a cold towel but he pulled away, mumbling, and screwing up his face. He looked in the little mirror over the sink and studied his face and finally a word, not just a sound like he'd been doing: "Jesus."

He opened his hand and thee was a little white triangle of something in his palm. He turned to me and held his mouth open. Drew the upper lip back and I saw it. Marty had broken his tooth.

In the kitchen we sat and looked at each other in silence.

"So what was that all about?" I asked as if it wasn't pretty apparent.

He swung his head a bit, saying nothing, squirming around in his chair some.

Does he hurt somewhere else I wondered until he finally settled down and a cell-phone appeared in his hand. His face was sore, that was also apparent the way he moved. I watched him as he dialed the thing. There was some kind of sound from it and then he was talking to the dentist. He was calling about his broken tooth.

"Yes, I have the broken-off part."

"Ok, tomorrow morning at ten."

He closed the cover, slipped it in his pocket and sat there looking at me, reached for the bottle I'd put out and poured himself three fingers, grimaced once, and sipped.

"It's beginning to hurt," he announced.

I got some patent medicine, pain killer stuff, out of the bathroom and gave it to him. He swallowed three pills after reading the instructions, then we sat and looked at each other, him pretty much staring at the floor and I watched. Finally, again I asked, "So what was that all about?" I avoided saying "I told you so." It was so unnecessary.

Finally, as if coming up out of a deep coal mine all exhausted, he said with a sigh, "I guess Marty figures Sara's getting a little bored and's thinking of taking on a boyfriend or something like that. I was over here the other day getting a tool and she gave me a good-bye kiss. Somehow Marty decided I was making a pass at her and comes over and pounds me." He made a face and finally looked at me.

"It must-a bin more-den dat for a beatin'." I surprised myself for I was in my old hayseed accent.

He was getting his hands in his pockets and slumping in his chair and staring at that spot on the floor. Neither of us said anything. Someone told me once that if you kept quiet the other fellow would start talking and give the whole story away. Presently he started in. Started in all over again considering the little private talk we'd had a week or so ago.

"What do you know about women?"

"Enough to avoid a husband's anger."

"Ummm."

"You think Sara's attractive?"

"I didn't know her, only by name. Seen her once or twice at a distance. Couldn't talk to her. Wouldn't even know what to say to her."

I was quiet. Presently he went on.

"She's good looking. Everyone says so. She talks easy, at least to me. We kinda got to know each other and so when we see each other in the grocery store or on the street, the library, wherever we end up, we have a little talk, you know: how are you and the family, what you doing, got any big plans, all that sort of stuff. Some of the guys on the job think she's one stacked babe and (giving a hesitant, embarrassed little smile) they kind of envy me. I guess he heard something and thinks I'm trying to make her."

"Are you? Or would you?"

He looked up. We were at the crucial part of our talk. "Well, she's sexy looking." He gritted his teeth and looked all around, head down, not finding my eyes.

"So you would if the opportunity came. Have you?"

He was shaking his head when his cell phone rang. He gave me a look and arose, went to the door, out onto the porch and started talking. Couldn't hear what he said but I bet you anything it was her. She'd somehow gotten free of Marty and was calling him to see how he was and apologize for her husband's behavior, clearing the air, maybe even making plans for another meeting, to sooth him, make love. All those things a woman after a man for permanent or temporary tends to do. Would myself, I suppose, were I a principal in the affair.

He didn't come back in. In fact, I heard him drive off.

Well, I said to myself, that fella doesn't realize how patently obvious it is, or was, the two of them getting involved with each other. I can't blame them in a way. They just have to be aware of what's starting up and harness it. If they don't it threatens the marriage. I got me out onto the porch and into the chair again, and stared at the sky looking for those two hawks and thought about what happened. It's my step-daughter so I guess it's my responsibility to counsel her. But then, shouldn't Marty, her husband counselor her? Then I realized that as the husband, he might not understand the extent of this marital rift. It gets complicated for my small, little mind. But oh, how I hate to stick my nose in other people's business. Jeff was so mixed up in his excuses. I finally assigned it to the Ash-Can-of-Importance and sank back in the chair. I bet I fell asleep, 'cause when I looked around, the sun had moved off to its noon position.

Chapter 19
The Three Investigators

This is what Sara passed on to me. She has a friend that works at the bank who passed it on to Sara with the understanding that she shouldn't tell anyone. It was just private observations that she'd picked up, so naturally Sara told me about it over our breakfast coffee. It was about those agents the government sent to solve the robbery.

The Chief Agent on the scene looked at his two agents. One was biting his ring finger's nail, the other looking out the window. He was the first to break the three minute silence they had endured following the Chief's moment of prayer that all who served under him learned to endure.

"It's the God-damnedest place I've ever been - to work in, I mean."

The Chief nodded a 'yes' , let his eyes slide left to see what the other was looking out the window at, which was nothing that he could see. He shifted in his chair, a big too-comfortable to be sure, but then this office at the bank that they had turned over to the investigators was more luxurious than generally available. The noise of the bank's daily business was insulated from them and the silence should have encouraged something more than dozing. J. Edgar Hoover, the seeming patriarch of the FBI, would have passed them a heavy scowl at least. At least that woman bookkeeper-type they shared the office with seemed impervious to them. She never looked up, never said a word. Maybe she had died on the job and was failing to topple over. He watched her a lot, but she did breathe which was reassuring.

Bates, the Chief Agent in this case, was in his sixties and close to retirement, seemingly trim but hemorrhoids annoyed him early in the morning and he sat slightly sideways hoping to avoid medical intervention "It's my body and no one messes with it," was his motto.

Romanske coughed.

Bates eyed him. "So what do you think of the situation at the moment? Who is our best suspect? Or is it suspects?"

Romanske coughed again, cleared his throat, and spoke. "It's the God-damnedest place I've ever worked. Obviously everyone owns a gun but not a one in sight. No one seems to be spending unusually. No one knows what happened. Everyone was playing this 'Steal the Flag' game and so were scattered here and there all over, everyone hiding or sneaking up on someone and no one pays attention to the armored car. It comes, exchanges money, picks up its allotment, starts off, the bridge was closed so it goes the other way. The bridge breaks, the truck is caught, the crew afraid it'll fall through into the gorge, no one answers the phone, the radio puts them through to Portland and help is on the way. They wait, get hot and hungry and despite the three mile hike head to town for a bite. That's against the rules but the world is unaware of their plight. The rescue comes but nothing can be done. No one hurt, the truck still locked tight as a drum, everyone afraid to touch the stupid thing for fear it'll go into the gorge. The three armored car geniuses afraid they'll be fired for taking the back road, but who can blame them? The semi had the road blocked. Still they're as nervous as snails."

"Snails?"

"You know what I mean. Not their fault, just a bunch of circumstances. The crane comes and lifts the car out, they get in to drive to Portland. It's been robbed. How? No one knows 'cept that someone had to have a key to the door."

Neal spoke up. "We've had the experts go over every inch of the car. Not anything, not a thing, different than when she was made. It had to be someone with a door key. Forensics took samples of everything around the car door, windows, any entrance but there was no sign of anything unusual. The same dirt, grime, and dust as on every one of their cars. They checked the other seven they have in their pool."

Romanske shuffled his feet. It had to be someone inside. Someone passed a key out to the right people and now whoever it was is rich.'

"Three hundred twenty-five thousand is rich?"

"God damned right it is, baby," retorted Romanske whose wife was pregnant for the fourth time and medical expenses for a man with normal sexual needs at a normal frequency were exceeding his normal income.

"Okay, okay," cautioned Blake. "For your information, there is Henderson and his group checking out the office in Portland, looking for suspects there. Who's got the key numbers, or spare keys, whatever. They're covering that. Our job is to check out that 'semi' business, whoever in this town has contacts to get keys and how'd they know the bridge would trap the car? It only weights about five tons."

"With a half ton of coin included," injected Neal.

"Okay, okay."

Romanske slid a folder onto the desk. "That's the engineering assessment. The bridge was normally worn out. No tampering with it to catch the truck. They think it was a natural breakdown of an old bridge."

The Chief said, "That's the whole problem. Everything seems so normal, an old bridge, an inadvertent break and the truck is stuck. The men go for something to eat. Walk three miles, can you believe that? Three Miles. 'Course, someone should have stayed at the truck, but they didn't. So that is a second mark against them, leaving the scene.

What was the first?"

"Communication break down."

Chapter 20
The Ladies

That bastard, thought Marty, messing around with my wife. Dad-rat his soul.

Marty talked to his wife, rather yelled, actually, according to what she told the ladies at the church. They gather every Wednesday for Bible Study. Good for the soul and all that, but this particular Wednesday they didn't have the assistant minister there until half way through the meeting. He was a young punk half out of college and doin' an internship as part of his training. All the big colleges seem big on doing this these days. It is supposed to round 'em out, according to the college professors.

Well, he wasn't there to "round himself out" this particular Wednesday so the ladies that met, old and young, experienced and simple, bewildered and on-the-stick, got an earful of Sara's trouble, as she saw it. There was nobody there to correct injustices or errors amid the spirited emotionalism. It went on pretty good, so I was told, and then this assistant minister having arrived, found himself, a man, sitting there with those ladies trying to pick up on a tale of lust (it had to be), illicit love, maltreated wives, mothers and girlfriends, and trying to present a rational answer to the kissing of a wife by some other man than the husband and if the ensuing violence was justified by a chalice of bubbling anti-man, subjugated womanhood and twisted Christian morality. Moreover the assistant had a lisp, acne and dirty fingernails. They had no respect for him, hence none for the churches approach as he portrayed it. For Sara it was a cheerleading group. For Marty, the even-tempered, defender of his family, it was accolades yet with a slap on the wrist for breaking a tooth and being so violent. For Jeff, the heinous attacker against the bastion of marriage, it was condemnation and castration (if only we were in the thirteen hundreds) but with an undercurrent of applause and who-will-be-attacked-next, the meat of fantasy in one's dreams. This Bible Study meeting had come to a high point. The assistant was glad to close it, and even here the ladies were noisy, disruptive, undisciplined, and impolite. No one was paying attention as he delivered the final prayer, phrased a synopsis and left. Pandemonium lived.

I heard a mixture of women's noise as I walked by on my way to the *Empty Plate* but gave it only passing attention. When I had been seated at a table, a woman came in with a great smile on her face, looked around, and started to sit at the vacant table facing the street. She saw me sitting there alone, looked quickly about the establishment, took a step closer and leaned slightly to me and asked if she could join me.

Well, when you're approaching your mid-eighties, and life is over for you, and a delicate beauty asks to share your table, you jolly well get a second life and that's exactly what happened. A whole new world opened up for me.

Believe me. A whole new world, and I'm not over it yet.

I half arose, pasted on my welcoming smile, and gestured to the opposite chair.

"I've seen you in here before. I hope you don't think I'm being forward."

"Of course not. You usually sit over there, don't you?" I'd seen her here from time to time in the mornings when I'm killing time until my half day at Bill's Garage. As an aside, it is noteworthy to know that, although free seating, people seem to use the same booth or table whenever they come in. That's the regulars, of course, and I've noticed that this one always had that booth over there. She's a nice looking woman, always well dressed in the casual style, and usually with a friend or two. This day she was alone, so it was my good luck. She was a Sara-type too, I might add. A good figure and pretty. And sitting with me. Oh I knew who it was alright. I'd inquired of her before, to Sara, and was duly informed that it was the woman from down the foot of the hill, 'Manda Cunningham by name. And here she was in person at my table. There might be some point in hanging around this little town a few more weeks after all.

Well we went through the machinery of meeting formally. We introduced ourselves and she nodded when I told her where I lived. "Ah yes, the gentleman staying with Sara and Marty. They live up the hill from me," and she directed the pointer on my mental map to where she lived on a side street at the bottom of the hill.

So this treasure of a woman named 'Manda Cunningham told me about the prayer meeting/therapy session she'd just left. She just had to talk to somebody about it and it was just my luck that she picked me. Sometimes people get that caught up in a thing. Told me pretty much everything I said already, so I had the whole story, a big deep problem in the lives of Marty and Sara. 'Fixable if we move fast,' she quoted one of the more elderly of the Gran Dams who were the fixtures of Bible Study and community morals. I pictured this 'Manda Cunningham standing up amid the upward looking members of Bible Study, raising an arm and intoning correctness, responsibility, and contributions to the church, this last quality pretty much being the main factor in honest judgment of good vs. bad behavior, really meaning financial contribution. She reminded me of the woman type that dresses the knockout in a somewhat rather suggestive manner and yet denies it all with words of sanctity and propriety. That bewildering (to men) mixture that always eventually causes trouble, yet so satisfying to watch.

Chapter 21
'Manda and Me

So here's me and 'Manda Cunningham sitting and enjoying her recollection of today's Bible Study and she's telling me about the Gran Dams and Sara. Then 'Manda says, "So Mister, I find out she's your daughter. What are you going to do? You can't just sit here and enjoy a coffee, you know."

I look over at her sitting there, hand on the glass, kind of swirling it around slowly. Nice looking woman, long hair down her back, gray with trails of blond mixed in, a rather pretty combination. But that was her, natural and good looking without a mess of pretext. She had a good figure to go with her pretty face, the kind of person that would attract me, so I let my eyes feast on her. Now here I am, an eighty year old man, and she's maybe thirty years my junior. We sit here and chat and enjoy the company of one another like a couple of school kids. Am I repeating myself? You betcha. After all, at eighty I don't have that much time left to enjoy a delicious woman. So look on, I say. Look on this.

I look up and find her eyes on mine and a slight smile playing at her lips. Shucks. Caught.

"Alright, it's true, she's my daughter. Well, sort of. She was my wife's daughter and we brought her up. She was maybe, I can't remember, I think about one and a half years when Betty and I got married so she's not my biological daughter; but for all practical purposes, yes, she's my daughter. And you think I've got a responsibility in this Sara-Marty-Jeff mess, right?"

'Manda nodded. "I do." she reached out and put her hand over mine, resting on the table like it was. She was looking serious, too. "I think someone's got to step in and save that marriage. It's not doing too well on its own. I've been thinking about it for a while already because it's well known all around the countryside. How could it be otherwise?

"And?"

"I have a solution." With that she looked at me intently.

"Well?" says I.

She arose, still studying me and I felt precisely like the smear on a Petri dish in a laboratory. "It might work. It might take the two of us though, I mean you as her father could have a significant part. We should talk again." She turned and started off, leaving the *Empty Plate*. Outside she stopped and turned looking back through the window at me, raised her right hand, index finger extended and gave a left and right gesture to it accompanied by a smile.

Well I was hooked. That gesture did it, in effect saying: "Don't go away, we will meet again." What is this idea this woman has to save my daughter? It wasn't my natural way to go about saving people who seem to be living life's way, even my step-daughter. Live and let live, I say, and let folks work out their own problems. I hadn't known this eternal triangle between Jeff, Marty and Sara was country-wide knowledge so maybe it did need help. And look at who I'd be working with: this snappy, good-looking woman who anyone would be glad to tie in with. Well!

You know, I was so caught up in this 'Manda Cunningham woman and my step-daughter that I don't really have any memory of working with Bill that day. My mind explored one possibility after another, going down one avenue after another with no end in sight.

Manda Cunningham was sitting in that same chair she had used last time, when I came in to the *Empty Plate* the next day. I saw, I went in, I nodded (to paraphrase Caesar) to 'Manda Cunningham who nodded back and I was in seventh heaven as I went to the counter. I returned with my coffee and there was her smile and a gesture to me and sure enough, I went over and sat opposite her and settled down to enjoy the spice of life. Her.

Idle chatter with this lovely creature that I had spent too much time thinking about overnight, and then she said the very words I'd hoped to hear: "I have a solution to our little problem." With that she looked at me intently. "Should you and I work together?"

"We are both adults and can work together if we so decide. Let's."

A smile burst over her that was as beautiful to see as were her words: "Yes, let's."

We shook hands.

"I have a solution. It may not be the best, but it might work. So here I am going to try it out on you. How broad-minded are you, Mr. – what is your last name?

"Heneke," I said. "Trevor Heneke."

So now she knew my name which was a step in the right direction.

"So, Mr. Trevor Heneke, how broad minded are you?"

"Try me." I put my hand out on the table and left it there for her to take, if so inclined. She took it and I was again in Seventh Heaven. Maybe even Eighth, Ninth, or Tenth!

I gave her hand a gentle squeeze and added, "May the two of us do well, a bond we have that each of us finds pleasure and success together." A little schmaltzy, but I wanted us to get over these beginning hurdles.

She gave a tiny squeeze back, laughed a little, a tiny mirthless, nervous laugh and said, "How much do you want to butt into your daughter's life?"

So, I think, it's me and her working as a team, as a pair of conniving busybodies going to straighten two adults out. Well, there's no question. Us two would be a helluva lot cheaper than a certified shrink in the big city, plus save a lot of travel money getting there. Those counselors, marriage or otherwise, never fix you up in one session that I've ever seen. Mind made up, I pasted on the smile and perked up my posture and, "Okay. How do we start?" Plus 'Manda and I would be seeing each other a lot. I could stand that. I smiled more, looking into her eyes again. It was then she slung the zinger at me.

"Sara's bored with married life, I don't mean all the time, she's always busy, you know that, but underneath she has spare time and she's starting to look around for some excitement. It's taking this form: Jeff, to be exact. Am I right?"

I was looking out the window across the street, not seeing anything, but thinking, so I spoke my thoughts. "You could make it out that way. Where do you want to go from here? You're thinking she just needs counseling? I always thought both partners ought-ta get it."

"Counseling?" 'Manda had a funny look on her face. "Do you think counseling would solve her problem?"

"Well now, if'n she's…"

'Manda interrupted, pointing her right index finger at me, jabbing toward me. "Counseling? You're the one that needs counseling. Will you cut that fake yokel accent? That's okay for a tourist, but I'm me. Get with it. This is serious, not some smoke screen to suck some impressionable city person to buy a cheap Taiwanese gadget they don't need."

"Oh." Maybe she was right, the accent was adopting me instead of me commanding it. I felt stupid in front of this good looking woman across from me, one I'd like to impress. "You're right. Sorry. And thanks for cutting me short."

She had turned from the table and now she was looking out the window. Her hand wandered about on the table, looking for mine I surmised. She turned back to me and shook her head slowly. "You are one funny man. Forgive me, you're not mine, so I shouldn't correct you."

"Oh that's okay, I don't mind. Need it probably. I was thinking a counselor, therapist or shrink was what you had in mind to straighten out Sara and Marty, that is if a therapist can correct a love affair gone sour or stop a budding one."

She had my hand and was squeezing it, shaking it. "What I had in mind was more direct than therapy. Let's consider your daughter's behavior."

"Whoa there," says I, "You're putting all the blame on my daughter."

She raised our two hands some, as if praising the congregation. "Let's face it. I think she's the seat of the trouble. She's always busy, anyone can be, but it's just busy work. I think, she's bored with today's life. She should have something serious to devote herself to other than a minor love affair with a passing man, however good looking he is."

"And that means?"

"She could have a child. That would give her something new to concentrate on. They don't have any kids yet, so why not? It does take up a woman's time. And not for just a few weeks like an affair would."

We discussed it. The way she saw it, it was the perfect solution.

I frowned at her, curled my nose. "So if she hasn't had any kids yet, and they've been married eight years probably, how do you expect her to get this kid?"

"The old fashioned way. You know."

I ignored that and replied, "Or could you be thinking of adoption?"

"The birth of a child, like I said: The old-fashioned way, but I have wondered about adoption. It is a possibility but I think we should opt for a biological child, don't you? It'd be more fun for both of them, her and Marty, at least in the initial phases of the process." She had a big smile, a healthy laugh from her, the minx that she was.

" 'Manda Cunningham, what a devil you are!" I had been told that her husband's job had him away from home a lot and irrationally I wondered how long her husband would be gone this time. An engineer, he traveled doing troubleshooting jobs for his company, or so I understood from Sara as well as our early introductions. We might see each other quite a bit in the next few weeks, maybe. Good company she was.

And that's how it worked out. I was certainly interested, being a now-divorced or pending-divorced, lonesome man for some time, and suddenly feeling like I was alive, well, needy, and very interested; while she was calm, collected, full of interesting things to do, a well-crafted woman with all the parts and apparently enough money to display the parts to her advantage. Short as our friendship had been, we enjoyed each other. Yes sir, we did. From then on we met at the *Empty Plate* every day, it seemed. We talked local gossip, national affairs, personal problems like what to wear to the dance Saturday night, good places to go picnicking, tolerable hiking places, canoeing places, sightseeing expeditions. I was free, having dropped the useless job at Bill's garage, and her husband was still away, due back in a week and then off after three days at home. Perfect. I could catch up on my sleep and be ready for our next thing. We were a match, a pair, and ready to enjoy this friendship. That's the way it was, had been for a couple of weeks, and satisfying to both of us, and hopefully would go on for a while longer.

Friendship, that's what it was. A good friendship.

We'd had several cups of coffee here in this little bistro, or was it just a cute little coffee shop, this small restaurant called the *Empty Plate*. We were discussing the "baby project" today after we had gotten our coffees and were in 'our' seat at the little table. Save the marriage between Sara and Marty. Follow up on her idea to get them into a real family; a 'real' family in this case being a husband, wife and children. We will start with one child. Should it be a naturally produced child in the old-fashioned way or an adopted one?

I can see it as a project worth doing and concluding successfully, having been in effect brain-washed by 'Manda. Well, to discuss, argue and come to a conclusion on whether we proceed with this, her great idea, or drop it - that is the goal for today. Is it a project worth doing, saving this marriage? Well yes, I guess it is, but I stopped myself. Where does this put Jeff, the man she's having the affair with at the moment? Does he just drop by the wayside on this road we're taking them down? And the fact that they were having an affair, or at least getting into one, is their love stronger? Should we be encouraging Jeff and Sara and thus make a strong marriage there, whereas something must be wrong between Sara and Marty that an affair should develop between Sara and Jeff? Big questions. And who decides which way it should go? Those were the questions lurking in the shadows of my mind.

"Ok, I agree," I said, but was getting practical. "Let's look at the existing marriage. What about Marty? If he can sire a child, shouldn't he do it?"

"How would I know? Eight years and no kids. That would suggest something. Even perfectly in-tune parents mess up and a baby is conceived. Least I think it's accidental with such types." That was what 'Manda answered and I was kinda glad. The only way she would know would be by trying Marty out, and that didn't appeal to me. 'My girl' doing it with Marty? Marty and 'Manda? That was not acceptable. This sex can get to be a confusing business.

"If they haven't conceived in eight years, what is going to create this miracle soon enough to override an affair? She needs a baby, okay. She needs it now, immediately, not another eight years from now." That was me talking.

"Do you know if it's a serious plan, no children till, say, Marty's job is secure. You live up there. Has she ever intimated something about their family plans?"

"Not that I know, but they are married so have to be having relations. I would suppose she's on the pill."

"Can you get her to go off it?"

"Subtly? I doubt it. We don't want to tip our hand."

"No. however, you could get into her medicine closet and steal her pills. Replace them with placebos, anything realistic."

"I hadn't thought of that. Okay. Get 'em something realistic to replace them with. You get something and I'll do it." I didn't like the idea, but I guess it was okay. People have babies, why not Sara?

"How long do we wait for results, nine months?"

"Oh, too long. We need to know immediately."

"How do you tell if a woman's pregnant and not wait till it shows?" I ask.

"If pregnant she won't menstruate. Can you watch her and tell when she stops menstruating? Watch the waste baskets, toilets, whatever. Find wrappers, whatever will give us the old info."

I visualized myself pawing through the waste buckets. "I suppose," I said. "Alright, but to have to wait two months might be too long. Jeff and she may try to get together before then. In fact I'd say it's guaranteed."

"Granted."

"Wouldn't it be funny if she and Jeff don't break up like the beating might suggest they would, and Jeff becomes the father?" she asked, rolling her eyes.

"As long as Marty doesn't find out."

"He might, and the marriage would break up, especially if she and Marty aren't playing the game."

That expression ticked me off: 'playing the game.' I looked at 'Manda carefully, trying to penetrate her mind and actually know her intentions. Is this whole exercise just a game she plays to entertain herself with and fill her days till her husband gets back?

"How would we know who's who, the father that is? We can't see into Marty's and Sara's bedroom. We won't know where Jeff and she go to do their thing, so won't know if they're trying."

She thrust a pointed finger into the air. "Then we must have them go somewhere where we can spy, and see."

Oh great. This is the stupidest thing. Now we must practically rent a motel for them. "Not possible."

"It is possible. We have to set up a place and somehow urge them to meet there. Have their little tryst there."

"Fat chance."

We fell silent, each thinking. Where?

She broke the silence. "The Hut" she said, it was a mite loud and she looked around. Anyone listening? Only two other couples in and well off from us. The clerks were messing with the coffee machines behind the counter and seemed preoccupied. Safe.

"The Hut?" I said. That's way off down the chasm by the rope bridge."

"Perfect. It's lonely, no one to bother them or look out for. It's private. No one would think of them going there."

I was suspicious. I bet she had this all thought out. She had just been trying to find someone dumb enough to join her in this little escapade. Someone dumb enough to take the blame if it all went awry. Me. And she is right. I am dumb enough to join her. I like this woman and probably would take the blame for her idea. I realized at this point, for the first time, I was falling for this woman. I looked her over. Me and her, let's say married. She was a knockout as far as figure went. She had ideas and was interesting. We could make it. But our age difference! She must be in her early fifties. And I'm about to drop dead from old age.

Would she really give it a try? Oh, heaven if she would, but she has a real, live husband off earning money somewhere.

I took a mental step backwards and looked at us again. Us? God! I must be out of my head. And she was still talking about it. Concluding the planning.

"Let's suppose she could go down the east side and he could go in and out of town by way of the rope bridge and cross over to The Hut." She fell silent, then added, "and into her arms."

I mused. That would pretty much insure that they wouldn't be seen together, each one coming to meet from a different direction. "Okay for a Sara and Jeff meeting."

I didn't think she had heard me.

She smiled. "Moreover, I could invite her to go down with me and clean it up, call it another tourist attraction and we want it to look nice. Take a couple of old blankets down, you know, rather set it up and she'll do the rest. See it as a safe place to go with her boyfriend. We could monitor it, sneak up, and listen or watch. If they perform as lovers do, we'll know."

"What you are thinking of is Sara and Jeff."

"Yes," she said. "This is true."

"But you should be thinking of her and Marty, her husband. Moreover, as far as that goes they could just as well stay home and do it. Why go all the way to The Hut when they have a bedroom at home? But if she and Marty aren't, and she gets pregnant can we assume he's the father?"

"We can assume that, but Marty and Sara will know the difference, which is where Jeff enters the equation. Everyone who knows of the bloody nose and broken tooth incident will make a connection."

"And if she and Marty aren't, and she gets pregnant, Jeff will be the culprit and that's not Marty and Sara."

"I agree." she said, and smiled. Is she playing with me? "Look," she continued. "Maybe we should get Jeff involved. He might sire an offspring."

I laughed. Here Jeff and Sara are the cause of this beating and the strain between her and her husband, and what are we planning? We're plotting to have Jeff conceive a kid behind Marty's back. I swung my head. "Unbelievable."

"But it might work. They purport to love each other."

"Well enough for Marty to beat him up." I snickered again.

"Yes," she said. "True. But think of The Hut with either Jeff or Marty. Remember, it would be more romantic than just another evening in bed. Marty could sneak down, meet her there, and the two would relive their courting days. It would raise their level of sexual enthusiasm."

But I had misgivings. "Maybe we should eliminate Jeff and concentrate on propping up the marriage and putting Marty in position to conceive the child. That was the original idea. Save the marriage."

She swung my way: "It's his duty anyway. So Marty, not conceiving, should possibly get into Portland to some clinic and have his sperm tested. Can he or can't he? If he can, then you suggest he go at it and they try for, let's say, three months. They could have a lot of trysts in The Hut. It could be the event of their lives. The events of their lives!"

I threw in the negative, "if she's on the pill, she might not quit it. One of them isn't into having a kid and I imagine it's her. He and all his sperm wouldn't have a chance in heaven."

"Talk to her. Maybe you could convince her to give it a whirl." 'Manda was having fun with this, I could see it.

"Lets be practical. If she hasn't until now, there's little chance she'll change right off, especially if I'm pressing her. I'm her dad but carry no sway now that she's married. If Marty did, he might get somewhere with her. She might quit the pill for him if she thought he was sincere."

"He could be sincere, but I doubt she'll give in. She's fought it off thus far. That's what happens in some marriages."

I felt sour and looked sour. "'Manda, come on. She won't, even for me, her dad. Besides to talk about it would make her wonder how I got that idea. No, besides, she loves Jeff right now."

Her hand on mine, squeezing it, "That's it then. We'll get Jeff to do it."

A discouraging remark. I had lost her minimal support for the husband to do the job. Discouraged momentarily, I said, "Am I supposed to talk with Jeff, then go to her and suggest she screw Jeff so he can have a son?"

She scoffed. "Course not. We've found the place to have a tryst. Make it regular, like every Thursday, meet and spend the night together and sooner or later she'll conceive. And don't talk so low caste."

"I can't afford some motel, and I doubt she'd have the money either. It's got to present a pleasant, safe spot, and well..."

"We have a nice, quiet place for them. Stop thinking 'motel'. We get them to The Hut and nature might take its course."

'Manda, bless her soul, had it all worked out alright. The Hut.

"Not if she continues with the pill. And how will we know if she does?"

"It'll show in nine months."

"How about four, or even three?"

Chapter 22
The Rope Bridge

So the river ran within a deep gash in the earth, more or less straight hereabouts, filled with all sorts of rocks broken off the sides of the mountain over time. The sides were just about sheer and the chasm was deep. It was a dangerous run most any time of year. In the winter when there was more water feeding this rough, splashy run, it was a most disquieting maelstrom to see; but in the summer when the drought was high, most of the rocks were pretty much exposed and you could see how treacherous it would be in any other season when it would be full of water. But in the summer during the drought if you got into the bottom of the chasm, somehow you could probably walk the whole length hopping from rock to rock, in some places maybe getting your feet wet a bit. In other places the really big rocks piled up and made caves or maybe just left cracks and crevasses between them.

Most every kid in the country had been down in there, playing hide-and-seek or follow the leader. It was cool down there in the summer, not one helluva lot of sun got to the bottom 'cept about dead noon in a few spots where the river ran due south. In the winter it was a flood of ice-cold water hiding a good deal of the stones and during seasons in between, it reeked of rolling and splashing to beat the band. Boy scout troops would run a day long excursion in dented and bent aluminum canoes and so far not a one has been lost, but there's been a few close calls. Still to do it and have a jolly good time occurs every year, spring to fall. Their folks will go to the bridge or a few lookout spots along the way and cheer their sons as they go by. No one can hear them though 'cause of the noise of the water rushing by, under and over and through the rock piles that stick up. It is quite a place, the chasm. It runs more or less about three miles long, and is in some places so narrow that each cliff side almost touches the other. And it's deep. And like you'd expect, people come to picnic and walk along beside it for a ways. At the place where old route 156 goes across, where the covered bridge is, it's about eighty to a hundred or so feet deep according to who's telling you the dimensions. The map makers say its mean average depth, top to water, is ninety, but you know how surveyors are without their instruments, no better than the rest of us. Geologists come through with college classes once in a while to prove in real life that earth cracks exist. They claim this is a minor crack in the earth's crust, or tectonic plate. This plate had a depression in it and, like always happens on a planet covered mostly in water, it filled up creating a gigantic lake, smaller than an inland sea. During the glacial periods the crack in the tectonic plate let water leak out along the rim of this basin cutting through to the lower land out east. As the plate rose during geologic time gradually the river cut its way deeper and deeper, and gouged this chasm where the water ran strong and free, and some of the sides collapsed for one reason or another and so now there's the chasm jagged and dangerous. Sounds kinda alluring and fun, doesn't it? A little bit of danger mixed in for spice. Oh yeah, none of the locals ever talk about it publicly to strangers. Seems that back a few generations, late 1800s I suspect, local folk realized outsiders were coming up to look at it and play with it. Canoes, barrels, row boats going down stream in a wet flurry or having a picnic and not picking up after themselves made life more than hectic around here so everyone agreed God gave it to us, and not to outsiders, so not one of the locals talks of it to outsiders now. Now hardly anyone in the world knows it's there. It's safer as a result and a helluva lot cleaner. Now down stream a distance, southeast of where the covered bridge is, there's an old hut on the north side. Some old codger built it way back thirty, forty years or more and lived there on this shelf where the land either side is bed rock, flat, and split in the middle by this river. The rock plates either side come relatively close, maybe a distance of fifty or sixty feet, it varies. The river down below is probably a hundred feet wide. Well, these two sides being so close tempted this old fellow to build a rope bridge across as he'd seen in pictures of Tibet or the Incas in South America. So he built one and somehow got both sides connected so he could walk over this bridge and visit the other side. It's one-inch hemp, or maybe it's one and a half inch hemp, four of 'em. And bits of branches, wood that is, tied in to make a walk way. Not too safe as I look at it, but daring folks have fun crossing over and back. The ropes have been replaced several times so I suppose it is safe enough, but let others do it, not me. It sways when people move around on it, or when the wind blows, and well, it ain't fer me.

Now back to 'Mandy and me. This old hut is where we plan to have those two meet. Solid wood place, old but solid, cracks in the sides and a plank roof, not the best in the world, but that's where we figured no one would suspect them being and that's where they are going to meet, have their little tryst, you might say. Stoke up a little fire in the old fireplace and have a bite or maybe a cup of coffee and sit close and chat. Or maybe make love, if'n it's gone that far. Marty and Sara, we're thinking at the moment, but if'n things got twisted up it could be Jeff. He would come up from the village, and she from where she lives with her husband. He would drive around, cross on the covered bridge and drive carefully down the old mine road to where this place is. A secondary plan would be to drive over from the village and walk across on the rope bridge which would be shorter. No going way up to the covered bridge.

So there's a little background on the chasm and hut for you, so you can see how isolated and lonely it is, a good spot for a couple of folks overly interested in each other to meet and chat and kiss. A kind-a pretty place too, the chasm and racing water and if you look off you can see the lower land to the east and the little lake that shows downstream, and above that, being farther away you can see the ocean and the line that is all that shows of the beach at this distance, and if it's a nice clear day, sunny and all, it's a real pretty view.

Now on this particular day, having checked out The Hut and looked at the rope bridge, it seems that I had spent a good bit of time (not so surprisingly) when who should I see when I looked away from The Hut, the chasm and the view, but (also not surprisingly) one 'Manda Cunningham walking along the edge with a little girl at her hand. Well, what a blessing that is.

I guessed they'd been up in the village buying bulbs and such for she had a bag with stems sticking out in her other hand. I stood where I was, rather watching her out of the corner of my eye. I saw her coming my way looking at the few wild flowers and stones and so on, entertaining her little girl and educating her about plants at the same time. It was late spring and gardeners were scampering to get their seeds, seedlings, and bulbs all together.

Well, here she comes, I thought. A nice looking woman by any standard. She was shepherding this young girl, maybe three or four years, along with her, talking to the child as they moved along the path above the chasm, looking at the varieties of growing things. She was two persons off now and it was time to move in for a word of greeting and hopefully a report on how the Great Plan was coming along at her end.

"Morning, 'Manda. I haven't seen you lately. How goes the battle?"

"Battle?" She frowned. She looked at me steadily, holding the child's hand in hers.

"It's an expression. Means 'hello'. I say too many words."

"It goes well. Jenny here, is my granddaughter. She and I have been visiting folks the last two days. She is Pamela's daughter. She and her husband are visiting, in fact their visit is over and Jenny's mother and father are packing this very minute. Expect to be in Boston by nine tonight, and Jenny and I must part, whereupon she spoke to Jenny and they talked briefly about the packing and leaving soon. "In fact their plan is to leave right after lunch. You should come by and meet them before they go."

"George isn't back yet?" I was referring to her husband, the traveling engineer.

"Come and gone. This time to Oregon. A major calamity out there in one of the plants. He'll be back in a week."

"Thank you for the lunch invite but I already have luncheon plans, maybe another time. Tell me, how goes the battle?" She looked at me, made a glance around and satisfied that in effect we were alone and said, "Jenny and I went visiting the other day, didn't we Jenny?" Looking down she shook the girl's hand and smiled. "It was fun, wasn't it, Jenny? Remember the chickens?" At which point the child went into a volume of speech and gestures at the end of grandmother's hand. To me, 'Manda said, "Jenny and I visited Sara the other day and she showed us their chickens. Jenny wants to raise chickens someday. Don't you, Jenny?"

The child nodded and spun around and there was a barrage of little girl-grandmother talk. During this display she said: "Sara said she'd like to have a family someday. I said to get started because time does run out, and a few kids can be lots of fun and this is an ideal place to have a family. Safe, pretty, decent schools and all that," she winked. It was a profitable visit. The idea is planted. Jenny and I encouraged her, didn't we Jenny?" Jenny bounced a few times and tugged at grandmother's arm. "How did you make out?" It was directed at me.

I shrugged. "Well, Marty's interested. Said he and Sara have been thinking about a family for years now. We'll see. I also saw Jeff and talked about the town and his place out there in the woods and mentioned that he ought to take in one of the Kalifer girls as housekeeper, you know, it might lead to something and he'd have family and grow old amid comfort and daughters to look after him."

'Manda laughed. "He bought that?"

"I doubt it, he scowled a lot, said he didn't want any more lost teeth and was off on another topic. But I'd say he's thinking. I didn't dare say anything about Sara or Marty, naturally. I think we've got to watch those two. They might slip off and fool us. Jeff and Sara."

'Manda nodded, and was moving off with one of her treasured smiles, and said, "Good for you. Keep your eyes open and the pressure on. We need to talk. Are you going to the library tonight? My company will be gone, meet at the library at seven-thirty. We need to plan." And with the invitation out, 'Manda and Jenny were gone along the trail.

So that's why you'd find me in the stacks at the library. I was looking for a book on submarines when I heard her voice out by the desk. So I stand back by the entrance to the aisle of the 400's until she sees me. She does, and she disappears down the fiction aisle for "F"s. I go down the back cross-over aisle, and there she is, seemingly absorbed in some set of books. She swings her head as acknowledgment and I come up beside her. She has a finger over her lips, the sign for quiet. I slip close to her, as if passing and she moves back, blocking my movement. "Where shall we meet," I whisper. There is a faint but pleasant aroma here.

"Here," she whispers back.

Her back is against me and I am looking over her shoulder, gazing down the slope of her bosom at the backs of books at waist level. Even though I am thirty years her senior and an old man, memory stirs and her perfume demands my attention. ' 'Manda,' I say to myself, 'good friend that you are, you stir me despite the short time we have been acquaintances.'

My hand wants to slip around her waist, to touch her. Would this violate a friendship with her husband, or with her? I am about to slide by, hands on her waist as if making sure we pass each other. She presses her elbows to her sides, somewhat locking my hands on her, yet weak enough to allow passage if I really want to pass. And she bends slightly for a book shelf below, a tight passage at best, and one I don't want to make. I stand, lean slightly to whisper to her, "Why here?" We are in full contact up and down her back and indeed she presses back against me. Why are we doing this like a couple of school kids? She's in her fifties and me in my eighties. Why are we acting like this? Cheap thrills or is it the last chance for healthy, old folks?

"No one would suspect us here."

Eighty years old and out of practice, the old man tries to figure out what she refers to, our secret plans for Marty and Sara, or us? Locked in some sort of friendly posture, enjoying this tantalizing woman, I puzzle. Are we reliving some desperate loneliness of old folk well past the age of innocence?

'Manda says, "I decided Sara is thinking of little girls since Sara and I visited."

"Likewise Marty. Not little girls but kids in general. Although principally considering the financial end, a family makes more expenses."

"I saw Jeff two days ago and made a point of looking at his nose as if I were the nurse. Giving sympathy I told him a nice looking man like him shouldn't be getting broken noses. I told him when I was fresh out of high school I had a couple of boyfriends and they got into a fight one night out by Cold Springs, a place near where I grew up. Pretty country. Passed him a hint. Think he'll follow up?"

I pressed against her, she straightened, us still in contact. "Only if he likes broken noses and smashed teeth."

She was moving away slightly, enough to turn and face me. I held steady where I was. She tilted her head and in the semi-darkness, looking at me, pushed at me with her shoulder. "You've got to say the most encouraging things to that young man, and I mean Marty, her husband."

"I try," awaiting her move.

"But we work at cross purposes. Who's going to be the father?" She had moved a pace away, and looked ready to move on. Should I preserve this moment? Invite her for an ice cream? You couldn't do anything alcoholic here in this town with a married woman, at least I didn't think so, but we should stabilize this situation and get on to greater endeavors. I made the sign of a cup of coffee, moving my cupped hand to my mouth. "Shall we?"

She stepped back to me, pressing left side into my right side and looking up into my face, she was half a head shorter.

"Maybe too public. We can't meet every day. We'd be spotted and the busybodies would be checking on us. It'd undermine our scheme." And then she was gone.

She was back, peeking around the corner at me, still in mild shock. The words, "But I'd like to."

Chapter 23
A Church Project

"Did you know some of the men and women from the church are fixing up The Hut?"

"No. Why?"

"It's to make it look nicer. Folk out on picnics might like to stop there and have their lunch. It's a pretty location right on the chasm, you know, and has a good view out the cut in the mountains there, you can almost see the ocean. Some say you can on a real clear day, with glasses, of course."

"It's a fair walk isn't it, to get there? I mean from the regular bridge."

"Well, if they ever finish fixing the bridge. But you can park on the other side and walk over. Tain't more than a mile maybe, and it's pretty."

"Well, that's true. Of course you could cross directly over to it on the rope bridge, if someone 'ud fix that bridge."

"Oh someone already has. It's got all new lines on it. And is a neat little bridge to cross on. Good bridge now. You should go down and look at it, cross over to The Hut. In fact we'll be there today, working on it. Cleaning it out so's we can give it a coat of paint."

"Who's the 'we' in that?"

"Well, different folks, mostly ones from the church today. Other days it has been just that Trevor man who's been coming to church the last few months or so since coming to live here in Portage."

"The one staying with Marty and Sara?"

"Uh-huh."

"That's his daughter, is it?"

"Uh-huh."

"I wondered about that; about him, that is."

"Good man, good worker. We all cleaned up the yard around The Hut. All that trash and wood and debris is gone now, hauled it back up to the road and took it to the dump. The grounds are cleaned up. Now it's The Hut itself that gets the treatment. Painted, or whatever it needs."

"First thing you know the school kids'll find it and use it for a hide out,"

"Different ones of us plan on keeping it watched. We'll chase kids out."

"I wouldn't want my kids fooling around there anyway, too close to the chasm. Someone could get pushed."

"That's why we're planning on some kind of guard, a guardianship, I guess you'd call it. Let 'em know it's looked after and they'll respect it. Stay away most of 'em."

Chapter 24
An Entry

So here I am sittin' in my bedroom separated from the others in the house for my "private time", as I call it, sitting at my little table with that little book with all the blank pages. I'm filling it up slowly with pencil written words. It's my diary, my journal. The history of me. No big deal. I never look back in it. No need to review my imperfections. Some grandchild some day might find it in the attic with other old stuff and get a kick out of it, so I guess it's worthwhile. I've been keeping it ever since Betty took off. I wrote my beginning line for today: "I'm looking off at the sunset." One nice thing about Marty and Sara's house, it is on a high point and the view excellent.

"Tonight, as most nights, I am thinking of 'Manda Cunningham, one very attractive female, if I say so myself . 'Manda, oh 'Manda. Why did you have to enter my serene little life at such a late date?"

And I filled a page of the diary:

She goes to church Sundays, the choir sings. Then it becomes another day and bible study, then it becomes helping out the little Peace Group starting up, trying to do some sort of Christian Good for the whole world. Choir practice at Portage Church fills another. 'Manda attends all these things. With her husband apt to be away for weeks at a time, it puts discipline into her life and gives her something to do. Something she had to do just to keep from slipping into a dowdy old hen. It worked. No fool, when she had moved here she had assessed where she was and what was happening to her and moved to make a new life, make new acquaintances. She attended any new group, volunteering for this and that, interacting with the members, then filling in for absent ones, accepting committee chores and soon was busy, busy, busy and a factor in this community. She met more people, folks she'd seen in church or at one of the committees, but there remained an annoying void. She likes men, and with George away so much, she had looked about her groups for someone free and interesting enough to develop a 'club' around. It would be the Presbyterian Art Club. With a name like that it would have an open agenda, could do anything. No limits. They would go to movies en mass, to museums, to art shows, take collective painting lessons, all that sort of mixing for pleasure and self-improvement. Men's outlook was so different than the things women found exciting. Therefore she opted for couples despite the fact that basically with George away she was a "single". She, the ipso facto leader, put together one meeting after another and one time, there, quiet, but looking healthy, well-dressed casual style, was a man who had kept his shape into his fifties and filled her candidate post. The perfect substitute while George was away. She approached during some delay in a program (Classical guitar, two students from Portland) and spoke to Mr. Quiet."

I put my ball point pen down, crinkled my nose and stared out the window. Why am I writing all this stuff? Stupid. Stupid writing what 'Mandy told me about her past here in good ole Portage. I turned over the half-filled page. I feel like I'm writing a story, another look at the sun setting beyond the far line of trees covering the low swells of ground, a shrug of the shoulders. Well, why not? It's something to do since I can't actually sit with her and talk. I picked up the pen, gave it a look, threw it in the waste basket with the words, "You have defied me enough with your gaps in showing words on the page. Be done with you, pen!" I picked up my faithful old Cross pen from the desk drawer, gave it a ceremonial kiss, and made some marks on the page. Satisfied that the dear old pen was going to work, I started my story, gathering memory snatches from the far corner of my mind, having adopted the mind of one 'Manda Cunningham and picking up from where she had last spoken.

"It is so nice to see a new face at our gatherings, but I felt someone should introduce us, so here I am 'Manda Cunningham, your committee leader. We hope you enjoy our endeavors and come again. If there is anything you would like to put forward, participate in, do, bring it to our attention, please."

"They passed pleasantries and 'Manda moved on. No woman attached to that man, and others said he was staying at Sara and Marty's. They thought he was Sara's father." It was me she was talking about, her thoughts about me while unknowingly I later sat in the *Empty Plate* and had fantasies of her.

"That was several months ago and it turned out that 'he' was her father and well beyond fifty, somewhere around the eighties. 'Pretty well kept, remarked Sister Jameson at choir practice. Sister was always there and talking like a broken record. She knew everything. George was home for the weekend and half the next week before an assignment in Indonesia. After the service Sunday, while George was talking with several friends, 'Manda, moved up the aisle and fell in behind someone she didn't immediately recognize but when Sara came up to him, she realized who it was.

Presently Jeff got a broken tooth and broken nose, the ladies at the Bible Study talked of it and when over she walked into the *Empty Plate* and Voila! There he was."

The rest is history. Oh yes! I'd forgotten about the afternoon Tea at the rectory. There was an afternoon Tea at the rectory, an attempt to draw more folks toward the church. A pleasant little effort by the pastor and 'Manda's art group, although I didn't know it at the time. Thinking this interesting looking woman might be there, I went and we met again, although a rather well-dressed man and more of her age than mine, name of Frazier, acted as if attached to her, so a short stay for me and out to the hill where Marty and Sara lived."

I stuck the end of the pen in my mouth and stared at the page I had just written. True enough, but I'd forgotten to mention that she'd given me a wink from behind Frazier's back creating a little tinge of excitement throughout my body. A more religious person might have thought God was pushing us together, at any rate I was hooked, another companion on the various educational or cultural experiences of the Art Club had been created. But she sure did look good. I gave a snort to the page thinking how the Art Club had rather fallen by the wayside for the moment as she and I were concentrating on saving marriages. She did say the other day that she thinks of me as hers (and I am tickled to death at it) for I am 'pleasant and somewhat interesting and positive in outlook.'

I put the pen down, stared out the window again. My novel is going to be one vast, red hot bunch of pornographic words. I hope to Christ Sara doesn't find this. I looked at the pages of my words. I didn't know, I really didn't, that I was so enthralled by this Mrs. 'Manda

Cunningham. What my hidden mind reveals to me! I thought that one over, still paused in my diary-writing, rereading, wondering where this imaginary tete-a-tete would eventually go. Maybe I really should write this more as a novel, instead of as my diary entry. I picked up my good ole Cross pen and started on this world-shaker of a tale again. "We started meeting for a coffee Thursday mornings. We were friends and she ceased feeling lonely and abandoned when George was away, nor did she feel as if she were the target of gossip for it wasn't just Frazier (who is Frazier?). You know, the man at the Tea. She explained about him. She had selected him as a sort of escort on Art Club ventures to keep gossip at bay, and now you (she pointed her index finger at me. Me and Frazier. Trevor and Frazier. Her two escorts when George is away. Now really, who is Frazier? Frazier had moved up from Newburyport, an old family friend, who had heard so many comments about the beauty of the Maine coast and Portage in particular that he had succumbed and moved here. Frazier also was available. Having two 'friends' to be seen with dissipated any gossip surrounding her choice of men to be seen with at coffee or any recreational event. Frazier had money, which was handy. They did occasional concerts, expensive ones in Portland. Once an invitation to go to Boston to something, refused on the grounds that she was married and it was improper. She pointed that index finger at me again and I wondered what was going to happen this time. She told me: Trevor is a different animal, not unfamiliar with the cultural side of things. Still he is more homespun, if such a thing can be said without diminishing his wisdom, conversation and experiences. And he was so old George would never consider him a threat to our marriage.

"Oh" I said I to myself. I'd be a little careful on that one.

I grimaced at myself. Am I the hero or merely the scribe in this thing? I'm not giving myself much of a build up. 'Course, Mandy may actually think that way. I, the next newest Ernest Hemingway, put down the Cross pen and stared into the distance through the window. Pines and deciduous trees mixed far off there. I could almost smell them in my imagination.

I hadn't heard too much about Frazier lately, since we'd gotten together to solve the Marty-Sara problem. 'Manda and I have found comfort in each other lately, an occasional touch, the taking of an arm, standing together sometimes very close.

If I weren't so concerned that I am too old I'd think of her a deal differently. And I should face it, I'm beginning to think thoughts like this more frequently. This stuff has got to come to a stop. It's okay in a story, but not in real life.

I picked up the Cross and stared at the wall. I'd better concentrate on Sara and Marty, our pact, rather than imagining me and 'Mandy getting into something. What's wrong with my head?

I can tell Sara knows I don't approve of that little kissing business with Jeff. So now I don't get any info from her on how it's going. Is she still seeing him, or trying to? Is he over getting poked in the nose and beginning to think of a woman again, and if so, I hope it's Sara.

Me and 'Manda had been working on getting Sara and Marty on stable marital ground, thinking about it, talking, fixing up the old hut down by the rope bridge, all that stuff, I'd rather lost track of them as people. Marty and Sara were just objects in the chess board of life.no longer individuals.

And here's Jeff popping out of my head as another piece on the game of Life.

"Huh" I muttered out loud. "By gum. Ain't that something." I go there and eat and sleep and Marty and me'll talk a bit, but it no longer seems like they're real people since 'Manda and I looked at this martial problem. I laughed a trace at the situation. It's all over in my mind. Maybe 'Manda and I didn't need to do all this, everything had settled down so well. There was no longer a problem that needed to be fixed by a baby.

Chapter 25
The Back Stairs

Jeena, 'Manda's youngest, had driven off toward college at dawn, expecting to arrive mid evening. Mom had seen her daughter off, giving her an egg sandwich, carrot sticks, three cookies and an apple for lunch on the road. 'Manda turned in her kitchen, watching the sun pour into the room, and then turned to start up the rear stairs. She went up six stairs, didn't remember closing the porch door, went back down to the door and it was securely closed, turn back to the stairs and start up again.

Up the stairs the light diminished as something blocked the light from the window farther up.

The noise was enough, but her husband's voice cascading down the stairs was a finale. 'Manda paused, thinking, I thought he'd gone out for a walk, If I'd known he was still here he could have helped say good-bye to Jeena.

She looked up into the dimness and sure enough, he was there, and something in his hand. Good heavens. His service revolver.

"George. What's the matter?"

"Ah-h. Mandy? That's you? Who's with you? Who just left"

She started up the stairs again from her surprised stop. "George, what in heavens is going on. You scared the b'Jesus out of me." She looked but it was gone, he was holding it behind him.

"What do you have that gun out for? George? Are you alright? Where are you going?" She followed him into the bedroom. "What is going on?"

"Nothin'." He was closing the drawer where he normally kept the gun, crawling into bed and gesturing her over. "I came up and started a nap, must have missed Jeena, right?" He gave 'Manda a gentle push to the bed and she collapsed there, then up on one elbow, watching him for whatever was next.

Next was the husband laying on the bed next to the woman who was the most beautiful woman in the world or so he frequently told her.

She rolled halfway on top of him with an arm around his chest and reached up to kiss him. "What were you up to?"

"Nothing, just practicing my civil defense. Nothing. Jeena just left?"

"Yes, your youngest daughter. Do you think she was the masked Zorro coming to steal me?" She giggled a tiny bit, liking the fantasy.

"Nope. Nope, nope, nope. Just practicing." He kissed her and lay back, letting his arm explore her side nearest him, and then rolled over and made a face at himself. I'm getting jumpy. I better be careful. Pulling a gun on my wife 'cause I forgot she was here. He closed his fist and squeezed. But by Christ, if that bastard comes to this house and I'm here, I'll blast his liver right out of him. No one man is going to come and sneak in on my 'Manda. I'll blow his liver out while he's sneaking down my back steps."

He was thinking of Frazier. He had stopped at the motel bar on the way in from the airport and some men at a table near the bar were talking about Marty knocking the tooth out of Jeff. It was over his wife, but it put his mind on Frazier and 'Manda seeing one another, Bible Study they called it, but you never knew what went on at a Bible Study after the pious ones had left, just another little coffee, sit and let's talk. 'Manda was home alone a lot, and long ago there had been some rumor. He remembered as it came boiling up in his fatigued brain. Now there's this Frazier and she's here alone all day and nothing to do, hang around, look for a little excitement. Jesus. I'd better be careful. 'Course, she'd never try something like that. His imagination pictured their big Victorian house with those back steps which someone could use and never be known in the front of the house.

All those empty rooms upstairs now that the kids were gone. She could invite that Frazier over and he'd be in the house and I'd never notice it. And he could sneak out after a little tete-a-tete, or worse. Slip down the back stairs and I'd never know the difference. But she wouldn't do that.

'Manda and George; our daughter Pamela married and the granddaughter, Jenny, and Jeena, college age. The Cunninghams, a nice family. Let's keep it that way.

But then there's that old codger 'Mandy has coffee with every once in a while. What's going on there, not that I need to worry. He's at least twenty, maybe thirty years older than her. Trevor, that's his name, met him at Church once. A bore. He must have powerful gift of gab for her to meet him there every week or so. 'Course maybe the town's people have dwindled in their ability to charm anyone. Maybe it's just that Manda's losing her feel for this place. We moved here, pleasant people, if not much inspired. Jeena's off to college now and 'Manda's alone when I'm off at some job. Too much off-site work, but then that's what pays the bills. Maybe 'Manda needs another kid. Something to keep her interested. He stared off through the window. It looked over the lower part of the town and off along the escarpment edge well off, a long view and a pretty one on a day like this. And he thought of Mandy, Trevor, Frazier, B&B, Bernice, and a few others. About Jeff and his non-tooth and swung around back to Bernice. He squeezed up his face in puzzled thinking. I wonder how B&B got that girl and what will happen if she gets pregnant. He snorted. Fat chance. B&B a father at his age? He shrugged, could happen, I suppose. A healthy girl like her, and with looks too good for this little berg. Of course all this about her falls into the gossip category. No one knows what happens when he takes her home. Maybe it's all innocent and all the talk and gossip and rumor is nothing.

I must have slept for short time. Looking at the clock, it said several hours had passed. The sun beyond the curtain confirmed that the clock was okay. He'd slept after his analysis of his little ol' town. Tomorrow it's off to Chicago and the next assignment. He arose, another look out the window. Maybe a little walk downtown and go into the *Miss Tracy*, the bar. Maybe Dan will be there. No, not likely. Let's call and see. Meet him there an' have a couple. Chat.

He called and Dan was raking the lawn. He readily agreed to meet for beer.

Too nice a day to drive, he walked toward the great business center down by the Chasm. An eventful walk as it turned out. Had to pass where the high school girl lived on the corner, B&B's girl. Abreast of her house he looked over the hedge, and quite by chance there she was, a striking looking girl in her last year of high school. How did he know that? He'd heard all the talk, and so he knew of her by reputation and the gossip. She was looking back at him, doing something beyond the hedge that he couldn't see and he lifted the least bit, as he hesitated there on the sidewalk, looking, and his eyes came back to hers and she spoke.

"Aren't you 'Manda Cunningham's husband, Mr. Cunningham?" She gave a lilt to her speech.

He gasped, hadn't realized she'd recognize him, he'd never been introduced which was natural since they were of different generations and she a school girl. He stammered, "Yes, yes, indeed. Yes, Mr. Cunningham. George. You know 'Manda, my wife?"

"Everyone knows your wife. She's active here in the community. I'm in the last half of History and Society, my last course in history at school. I've got the terminology, finally. She hesitated in what she was doing, still looking at him, her smile lingering. How are you, Mr. Cunningham?"

"Well fine, thank you. I didn't mean to stare."

She was across the hedge from him now. "Oh you weren't. I was stretching one of my sweaters out like mother showed me. I just washed it. You may come in if you want to see it. Do you know how to do it?"

"Me? Oh no. 'Manda does that, I suppose" She has on some kind of rather tight, light sweater. It's old, spots on it where she'd done some painting or something, and small for her. No wonder B&B takes her home. She's big too; almost as tall as me, and heavy in a high school girl kind of way. B&B still taking her out like it's almost a year. Or is it? And the question of the century, is he getting it? I wonder if she's on the pill, and is B&B up to that kind of thing? People used to talk about them, and the disgust in it all. But no one talks any more, used to it, I suppose.

Her hair was in some kind of bandana thing which partly dislodged and her hair fell to the side as she moved. She made a face and flicked her head repeatedly. "Mother showed me how to do this. Do you think it'll lose its shape? Please don't mind my hair it's getting longer and I don't want to cut it. B&B likes it this way and I do it to please him. He treats me well." She held the sweater up to her chin, smoothing it across her bosom and stomach. It didn't seem to reach her waist, her belt. Thus encouraged, he looked it over carefully. Spread across her bosom it gave him the most perfect right to view her. She gave herself a shake and everything jiggled. "Do you like it?"

"Yes, pretty color."

"I think so, too, that's why I agreed to try this. My mom said that it was worth a try, but not to be too concerned if it lost shape because it's an old one, and too small for me."

He raised his eyebrows. "It doesn't look it."

She somewhat laughed with an eye on him and, "Mom may be right. What do you think?" She hesitated, then added. "How come you are in town today walking around? Your wife says you are away an awful lot on business."

A healthy sigh, "She's right. I leave tomorrow on another business venture."

"Oh? How long will you be gone?"

"Can't tell. Business varies with the kind of breakdowns of the machinery. I fix broken equipment."

It must be interesting. I wish I could do something different."

"Different than –?"

"Oh you know, school work." She looked shyly at him. "You know B&B gives me rides home?"

"Yes, I've heard something of the sort." his eyes widened. My God, she openly speaks of it, but then, why not? Everyone knows anyway.

"He's nice, but every dance, or trips to the library, or for groceries he seems to find me. It's nice of him but each time? A girl needs a change once in a while."

He thought of 'Manda last night or was it this morning? 'Manda needs a change too. Would a pregnancy do it for her? At her age it might be touchy. Older woman having a baby? To the girl he said, "Yes, it is nice for a woman to have a change once in a while. Makes her think things through."

Her face was on his and he felt her hand go to his arm over the hedge. "You're right. A girl does, before she gets married and everything turns on him and his wants, whatever they may be."

She had taken her hand away and was moving the sweater and stretching it out on the picnic table again, "Do men feel that way, ever?"

He snorted. "Oh yeah, but usually when they're in their forties, early fifties."

She was looking surprised, and turning again to him approached the few steps to the hedge, and took his hand and held it in her two. "You and I should take a day and go to the country and talk this out. I'm fascinated. In school it was alluded to once in that same history class." She was close. "Imagine. Finding it right here with you, that very thing we were talking about. B&B doesn't talk about things like that". She moved slightly to the left, "Come in, it'll be easier to talk. Come." She had moved to the small gate in the hedge and opened it, drew him in, guiding him to the table, stopped and smoothed the sweater again, turned slightly to him, her hip against him and her voice almost a whisper. "Mr. Cunningham, I've watched you when I go places. I never thought you'd be so understanding, but do you really feel that way, like you'd like to change if even just for a day? Are you really feeling that way, even now?"

Dare he put a hand on her waist? Her face inches away, eyes moving somewhere. His hand went to her waist, gently, softly, and she was still talking. "We should do that some time when B&B's away. Talk. It would be good for us. At least for me. Would it help you?"

Should I? He asked himself, intrigued with the thought and the potential.

Her face was close and she whispered. "B&B's away daytimes. We could. But your wife, would she mind?"

"I think she'd approve," he lied.

"We should. It'd be good for my mental health."

"And mine."

From her a smile, a quick kiss to his cheek. "Lets."

He drew her close. "Okay."

"When? Where were you going now?"

"Today?" he questioned, sensing his voice crack as he whispered to her. She was still leaning against him." Why are we whispering? He spoke aloud. "We couldn't. I don't have the car."

"Why do you need that?" She was away, pulling him. "Let's go in, I'll make coffee for you and we can talk inside. Just like in the country. No one will be home 'till after six."

And inside life ran its course. The high school girl in her last year. B&B's girl and 'Manda's husband.

Chapter 26
Not Us

George Cunningham laid on his back, arms folded under his head and stared at the ceiling. Outside, a middle-aged man scurried along a street, a young lady beside him held his hand. They reached the rope bridge and stopped and looked at the repairs, someone had strengthened it and replaced the worn and dangerous foot treads. The two came together and kissed, and he took her hand and again led the way, quickly, not trusting their good luck at finding the bridge in such good shape. Forbidden thoughts arising as they hurried, basking in the anticipated pleasure of being alone together in the little hut on the other side of the gorge, a place where they could be together for a few hours. 'Mandy looked so young and vibrant. A memory of another, much younger girl passed before his mind: B&B's girl, Bernice. This is better. 'Manda and me. Us together, enjoying this. Forget Bernice.

Days, weeks ago, he had been concerned about someone sneaking up the back stairs and visiting 'Manda while he was asleep in bed. Maybe Frazier, that swine. Possible that old codger Trevor that she talked with in the coffee shop. According to her, they talked about fixing up this very hut and getting a love nest out of it, the abandoned and remote place that it was. He wasn't sure where her talk was going, but wondered what it meant for her subconscious. Is she having some sort of crisis?

The idea was to lure Marty and Sara to a different location than their own bedroom. A different spot, a trusted spot that would heighten their love-making and put some spark in it. A different place than the usual bedroom and all it had come to represent, the hum-drum existence of a marriage slowly going sour. George frowned. An interesting thought, an interesting therapy for a bored couple. The secluded hut, warm and cozy with a fire in its little fireplace, blankets, some little meal. Perfect for an old couple once bored, to now become enamored again.

George curled his lip in partial denial of this idea. He dismissed Marty and Sara, the oh so needy couple according to his wife. Just baloney, he decided. They weren't that old yet that they needed such an artificial situation. I bet the real focus, and she may not know it herself, is Mrs. 'Manda Cunningham, my wife. It sounds completely too familiar. Her real concern might be me and her. "Manda and me going sour on each other. Maybe she even heard I spent an afternoon talking with Bernice. My God, that could have made her think.

And then another thought. She'd mentioned Sara having a baby as a result of this little tryst in The Hut. What if she was really thinking of herself. She and me having a little tryst there. My God, does she want a baby? Jeena is gone. Pamela is gone. Maybe she thinks she needs another kid. My God.

The Hut: a place where we could let ourselves go in a renewal of past passion. She pretends to me that Sara needs a baby to complete their family, Sara and Marty but it's really her and me. She has convinced herself that she must unleash her sexuality on me and arouse my desire that I follow God's Will and go forth and multiply. At her age! At my age! She's going to save Bernice from me by getting pregnant herself. Warped! That bastard Trevor is probably in on this too, she mentions him helping to clean up The

Hut. God. I have been away on business too much. What possibly could happen next?

I can't believe it. My wife has convinced herself that Sara needs a baby to complete her family and it is up to Marty to do his duty to his wife, and after she tells me this preposterous idea would jab her elbow into me and wink. His duty. It makes me feel that somehow she is trying to egg me on. For Christ sakes, what does she want? Does she really want another baby? And what's wrong with our sex life? Nothing. Maybe not the greatest in the world, but adequate. It isn't that I can't or don't want to, it is just that I'm away so much, and tired and wanting relaxation when I get home, and don't always feel like responding to my wife right away. Sure I'm tired and exhausted, but I get over that. I wonder if 'Manda is trying to get another baby? She must be nuts.

George Cunningham, mid-fifties; beautiful, healthy wife, yet after an afternoon with an unimaginably well-built high school senior, touching, feeling, kissing, and contending with the serious thoughts of a young maiden searching for meaning in her relationship to elderly B&B: and her thrill at being with a somewhat younger man and his mature advice in matters of love, George Cunningham moved somewhat on the bed and reached out and down with his hand, felt around two inches and connected with a glass bottle, lifted it, drank two swallows worth and repositioned it on the floor, swallowed in pleasure, rewarding himself, orange flavored vodka; laid in his bedroom, waiting for the beautiful, healthy mid-fifties wife to come to bed, and wondered what had happened to him this afternoon. A seventeen or eighteen year old high school girl? He had been worrying about some unknown man sneaking up the back stairs to his wife while he slept the sleep of exhaustion, mental and physical, of a high tech repair engineer always away from home, and here he was pulling that very stunt, sneaking up the back stairs to bed for a nap? Was he losing his marbles?

No, just relaxing. But now that he had resurrected that idea of the back stairs, it persisted in his mind.

Although he had never seen anything amiss, Frazier was a real threat. Wasn't he? And who else was around this cute, picturesque, little isolated village that could jeopardize the peace of coming home from another trip?

No one. Some young punks around but not interested in a mid-fifties, married woman. All the rest were like B&B, too old for that stuff. 'Course, Bernice was his girl and must in some fashion satisfy B&B. But that was their business. So be it. Every other man in town was settled into their marriages which for all I know are all getting stale. Certainly not mine, nor 'Manda's. And she doesn't need another baby. I'll have to be subtle and persuade her out of that. What a stupid idea.

Chapter 27
The Triad – A Third Encounter

"That Steal-the-Flag game is the dumbest thing I've heard of in years."

"We gonna go down and watch it next year?" Marty scowled. "Go down and watch that stupid thing? All those na'ar-do-wells running around like hyenas playing some teen-age boy scout game? There must be better ways to spend our time. Maybe take a Sunday drive out around Ellsworth and north. It's pretty out that way."

I noted Marty was getting ready to drop into his I'm-a-poor-dumb-yokel way of speaking, a sure sign that he was willing to be dissuaded by these brilliant, college-educated people that surrounded him, me and Sara.

"There's a nice restaurant in that little berg," noted Sara sitting there studying her husband's belt-line. I looked it over myself. What was she seeing? The belt went from the rear at his waist-line back there around front and down below the front waist-line by several inches, his stomach protruded a bit, not a lot, but a bit and hung over the belt. He's putting on weight and in two years will have a big gut sticking way out and the belt will be down almost to his groin in front. He'll look like any other construction worker. I wondered if she was thinking of Jeff. I'll have to give him a look too, see where he's going with that. And me, what do I look like? So what about Sara? No baby-stretch marks on her yet, but give us another nine months and we'll see. Her tummy is still in. Give 'Manda and me time, and our great scheme will see to that. She was looking herself over, looking down past the breast-shelf at her flat stomach. She looked up at her husband. What's he saying? I should pay attention.

They were out on the back deck, smelling hamburgers sizzling away on the grill. I looked away from the grill and off over the hemlocks, pines and deciduous tree tops showing off there swaying in the breeze. One nice thing about where they'd built this house, they had a good view. The sky was deep blue today and not a cloud to be seen. Beautiful. And these two were arguing again. Like Mandy said, maybe she does need something to really occupy her mind.

'Manda. Thinking about her reminded me of something. What the hell was it? Not anything about this Sara and Marty pair but her and George. What was–, oh yeah. One of the neighbors had given her a bit of not too delectable news at Bible Study Monday. Something involving B&B.

A lady next door to Bernice's place had reported to some in-between who had naturally, nothing out of the ordinary, just reported something, just a remark from a neighbor the lady had said, that George had been talking to Bernice over the hedge the other day and she couldn't hear what they were talking about but they were having an agreeable conversation, and the next time she'd looked out they were both gone.

Now what in hell did that mean unless someone was trying to make a story and get something started. People are so damned curious and trying to live an exciting life watching the more daring among us parade about. So George was talking to B&B's girl, well, not really his girl, just giving her rides around the countryside after events like dancing and such. Nothing wrong with that especially as her parents didn't seem to mind. And she always went.

I was smelling the cookout coming along and watching a hawk soaring off a half mile or so, slowly making lazy-eights in the sky.

So now why did 'Manda tell me that? I didn't say anything to her, just went on listening, wondering what she had up her sleeve this time. So George talked to Bernice. Well, I haven't seen Bernice in a month, maybe, but I'm sure she's still the good looking piece she was back then. I guess the question is what is George up to, talking to a high school senior? Another adult to give her a different perspective on life. No harm there. 'Course he isn't around that much being off working in some far away place. Tough on Mandy, though. Must be lonely especially with their daughter gone this year. Look ahead Mandy. She's off and you're alone so you need to fill in your life with something else. That's the way life's going to be from now on. Jeena'll get married and be gone for good. You'll be alone.

I realized I was frowning at the hawk. Huh. Now maybe that's why Mandy and I are hitting it off so well. She's ahead of me, realizes already that she'll be alone and is building up a clientele of friends to fill her life with. Wonder if I should out and ask her? Maybe not. Might squelch our friendship, and she is pleasant company.

'Manda and I were in the *Empty Plate*, we were beginning to call it a 'coffee house', making us sound uppity and always laughed when we did, interrupting our putting the final move to the 'Sara and the baby' plan. The rope bridge had been woven with a new main rope, the grounds around were clean and I'd say the place looked good. The hut itself had been cleaned and painted and the insides furnished with a couple of benches and a picnic table. The big two-person shelf, originally a double bed for hikers to sleep in, was very clean and painted. Fact was, everything was ready. It just needed Sara and Marty.

So that was our thinking for today, not that each of us hadn't given it some private thought as we'd worked. As of course so had the others, those that had volunteered and the others who'd just come by and donated some work as they passed through or finished off the day before going home to lunch or supper. Everyone was happy at a small community project successfully and tastefully done.

"What'd'ya think?" That was me talking.

She reached, took my hand and gave it a squeeze. She nodded.

"The moment of truth awaits expectantly."

Mandy smiled. "Ah, the magic word: EXPECTING! Well, put, Mr. Trevor Heneke. Well put. The object of our work!" And 'Manda snicked away at the play on words.

By gum, I sure liked that woman. She had such a natural way about her, and such a good worker, and good with ideas, too. Now let's see what we can find out. I said all that stuff to her, watching her look away somewhat embarrassed over the comment and then one-up me with her comment. Well, we were two people in sync, that was for sure.

Looking me dead in the eye, in her quiet voice so that others in here wouldn't hear. "I've enjoyed working with you. Do you think we should cooperate on something else, some other needed project here in this dead country to the east of Portland?" A half-smile lingered on her face. She was teasing, or was she?

"Yes, I do." And you know, I was feeling good and full of energy, and said, believe this, "Absolutely, but maybe something more akin to our own needs, and something not so visible. This working together in the daylight is okay, but let's try a night project?" I let my teeth show, my big smile to be taken either as a flirtatious remark or as a clandestine suggestion. I suppose either one could be flirtatious. So I added, "Maybe putting up public lighting in the park." That was pretty bland and maybe misunderstood so, "to keep the high school contingent from hanging around there day after day. More safety." That was alright but needed more explanation. "Maybe more adherence to the customs of our elders." And not quite fitting my thoughts, so, "Fewer pregnancies among the senior class." And that was too much, so I shut up.

She had one eyebrow lifted way up high and a full smile, laughing at me trying to express myself, or something. Her answer came out slowly.

"Maybe we should follow B&B around and see what he and Bernice are really up to when he takes her home."

Just like a taut rubber band snapping against an empty paper bag. A nice 'snap' in my head. I knew what she was thinking. It was that gossip about George and Bernice, I'd heard the gossip, too. My little jumble of badly phrased talk about teen behavior and pregnancy had brought a concern about her husband to the fore. Why did I say that stupid stuff? But it revealed a concern she had about her and her husband. She had said last week that she'd hardly seen him when he was home last week. It had never occurred to me that she could be worried. I hadn't even given it any real thought until now. I'd more or less forgotten George existed. In my head it was me and her together. Me and her walking hand in hand off into the sunset. The perfect pair. And now I find her worried about that. So much for my dreams. So George and Bernice talked friendly-like over the hedge. And someone claimed to see him out by the roadside pull-off on the way into town. Bernice and George? He's twenty years older than her. My God. What's he up to? 'Course B&B must be close to thirty years her senior. This can't be happening.

I looked hard at her, and there she was, eye to eye with me again, only no smiles this time. She's worried about him fooling around.

We looked at each other too long.

I flung my head to the side. "Aww-w, that's a lot of hog wash. George is a nice guy, friendly. He wouldn't mess around with a high school girl."

She drew back, shifted in her chair, asked, "You want a refill or should we be going?"

Now I was watching her all this time, and getting concerned. She looked edgy, not exactly upset but sort of. You know how you can tell when you know someone real well? That's the way it was and I liked this woman. I tilted my finished glass, rolled it in a 360 on its base, round and round, thinking. She was on the edge of the chair, waiting.

"Yeah-h. I could stand a refill, I guess, providing you're going to keep my company."

Her free hand on mine for just a moment, and she was getting up. "I'll stay with you. However long it takes."

Now what did that mean? For time to drink another Smoothie or for the years ahead, the two of us facing an unfriendly world. Stay with me? I was going to ask her, but she was gone.

When she came back she had someone with her. It was George, and she was acting like a flustered hostess, leading him to our table and I stood, got introduced and hearing his reply, "We've never been introduced, but I've seen you about town. Trevor, huh?" She was sitting, then up and gone, back to the counter for another drink and bringing the three back, one for each of us. I didn't know what to say and we sat in silence, watching her. Why were we sitting in silence? I felt like we'd been caught, but of course that wasn't it at all. I was thinking of B&B and Bernice and this guy, the whole town watching to see if he, George, was cutting in on B&B's girl or watching him and his wife to see if there was anything developing over B&B, or if their marriage was any way in jeopardy. What a mess and here I am, seeing Mandy again, like always, and maybe they're watching me and her, too. I hadn't thought of that before. He and Mandy were talking about something and I was sitting here totally out of it, acting, I'm sure, like an out of place suitor.

I finished my second Smoothie and having listened unsuccessfully to what they were discussing excused myself and moved off. Walking along the street, I passed that new building they were erecting and stopped to look in. A big sign said "No Admittance" so being an American I knew that was an invitation so stepped past the sign and stood in the open doorway. There were voices up above and hammering sounds; the first floor pretty much laid out as if ready for the plasterers to come in and do the walls. The building was at the edge of one of those minor chasms that show up in parts of this country, not like the big, deep one next to The Hut, but similar although smaller in all ways. Still I was surprised it was so far down to the river. Moreover the river had backed into this place and made a quiet pool there. Below, were a few skiffs tied up. Over to the right was the stairway that went from the street down to the small wharf backed up against the cliff side. It was a steep cliff, but not as sheer as the one over at The Hut. A hoist-rig was there, too, at the top, an 8x8 with a block and tackle attached and some boys hanging around it, looking my way from time to time without wanting to let me know. They wanted to go down on the line but knew it was against the rules. I backed off, watching. Out of my sight they thought, they only waited a moment before one grabbed the line and down he went, the line playing out with that rattling rustle, his weight carrying him down. He landed on the tiny wharf and yelled for the next. They were all going to do it, I knew. Kids. I went upstairs to see how they were doing and found Marty and Jeff and two others struggling with a wall assembled on the floor and being pushed up and levered into place, nailing it home.

They got it in place and I congratulated them and moved on, thinking about B&B and Bernice going out in his car after dances, and George and Mandy. Nobody knows what they do, B&B and Bernice. So later on I heard one of the O'Hara men had decided to find out. Of course neither B&B nor Bernice would tell, it was some pact of trust between them. O'Hara wouldn't say after he, according to him, successfully completed the mission. His advice to everyone was to leave it alone. The nature of the advice and best for him as well as for B&B and Bernice was such that others observe their privacy. No one else mess around trying to find out. Of course the interesting thing about people is that seldom can anyone keep a secret well.

Chapter 28
That Guy O'Hara

I had taken my paints and other equipment and gone out to the lake out back a few miles, parked at the public boat ramp and walked along the shore a ways to a place I'd picked long, long ago and set up. I sketched in the mountain and some other broad details and moved off a bit and was just sitting. Old men do that, sit, sometimes nap, but lots of just sitting, thinking back on life and the mistakes and small successes most of us suffer. Presently along comes John O'Hara, crunching along the sand beach heading my way.

"Paintin' somethin'?" he said, as a sort of greeting, and sat down a few feet off to chat one of those slow, meandering chats folk have when there ain't no real business and the day's a good-un, sunny, warm and the air quiet.

At one point he asked, "Hey, Trevor, how much longer you planning to hang around here, I mean Sara's place. You been here a bit already. I should think you'd head off for Arizona or Florida where the sun still shines in the winter."

"Ain't given it much thought." I had fallen into my yokel patois. "I got me a bunch of friends 'round here, I've been here so long I might stay the winter. Who knows? Far as that goes, who cares?"

He shrugged and kept staring off across the lake, watching the far shore where a canoe with two people was drifting, so I finished for him.

"Sara don't seem to mind having an extra mouth to feed around the place, so why move on now?" I bolstered it with something like enthusiasm. " 'Sides the dullness might come to a close with some action. Look here, I'm out trying to be the great painter. Who knows what's next?" Reinforced with a fucking big smile.

"Yeah, yeah. Everyone knows ya got friends. Like that 'Manda Cunningham. According to the Ladies Aide from the church you two're out sucking coffee every morn at 'The Plate'. So my wife tells me."

"Good God. People watch us drink coffee in public?"

A smile from him. "A-yup. If'n you miss a day it gets reported."

Now a big grin from him. "That's what the Ladies Aide's for, see that everyone stays in line, one way or another. Now for example, I went out one night..." And here he stopped dead, dropped the grin, stared after the canoe. Silence.

Now we sat that way for what seemed like six months, course it was only a minute, maybe three. I'm wondering what the hell he had been about to tell, figured I'd never know, and then he started talking, and of all things, about B&B and Bernice. He'd been thinking about them for some time I guessed and just had to let it out.

"You must know who Bernice is," he said.

"Oh yeah. Pretty girl, good figure. 'Manda's husband was supposed to have had a conversation one time with her."

He looked over at me, did that grin again. "Oh yeah. Worst thing he ever did. They disappeared somewhere, probably in the house, and everyone's still contemplating that. She is a real neat woman, looking-wise, and I wouldn't blame anyone for studying her, and that's what happened to me. The misses got carrying on about B&B and her, probably spurred on by the Ladies Aide or maybe the Bible

Study ones and their mouths, so I decided to find out what they really did when B&B took her home and they don't arrive for an hour or two." He turned to me and began working out what happened using his finger to emphasize points.

"I'd follow B&B's car for a ways. Then another night I'd lay out ahead of time and when they passes would pick up the chase. Drop it before they got anywhere, and pick it up there next time. B&B was consistent. Always the same route it seemed, at least that's the way it went. They'd go out to Darling's Grove, pull in among the trees and shut down. They'd talk a while. I know because I'd sneak up on the car and watch and listen. It was always the same pattern, B&B's an old guy. They'd hold each other, she'd slump into his arms, talk and him feeling of her. Not much kissing, but some. So that was it. A little affection, feeling and kissing a pretty girl." He fell silent, looked away, watching the canoe and the mountain and so on."

I didn't say nothing. What's to say?

Finally I got an idea so said, "You told the Ladies that, I suppose."

He nodded. "I didn't say nothing to my wife for a long time, thought about it all. I knew it'd get back and get picked apart like they do so well. This is a small town and most everyone knows what the others do, and how. So I played it discrete. That's the word, isn't it?"

"Yep," so I nodded.

Silence while the canoe over there loaded its people and they started back along the lake. Out for a picnic, I suppose. We watched from way off here what they did way off over there.

He picked it up, twirling a stick in the sand where he sat. "According to my wife what the ladies said pretty much was 'What do you expect. He's such an old hound dog he couldn't do much at all. Kiss and hold on to her, and according to my wife they'd laugh at about that point, laugh in a sort of an embarrassed way. It's pretty much over now. That was weeks ago. They get together to hear things to talk about. Gossip. Like you and Mandy."

I didn't like that at all but what do you do? I was sitting there smarting from the sting of that when he said, "What I told them was all cleaned up to give them something to talk about without really hurting no one. Don't you think that's a better way?"

"Well, I do."

"He had this poor girl pretty well trained. He was quiet and kind and no one else knew what they did and no one dared ask. And she was smart enough to keep her mouth shut and enjoy what he gave. The ladies were right, he couldn't do nothing like make her pregnant, maybe that wasn't his goal anyway. Just have a pretty girl make him feel good. And she did that. They'd talk, mostly him, pouring out how he felt about everything, private talk, personal, stuff he had to get off his chest, anger, plans, pain, hate, and nice things too, mostly over her. I think he really does love her in his old man kind of way. She makes him feel good. I guess that's it. Just a nice old couple, well, him anyway, but they can't let on publicly leastwise not in this town." And he sat there, staring off and twirling that stick in the sand and looking into the distance, wondering why he'd gone to all that bother, probably.

What could I say? Not much, 'cept you did right by them, I guess. I said it.

B&B. Big and Burly, seeking his last love. And Bernice, finding out about love and care for someone else and on the verge of being put through the ringer. What can you say?

O'Hara left, but broke up my day of painting so I sat there a long time, watching nature all around me and thinking it over. Now ain't the world a funny place?

Chapter 29
Spying at the Dance

They were at the dance at Berman's Hall. A four piece band playing and folks dancing and mingling. I was over at the south wall where a small group of friends and I were chatting about yard care at home, and each had a story to tell about it, humorous, difficulties overcome, how-to, all the usual variations on a subject that fills conversation and some of what is called 'male bonding'. I had been standing near the in-desk where the admission was collected and people came and went, a crossroads where people moved to the rest rooms and coat rooms and other places. The bar was there, nearby, and I was sipping orange vodka and looking around, assessing who was there and what they were doing and so on, the usual inspection you do entering a public affair for whatever purpose.

Sara was way left near the bandstand talking with two other women. Good, that was my ride home. I'd walked in tonight so I'd have a chance to talk with myself. It was getting time to leave, sort of, so a month or two away I'd be leaving, heading back to North Carolina or wherever I was needed.

Marty at that moment was dancing with Mrs. Ferguson, doing some square amid all the others and having a good old time, or so it looked. I could go over and get a dance with Sara, I figured, next set coming up.

George was there, amid that group of men and, yes, there was Mandy dancing with some man I'd never seen before. Chances are he was from along the interstate to Portland, one of those little towns along there.

Eyes swing back to George, smiling and apparently settled into that bunch of men, but his eyes were not on his current companions, but on 'Manda, his wife. He wasn't enjoying his wife's proficiency at square dances, or her manner with her partner, whoever he was. They came out of their moves and stood in place, a third couple awaiting the next call. Her hand on his, and his arm around her waist, her looking up at him and laughing with him at something, breathing heavily from following the last call and the swing at the end. George watching carefully, suspicious. I could tell.

Later on they were dancing some schottische together, pretty good dancers as a couple, I noted. At the end they parted and when she returned to the hall he was doing some fox-trot with one of the Hansen's. She slid across the floor and I suspected she was coming my way, but nope, on beyond to a couple of men talking near the bar, entered their conversation easily, they greeted and swung into an animated talk. 'Manda does have a way of just entering conversations and is lost to the world for a few minutes. George, dancing now, didn't miss it either. I saw him out there on the dance floor where his eyes, presumably on his partner, were over her shoulder watching 'Manda getting on with folks. Seemed natural to me, but I figured what he was thinking. So I thought about the two of them for a few minutes. They've got to get over themselves, I reasoned. I dropped them from my concerns and enjoyed watching the others dance. Jeff, over there on the far side, keeping away from Marty. They work all week together so guessed he'd had enough of him. I did note Sara keeping her eye on him all night long. I rather wish our little plan for Sara was moving along faster. The Hut and bridge done, all we had to do was keep her down there and see that Marty discovered her there. Watching her and Marty dance made The Hut scheme so far fetched. Luring her and her husband together like a couple of barely-aware-of-each-other folks for a lovey-dovey evening seemed so far fetched. Maybe 'Manda and I should reconsider.

I saw Bernice come in about a third of the way through the evening. Her dad was with her, I noted, but left shortly. Gotten her here safely and knew B&B would take her home. I watched her get swept away for the next set of squares and watched her awhile, enjoying herself. Now why, I wondered, would her mother and dad permit B&B to escort her home. Maybe they figured it was safer and cheaper to let their daughter become something special to B&B, not just a companion as O'Hara seemed to feel she was, but an actual mistress to him. She might get a house to live in, or maybe a nest egg for the day when he passed on. B&B was probably in his fifties, so had a bit of gumption left in him. Would she eventually have his baby, and lead a life without a financial care in the world, she and his offspring? It puzzled me as I watched, although I tried to conceal what my real focus was tonight. People might think I was interested in her, like George there, who I also watched.

Now George there was a real case. He kept his eye on 'Manda, who she talked with, how long, how they seemed to favor each other, she and whosoever she was talking with. Bernice and 'Manda came together once during the evening and I bet twenty seconds hadn't gone by before George was there with them making it a threesome. What was up? I noted B&B come to attention, sitting in a chair not far from the orchestra, that's what made me realize it, and followed his eyes over there. George was smiling and had the two by the waist and they were all animated like you wouldn't believe. Some guy slipped up about then and 'Manda went off with him to a round dance so George had no option unless he wasn't a gentleman, an obligation then to dance with her or keep talking. They went off dancing and it was the funniest thing to watch. The dancers slowly rotating counter clockwise about the floor as dancers do, and when way off on the side away from the orchestra she'd step in close to him, or vise versa, and the two seemed to understand the ruse, that is when they got in a position on the floor where B&B might observe them, they'd separate somewhat, otherwise cheek to cheek, the longer they danced the closer they got till plastered body to body. Quite unseemly being as they paid no attention to where 'Manda was on the floor (and no doubt watching), but they kept a proper distance when B&B was in sight.

Well, that was worth watching because what did she do when dancing with some other young man? She danced five round dances: fox trots, a waltz, a schotische with others, mostly, I noted, some red-faced young man from out of town, then Jeff four times during the evening. Tight on with Jeff and George. Tight as all get out, the two plastered together like bricks on a wall.

Mandy and I did a dance together, a slow fox trot. I gathered her in, being in a friendly mood and the feel of her against me made me forget most of my admonishments, so about ten minutes later, standing watching the youngsters having a good time, was some taken when George came over to me and chatted. Suddenly I realized he was warning me off. I looked at him a minute, and then burst into laughter, which made him look funny and he turned and was off along the side of the floor, and guess who was there? Bernice standing next to two other girls, and just like that he was on the floor with her. Well how about that.

Chapter 30
The Califer Housekeeper

'Manda and I were in the coffee shop again, sitting there and trying to lay some scheme to get Sara down to the hut. I told her about George the other night at the dance and she looked at me funny.

"So what's wrong?" I says.

She shrugged and made a face. "We've got a housekeeper to help out. Now would you believe that? All of a sudden George has the money to help me with the work around home, even the gardening. It's disgusting."

"I'd say you should be pleased. A little late, maybe, but you can't say he's not interested. Some women lose out when a man goes into his mid-life crisis."

"All the years when Pamela was little and I could have used help and we couldn't afford a helper. Now Jeena's in college and he's got me a housekeeper."

"My take on mid-life crises is that men look around, looking for a new love for a few nights trying to relive a lost youth or whatever it is, but come back when they get spurned by the young women of today." I pasted on a great engulfing smile to take the sting of George away for causing trouble because she danced with someone else the night of the dance.

"A spy, I'd say. Old enough to know what it is all about, and probably instructed to the letter by my suspicious husband."

She carried a look of disgust which made me think of last week's gossip about him seeing Bernice, and what then for her and B&B, or is it George? So ridiculous I wanted to laugh; but Mandy was not in for a good laugh at the lascivious ways of some men.

"He thinks I'm out running around, and he's the one who's doing that. I swear it."

"I rather doubt that. He's just being a man, looking at other women for some reason, probably can't help himself. Men are attracted to women, something to do with basic drives of the species." Sometimes I am so far ahead of everyone else in knowing exactly what's going on that I am a pain.

"I shouldn't be talking to you like this. I'm sorry. It's my problem, no one else's."

"You are a nice looking woman and he has to be away on business and so wants to protect his nest. He got onto my case the other night for dancing once with you. He's probably in a I-don't-trust-anyone-around-my-wife kind of mood. It happens to men. Maybe 'cause he's in the mood to fool around himself, so suspects everyone near him feels the same." I decided to check on how brightly this fire of passion was burning in her, according to her husband.

"It's just that I've got too many irons in the fire: this business with Sara and Marty, the church work, Garden Club, golf with some of the girls from the school. We play afternoons. Fixing up that hut with you was a revelation, though. I found out what's going on round town and I suppose stuck my nose in too many places. I hope I'm not a word in everyone's vocabulary round town."

I recognized it. Being all wrapped up in her own problems wouldn't let her see the humor in it all, or the background of the phobia as I saw it. "Okay," I said. "So let's get one of your problems sorted out and it'll be gone from your agenda. Lighten up your stuff one by one and you'll be back to basics with him." That was my contribution but as spoken I realized I liked meeting with her.

She took my hand from across the table and gave it a squeeze. "I enjoyed the dance with you the other night."

"And I you." Dare I say more? The feel of her in my arms awakened desire. I'd thought of it nights since, but it wouldn't work. I'm smart enough to know the situation, the limits. It wouldn't work. Don't bait her into more. It wouldn't work and was not proper. Be friends, enjoy her company, but forget anything else. No, I would not dare to say more. "Okay," I said. "We enjoyed a dance. I like you and call you friend. That's it. Let's get on with our Marty-Sara project."

Thus the declaration scene in our romance was shoved into the closet and I had a moment of remorse. I lifted my hand from the table, about to speak, deny this decision that was declared between us, take her hand, hold it, tell her how I truly felt, then out of sight and a quick kiss, a hug, a declaration of love.

No. That wouldn't work, not really. I let my hand fall. She returned to the table with refills and we entered the new phase, solely a business relationship. I can handle that. And she told me of her latest effort in the Marty-Sara saga.

"You know where I live?" she said.

"Aye, lassie. That I do."

"Well, I cut a swath."

"So?"

"I cut a straight swath through the empty lot next door so that I can go into my back yard with glasses to see Sara's house on the hill way off up there."

"Big deal," was my contribution.

"I hope to know when Sara is in and out, in preparation for the tryst."

"Sounds like a sound move, I'd say. Somehow you'll be able to stock The Hut to be like honey to a bear. They'll want to get there and have fun." I put on a smile, really thinking it'll not work out.

"You know what happened?"

"Not the slightest."

"The man next door discovered me alone out there cutting the field. He's not particularly friendly and I detest him. His wife's alright but he's a dead beat pill. (I let my eyebrows go up in surprise. Not the way my 'Mandy usually talks of people). So he came out and approached me, all hot and sweaty from work and he's not wearing any shirt, absolutely disgusting with his usual innuendo kind of speech. He just wouldn't go away. He kept talking and I fell for it, many times. She looked expectantly, watching for my reaction.

"So what happened?" Where was she going with this?

"He invited me in for a cool drink. Like I said, he's unfriendly, but I've always wanted to see the inside of their house. So stupid me, I accepted. I've always wanted to see it. We had coffee and George finds out, immediately suspicious."

"Okay, you went. How was the house?" I could see it now. She goes into the house, drinks, chats. Time goes by, her husband wonders where she is and goes looking, finds her with another man, and gets ideas. Trouble. "What happened?"

"What happened? Nothing. We sat down and talked about the town, the weather. His wife keeps a clean house.

She was out shopping, he said. All his innuendos were missing, thank God. It was okay. I left."

"And –?"

"I found George in the field looking at my hedge clipper, the weed whacker and trimming saw. He wanted to know where I'd gone to."

"So you told him and he got sore."

She looked at me, frowned. "How did you know?"

I shrugged. Is this the woman I started to fall in love with? "You don't know?"

She gave me a long, long look.

I started to say: He's suspicious of you to begin with and you don't know why? I didn't say it. I was questioning her ability to connect the points, her analysis of situations. The apparent stupidity in this negative relationship with her husband which she had told me of, complaining of his unstopping questioning about what she did, his show of interest in other women as per the gossip about him and Bernice, the meaning of these situations for some reason had gone right over her head. She can't be that unaware. My 'Manda missing the point? My God, she's not a goddess after all, she's a human with all the frailties, misses things sometimes, just like ordinary people. I wonder if she's missing the impact she's had on me, and how I feel about her? I looked off into the hazy distance, momentarily disgusted with her. At that point I got real dumb, too. I dismissed myself, got up and left.

Whatever was said between her and George had one beneficial effect. I don't know what she told him, or what she did, But next Wednesday when we were in there again, having coffee and talking away, she told me he'd dismissed the housekeeper.

Chapter 31
A Big Boat on the Horizon

From the top of the new building you could see a good distance, even as far as the ocean. No big deal, because you could pretty much see the same distance from where the rope bridge crosses over to The Hut. It must be that the terrain rises gradually from the town to the rope bridge. I was out that way. 'Manda had driven us out there yesterday morning, we making a dry-run on how Marty would feel sneaking out there to meet his beloved wife some evening and wondering how we could get them to do it. So there we were, at the rope bridge, venturing out on it, looking down and marveling at the great rush of water far below, and all such childishness. The place was deserted as always at this time of day, and it was a beautiful day with a clear deep blue sky and a few puffies drifting overhead to help us finish our coffee. George was off in some California factory town not too far from San Diego so I was relaxed. I'd had enough of his suspicious looks and spoken innuendos and so had she, and this was our perfectly innocent venture. The bridge is tight and narrow with both of us on it at the same time. It swings, dips, sways, and rolls like rope bridges can. We were laughing and having a grand old time and then when we were near the center the bridge moved again and we found ourselves hanging onto the lines and each other, very much together. 'Manda and me, holding on for dear life waiting for the bridge to run out of life, and my arm around her waist, and hers on me someplace, and our heads close, and her face right there, and it was the most natural thing in the world to kiss. It was a long kiss. Our lips held and our arms held each other and the bridge and the kiss went on and on. The bridge quieted and there we were, looking into each other's eyes and knowing that something utterly unplanned had happened.

"Well dog-gone" I said, and she laughed and put her face to mine again, rubbing quietly and that was it. I haven't kissed a woman in twenty years, well maybe ten. 'Course she has a husband so probably got kissed yesterday when she drove him to Bangor for the plane. Then again maybe his discomfort over his suspicions had set in and they didn't kiss. She mumbled something and swept her head closer, her body clasped to mine. It was really quite nice, and the memories and feelings of long ago returned.

I'd probably never get another kiss like this. We both knew better. So thinking that, I opened my eyes and looked off south the way the chasm ran from somewhere way off back in the hinterland where millions of years ago the river piled up by the glaciers had chopped this channel out to the sea. And out to the sea I looked, feeling that most wonderful female body, starting to move my hands a small bit and her letting me, almost guiding, and out there on the horizon a ship was standing. Far off, just a great vessel standing off out there. Now moving, or was it? But I wasn't interested because one of the finest women I've known had her hands on me, enjoying my subjugation to her as much as she enjoyed being the goal, the recipient, the focus.

I was panting, or was I? She had on some sort of safari outfit, very chic and very expensive from one of Portland's better stores, and now my right hand had slid between the two sides of the blouse with its slots for cartridges, five over each breast, and open slightly at the belt. My hand burrowed in and slid a few inches along her stomach and she stopped it.

She held it there firmly and our lips touched again for a long, long moment, as if starvation for honest affection had struck us both.

My hand moved by itself, right some, left some along her tummy line at the belt of her safari shorts. Very soft, very smooth. Her hands were down my sides, reaching behind me and stroking me down and up once. "I guess we had better get going, what?" It was me, breaking the charm.

A nod from her, a part turn, her hands each side of my face and a quick kiss. "You are right. Will the bridge behave?"

"Probably better than us," I returned, and pushed at her moving us along the narrow step-walk between that held us safe.

Now I'm an old fool, we all know that, and she's thirty years my junior and so desirable, and the spell still working such that when we stopped at The Hut end, I closed on her and slid a hand around her again and she crushed herself against me and we stood not twenty seconds and both spoke in unison the same words, "We must stop this."

That simple, the two of us laughed and released each other and she pirouetted once and crashed against me in mock error and we clasped again. All this was so unexpected and so natural from us two friends that we both laughed, and that broke the spell. "This is so pleasant. I haven't felt such a spell overcome me in a long time. Thank you. But we must be more careful."

She was right and we both walked to the door of The Hut, her hand sliding into mine for the last twelve feet. She talked about Sara's great need, and me thinking, of all things, that there was a big boat on the horizon. I frowned, puzzled. We never see big boats off our section of coast. I resolved to ask some of the lobstermen what it all meant, if anything; and stepped to the door to take another look out along the course of the chasm and verify that it was there. And yep, it was. I mentioned it to 'Manda and she came to the door and stood next to me, her hand to my shoulder and mine around her waist. It was so natural.

I think Mandy and I are entering a new phase. And I'm not sure it's for the best. What do you think?

Where am I now? At home where Sara and Marty live, where I stay this summer, and thinking this all over. I'm looking out over the trees toward the ocean way out there. Is the boat still there? I can't really tell. The top of this rise is not high enough to spot the ocean and its boat, but I wonder.

I'm so silly. The vessel has assumed the spirit of our love, and I want it to stay anchored out there forever.

Chapter 32
Old Folks

A dangerous game, romance. To be specific, to pursue a beautiful woman is a dangerous game. Why? Her husband or boyfriend could get ugly. Ugly like a poke in the teeth, like Jeff got. Which at the time I thought was funny, but now it's me I'm worrying about. Or I'd look ridiculous. An eighty year old man chasing a young girl, and let's face it, at my age they are all younger. That's the cool, thoughtful, philosophical side of me talking. So do I follow my sage advice? Sort of, but not exactly.

That business with Mandy yesterday out on the bridge and all that was really out of character for me, yes. And for her, I'm sure. Kissing like a couple of newlyweds, clinging to each other as if we'd never hugged before. Me touching her like some gawking teenager. Really something got into us and it wasn't the wisest course either of us should have taken. So I know, absolutely know, that we'll never have an early morning coffee again. We'd be nuts to carry on some sort of obscure love affair and run the risk of being seen and that would be it.

I figured, since I knew I'd never see her again and if she had half a brain in her head it would be this way, so decided to drive into town and go by the *Empty Plate*, give it a look, and maybe stop in for old times sake. If she saw me there she would probably shoot me, hugging and kissing her and all that foolishness.

I drove by slowly, looking in. AND BY CHRIST. SHE WAS SITTING IN THERE IN THE SAME TABLE WE ALWAYS SAT AT. MY GOD!

I had the car parked and almost ran to the coffee shop. She gave me a look as I came in, almost panting for trying to run. I hesitated at the table, looking down at her, my mind a tumble of thoughts, self recriminations, blame, desire. All that and more. She looked up at me, I was standing reasonable close as you would passing another table, her eyes on mine, a smile, and, "Trevor, how nice of you to come. I wasn't sure you would."

I splattered the first half of a laugh, more an exhale. "I didn't know you'd be here. I thought that maybe, we, well, maybe it's better left alone." Standing there with that sick little choice of words I began to feel out of my depth.

"I was afraid you might stay away today." And she had my hand and was pulling me to the chair opposite where I usually sat. I was speechless.

The waitress came over with my cup and "the usual". She knew us.

'Manda gave it a squeeze and released my hand. "Trevor, Trevor, Trevor. What happened to us yesterday?"

I shrugged and fixed the coffee, took one sip. Looked her in the eye and lost my confidence. I was going to tell the truth, but somehow it wouldn't come. "I'm glad you came. Can we pick up life from where we left off yesterday?

"Or should we from the day before, before yesterday happened?"

"Yes" and I folded my hand over hers.

"Yes which?" A big smile from her, a squeeze to my hand, and she released and folded her hands under the table and looked at me. "I'm so glad you came. I think I needed yesterday, so let's not spoil it by talking about it." We sat silent for maybe a minute, and a minute can be so long sometimes.

I looked at her, nicely put together as always. "I was afraid you wouldn't want to see me again."

A bright, pleased look crossed her face. "I don't know what I'd have done if you hadn't come. I prayed and prayed that you'd be here." And then an exultant look, she had my hand again. "I want you. I want to be your friend, I do. I feel so girlish about this, but I do. I want you in my life and don't know how we'll do it, but I want us with such intensity. I almost called you last night, but then decided to be more discreet." She took a deep breath.

I had her hand and raised it to my lips. "Let it be so."

So there we were, locked together in some strange pact and ignorant of the rest of the world.

"George called last night," she said.

"And?"

"Checking on me. He's so sensitive lately, thinks I'm playing around and it's not true."

"You're seeing me."

She was silent awhile, thinking out how to say it, whatever it was going to be. I watched her take a deep breath, and quite frankly noting again that she had a nice figure.

"Yes. I do see you. And I enjoy our moments, and what happened out on the rope bridge will not happen again. That was an aside, in a manner of speaking. George worries needlessly, but you can't tell someone that and expect an immediate cure. It takes time, so I must be a model of Puritanical Purity for a while, maybe a year, till he gets over whatever bothers him. In the meantime, it did happen, that thing between us. I enjoyed a moment of affection. I don't know how to interpret it, but I, you were enjoyable and – ." She shrugged.

I seized the moment and said "we should go out there and check everything, make sure the scene is set and then concoct an excuse to get them to come together. Will you go with me?"

"Yes."

And it happened again.

She nestled back against me, my arms encircling her, feeling her stomach and her skin under her blouse. We were releasing decades of propriety with a touch. She would turn, my hands encircling her waist and exploring, her lips against me; her hands here, there, undoing buttons and on my chest, and down my back to my buttocks, each pulling the other's string so fruitlessly to join together. Twenty minutes and we realized it was impossible, our sub-conscious desires struggled to remain hidden from the other, even ourselves, and we would break apart only to be back together with more fervor. We were terrible, and were we at home we would have been fulfilled. We were just lucky that no one was about to see this shameful behavior from a couple of "over-the-hills"

But someone was watching, maybe two.

Word reached George and he came home from the west coast on a weekend, something he had never done before. Usually he waited for the job to be done.

She wasn't there at the coffee shop for five days. She sat apart from me when she came, and stared out the great window. I waited until she had left and followed, maybe twenty minutes later. Her car gone, I went over to the rope bridge just to check it out and her car was parked at the side with no one in it.

I found her in The Hut alone with a blanket to sit on. It was awkward at first, getting readjusted to each other, what we could say, what should not be discussed. She beckoned and I joined her on the blanket, and then we were laying next to each other and our desires swept us and our pleasures joined for we had collected new sins, an eighty year old and a fifty-fiver. No one would believe us if we told someone, and yet here we were, unable to stop ourselves or each other.

Chapter 33
Stage Set

The stage was set for Sara and – who? Her husband? Possibly Jeff? 'Manda and I discussed that: if Jeff was still interested in her, well? He could still be, they could still be having their little trysts for all we knew. They were much more careful, if such was the case, hiding their love much better. Still Marty was the husband on the scene and maybe he watched her more closely, or maybe the old pre-marital spark had returned. We had no way to know. So how do we get Sara to meet him and get pregnant and have a more rewarding life in the long, long-range look at "family." And of course that sort of thinking always ranged around the fringe of the Sara problem, we trying to figure it out for a successful "family" for Marty and Sara. We were hoping for success, thus the working together and that made George suspicious of 'Manda and me. We had to be careful that our mutual "interest" didn't become too infectious and we ended up meeting at some time when we would be spotted kissing or something. That "something", once broached, could become the most infectious of diseases. If known it would set George off and she didn't need that, nor did I. Yet our affection was real and in moments of true being-alone it expressed itself. We weren't going to "break-up", as they say, but wanted to stay close, just something about it that felt so fine to us both, but no one was to know. So we were careful. She made it plain to me, and I accepted it, that she would not leave George. He was the economic support for the family, she and George and Jeena, the daughter off in college. So we could never consummate the desire in marriage. To consummate it out of wedlock, such an acceptable union these days for men and women, even if married, seemed to suggest that everyone did it. Gone were the days of a proper Victorian marriage. Well, so be it. We agreed that there should be no tryst between us. We must stick to our purpose until satisfied and then could break forever our little bit of love. Acceptable, I guess.

One day we found Jeff at The Hut, looking it over, as a carpenter checking it out professionally since all us folks who had donated time and effort to the project weren't necessarily qualified to do it "right". Jeff looked at the two of us as we stood together in the doorway surprised to see us He'd said nothing, us standing there caught, holding hands like teenagers. We entered with questions about how the committee had done fixing it up. Okay, was the verdict.

'Manda, at a quiet moment in the conversation, mentioned seeing Sara down here one morning, and said something about her idea of having a general picnic Saturday afternoon. She knew that Marty and some of his cronies went off to the coast for some beach fishing or even getting one of the guys to take them out in a motor boat. I didn't know anything about that but found out later it was a spontaneous idea. Get Sara down here with a few others, and dropping the hint to Jeff so the two could meet, admittedly amongst others, but then they could make plans, if they were still interested. That was her idea.

She didn't want me there, too much talk about us, she feared. My task was to hide in the rocks among the cliff side behind The Hut and wait and watch. See if they met after the hut was empty.

"But it's Jeff. Not her husband," I argued.

She looked at me, disgusted, as if I were a child in this situation, and I had to admit to myself, I guess I am. And later, hiding in the rocks with a set of sandwiches and bottle of water after four hours of watching and listening to the sounds of moderate pleasure from the picnickers, it came to me that 'Manda seemed to know too much about this sort of thing and a tinge of suspicion that she had done this tryst thing with others before I entered the scene, came over me. Suddenly I felt like George must feel, suspicious.

Jeff left about 4 pm when everyone was breaking up. Sara was there helping 'Manda clean up, and then they split. Sara heading up the path toward the covered bridge and 'Manda gave a glance at the rocks where she thought I was lurking according to plan to see if the two returned. Jeff and Sara, and with that last glance she was gone on up to the bridge to her car and town and home.

Ten minutes later Sara was back, muttering, going inside and coming out with a bag, muttering to herself about forgetting this bag. She waited about ten minutes, I awaiting out her watch, and started away just as Jeff appeared coming over the rope bridge. Then they were in each other's arms and moving to The Hut and I couldn't hear a damned thing, nor see them, so I waited another stupid hour, then fifteen minutes more and she and he exited, kissed, talked about meeting at that wide spot in the highway on route 32 at some time, then I couldn't hear a thing, and each disappeared to the paths to their cars I suppose and that was it.

I met 'Manda and we talked.

"Should we try and follow one of them?"

"How would we keep from being caught? I mean seen by one of them."

"Somehow we need to know that they're meeting."

"We do. By the wide spot on 32."

"You're sure you want her having a baby by Jeff?"

She moved her head all over, spreading her hair as she did it and looking beautiful to me. "That wouldn't work would it."

"It would be nice to know, though."

"We may have to wait two or three months to see if she swells."

I shrugged, uncertain if Jeff should be the one.

"I'll take my granddaughter around again so she can keep being reminded of how much fun and how pleasant it is to see a well-behaved son or daughter. Keep her thinking of children."

"I suppose she could be having relations with her husband."

"She's supposed to. They ARE married." She remarked.

Me and the shrug again. "I know."

"Married people do have children," she commented, looking at me like I was the most foolish man in the world. "Oh yes, George will be home tonight. I don't know if we should meet for coffee or not."

"I'll be there."

And I was. Sitting about an hour looking out the window and chatting with others at nearby tables when finally the door opened and there were the two of them, George and his wife, 'Manda. She greeted me and pulled a chair out for herself, slid in to it and George was sliding into the one across from me. She spoke to me like an old acquaintance, which she was, "Well, Trevor, what's new with Marty and Sara? I haven't seen either in weeks. You live with them. What's the news up that way?" Making it sound like an enclave of gypsies and na'ar-do-wells, a virtual walled village a-la the Middle Ages. Old friends, we were, and did our best to act it, chatting of things about the countryside and general gossip which we had already heard, but it drew George in and away from the suspicious look that rested on his face the whole time. He began to unwind after about twenty minutes and joined in, more natural like, but believe me, I was one careful dude about how I spoke and acted to 'Manda. He asked me about some new guy around town who I hadn't heard of so I peppered him with questions to no avail. I was about done, shrugging uselessly inside when this tall, gangly fellow with a tanned complexion and blond hair came by. Nice looking chap with a dimple in his chin and a serious face, muscular, and a kind of funny way of walking, not exactly a walk but more of a kind of saunter. He'd move his feet out, and then the rest of his body would sort of catch up, so to me he always looked like he was sloped backwards during a walk. George motioned him over and I watched Mandy look puzzled then straighten her face. This fellow seemed a bit too familiar with George to be new to him and for a brief moment I wondered if he was some fellow worker in the electronic production business like George was, but he began asking questions about where the best surfing was.

"Well, not around here," said Mandy.

George was hostile acting. "Now that's not true," he started. "You could go down the river on a surfboard and out to Whethersport on the coast, even out to the ocean there, and pick up surfing on the beach, it'd be great."

I pictured someone trying to surf down the river and rejected it. You could float on the current and avoid all the rocks and debris that catches in all those pockets and it'd be fun, but more like white water work than anything else. I started to say that when shucks! 'Manda was saying the very same thing. Now doesn't that prove that we're well suited for each other, thinking the same?

George was picking up the conversation and saying how the gorge, 'the chasm' we called it, was too narrow and too filled with rocks for paddling anything there, even white water people respected it, and so on, but how farther down, maybe a mile or two, the land flattened out some and it got quieter and smoother and you could paddle out to the ocean easier and surf there. The fellow was looking at George with a disgusted look on his face and picked up his coffee and walked away. So much for that.

George was picking up the tab for the table and moving off, kinda following that fellow, and Mandy and I were alone, waiting. She looked at me and said," What d'ya suppose all that was about?"

"Don't know, why?"

"George never invites strangers. I'm suspicious."

But I didn't find out about what 'cause George was back and she going off with him and I'd have to wait to see her some other time

So there I sat, alone, and wondering what to do with myself, but that passed pretty quickly for I thought of the building going on over at the edge of the chasm, so I went back there to talk to the boys in Marty's construction company. Two were on the lower level and Marty and Jeff were upstairs working on some doors. They're talking to each other again, and have been for a few weeks, since they ironed out who Sara's husband was. It's not exactly the same, more restrained you'd say, but they didn't want to break up the company 'cause work's scarce and who wanted to just quit and slowly starve so there they were not talking much but getting the work done.

Marty went off, and I stood over there by the window that looked out over the edge of the gorge way up that a-ways. I stood staring and rather reminiscing aloud. It was a set-up. I had it planned days ago, just didn't know how to go through with it, or when, and now was the time.

"Jeff, you used to know Sara pretty well at one time –." I said all this with eyes fixed on the distance, "Now why would she want to go for a walk down to The Hut, do ya suppose?"

He came close, I could sense him there. I finished up with, "The other night she walked down, and I think last night," I was facing him now, crinkled up my face and said something about exercise, had an apple with her to keep up her strength, she said. "Now ain't that a foolish thing? Come way off down here with only an apple, but I suppose if'n yer into getting skinny that would do it."

He was close, looking out the window, too, and listening. He turned to me and said, "I guess she's as worried about a layer of fat as much as the next girl. They all do that. She should go out at night with one of her girlfriends. Not so good to go walking alone at night way off down there. Maybe her husband'll go with her."

"This is his card-playing night at the Legion. She'll go alone. Bet ya anything."

He was real interested, I could tell. I couldn't believe it was this easy. 'Manda and I had worried about how to get them together, and this apparently was it, and way too easy. Things by chance get that way sometimes. I figured I'd put a solid stamp to it for Jeff. Of course 'Manda would opt for him, not her husband, as the first concern, but here was the chance and I'd taken it and it looked like it was working. Still the fact that 'Manda opted for him as first choice puzzled me. Odd. Did life with George color her feelings, someone different for a change even if she was thinking of another woman?

He was talking. "I guess you're right. T'aint a good place to go to alone, that is if any bad-'uns are around, But since the robbery everybody's been good as gold, in bed early and off the streets. It's all because no one knows who's going to get blamed for it and they all want to stay out of it, leastwise out of suspicion."

Jeff was staring at me now. I'd have to drive in the last nail.

"And Marty's no good. He always stays down there playing cards till they close.

"Cripe, Sara was back an hour 'fore he got back last week. He wouldn't even have known she was out walking if I hadn't mentioned it to him."

"Last week?" from Jeff.

"Yeah. She went experimentally last week. Trying it out to see if she could do it, I suppose. It worked out, she was back home before Marty, too. It's interesting watching how a family works. I'm glad I moved up here with her. I'm planning to head back to the old haunts in a month or so. Did I tell you that?"

He wasn't paying attention, thinking over Sara and her walk. My guess was he'd meet her there. Either Mandy or me should go down there to check on 'em. Or should I keep it from Mandy for a while? She really wanted Jeff there. But like she said once, the thing is she must get pregnant. No one'll know who the father is anyway unless Jeff or Sara or me tells. They won't. I won't. I smiled.

Heading on home I remembered the other time he and Sara had been together there. He hadn't even mentioned it, of course why would he. I wasn't supposed to know about it.

Chapter 34
New Face in Town

We'd been in the *Empty Plate* about an hour and a half, passing the time. 'Manda and me being oh so proper while George chatted like everything was normal, so I guess he was getting over his fit of suspicion, at least of me. Frazier was another thing, but who knew what George was thinking? We chatted comfortably, like friends.

George and 'Manda left, so five minutes later I gathered myself together and was off, too. Maybe I'd go out to the coast and check the shoreline, look for a tie-up place for a boat. I was thinking of building another and keeping it up here, while continuing to live with Sara and Marty, by then the baby'd be here likely. The boat would be a small one, like Hamilton's Sharpy, not too big to haul around on land for repairs, but too big to haul home after every sail so necessitating a tie-up place.

I was standing at the corner where the street cut off to go to the covered bridge over the chasm where the armored car had gone awry when I heard a voice. Was it directed at me? At the same time I heard other footsteps on the board walk. This section of the street had a board walk. Water collected here during a rain and the town Fathers had decided anything more permanent was a waste of effort. A board walk is easily repairable. The sound I heard was someone coming. I looked, taking in the stranger at the same time as he saw Bernice. Where is she going? Is he talking to me?

Question one easily answered as she nodded to me and passed on, headed toward either the library or one of the stores down that way. I glanced at my wrist watch and heard again the stranger's voice, "You. Weren't you at the table with the Cunningham couple?"

I faced the man, nodded, and admitted I was there. "Yes. And we were introduced. I'm Trevor Heneke. You didn't give us your name."

"Maybe I don't have one." he retorted, his head swiveling to follow Bernice down the street. She was a nice looking girl and I began wondering again what she got out of always going home with B&B after a dance or whatever else she did that took her out evenings. I didn't keep track so really couldn't verify that he always took her home, but then it wasn't my main concern in life

This new man broke my train of thought. "Where do you live?"

That was okay. Everyone knew anyway. You can't keep secrets in this town. "I live up the dirt road with Marty and Sara. She's my step-daughter."

"How come you don't have a place of your own? You got a record or somethin'? Can't get a place on your own? No money?"

"Well, Mr. Whoever-You-Are, I can pay my way. I give Sara some money for being there. It helps them and is only fair. Why?"

"I'm just asking." He was still watching Bernice, a half block away now. "What's that one's name?"

Boy, this fella is one inquisitive soul. Mean sounding too.

"She's in high school, her last year. Her name is Bernice."

"Where's she live?"

I told him. "Everyone in town knows her so I wouldn't get any ideas."

He stepped several steps closer, was right on top of me, chest to chest, and being a big guy was rather overpowering. He looked down and said, "What's that mean?"

Me, shrugging, said, "Just a word of advice. She's got a boyfriend so you'd be homing in. Cause trouble, maybe."

I had backed off a pace or two to his retort which was, "I love trouble. It's my middle name."

I stood watching him turn from looking after her again and said, "You didn't mention your name. How do we call you? You do have a name, don't you?"

He looked down at me. "I have a name. You damned well know it. What's yours?"

Why wouldn't he tell me his name? "You were there at the table, you heard my name. And I just told you." I wanted to be surly and say: Don't you listen? But he was too big to monkey with.

"Ok sonny, actually, I missed it I guess. Let's try again."

This stranger was awfully inquisitive, but I was being affable, or trying to be before he 'Jeffed' me, the latest way around Portage of saying you got busted in the nose. "My name's Trevor Heneke. Yours is –? And how can I help you?"

He was on me again, shoving me back. "You're an inquisitive little prick, aren't ya now. Get out of my way." He shoved again and stepped by me and was going down the street where Bernice had gone. I stood watching him go and then sensed a person next to me. It was Henry from the grocery store.

"Who's Mr. Mean and Ugly? He trying to pick a fight or something?"

"I don't know. I've never seen him before. I was in the coffee house with Mr. And Mrs. Cunningham and he came in. Says he was introduced, but I don't know by whom because I didn't hear any name. Mr. Cunningham seemed to sort of know him."

"I was watching from inside, and moved to the door to listen. A surly bastard, huh?"

I hunched my shoulders. It seems no matter what you did around this country everyone knew about it. He was still going on, intrigued by the stranger that I'd just as soon never see again.

"We should report him to Constable Jones or B&B. Hey now, he was asking 'bout Bernice. What's he want that for?"

Oh God, here we go again. Bernice at the center of something. I was momentarily glad I didn't really know her. "Your guess is as good as mine."

We stood there talking of other things and presently he said while facing the other direction, "Here he comes again." And with that he retreated back to the store and left me to face this stranger.

"Hey you stupid Dane, I got a question for you."

I turned to face him. I should have gone five minutes ago.

"Didn't you say that girl's name was Bernice? Well?"

"I don't know her personally but I'm told that's her name. As I said I wouldn't bother about her. She's got a boyfriend to my knowledge."

"Well now, ain't that nice. You tell your friends around here to answer up when I ask 'em questions. I'm a private detective and want answers not giggles and turned backs, ya hear?"

I tilted my head and moved away a step. "I'm not in charge here and don't give orders to folks. If you're a private detective you need to take care of your own business. If you want information you should probably check in with our constable."

"Screw your constable. I got my own ways."

So now I shrugged, not wanting to talk to this man, couldn't predict what he'd do next. "I've got to be going. Good luck to you."

I moved off only to be grabbed by the shoulder and abruptly found myself facing him again. I should have left sooner.

"Look you small town bastard, I want answers. What's that woman's name?"

"I already told you. Bernice. That's all I know. Ask Mr. Cunningham, he may know more about her. I don't. You were talking to him earlier. Ask him." He still had my shoulder.

"Why didn't that guy down the other street tell me? He lives here too."

"I don't know who you talked to, but it should be obvious, shouldn't it? Folks hereabouts don't take agreeably to strangers asking questions, especially those trying to use force." I bowed my head to his hand still on my shoulder and looked back at him, trying to be firm. It worked for he withdrew his hand, saying "That's their tough luck, isn't it! Who's that girl?"

I started to tell him again then changed my mind. "One of the local girls," then decided to give her a measure of protection. "Going to marry one of the locals. Nice girl."

"She old enough to marry?"

Knowing how I felt about young folks, and old folks too, getting married, I replied, "She is. Ask her parents if you want to discuss it. You some preacher up here to put codes of behavior on us, Mr. Private Detective?"

He snorted. "Not likely," then he changed his mind and said, "Actually, sonny, in a way that's my job." He laughed and turned toward the way she had gone, looking. "She coming back?"

So I'm "sonny" now, huh? Just another kid to him? Me at 84? I moved off and when I heard his voice again just kept going. I heard several hours later that the new guy in town had smashed some town person in the face and given him a 'Jeff', a bloody nose. Also he'd been down more in the center and offended some fellow and they'd raised fists and he got a good blow in. A private detective? I wondered. Working for who, trying to find out what, and knowing in some fashion or other Mr. Cunningham. Maybe 'Manda could fill me in tomorrow morning when we meet for coffee. Private Detective? He could be working for the insurance company investigating that robbery.

That Saturday night there was a dance with all the usual people, the usual band, the usual dances, and that detective showed up about mid-evening and stood in the doorway watching. Bernice was there, sticking way out in front like some of the girls did, knowing what they were doing and teasing the men. The detective had a dance with her and I suppose everybody was watching them, I know I was. And of course he no doubt knew it, too, so he was reasonably careful.

The end of the evening came and things were winding down. He was on the other side of the hall, near where she and her girlfriends were. She was separated from her friends for a moment while gathering her things, and he took the opportunity to be there at her side. There was no surprise on her face, like all of us she had probably been watching him all night, too. The noise and distance made it impossible to hear what he said, but each of us could imitate it.

"Say there, Bernice, thank you for the dance." She acknowledges by a nod of the head.

"I was thinking, why don't you and I go over to the coffee house and have a little something, it'd be a fitting finish to a real pleasant evening here."

We all watched, seeming to be focused on something else: the windows, the decorations, other groups, our coats. B&B was over by the bandstand chatting with the leader. We watched him, too.

She smiled broadly and seemed to shake her head while speaking, but we couldn't hear, it being off across the room, almost as if they were separated by an invisible wall from the rest of us. The girls in her little group were watching, too.

She probably said something like, "I already have an escort, but thank you so much." And then maybe added some dangerous remark, like "Some other time, maybe." Innocent and polite, but not too smart when you consider the implication to a man like that, but how would a girl know, just being polite?

She had turned and was moving back to the girls, past him, and he reached out, taking her arm and we watched him go on talking, probably uping the ante, or lowering it depending on your imagination and expectation. "You might prefer going over to the *Miss Tracy*," our one saloon in town, or night club if you prefer.

Her smile was strained now as she moved more toward the girls, but still a smile. The girls were dead on staring at him somewhat horror stricken. I got in a fast glance around the hall, and you betcha, everyone was watching, and B&B was over there takin' up the challenge.

He was moving toward Bernice and the Private Dick, Bernice frowning and pulling her arm away, or trying to. And from the other side by the main exit door there was 'Manda moving toward them, George following. His face looked some upset, it did. I should go, too, I suppose, before something came unhinged here and there was another fight. Word had gotten all round town that he'd already beat that guy up downtown, and the Constable had been looking for him to register a warning and protest about public behavior.

B&B, big and burly, as tall as him and twice as thick, and twenty years his senior lumbered up, gripped the Dick's arm holding onto Bernice. The Dick jerked, his whole body flicked at the grip for it must have been a strong one, B&B was a strong ox, and a surprise, probably no one had dared touch him for years. He somewhat lowered, going into a fighting stance and his other fist coming back in a prep move, but also behind B&B, closing in, were 'Manda and George making faces that said "NO," and George shaking his head and behind him some of the guys from the doorway, a mob backing up B&B, you might say, or maybe backing up George. The Dick took it all in in one big look and dropped her arm, straightened, and somewhat faced B&B and the mob and backed away, closing his back against the wall, less area to be attacked from. One smart bruiser, I'd say.

And I found myself at the back of the mob hearing him say, "Yes you fucking bastards. What do ya want?"

Silence.

That was it, it was over. B&B reached for Bernice's hand and drew her away from the girls where she'd fled. She came willingly enough, maybe eagerly, to her protector, her whatever. She went right up against him, the first sign of real closeness the two had ever shown publically. She turned back to him, and stared along with everyone else at the man against the wall. He had that sardonic smile on his face, and seemed to grow another foot or two as he stood there, and suddenly brushed into the nearest young guy standing there, and past, and moved like a phantom though the silent hall and out the door.

So that was the end of the evening; a little incident to whet everyone's interest. B&B and Bernice were out in front of everyone like they'd never admitted to before. B&B was the envy of every unwed man in the district, and now there was an ugly vendetta over Bernice to boot. Detective Dick didn't score any points.

I wondered if Bernice was the kind of woman that liked to stand and watch two men bloody each other over her.

The next morning I met 'Manda at the *Empty Plate* and she sat next to me, rather than around on the other side. She told me that late at night George had company. She wasn't sure who, but suspected it was that Private Dick. She wondered why her husband would be seeing him, more to her concern was why would he come to the house? I couldn't answer her questions, but it certainly added a trifle of mystery. "George is going out to Washington State tonight. I drive him to Bangor for the plane," she told me and inwardly I sighed relief. She'll be alone and it'll be easier for us to meet and chat. I like her company, no question

Chapter 35
George, The Dick, and Angel
What's the Relationship?

As a side note, today Bernice did not show herself in town or at school all day, no doubt glad she didn't have to suffer those stares from other girls and the community. She was B&B's girl and the event at the dance drew attention to it, if anyone, perchance didn't already know. Late in the afternoon I saw her out in her backyard again, leaning over the hedge and talking with George. I'd gone into town to get some things for Sara before supper and who should be in the line ahead of me but Angel.

Now Angel has the reputation around here as being the big drug dealer in the area. He doesn't drive a big car, or have a string of women that I know of, so you can tell he's either a poor pusher or poor organizer, a poor teacher for getting young folks, or old, into using drugs himself, or the country is just so poor that drugs can't be afforded by anyone, or another possibility is that people just don't want that stuff. I know I don't, but I'm not everyone so it's hard to figure, know what I mean? So he's a no-account pusher. Oh he's got a following, but not large and the followers are basically the kind of men mothers keep their children from, so he's got friends, but not lots, and the kind that are always suspected of being on the off-side of the law. So there's Angel, bent over like he is, a mess of black hair, hunched up shoulders, I suppose he might smell, too, but I've never gotten close enough to tell. Who's he talking to in line but that private detective; the Private Dick. That's interesting, but then it might be in a private detective's line of work. Otherwise, why is he here in our town?

So I watch. I'd like to know more, but I'm not willing to make friends with Angel; to find out who he sells to, who he hangs with, what they do to get money to buy his stuff, just to track this detective's behavior.

Sara, Marty, and I ate supper and I was thinking of 'Manda so it wasn't surprising to find myself wandering down to town and cutting through the streets such that I was passing by Mandy's house about dusk and I wonder if she's back yet from taking George to Bangor for his flight. The house is dark, I stand looking at it, thinking of George talking to Bernice, and liking it to me talking to Mandy. Is it altruistic or just good friends? That would be the best way to look at it. Avoid the complications and disappointments of a girlfriend, especially one that is already taken, like Bernice, or like 'Manda. I start to move on and WAMBO! Someone had me by the back of the neck. I got jerked around and found myself facing The Dick.

"So what's a nice guy like you doing hanging around Amanda's house at nine at night?" he asked, a little ugly sounding.

Get it right, I thought. It's " 'Manda", not "Amanda". What's a creep like you doing around here? I was about to ask when car lights showed way down the street and his grip lessened and he was gone. I don't know where, into the shrubbery and off to who-knows-where. I was alone. It could be 'Manda coming in the car, so I waited to see. We could have a chat or something, but it went on by so I skidaddled off myself, puzzled about why this Private Dick was hanging around George and 'Manda's place.

Chapter 36
More of The Dick Affair

We met on Monday for coffee, our private little meeting, usually just the two of us but once in a while someone else would be there. These times were always pleasant, friendly, and newsy, and like a couple, we enjoyed the company of others at our table. A 'couple' I said; and that was the way we were becoming.

So here we are on Monday and George is away on a business trip again and she and I relax together and we're wondering about how to get Sara down to The Hut. That lane she cut in the undergrowth and trees across her yard made checking on Sara and Marty easy, just go outside with the binoculars and look up the lane to the house. Were both cars there? Then they're home. I live up there too, so she can check on me, but I walk to town and she could miss that. I told her once I'd put out a flag when leaving, and she'd know I was gone. This was a little crackpot scheme done more for the amusement than a true need.

"Why don't you bring Marty over to the rope bridge on some pretext or other and I'll bring Sara down for a little walk. All four of us meet and you and I, everyone knows we meet for coffee and are friends. We could go off for a walk and never come back. Leave them alone and see if it takes."

That was 'Manda's suggestion, and not a bad one. Usually she seems to opt for Jeff instead of Marty so I was pleased. It must be her personal preference for the Jeff-type so she foists it on Sara.

That was the best we could come up with, not very sophisticated, but simple enough to work. So it's a "go" for tonight, and while we're sitting there rejoicing in our action-plan, who comes in but The Dick. Everyone around town calls him "The Dick" now.

Chapter 37
George and The Dick

"You almost blew it," George said to The Dick.

The Dick's mouth curled in a surly way and involuntarily he sat straighter, an imposing man when stretched for his body was long and powerful. He involuntarily swung his torso slightly to the right, showing the strong muscle mass of his left arm biceps. It was an intimidating pose. George thought: wouldn't it be ironic if in his prancing around while looking for 'Manda's current heart throb he began to get ideas about her and she took to him? He slapped the table. He looked at The Dick, trying to imagine how a woman would feel seeing his imposing figure. He tried to imagine how she would feel receiving his arms around her waist, or taking that arm in her hands and feeling its size and latent strength. George curled his lip and gave his head a little shake. Maybe he'd made a mistake in hiring this guy. 'Manda and The Dick had had chats, he claiming she was giving him leads, and yet all he reported was that that ignoramus had coffee with her every morning in town - that old guy, Trevor Heneke. I probably should never have hired him, George thought. He probably knows more than anyone who she's taken a shine to this time. He grimaced to himself. Actually I want a history of this flirtation business going back and back. She's only got so much time so can't have too much going on in a flirting, overly-friendly manner.

"Let's go back a dozen years and see who it was and get some idea of how far they went." He's got to come up with more that he's unearthed so far. Maybe this whole thing is stupid.

The Dick was smiling faintly, staring at his employer. "So you want to know how far back she's had these boyfriends?"

"That's the idea."

The Dick tossed his head. "We can do that. It'll take a lot more digging. And by the way," leaning closer like a secret was coming "The other night I found that old guy, Trevor Something-or-other, skulking about your house."

"Where was 'Manda?"

"Inside, I suppose. No lights on. He never went to the door, just hung around like waiting for her to come out, which she didn't."

"You sure there's nothing between those two?"

"If there is, I ain't seen it."

I wish to hell he talked better. He looked at The Dick with disgust. I should dismiss him. Maybe everyone from California talks like that.

"But you know, she is always ready to talk to men. I posted myself out by the construction on 103 at the bridge and pretty soon she comes along, driving in that white car of hers, and the flagman stops her and she starts a mighty conversation with him. Made his day I bet."

"What were they talking about?"

"I got this electronic listener thing and can hear up to one hundred feet on a quiet day, but there was equipment working so it was harder to hear from where I was. He was a skinny codger, like the Trevor one, and they talked about the next dance, she inviting him to come in the nicest way." George could feel his fists clenching. The Dick took time to smile at his employer, and left out the part about the

Flagman's family and his wife's garden. "And they talked about Church." He fell silent, thinking, and then blurted out about how two-faced some Church people are, muttering how he hated it and the churches should clean up their acts. He added how Church women shouldn't flirt. It was God-damned unchristian, and how he was going to find the minister and let him know. "Does she go to Church?"

"When I'm home she does. We do. She says she does when I'm not home."

"There's some guy that comes out of the Church any old time, I suppose the minister."

"It's him if he's average height and always wears a jacket. He talks with 'Manda too long?"

"Him, then. And they have talks, she snuggles up to him sometimes, but always draws away. She spends time talking with the workman at the office structure they're building."

"Which one?"

"There's that big one from up the hilltop who owns the company. Another named Jeff, and two others. She seems to congregate to Jeff or the owner, one or the other. Last time she invited Jeff to go for a walk to someplace after work. But then she added in that old guy, too."

"What old guy?"

"The one they call Trevor-something-or-other." He fondled his chin. "They spend a lot of time together, come to think of it."

That evening George tried to draw 'Manda into a conversation about Trevor, but got nowhere.

Chapter 38
A Field Ripe for the Corrector

The Dick followed the path from the new office building being constructed there by the place where the chasm did its loop and got in close to the town. The building was a bit removed from the town, just as well, the roar of the river occasionally got louder for some reason and would blot out casual talk so I suppose they were insulating it well, for sound, not heat and cold.

Well anyway, this evening The Dick decided to follow the path a bit. There were plenty of things he didn't know about the town and its surrounding parts and bits, so why not? He knew the path was along the chasm pretty much, and he was suspicious of heights, but what the hell, take a chance once in a while. That's how he felt. He'd never taken that path before, too close to the chasm and all its noise. You couldn't hear it a hundred feet away because the noise was directed upward, but what the hell, one time wouldn't hurt.

He'd been standing in town, a block or so from the church, in the shadows between two buildings. It smelled faintly of urine, so someone had been in here before and there are never any public toilets in American cities so the country dirties itself. In the Service he'd been to France once, Paris, and there'd been places to go when you had to, but not in the USA, the greatest country in the world.

So here he is standing in the shadows and it's Wednesday; mid-week Church services are finishing up. Out of one of the Church's doors come a teenage boy and girl. He starts to look away but then catches them kissing. Right there on the Church's steps! He watched. He'd do the same thing if that Bernice were here, but she wasn't his girl, she belonged to that B&B fellow. Disgusting, their behavior. Kissing right there in public. Well, it was dark and so they could get away with it. Now who would know what they'd do next, or be doing this very minute? He peered harder, trying to pierce the gloom of night. Maybe he should walk over there and stop them before they went beyond God's dictates in the Bible. Now take George and his wife. If her mother had taught her better, kept a close bridle on her, George wouldn't have hired him to spy on her. He didn't trust her talking to other men, she so free and easy and him having to be away working so much and not knowing what she might be doing. George was some sort of fool. Checking up on his wife and yet when he comes home he waltzes by Bernice's place and wants her to come out and offer him a cool drink like she did one time. I bet he's just waiting for a chance to take her. He thinks his wife's cheating on him and it's him who's doing the cheating, if he gets the chance. People certainly are despicable! They should pay more attention to the Bible and what it really says about that stuff. A look toward the Church and the two were still clasped as one as near as he could tell. I've got to go down there before they deny their chances in heaven later on.

The Dick pulled himself up, one shouldn't look sloppy when you do God's work. He walked toward the Church, seeing the single silhouette split into two and move away. They had seen him. He should stop them and give them a few words from some verse, before they repeated their sacrileges somewhere else. A lesson is what they needed. If he weren't a stranger he would get into the Church and lead some lessons. This town was so full of blasphemers and non-believers and fornicators and cheaters and two-timers that it should be bathed in fire and purified.

He started to run, slowly, steadily, at a pace that could carry him ten miles without a second breath. He would overtake them and share a couple of words. They were moving away, maybe running, too, toward the chasm, stupid kids. Didn't they know chasms were dangerous?

They had disappeared. They probably had a couple of blankets cached nearby to stop and have a few cherished moments before going home to Mom and Dad. They needed a lesson.

Where could they have hidden?

He looked curiously among the rocks at the end of the street where the new construction was going up. Nothing. They could hide in the building in one of the rooms. No one would know. He scouted quickly, hearing the roar of the chasm now that he was close. They didn't go to the chasm or the side of the building. He hated heights. He hated the noise. Two kids somewhere around here, making love in the brush, knowing it was wrong but not having a mother or father hard enough on them to leave an impression. Disgusting. Useless kids with no morals. Maybe he should go up to the school and make plans for lectures when it opened in the fall. It'd be good for the whole family. He walked out, leaned against the unfinished doorway and stared up the street in the dark. He could probably see the same distasteful ignorance of God's Work in any window he peered in.

He started walking up the path.

Chapter 39
The Dick

The Dick was standing in the clothes store alleyway, his favorite spot. It was shaded and cool; a good place to watch from. He could see the coffee house where his target and that old codger sat and chatted until around eleven, sometimes leaving separately and sometimes together, usually walking over toward the chasm way and that path he'd found over there the night those two kids had eluded him, all set to make love he was sure, and he stopped them. He'd talk to their parents as soon as he found out who they were. They weren't his prime problem. Sort of a private little task more related to his religion that his real job. Both needed to be done, but he was getting paid for one, so that's the big one. So you could see plenty from here, and then move off to his next spot. He had several spots from which he could watch George's wife from since she was a sort of public person here in town. Following her and spotting the men she talked to was his real job as well as doing that research way back to see her past behavior. Following each one was a chore, and finding out their names was difficult. One time, not getting any clues by asking passers-by, who THAT man was, the next thing he knew the man was standing in front of him and asking who HE was. It ended in a fight, no big deal, fights had their place and although the man was big and strong from working out, he couldn't do a street fight, a bar fight more like it. He'd caught him with a false karati kick, the man expecting it and ready to grab the foot coming at him but a full lunge, twisting and left-right did him. His rib hurt for the rest of the two days but then that was part of the job. He had a notebook with almost every man's name in it now, and –

Wait! He came alert. That Sara woman from up on the hill out of town was walking on the other side of the street. Going where? Nice looking broad. It was satisfying to watch a well-endowed woman walk. Hm-m-m. He watched. A woman like that was potential, as he looked at it. And where is she going? He came out of cover, trying to figure her destination. Going that way there was only that new building going up, the chasm, and off to the side the path along the edge.

He looked around. No one about, usually wasn't. Down by the *Empty Plate* his focus, Amanda, was standing by the door having last words with that old codger. Ignore them. He stepped out, following, and puzzled. That Sara woman, sexy looking bitch, was going into the new construction. She wasn't soliciting, was she? If so, she was fair game. Following Amanda and the old man would have to be postponed this time.

There was no one on the ground floor in the building. He walked through the unfinished rooms looking, and returned to the foyer and the stairs up, some pails for wall compound stretching up the steps, some tools, and voices above. They were indistinct, but now he heard laughter. He tip-toed up. Two white coverall-clad men in a side room were doing wall board; he gave them a nod. They looked at each other.

At voices to the left, he went through the room and hesitated. They were in the next room talking in low voices. Had 'em. Good.

He stepped around the corner in full view and leaned against the wall unaware that that cynical, sly, all-knowing smile was on. The bitch was tight in that guy's arms and in the middle of some super kiss, their arms entwined. One hell-of-a kiss. They didn't know he was there. Good. Get some pointers. Bitches. This town is ripe for some good God-fearing lessons. It's not just the teens. It's even the adults. You can always tell. Off the main stream and they do anything they want out in these podunk places. He was losing patience. It was time to move in and save this man from committing himself to a slut like this. I wonder if she did the two men back there, too. His hands were on her rump when he came in. Too bad this wasn't that Amanda, then he could report some real transgressions to George. Maybe he should report this anyway, let George think she was this one. Don't tell. And he wouldn't believe her if she denied it either. Perfect.

"This fore-play is going too far." He spoke.

"Okay you two, break if off," he added.

It was like cold water showered on them. Yet they didn't stop. Still arms about each other, the two heads swung to the doorway and stared. They were surprised, but stayed clasped together. A disgusting display.

"Break it off. I should report the two of you for indecent exposure, public display and all that. The Lord God would have your tails in hell for this kind of thing. Thank the Good Guiding Christ that no one else is here to see you."

The man was slowly unwinding from her, placing her to his right, still his arm around her waist. "What the hell you talking about and what're you doing here. Didn't you see the No Trespassing sign down by the door? Get out of here."

"Sorry Mister, but the Good God doesn't want men fornicating with wanton and loose women. You are warned and will be punished in good time. She has no business soliciting in a work place. I am surprised at you and can forgive, possibly The Good Guiding Christ will accept your penitence in due time. You –" Interrupted, he still stood there with index fingers in the cross formation.

"Get the Fuck out of here yourself. Now beat it."

The Dick was aware of another man, also with white coveralls, entering by another doorway. He had a puzzled look on his face and was frowning.

The Dick turned to the newcomer. "Friend, do not enter this room of evil. These people are committing a wanton act and –"

The man had a look, the frown deepened and he said, "What's going on Marty? This man trespassing?"

The woman was pointing at The Dick. "That's The Dick George hired to watch 'Manda. Now he's on to us." She laughed.

"The woman walketh in the steps of the prostitute. Don't enter and be contaminated," He placed that rather superior smile to his face. Effective at times. "She –"

The newcomer was almost at his side and he dropped his right, readying. Whose side is he on? He heard him saying: "Sara. What's going on?"

The kissing man was coming close.

"Look here, mister. We got work to do, You saw the No Trespassing sign, why don't you move on. Take your business somewhere else." Jeff stood next to him as he spoke.

The Dick faced the two men and slowly raised his arms high. He intoned, "Lord God above, look upon me, your humble servant, warrior for your Truth. Enter these two and purge the Devil from their bodies." He looked over at Sara standing by the window where Marty had been. "I pray for your soul. May your ways swell to reach these men in their moment of passion, that you, the Mary Magdalen of today, bring the True Way to your men."

Marty looked around. To her men? What does this quack know of our lives? As he watched he saw her eyes leave The Dick and go to Jeff, still standing there and staring at The Dick, probably wondering what he knew of his black eye and hurt nose, broken tooth and him and Sara. Dare he look at her. Things were always tricky between him and Marty these days, and this guy comes in and breaks the issue plum open again.

Marty moved to Sara and put his arm around her while The Dick recited some poem from Psalms about marriage, at least that's what it sounded like. He broke in on the man. "Now shut yer God damned trap and listen. This here's my wife and I'll kiss her any time I want. He was yelling over the words of the poem. "This is a work place and you're interfering, YA HEAR! A WORK PLACE. NOW get the hell out."

The Dick was on his knees, arms outstretched forward, hands gripping themselves, tears starting to form and his voice now more quiet. "Lord, Lord, help these poor misunderstanding people. A man, two men, and a woman, and it be a sin in your eyes for a woman to take two men. Married. Be they married but do they illustrate your Godly intentions? Now as they profess in this room. Nay, deny your Heavenly Guidance. Nay to the woman to open herself to two men. Let her be the wife of one and the other to go on his way." The three were looking at him, surprised.

"YOU. YOU, the woman to many men. While your life lives let it come to the Christ and be blessed that you adopt a life of truth and Christian behavior. LET IT BE SO!" He was on his feet, tears still streaming and advancing two steps. "GO WOMAN with your man, and leave these premises before the Christian dictates are violated. You must, to keep God's integrity. GO NOW. GO WITH HIM." He took her arm and shoved her at Jeff, into Jeff who backed a step in the doorway and Sara fell against him from the unexpected shove. The Dick had both arms raised on high and was shouting the Lord's Prayer at them, forcing them together with his bulk and back out the doorway. Marty snatched at his arm looking beyond Sara against Jeff and all the pent up feelings about the 'affair' poured out. He started yelling to Sara and Jeff and they separated but The Dick, filling the doorway, kept her pressed at Jeff. A whisper in her ear. "I have longed for a moment like this." and with that felt him drop away from her, stepping back and she watched Marty's eyes behind The Dick following Jeff's departure. The dumb Dick had thrown us together, was that a subtle hint from the Lord through this man?

Marty was yelling about his wife and trying to point and get past The Dick to her for The Dick blocked his way. Then The Dick made a twist and with room for Marty to squeeze pass, slipping by the man and to Sara who accepted his arms around her neck and planted a kiss on his lips. The yelling about worship to your wife and the children she would bear and a man's duty under God to her came thundering through the room just as Marty, her husband, swept her around lifting her feet from the floor and she felt the thrill of the moment and hearing Marty's great voice calling forth about his wife. The Dick looked askance at the two and beyond her to Jeff disappearing through the room to the far side where he had been working. Sara, being swung about in Marty's sudden emotional enthusiasm, looked pleading arrows flying to Jeff: Jeff, come to me. This is my husband but Jeff, Jeff, it is you. Yes. We must meet.

The Dick and Marty were squaring off, moving warily around each other, like two bears ready for a scuffle. All the while Jeff yelling about mistakes and wives and husbands and get the hell out and mind your own business and The Dick shrieking God's commands to Moses and the seventh commandment and the words of Moses to his people to follow the tablets, and then a bigger noise for about seven men and women and some kids in the doorways, drawn to the noise going on here in the new construction. And that was it. The Dick drew himself up and said something in a voice that was indistinguishable in the noise and thrust through the people and out.

Over.

But I have to see Jeff, was on her mind.

The crowd closed behind him, turned and followed, watching, awaiting another blast of God-tinted shouts. Whatever was it about? And they got their wish.

The Dick drew himself up full height, raised a fist aimed at the building, the roar of water from far below in the chasm beyond, and let off volleys of curses and exhortations to the workmen inside and the prostitute waiting in there for her chance, he yelled and yelled. Saliva dripped and the voice became hoarse.

God. The holy trinity, the ten commandments, Moses and Paul, the true life, the sin of consorting with the unclean, the retribution due a man who succumbed, the purpose of life, Mary as the perfect example. The unclean, the holy word, the intentions of God for mankind, the passions of the disbelieving, the Lord's prayer, the place of Mohammed, the plague as God's weapon, the four horsemen, Crusaders in the Mideast, crusaders against whores, venereal disease, AIDS, lack of scruples, morals trodden, the failure of Churches, ministers shirking their duty, unfaithful women, the teasers, wantonness, the failure of the missionary position, sex for procreation only. The duty of each man only to his wife, women give yourselves to your men. Never dwell on sex, the foul movie industry, Hollywood the center of pornography, grace, saving one's self, the fire on Joan d'Arc, the true power of God.

Chapter 40
I Talk to Marty

I was there, I could hear it all, and what I couldn't see which was about everything, I filled in out of my imagination. Imagine!

I had gone into the new construction during their coffee break, been hiding up on the rocks near the path to the rope bridge since leaving. This is how it went.

Waiting outside there, I was wondering how I could get to talk to Jeff when I saw the coffee truck coming, chuggin' along like it does because he never bothers to have the engine inspected and fixed. There I am, and I see him pull up with that honk of his horn. The two hired hands come out, and then Jeff (Damn! Missed him.) and Marty after a minute or two. The five of them walked around the corner of the building, I suppose to get out of the sun and chat while they had their little mid-morning snack and coffee.

This was my chance so I was down out of the rocks and running up to the side of the new construction, they were away on the far and shady side, and me inside and up to the fourth level – floor, they called it. Hiding up there seemed safe, it was offices mostly done since for some reason they had started from the top down finishing things off. It was more like an apartment building than an office. So I hid, and heard Sara come in and then The Dick, and it started. The locals began to saunter over to listen and watch 'cause that bastard Private Eye had the biggest voice in all Christiandom. They came, siddling in, listening. He put on a good show, and then off into the street and more people, and yelling his Christian message to the world. He's one of them believers big time. It was close to lunch and bit by bit the street cleared, a bunch following him on down to the central part of this little berg and it quieted here. No one was walking downstairs below me. I heard Sara saying good-bye and presently the others cleared out. Marty got in his pickup and left for lunch. I sneaked out, up the path and at the rope bridge cut over, there was no one in The Hut, and I went on up to the highway and the bridge and back into town like an innocent little choir boy. 'Manda was leaving the church and she gave me a nod, the nod that said let's talk so I was off with her to the diner. "Jerky, Fish and More" is the name of that cussed little hang-over from another era, but the food is good and we stood by the door, waiting for a place like everyone else.

"What you been up to in the last two hours?" she asked as way of introduction.

Always the delicious looking woman, at least to me, and I had to break away from looking at her, waist up only as she was in the booth now and I couldn't do hips and legs without being obvious. We talked like two civilized people, discussing the weather, the summer, the heat and how to get Sara set up with a family, our prime objective this June. A February baby is always welcome. She told me about the meeting with the minister and how she almost spilled the beans about our plans, and how, fortunately she was interrupted by the mob massing outside under the leadership of the jerk private eye her husband had hired. He exhorting them to greater volume in their singing for he had led them down the middle of the street all the way from somewhere (I told her where) to the Church singing Christian hymns of which he seemed to have an unending number, familiar and unfamiliar at which time he'd call out Christian phraseology interspaced with hymns.

'Manda curled a lip and noted that some of them sounded more like army marching songs, and, "– you know what those verses are like."

I had to laugh, and she finally did too, took my hand and gave it a squeeze. Now there's a woman I could go for, if it weren't for her being already married and having her own Private Dick watch-dog and a husband as eagle-eyed and watchful as the eagle scouting the sky for his wife out for a little fly.

So we enjoy each other's company.

I told about the beginning of The Dick's episode today, how he'd gotten Sara mixed up thinking her married to Jeff, but also racking her with his venom – today her being the classical prostitute in his eyes. It had blown my part of the plan. 'Manda was to see Sara and suggest an evening meeting at The Hut for the two of them, and I was to get Marty to meet her there. It was blown as far as the original plan went, but the longer we sat there over american chop suey and her lobster roll, the more we resurrected a new one. I'd be home tonight, start talking with Marty and get him to: "Let's go down and see what Sara and 'Manda are up to." Then 'Manda and I would wander off for a little walk farther down the chasm, and leave them two alone, husband and wife together, a new place, a chance for renewal of their marriage, and the magic of the night would carry it along. Thus the February baby would be on the way and Sara and Marty would have a real family, and all the past would be over. The threat of Jeff stealing her would be done. Sara'd be busy preparing for the baby, and Marty would see a family of seven marching toward him on the

horizon, give him four or five years to do it now that he
knew how (ha, ha), and 'Manda just shook her head at me
and gave a mock frown at my suggestive remark. That was
the plan.

Of course, I knew nothing about Jeff whispering to her
during the episode with The Dick so things that started out
got twisted in some fantastic God-driven way, I guess that's
how you'd say it.

So after supper, my eye on the clock, I sat down on the
evening porch across from Marty who was reading some
book about World War II, and I wondered out loud if he
knew where Sara was.

More interested in the book than me, he muttered she'd
gone out with the girls tonight. Someone's house in town.

Okay, thinks I, 'Manda and Sara are starting their walk
down to The Hut as planned.

I sat there quiet for a bit, thinking about "the affair"
Mandy and I were setting up between this husband and
wife, and congratulating myself on doing some kind of
Good in the world. I thought about Mandy and me like any
red-blooded, healthy man would do. Of course my thoughts
went to Jeff, and then to Mandy's husband off on his
business trip and hiring that private detective to watch over
her like a good Catholic nun. Every single man in town, and
a few marrieds, too, I'm sure, must envy my friendship with
her. Mandy and I drink coffee and chat, and have the best
time, and I'm sure folks even see us walking off here and
there in town, checking on things, you'd say, putting
together that little work group that fixed up The Hut for
folks to picnic at or hide from the rain in, or maybe meet
some loved one and have privacy for talks and a few kisses.
Too bad (oh well, probably just as well) 'Manda and I never

really got into the kissing stage of friendship. A few times, but not really serious, at least so far.

Sitting there on the porch Marty interrupted my day dream. "You know that there's a Dick around town? He is the most absolute pain in the ass I've ever known. I don't know why 'Manda's husband hired him. I hear one story after another and I'm damned sure not one of them is true."

My ears perked up.

He slammed his book down on the coffee table Sara had put out here to encourage them to get outside more in the summer to get fresh air and sunshine to offset his working inside so much. I was looking for my chance.

"Now you know what he did today? Everyone in town hates him so I'm not surprised. A whole town full of people can't be wrong."

I knew he didn't know that I was hiding in the building when The Dick was there so I played ignorant. "I get that impression, but let me play the Devil's Advocate. You tell me what he did was bad, and I'll explain why it was good, all right, and had needed doing for a long time." I plastered a smile on my face.

Marty snorted. "He came in the construction zone this morning. Sara had just come in, being in town she thought she'd stop by and say hello –"

"She loves you, you big hunk. She's your wife and wanted to see you and get a kiss or two."

He ignored me.

"– I don't think she'd been there more' un two minutes and in he comes. He probably followed her half way across town. So he prances inside and finds us all and starts bawling us out for meeting there. Well, fer Christ's sake, she's my wife and comes in if she's in town, and he starts

talking as if he'd broken in on a prostitution ring. Jesus
Christ! I should have plowed him one in the face and kicked
his balls out. Jesus! My wife right there and talking like that.
I was too surprised to do anything but stare. And Jeff
comes in. Now this Dick can't know about me beating Jeff
off when Sara and him started that little pact– him and her
and kissing and all that. Jeff was astounded, too. That Dick
calling Sara a whore.

Well! I was on my feet and smashing my fist into my
palm and shouting, "Sara's my step-daughter and she ain't in
no way like that. Wait'll I see him. I'll –"

He interrupted me, pulled me back to the chair, and I let
him. Just maybe I could twist it into gettin' him down to
The Hut. I could see him getting gradually more upset and I
wasn't supposed to know anything.

"Now you just quiet down, Dad (He never called me
'Dad' before) and listen because I AM THE ONE WHO IS
GOING TO SMASH HIS LITTLE FACE IN. Let me do
it. Understand?"

I nodded.

And the other two came in, hearing him carry on. And
he started in on some Christian Fundamentalist stuff about
God punishing us all and we were evil. Jesus, she's my wife!
She can do anything she wants with me. And him! Oh-h!"
He clenched and unclenched his fists.

I rose up and grabbed his arm thinking I could get us
going. It was perfect timing, go into town and out to The
Hut looking for 'the girls', and find that Sara was out at The
Hut and go out to meet her and with him all wound up like
that they'd have a meeting that would out do Anthony and
Cleopatra. 'Mandy would have gotten her out there and all

excited about romance and sex and it would be the perfect meeting we were looking for.

But he didn't get up. He jerked me down and shoved his index finger in my side and lectured me on the married life of two deeply in love and almost got into blessed details and various ways to perform the act and all that sort of thing, the kind of talk that excites teen-aged boys. I don't mean his talk was dirty, or anything like that, it was just that he was excited over his wife and what had happened and how it seemed to awaken a new awareness in him. It was interesting to me to see him carry on so aroused, I guess you'd say. But man, it was there! My mind came and went as I listened, and occasionally I'd replace Sara with my local heart throb, and his name with my own and I'd just vegetate in his excitement.

Marty looked at me, his face growing fierce, "That man come around again and start calling my wife a whore he'll find himself dead in the gutter. I'll kill the bastard. I will. "He looked at the bottle on the table, pushed it aside and looked again at me. "That damned bastard. Sara ain't that way, and you know it. She's your daughter!"

Well that was true, she was. And I'd never seen any hanky panky going on, even that black eye on Jeff was something I didn't see done although I did see the nose and tooth part of their fight, and it was over a supposed kiss between her and Jeff. Men and women have these little times when someone else comes along and gives life a jar. A presumed love affair never to ever end, but it does because both parties come to their senses and realize their marriage and children are more important than a few kisses. So Jeff and Sara found each other for a few days and had a few kisses, it never went beyond that I'm sure, but Marty found

out and put an end to it. I'd never seen neither of them do it
again. Of course I had to admit that Jeff looked on her
rather fondly, which I saw, and I suppose Sara did too, but
we all ignored it and life went on. Marty was supposed to
get on into town with me, but he was getting pretty high on
the whiskey and I'd better wait a bit 'fore taking him in, or
getting him started to The Hut and that clandestine meeting
'Manda and I had set up. I looked at Marty, wondering what
kind of father he would be and was satisfied. He'd do well.
Be proud as the Dickens, teaching the kid to throw and
catch and hit with a bat and drive a car and grow strong and
healthy and take a wife and give Marty all the grandchildren
he could stand. I chuckled. Marty poured another three
fingers into his glass and looked at me offering another and
I shook my head, wondering the while if I could get him to
The Hut on time. I was relaxed and felt like sleeping but just
stretched while sitting there in the chair listening to him still
talking away about the evilness afoot with The Dick stalking
the town looking for un-Christian behavior. I wondered if
George had really intended that The Dick clean up the town
or just look for guys hanging around his wife. Stupid
George, I was thinking. Spending money on someone to see
who she saw and talked with while he was away. I guess she
had just been too friendly to other men when at dances or
other Church activities in George's presence to start him
thinking she was "looking" and "susceptible" and liable to
get laid by someone. What stupid thinking. She was as
trustworthy as any woman and I knew 'cause I saw so much
of her. And so that's what I was thinking and well, let's face
it, thinking of her was relaxing and pleasant even for an old
'un like me. So there I was, enthralled, and relaxed, and

comfy, and I fell asleep during one of his descriptive passages.

Well, I looked around and sat up, sort of. Something didn't seem right, yet everything was the same: the warm night, the light on overhead on the porch, and I was alone. I figured he'd finally got tired of me, ran out of words, whatever, and gone on up to bed. But that was wrong.

We were supposed to get him down to The Hut, and I'd been sleeping!

My God, for how long? I was still on the porch in the chair and Marty was gone and it was dark and slightly chilly. Had I failed at my end of the tryst-makers scheme? Of course!

I called, quietly, but no one answered, so I walked up to the bed rooms figuring he'd gone up to bed to wait for Sara, but no Marty.

Ah, He's gone in to town himself. Good.

Satisfied, I got ready for bed, brushed my teeth, the whole bit. Let them work it out.

I awoke with a start. Again! Noise in the cellar. A machine tool running. I was out of bed and down stairs and at the cellar door. It's Marty working on that little pram he's been building. A turn and to the clock and I saw it was after eleven. Too late. He's here, not at The Hut. She's there with Mandy and no Marty. No romantic moment. No baby in February. No point in going now. It's past, the time gone. My fault. It'd be after twelve when we get there, no use. Over. So Sara's going to come walking in any minute now. Oh Jesus Christ. I softly closed the cellar door, leaving Marty to his hobby, and returned to my room.

I awoke when I heard the noise next door in Marty and Sara's bed room. The clock said three AM. She's just getting in? And I fell back asleep.

Chapter 41
Mandy and Me Check the Times

Mandy looked tired when she came in for coffee. I'd had a reasonable night and felt alert and perky and the sky deep blue and had hardly a cloud so far and a slight chill in the air. A cold front had arrived and a high pressure area and the animal body was tuned to the change and feeling first class. Active, alert, and ready for the world. A wonderful day ahead.

Mandy looked tired. Oh yeah. The botched tryst we had pulmigated on mankind last night, at least on Mandy and Sara, the tryst I botched by failing to get Marty down to the spot. The spot where it was to take place, the moment of husbandly love. The moment to be the turning point of Sara's life. From just hanging around and doing wifely things, to having a real family to look after, to guide, to love, to enjoy. Nothing to it. But I had botched getting Marty to the Church on time, you might say, or sing if that befitted you.

She didn't accuse me. She was totally content, although she had been up late.

"You were up late." I said as way of introduction after she had her English muffin and coffee, plus orange juice to kick it off. She yawned, stretched. What a wonderful presentation from a woman I spent too much time thinking about and too little time seeing. Now that the whole tryst business was over. I must find something else to do rather than be with her as much as I was. After all, she was George's wife.

Of course, George was never home and had hired The Dick to fill in, maybe be her escort, but she never did anything else but the usual daytime chores. Oh well. "How'd it go?"' I asked.

She touched my hand as she moved for the butter.

"Fine, I guess. She and I were there on time, dark, nine o'clock. She had a little sack of apples and cookies, and a thermos. We chatted and I told her how nice it was here at The Hut; but had to get on and would leave her to enjoy it. She was quite willing, thank God, otherwise it'd have been a job to keep her there, remote as the place is. So I left. I waited up by that big rock where I could see some, and know if he arrived, I waited a long, long time, it was late, but she never left, maybe fell asleep. One could sit there, it's so private and secure. So I waited and eventually I heard the rope bridge squeaking and groaning and knew someone was crossing over. I figured it was him so I gathered up my stuff and came home."

"When'd you get home?"

"You know that's funny. I was thinking how I was tired and ready to sleep so may not have seen the time right. She looked at me. I thought it said three AM. Is that possible?

Three AM, I said to myself. Three AM? Mandy got home at three AM? And sometime around twelve or one I saw Marty working in the cellar, and heard Sara come in at three AM. Or I think it was three AM.

I looked at her. "Mandy, you look tired. Did you get enough sleep?" This time thing was tricky. What had happened, really, and when? I felt suspicious, and that was when Jeff came in with the coffee order for the men. The coffee truck was broken down this morning and not running. Jeff was doing the chores and looked like death warmed over. He got the order for four coffees and two buns, a Devil dog and one English, and left. Gave us a nod as he passed.

He and 'Mandy looked a pair. Tired like an all night card game.

She caught my attention. She did one of those big stretches again, a wonderful presentation just for me. I'd been lost in thinking; and although she did it for me all the other clientele had a taste of her beauty, too. She knows she's a good looking woman and takes pleasure in it, although not wantonly nor indiscriminately. She presented herself to me and I loved it. I'd tell her later, maybe when we were in a more private setting. But she did look tired. Mandy looked tired and Jeff looked tired. When had Sara come in? Three? And Marty? I hadn't seen him today, he was off at work before I got up. I should walk on down to the construction and check.

If Mandy saw him come over the rope bridge, then he must have sneaked out after I saw him in the cellar. Wow. That's one way to lose your health. Work all day and sneak out between one and three in the night for a little nooky. But that's mankind for you. Always ready for action.

So what about Jeff? What does he do, stay up reading, watching that terrible television crap, or does he have a new girl? Hardly. He certainly looked like he'd been up all night too.

Mandy was eating the English muffin and probably worrying that she'd be putting on weight. "Mandy, who crossed over on the rope bridge?"

She shrugged. "Don't know. Someone."

And she looked at me hard. "You got Marty off on time, didn't you?"

I shook my head and she looked at me harder. Then she turned her head half-way and looked at me out of the corner of her eye, a coquettish trick of hers, very charming. "You don't suppose it was God's representative on earth checking out all the trysting spots, do you?"

I had to smile. "The Dick? Sneaking around at night getting all the un-marrieds broken up and at home and the marrieds lined-up for Gods vengeance?"

She laughed. "It crossed my mind."

"Let's go find him and see."

"If he sees us together it'll be another mark against me when George gets home."

We left hand in hand almost. My hand grazed her hip as she moved and it was just too natural not to let it happen again.

Outside she said, "If George sees this he'd be suspicious."

"Well, possibly, but remember, he thinks I'm safe as I'm over the hill."

"Yes, he did intimate that." She laughed. "Let's do it anyway," and she grabbed my lonely hand.

Ah-yup. Another nail in my coffin.

Chapter 42
Did It Work?

We walked together, holding hands for the first block and then dropped them, people moving here and there and we really did not want to start a talk about us being a "pair". With The Dick around everyone seemed to know he was looking for Mandy's boyfriend as well as chasing down every non-Christian alive and working a conversion. So we had to be careful. People probably talked about us anyway. I looked at her and she looked at me and we had this unspoken conversation, and then, action established, we approached the first couple we ran across.

"Excuse me, we're looking for the Private Detective. Have you seen him this morning?"

A shaking of heads, a polite 'no' but a muffled smile. Everyone already knew he had become transferred from "Private Dick" to "God's Agent on Earth" – "THE DICK" for short.

We passed on to another couple. A 'No, Ain't seen him." Then a woman with a three year old, out shopping. Another "no".

We walked all the way to the new construction. One of the white coveralled workman was outside, burning sweepings from inside. "Naw-w-w. Ain't seen him. The other day was enough. Yer outta yer heads looking for him." We turned and started back only to hear his words behind us. "You stay at home Mrs. Cunningham and he'll be there to report to his employer, George. Check it out." Meant as a joke it fell flat on the two of us.

We checked more folks out walking the town on their private business. No one had seen him today so far.

"George is away, still. You want to come over for lunch?"

I crinkled my nose. Yes I would, but it really wasn't a smart move. I was above suspicion at the moment, but George hiring a private detective was a dead give away that he was alert to whoever she was interested in. "I guess maybe not. I'll go up and have lunch with Sara and Marty. He generally comes home for lunch." She knew what was in my mind and nodded. Gave my hand a squeeze and we parted. Two women walking along were watching us. So it goes. They'll surely mention it to The Dick when he asks and he seems to ask everyone.

Sara was in, looking like death warmed over. More like she hadn't sleep an inch last night and actually that was a good sign, or was it. Out all night with her husband was exactly what we had wanted. I looked at her tummy when she was preoccupied elsewhere and it looked normal. No baby yet, but then it was only the first day of the first month of this trimester. Or something like that.

Marty came in.

He looked pretty ordinary. I regretted not staying up to make sure he left on time, or at least left to meet her. Also I noted they gave each other an ordinary kiss, no kiss like they were both thinking back to last night's experience. Damn me for being so wrapped up in my own need for sleep.

So we had a hurried and ordinary bowl of soup and tuna fish sandwich and a bit of chatting. She was going shopping this afternoon, would walk in, wouldn't need the car. He offered to give her a ride down, but she shrugged that off. He mumbled about the job on the new office building, asked where "God's Ground Agent" was today, that question to me as he knew I usually went into town early and saw Mrs. Cunningham. He asked when George was coming back. It seemed George was thinking of setting up an office and running a consulting business from here instead of doing all the traveling.

"God's Ground Agent", a new term for The Dick that was running about the gossip circles now that he'd established practically a new Church in town. At least he had a congregation hanging around amongst the people from the other day. It was a joke among the steadier folk round town, worth watching for the laughs. I privately wondered how much George was paying to entertain the town like this. So be it, whatever.

Sara asked if he'd picked out his office yet, and Marty said, "Yeah the one on floor three out back overlooking the Chasm."

"The cheapest one in the place?" put in Sara, and they both smiled.

"Well this private detective can come and go and no one'll know he's reporting."

"When George let's that one go then he'll only have the office to pay for."

Marty shrugged. He looked at me. "Well, it is his money and he can blow it any way he wants. Are you on his list?"

I guess they more or less figured George for some kind of cheapskate but was burning money on The Dick. And I was in his sights. I answered, "I'm sure I got reported. I see his wife about every day. We had that committee that was fixing up The Hut, remember. I'm sure I got reported."

Sara gave me a long look.

Marty said, "You gotta stop seeing her. Ole George sees your name on the list too much and you'll be a goner." He laughed.

Sara wanted to know what list.

Marty gave his wife a look. "You need to hang around town more. Everyone's got it figured that The Dick is sending a list of 'Manda's male acquaintances to George every day. Apparently George is considered a spend thrift, as he's hired a 'Dick' to keep tabs on 'Manda. He's jealous as all get-out."

"So he's just watching for who hangs out with his wife?" Sara asked. I bet she was wondering if he was spotting other transgressions of the Ten Commandments variety and reporting them to George, too.

And you know, I was listening to these two talk on and they didn't in the least sound like they'd been having a little private tryst all their own. Maybe Mandy's idea of a special little place to bring love out was all wrong. They had a bedroom and each other and no doubt went through the motions of love like any other married couple. So why the special little tryst? I'd have to run over that with her again. Maybe she was just an ordinary busybody messing around in other people's lives. So I got to thinking about that and kind of lost contact with what my step-daughter and her husband was talking about.

Chapter 43
God's Ground Agent

They pretty much had a rally in front of the Church, all those people that had followed him through the town when he left the construction site a couple of days ago. All those people that had heard the ruckus and gone over for the entertainment, which was probably about everyone available late morning, like housewives and the out of work folks and the old codgers sitting around on rockers waiting for excitement to appear one last time 'fore they took a journey into the hereafter with the Grim Reaper. Quite a bunch. But as I looked around at the folks and kids I could tell there was more than before. Folks I hadn't seen before or in a long time. That Dick was getting a high reputation for preaching and leading the world pell mell (if he had his way) to a great Christian Community right here in good ole Portage. I ain't exactly a joiner so was able to look it all over more scientific-like.

First off, it was a week day so there shouldn't have been that many folks around, but there were! Unbelievable. The minister came out at all the yelling and cheering that was everyone's responses to The Dick. It was like some parts of the Church service, him yelling out things, platitudes, threats, promises, and the mob would yell them back, a regular responsive reading from the Good Book of Church stuff. When Minister Prezzell came out, The Dick turned the program over to him, coaching him along with quotes and readings and exhorting everyone to call out louder, and then grabbing a few women, one at a time to come up and repeat what they felt about booze and bad women and their husbands falling into the ways of Evil. "The Devil walks among us," he would shout out and get a huge call back, "THE DEVIL WALKS AMONG US."

I came out of hiding and went to the rear of the mob so I heard it all and watched, thinking how dangerous a demigod like This Dick could be to common sense and intellectual truth and so on. I could see the minister getting swept aside and put in a position of supporting some of these extreme positions. The Dick was working everyone up, too. I could see Prezzell gettin' upset and finally he spoke out, shouting the greatest for once, calling to the people to settle down and stop chanting everything this man said. He didn't want to call The Dick a false God, but he was doing that, and calling on folks to disperse and go on about their business. There was some confusion and The Dick shaking his fist to heaven and to the minister and yelling stuff and then Prezzell was yelling back and of course the constable appeared about then and that settled it, people moved on away in singles and groups and suddenly the town was quiet, the mob gone, the street clear. Amazing. I guessed they'd caught it at the right moment, the preacher and the constable and averted who-knows-what? Well, it was good. The minister was still on the steps of the Church where he'd done his part and I stepped up to him and said, "Well done."

I didn't get to say more because he recognized me and started right in, venting about it all, and ya know, he said, "I don't usually say things like this but I know you'll keep your mouth shut, but you know that man is the most dangerous folk that ever walked into this town. Now George is a sensible man most of the time, but by now everyone knows he hired him in here for some dumb reason and he is the biggest danger we've had to common sense and responsibility in a generation. Someone should shoot him before he really does damage to a good, God-fearing small town like this. George is in no position to see what's happening, or he'd get rid of him. Someone's got to."

That was the first time I heard that idea, getting rid of God's Ground Agent, as some called him now.

But it also told me something else. He was talking to me like I knew George well enough to convince him, which I didn't, and then it came to me, he knew about 'Manda and me sipping coffee together day after day and therefore I could influence George through 'Manda. Christ. Everyone in the town must know about us and our meetings. What don't they know? Well, who is to say, but if they don't know, and I don't think they do, then they make up stuff. That's the way these people are!

Fact is, at that point it occurred to me that I should get that Frazier-guy over here with us. Let him take some of the blame.

Chapter 44
Skip Day

"Jeff was at the game the other night?" I asked B&B.

"First part," he grunted and that was all.

I was having suspicions.

We were up at Tracey's, a food spot and beach on the million-year-old lake way up country. The high school class of something-or-other was having a truancy day and half the school population was there in the water and on the beach and having a free loose and fun day of debauchery. What was I doing there? Trying to check up on all my participants in the Great Tryst. Just getting to know which way the wind was blowing. Marty came home from work early, he was tired, he said. And he looked it. Sara was home all day fussing around with things and I was in the way. I drove up to the Tracey place to escape only to find the whole fucking high school up there. Everyone but the staff, it seemed. It did not look like a relaxing place to go, but there's no sense in just leaving again, so settle down, observe the doings of human youth just as an anthropologist would.

Bernice was groveling around on the sand at B&B's feet with a couple of girlfriends, bikinis and all. B&B would have a heart attack if he was six months older, a quart into the booze and his eyes no longer twenty-twenty so it was every time Bernice squirmed about he had his hands caressing her from shoulder to knee. I don't know the odds, but this was either going to give him an extra ten years or take ten years away. You name it. She was a looker, alright.

And wouldn't you know it. Someone called 'Manda Cunningham has arrived the same as they'd been announcing every adult non-school person since I had arrived. It was around one-thirty. She must have spotted me immediately for she walked up to me, sitting under one of the umbrella-tables on the deck and gave me a blow like an elephant's. Almost sent me and the iced tea (with vodka) to the floor. "Yes, of course I'm glad to see you." She hit me again and then sat on me, much to the enjoyment of a bundle of those highschool kids who were too young to know anything about adult play.

Mandy and I had a nice chat. I do like that woman, even if I am thirty years her senior. So we talked and maybe if I was six months older I'd be the one to have the heart attack. Aside from that our job was over. We had brought the participants together and if nature took its course, I mean OUR COURSE of course (It's the vodka) the act has been committed and our job is done.

She looked at me, blew the cover off a fresh straw at me and said, "Should we seek another good deed to expend ourselves on?"

"Well, why the hell not?"

"Swearing does not become you." Whereupon a great shout went up from the beach. Danger. A drowning? Someone break a bikini strap?

It was The Dick, driving one of those golf cart things along the beach, pretty much hands off the steering while he manipulated a video camera with both hands and squinted into it.

Chapter 45
Did it Work or Not?

So they say there's no fool like an old fool, and that could all too easily be me. Or so I thought when I got into bed. I'm sure enough on George's list, no question about that, so why doesn't he do something? Like speak to me about bothering his wife? Or maybe have The Dick give me another talking to? Being almost the oldest man in town, maybe he figured my presence kept the others away.

And being the man of action I think I am, in the morning after a sleepless night more or less, I beat it on down to the coffee house and moved in, a little ahead of schedule.

"George called," she told me when she arrived and had gotten her coffee, roll, put her sweater over the chair back, and gave me that long, strong look, her morning smile, and I felt her knee brush mine. She smiled more.

Is she a tease and I'm just here as a prop in her game?

She certainly looked good to me, with some kind of ethnic blouse on that was a little tight with a scoop neck showing a lot of cleavage. For one un-responsible moment I wondered if she and I should have been the ones in The Hut the other night having a moment of bliss together instead of Marty and Sara. I allowed my eyes to leave her bosom and move up to her face and there she was smiling at me some more. She knew what I was studying so thoroughly and smiled even broader. Then she fooled me by reaching over to squeeze my hand, instead of acting incensed at my too obvious study of her prominent anatomy this morning.

"We're going to have to find you a girl," was her comment, outsmarting me again.

"No-o-o," was my response. "I've found what excites me right here in town." And that wasn't what I had started out to say, so my face started getting red, me at 84 years and her at a young 55.

We sat there a long time, looking at each other, thinking things, I suppose.

Finally, to break out of this deadlock, I offered, "You look very nice today. I applaud you."

"I knew I would see you and thought I would put on something you would like."

"You have succeeded."

"I am pleased." She hesitated a long time, her face changing slightly, then a breath and: "Trevor, I have never known someone that makes me feel so special." I started to speak but she held up a hand, the 'no' sign. 'Stop,' 'Say not a word,' all with that one gesture. "My husband returns tonight, and I will be there to greet him. If not I might be tempted to do something foolish." She looked at me a long minute. "Have you ever felt that way?"

In my gallant and flirtatious mood I said, "Every time I sit here with you."

She snorted.

"Trevor, you are a devil," and laughed.

In this mood, I picked up my cup, saucer, and plate, and moved over one chair to be next to her. Immediately my hand, beneath the table and out of sight of the world, moved to squeeze her knee, but ran into her hand coming in my direction. We each started and laughed. Aren't we a bunch though!

"Now tell me, Mrs. Cunningham, what time does he arrive?"

The plane gets into Bangor around ten, by the time he gets his car out of the lot and on the road, he'll be here at the house about twelve fifteen."

"And you are ready for him?"

"Yes."

"You have the bunny costume on, holding a silver tray out to him, his welcome home Martini, and what else?"

"That pretty much is it. Not a bunny costume but I have a special dress that fits me well and reaches almost to my knees. It suits him." She waited a moment, watching me absorb that, and then added, "It works for him. Would it work for you?"

"Try me," I said while at that moment I gave her knee a good healthy squeeze and thought of tossing an envelope of sugar down her cleavage, but didn't, lost the moment, and we were talking about Marty and Sara.

"She's two or three days pregnant, right?"

"It' kind of hard to tell at this point."

"She did come in late and looked tired in the morn."

"And Marty? He came in with her?"

"You know, I don't know. He was down in the cellar with his woodworking skills and I went to bed. I gave him a lot of talk about The Hut where you women folk were going and I thought he was pretty well primed, but didn't stay up to see him off. I was out blotto the minute I hit the sack." I looked at her steadily. It was plainly obvious that I'd let my end down, being as I was supposed to see that he went there, even take him, if necessary. Cripe! I had flubbed up.

Jerk Johnson, son of the ex-mayor, and on unemployment came over and sat with us at that moment, which saved her chewing me out privately. She did it publicly, more or less running over my responsibilities as if I was her sick cat we were talking about so he wouldn't know. It was dumb, I know. I could have fallen back on my advanced age as an excuse, but knew she wouldn't buy that, so I took a gentle tongue lashing.

Jeff came in. He stopped by for a few words, got his order for the men on the job and left.

"He looked tired."

"But he was happy about life." I said, and then we looked at each other. No saying what we were thinking, but we both knew.

She finally said something like, "Oh my God." And that was all.

"Don't think it," I added.

"You're right," she said, and took my hand as I squeezed it. I like that woman. And she certainly looked well put together, and she said it was for me! Well, I can accept that. I got up to leave, seeing that my hand ran up her arm as I stood. She held my hand at her shoulder for a moment, and then we were separated for the day. Unlike my usual pattern of walking about town and talking with one and everyone, I beat it on home, wishing Mandy would be there to meet me.

Sara was home getting a lunch put together and I sat at the table watching her and chatting, all the while wondering who met her there since she got in so late. Mandy had said she left there on some pretext and went and hid up by the big rock, listening. As I looked back on it we had both flubbed up: me with Marty and she with Sara for she should have waited to see who came. Well, it was over and done, and then I perked up. We could arrange another tryst. Why not?

So in this buoyant mood I watched Marty come in for lunch and after a routine type of conversation with his wife ask her why she got in so late.

Got in so late? Why would he ask her that if he was with her?

And presently she said that she'd been with 'Manda and they'd lost track of time and all of a sudden it was late-late-late and they both beat it for home. Marty nodded the way husbands do, not really paying attention, but I came alert! They left together and it was late-late-late? That wasn't what Mandy said. So what was going on down there at The Hut late-late-late in the evening, or rather in the morning. I must have looked at Marty too long, for he asked me some question about where 'Manda had been last night. I shrugged and said, 'The Hut, I guess. That's where she said she was going, I think." I looked at Sara.

He interrupted my stare with, "You see 'Manda a lot, what did she say this morning?"

"Huh? Nothing. Why?"

"The two of them were out together, going down to that hut for something. She didn't say anything about what?"

'Well, I don't think so. "What's going on down there?" I wanted to act dumb.

I must have succeeded because Sara started talking and he, ignoring my non-answer joined with her and I was left alone, the two of them bantering away and giggling. Something about that place that had happened in the long ago and I was left out. The two getting on too well, which was as it was supposed to be, but it somehow didn't fit how I thought two lovers would act. They should be making references about last night, not ten years ago. Well anyway I thought I should get back to 'Manda and see if she had any clues. I knew she didn't, or she'd have mentioned it this morning at the coffee house. I left the two and went out on the porch where I could look down the hill way off down there and see 'Manda's house, where she'd cut the brush so she could see up here and check Sara with her binoculars. That lane was empty of people, 'Manda was off somewhere on one of her personal missions for the church, or library work or something else. I could see the car way down there and that gave me a shock. That meant George was home, early too.

I went down there after lunch, and of course my walk went by Bernice's house, and a voice caught my attention. I kept going, pretending I'd heard nothing, but it was a familiar voice, George's voice there at Bernice's, just like weeks ago.

Dare I hesitate and listen? No. But I did.

Didn't do no good, couldn't get the words. It was a quiet conversation and I heard nothing. B&B was mentioned, and the detective, and I heard 'Manda's name. What, why, news, gossip, nothing. So on, making a pass within seeing distance of Mandy and George's house, on to the barber shop and three guys sitting out front. I greeted them and they reciprocated. I waited, and got included in the conversation. B&B was there, him saying to me, "That Cunningham man still talking to Bernice?"

I nodded and B&B nodded too, and said, "That Cunningham's getting as bad as The Dick." and looked about and the three of them laughed. "I'm going to have to do him in, too."

This was interesting. I hadn't realized that B&B knew of George's talks with Bernice. How many were there anyway? I asked.

B&B shook his big body a trace and thumped his index finger into his other palm 8 or 10 times. "Too many, I'd say." He looked up at me, gestured to the step next to where he was sitting and I sat. "Now I'll tell ya, sonny. A woman accepts a man's good intentions and that means something. Later on, be she young, when she's grown a bit more she could do a man a few favors, ya know what I mean? Seems only natural, ya know?"

I allowed as how it was possible, but then wondered about how long a B&B type would wait for the pay off. "She graduates this coming June. How long do you reckon it'll take for her to realize her obligation?"

The other two were paying attention. No one spoke, and I bet five minutes went by as we greeted passer-bys. Me, I was looking, watching up and down the street, and was pretty sure that was 'Manda way down with two other of 'the girls' coming this way. B&B broke the silence.

"Tuggy. You go into the refrigerator inside and bring us a few beers," and Tuggy was up and going inside as B&B spoke. "Didn't want Tuggy hearing this, he's not big enough, but you know, I got half a mind to tell George Cunningham if he don't get that Dick out of here within a week I'll burn his fucking house down."

Bassett, not the swiftest, replied. "What's wrong with his house? I always thought it was okay." He looked around at us.

"The Dick's going to carry Bernice off?"

A sincere and penetrating look from B&B. "He's trying his best. And she may be at that spot where she's adventuresome."

"You're going to keep her then?"

"Of course. Damned right. She's got good tits and swings that ass nice. She's worth the bother."

"She agreeable, or she getting to argue?"

"She'll do what I say. But these guys, The Dick and now Cunningham hanging around and talking to her, I ain't saying they're being indecent, she don't have an indecent bone in her body, but they'll wear her down."

"Could be she'll be offended by all the attention and come to hide in your arms."

"Now wouldn't that be just nice? But I tell you that "The Dick" was there by her house most every night when I brought her home. Damned annoying. George has got to send him back to wherever he got him. If he don't I'll have to do it."

"Why that? Since he could run a Christian class outdoors he's got plenty to do. It might take up his time."

B&B pointed a finger at me. "Well maybe he could, but the minister don't think it's too good an idea. It's a contest between the two of 'em, who's the most God fearing? Maybe those two can fight it out."

"The minister's too small, a wimp. But I'll say he's getting more spruced up about this matter than he was at first."

."I suppose like lots of meditative type men he could go on for years and then finally get riled and lash out and kill him even. Trouble is, I don't think I can wait that long."

"You got serious long range plans for Bernice?"

He just smiled and looked at me rather out of the corner of his eye. He nodded but would not speak. I wondered if he and Bernice had reached some kind of agreement. It set my imagination running and I could see George in my mind's eye, leaning against Bernice outside her back door, George going total jerk, leaning against her, and fingering her skirt around her thighs, and as she moved past him his free hand holding onto her rump and where would that fantasy go from there? Him with such a nice wife and letting his forty or fifty year old adolescent desire lead him into an affair that would wreck his marriage. God, some people are so weak minded, or so led astray by today's television entertainment or the oh so public lives of the theater or TV or Hollywood set and their no-moral limits.

I heard B&B saying he'll get the raw end of his shotgun, once and for all.

"You'd do that to George?"

"Hell no, don't you listen? That big detective with all his manners and ideas has no idea how to catch himself a bed-mate. George? George ain't got the guts to strip down Bernice and have a little nooky." He stopped abruptly, looking at me, a frown forming. "I gotta keep my mouth shut."

It wasn't lost on me and I popped up, spontaneously, with, "She pregnant? Is she?"

It was no good. No more lapses of confidentially from B&B tonight. "So shoot him." I finally offered and he took it seriously. "Damn right. If someone else doesn't, I may have to do it myself. She's my girl and stays that way."

"She's going to college in a couple of months." I put that in to see if he had any expectations for after she was gone.

"Naw, no, she ain't. Might send her off to hospital training in the fall."

"She'll have her baby while working there?"

Big frown. "You certainly do have babies on the brain. Why ain't you messing around with someone?"

I was, actually. 'Manda. But I wasn't saying nothing about it to him. He'd tell his cronies and a wonderful thing, a wonderful friendship would go sour.

He said two guys down at the bar were after The Dick's hide. "Seems he punched one in the face for some infraction. It seems that some man's daughter came into the bar to get her father and Dad wasn't ready to leave and said so, and the two got in a family squabble there in the bar and father finally gave the girl a wallop back of the head that sent her sprawling and The Dick got into it and beat the daylights out of the man for talking badly to the girl and whacking her. He picked up the girl and escorted her home, so the story went. Don't know how that would set between the two of them when Dad finally came home, broken nose and all, but that's the way things go nowadays. So the guys at the bar have no love for that man. He'll get his someday."

It certainly looked like The Dick was making a fiefdom of the town and it would run in his way or not at all.

One of the guys that had been listening to us chat came up to me after B&B left and said, "You weren't there Saturday night, were you?"

"At the dance? No, I was there late but not 'till mid-time, I'd say." ('Manda and I had come at about the same time and went off for a stroll together). "Why?"

"Couple of big fights."

"They always have fights when I'm not there. It ain't fair. So what happened?"

"B&B was getting up to get his girl and some out-of-towner burst in and grabbed her wrist and pulled her toward the door. Barry Gelatin had been talking to her and she got pulled right out from under his gaze, so he took after the two of them. It was funny for Bernice went along pretty quick with him, that-out-of-towner, almost like she wanted to go."

"The out-of-towner gave Barry a cuff to the shoulder and Barry, he's skinny but gots muscles, you know, works out, yells, and punches the guy and they were at it. At first Bernice got in it, someone's fist ripped the shoulder of her dress and when I looked next it seemed like the whole left side was bare right down to the tit, that half of it. She jumped around trying to fix it decent like and these two fight around her. Damnedest funny thing I ever saw and somehow she lost the back of her dress, down and ripped wide, well, most folk were trying to get around front of her to see her, you know how she's always been the one with the biggest pair in the high school class, well that forced the fight around twisting to the left and the people trying to see her and blows here and there. She got her front covered and away from those two and then B&B was there and people falling away, you known like they do, letting him in and the fight was over. So off they go, but, BUT, The Dick appears out of the dark while B&B is chiding people for not stopping the fight and pulls her into the dark and then here's B&B and the Dick circling each other like a couple of banty cocks and her over there in almost a swoon and other women about her and she's all together and B&B walking away from The Dick and coming and taking her hand and leading her away. Did ya ever wonder what those two do?"

"Not me brother, I got enough problems"

"B&B said he'd wipe that guy off the earth."

"Everybody talks tough, but no one does anything."

"I guess I saw you and Mrs. Cunningham come in about then."

"Yeah, I guess we missed it."

"Yeah, well, that's the way it goes."

"B&B put her in the car and drove off?"

"A-yep, like always."

"What d'ya think they do, those two?"

"Can't say, maybe he just drives her home."

I rolled my eyes. "What do you think they do?"

He smiled, made something of a face and curled his left index finger and thumb into a nice little round circle, and thrust his right index finger into it

Later on 'Manda and I talked about it. I asked her, "What'd'ya think's gonna happen?"

"It doesn't matter. They'll go on until someone gets hurt bad and then it'll stop."

"Yeah, winner or looser, one'll have Bernice and the other'll have nothing but hurt bones and a messed up face, and a grudge."

She looked up at me and said, "That's what it's like going west."

I laughed and pulled her tight to me, my hand being around her waist. She felt good. Soft and curvy. I did want to kiss her. But we've kept it pure and simple all this time and to start into an affair would be real stupid.

We walked down Main Street a bit and then she said, "We shouldn't be parading around with you on my waist and me all empty headed and waiting for you to take me here in the middle of Main Street."

"You're right." But I did it anyway. I bent slightly and kissed her forehead. Foreheads are foreheads, but this one felt good. And then I felt her arm go around my neck and I was pulled down again and our lips went right to the target. We kissed. A long and soft one. Her lips were perfect. We held it and held it. I think I've never felt such a nice kiss, and from someone I wanted, had wanted, for days or weeks or months, ever since I'd set eyes on her. And it wasn't a kiss alone. I was with her body pressing up into me, and me down onto her and I'm glad we were in the middle of Maine Street. Yep, she felt so-o-o good.

Then a voice. "Ok you two, go on home. No doing that in public."

He came out of the dark by the barber shop: The Dick. There were no street lights there and he hadn't seen us clearly. Now he recognized me and out of his mouth the old swear words. "Jesus Christ. You, too? For heavens sake this whole bloody town's one great berzerk!"

He was coming out into the street and I trying to step left or right or whatever it needed to keep him from seeing it was 'Manda. She was dancing left and right too, slightly, trying to back off toward the other side of the street an get behind a building and away, but it wasn't easy. It was up to me now.

"Who's that with you? That Bernice? You bastard!"

"It weren't her," spoken in my best lower-class talk.

She was across and headed into an alley, and he spying out and not seeing clearly in the dark and saying, "That ain't Bernice. Who is that?"

So 'Manda got away, and I took a half-blow in the gut which was tolerable and staggered off toward Marty and Sara's.

Chapter 46
The Best Forbidden Kisses in the World

That night I was looking out my bedroom window down the hill to the lane 'Manda had cut in her gardening enterprise and saw, maybe after twenty or thirty minutes, what looked like the wink of a flashlight. A weak little pin prick of light in the dark. 'Manda had said some time ago that she'd cut out that swath so that she could step out and look up the hill, way up here with her binoculars and see what Sara was doing, part of our attempt to find the perfect moment when we could get her alone down there in The Hut so that she and Marty could have their tryst. Why blinking now, and a signal to whom?

I bounced out of bed and into my duds and was downstairs in a jiffy. It had to be me, selfish, self-centered man that I am, besides I knew Sara wasn't home, out with her girlfriends tonight and that brought me up short.

Out with her girlfriends?

Where? With who? Out?

Marty was snoring away in his bedroom as I went by so when I saw the bike standing by the rail to the porch, off I went scooting' down the hill.

"I could see someone coming with the binoculars when you passed under the street light up there," she greeted me as I slid to a stop next to her. 'I didn't know if you'd see my signal or not." And with that she was against me, her arms around my neck and I got a kiss. The bike fell to the ground and I was grabbing her around the back and pulling her tight and she was sort of quietly giggling as I swept in for a real kiss. She did great kisses. And me, reaching around I realized that she was in her pajamas. A house-coat was over them, and I realized about then that I was under it and only the light pajama separated us. She was mumbling something, badly interfered with since I was extending the kisses around her cheeks and face, and I hadn't really realized I was so hungry for love, for her. Then the words took form "George went off several hours ago and I don't know where he went, maybe to see that brute of a detective he hired."

"Oh Gawd!" was my reply.

"He thinks we're like lovers, always being seen together as we are."

"Oh Gawd!" my reply again, then, "George or the detective?"

"The detective. George has already dismissed us, thinks that you are an old codger trying to act like a teenager." I could see her staring at me, waiting for the reaction. And I did feel put down. Christ. Me? Acting like a teenager?

She laughed suddenly and grabbed me to her, pressing into me with her head sideways and rubbing her cheek against my lips. "You look so positively dejected! It's funny. Don't feel that way. I think I love you in some impossible way. I realized it a few days ago." Then she pulled away, holding onto me by the shoulder blades and pressing off me, still connected waist down. "Trevor, I love you!" and she was shaking her head at me as if unable to believe herself.

"Well by gum," was my thought. I pulled her in for another kiss, or three or four, and then we separated, holding each other by a hand. "And I love you, but you've probably known that for weeks."

She nodded, her eyebrows up and then a soft kiss. She gently said "Yes. And it's something we've got to deal with, but not now, later. Listen, I think he's ready to give a report, a comprehensive report to George and we'll be included in it."

"George already knows we see each other for our early morning coffee. What's the big deal? You said he'd written me off. Actually he's right. I'm too old for love."

She gave a snort. "When he's around, not off on business, he shows up everywhere I am, spies on me. Thinks I'm with some man, or if not, on my way to some man to have a meeting, and so on."

You are. With me."

"Yes, but it's not universal like George thinks. It's sterile, one man. You. He thinks I'm making myself available to every man I see."

"Our love is not sterile. It's very much alive. And we've hardly started."

"Harumpf!"

I held off from kissing her right ear and looked at her. "How would you do that, make yourself available?"

"Oh come off it. You know. You've seen girls making gestures or looks or posturing all your life. I've watched you at the Saturday dances. You watch them. You watch me."

"Are you, do you, posture for me?"

"I try to be more discrete. Like right now. I shouldn't be out here talking with you. He'll come home and we'll be caught. We're not doing anything wrong, but he'll put some determination on it. I must go in. Out here in pajamas and a house coat is asking for trouble."

I had her, hands around her again, and we held that way. The old comment about two people against a cruel world came to mind and I released her. Too far fetched for us. No chance we could be that close, so I pushed her away gently and turned my back and looked down the hillside, down the street past the street light farther down where the hill sloped into the flats of the town, a mess of confusion running about my head.

When I turned back with desire at my right elbow, she was gone.

Gone. She took the best kisses in the world with her. Forbidden kisses.

Chapter 47
The Lure of The Hut

I was panting, as usual, when I got up the hill and entered the house and there was Marty looking at me. "Seen Sara?"

I glanced at the grandfather's clock by the staircase. Eleven twenty-five. I shook my head. "I went down to Cunningham's. Saw a light down there and wondered if Mandy or George were in trouble and signaling for help. Why? Didn't Sara go out with the girls? I thought that's what she said at supper." It dawned on me that this was the night 'Manda and I had figured on getting the second tryst, the make-up tryst to replace the botched one days ago. We were so engrossed with each other that we didn't even get to the real effort, the effort toward reproduction, to put it bluntly. What was Marty doing here? He should be down by the chasm in The Hut making love to Sara. I looked seriously at Marty. Why wasn't he down there? Krimminy. Neither 'Manda nor I had given it a single thought in our little meeting, she being so wrapped up in propriety tonight. That is what it was. Our own kisses had so googled us up that we'd both forgotten. Cripe!

He was supposed to have gotten a tiny envelope in the mail today, a tiny envelop that Sara and 'Manda had slaved over, a very private and somewhat sexually slanted invitation to "meet me at The Hut. I'm going to slip out of my friends' grasp and be there at eleven. Meet me, dearest beloved." Something like that. So what do I say to the missing swain, "Did the mail come today?"

He looks at me funny. "Nothing for you. You expecting another Social Security check this month? No way. Once a month only, my friend."

I shrugged, wondering if it came tomorrow, what would that do? Obviously the dates wouldn't match, although maybe we could get Sara to go down again. Meet him, fall in love again. Become pregnant. 'Manda had done a lot of research finding out when Sara's fertile period would be. It was supposed to be tonight. Cripe!

"So what was going on down there? You say a 'help' signal?"

"Naw. Neighborhood boys with flashlights looking for worms. Going fishing tomorrow, I guess."

A thought occurred to me. Who was supposed to mail that note? I don't remember 'Manda saying.

"Just as well. The Dick is beginning to think you and 'Manda Cunningham are in the process of getting tied up together. He could tell George and stifle that in a jiffy. You two are being seen together too much, lately."

My heart jumped. I thought we were in the clear. I made a scoffing sound and stepped to the stairs.

"If he knew you went running down the hill to her for a bunch of flashes he'd think you were well beyond first stages. He thinks everyone in this town is looking for a change in their matrimonial setup so you're no exception." I could see he didn't believe that and was teasing.

"You talking about George or The Dick? He is a nut, The Dick, I mean. A total nut, but then George hired him so I suppose they're much the same. I should take a pop at the Dick myself, everyone else seems to want to."

"Hey that's true isn't it. Might myself. But he's stayed away from Sara and me. Remember he came into town just after I bopped Jeff's nose for starting to mess with Sara, so he probably thinks we're the only three left in the valley that ain't into tryst and love nests and all that stuff."

"Could be perfect for you then, have a little tryst and enjoy it and he'd never suspect."

"Maybe you and 'Manda."

"We're good friends, that's all; and George knows. You should pop onto yer hoss and beat it down to The Hut and see if there's a lonely woman waiting there. Give it a shot."

"Ya know I was going out for a walk when I heard your footsteps. Another one sneaking up my back steps, so I waited and it was you and of course Sara ain't here so what's anyone not in the family doing here. I was about ready to blast yer head off." He gestured to the wall where his shot gun usually hung. It was gone.

"Well I'm here to protect the misses so go take your walk. Go down to The Hut and scare the hell out of someone." I gave a laugh and went on up. Would he? Would it be too late to meet Sara there? I wanted to call 'Manda and tell her we'd blown the whole deal. Him here and Sara off with the girls, but should I? Should I call her?

I called.

She'd been outside in her jammies and house coat which meant that George wasn't home, or so I thought. Well, he answered the phone so I kept quiet while he gradually yelled into it, "Who is this? You bastard, answer! Call up my wife, will ya, just wait 'till I find out who you are," and stuff of that nature. I hung up rather upset. I'd encouraged the worst in George, and he'd blame Mandy and it'd get worse between them. He'd think all his suspicions were true, and that would be my fault.

I laid in bed, unsleeping, thinking. Sara was out, someplace hopefully waiting for her lover, supposedly Marty, if he got there. So an hour had gone by and Marty was still gone, supposedly meeting her at The Hut, if he went where I said.

I wasn't sleeping and after another forty-five minutes I got up, dressed in my blue pants and black shirt and headed out. Down the back stairs, onto the bike and into town, an old codger like me riding a bicycle in the dark, a little on the more stupid side. I left it in a clump of bushes near the bridge a little farther back than I'd have liked because there was a car parked close into the brush beside the road. I figured it was some young couple and that wasn't my business. I had to keep focused on The Hut. So bike out of sight and me being undiscovered as far as I knew, I went through the brush to the path, in the dark it looked a helluva lot closer to the chasm's edge than in the daytime. Still I had to do this so I moved along the path as quickly as I could, being extra careful. If I ran into Marty along the way he'd wonder what the devil I was up to but I had to know that he got there and it was going along as planned.

I was by that twisted oak that almost blocked the path, meaning I was getting close, several hundred feet away but too far to hear their sounds, if they made sounds while making love, that is. I'm by that twisted hunk of wood that almost blocks the path and stepping on tip-toe to avoid stones clicking and twigs snapping revealing my approach. A regular redskin I was. Silent as a breath of air. I never thought I could be so quiet.

That's when a stone hit the path in front of me. A gigantic big whump. So much for stealth.

I was stone dead, that is not a movement came from me for fear of revealing where I was and what I was up to and who I was.

I waited.

I started breathing again, listening for all I was worth. Who heaved that stone at me, or into the path, or whatever the hell they were up to? Was it Marty, hiding, waiting for Sara or was it Sara hiding and waiting to see who'd come. It was supposed to be Marty, leastwise that's what 'Manda said she'd told Sara. She and her husband supposed to meet like in the days of their courtship. Slip back a generation to put them in the mood and then the ninth-month penalty.

Then I heard very quiet noises. The snap of a twig, the splat of a branch against a body. A sound like a foot feeling for footing.

My body slowly, quietly rotated in place until ready to see, to run out of there and back up the path, or put up my arms and ward off a blow.

Something whitish was out there moving my way, very slowly. Not as high as me, but still coming, becoming more distinct.

"Mandy!"

Mandy in her pajamas and suddenly she was here next to me, in my arms and whispers. And she was kissing my lips, and I was holding onto her like we were meant for each other. Me feeling her body, maybe making sure I wasn't dreaming, but whatever she was she was warm and soft feeling and sure enough it was Mandy.

She didn't stop my exploring searching hands, but broke off the kiss and asked, "What are you doing here?"

"What are YOU doing here? I just called your house a half hour ago and George answered. Why are you here?"

"I heard. He was angry. He's back to his old thinking. He thinks someone was trying to reach me. Jealous. Why'd you call? It set him off. I knew it was you. No one else would call me at that hour."

"Marty was home, and I thought he wasn't going to get to The Hut and wanted to talk with you about everything going wrong. He's gone now. Or was when I left. I came here to see if he made it. If she was here. All that."

"After we talked, and then you called, and I knew it had to be you, and I guessed why. So I came down to see. What are we going to do?"

I still had my arms around her, she warm against me, the pajama's light material separating us. She was no skinny piece of pipe; she was a real woman with solid parts and more than lovely to hold. Who was supposed to be having this tryst, us or Sara and Marty?

We whispered our way into a decision. "We've got to get closer and see who's in there and then get the hell back to our beds."

I might have been silent as a zephyr when I came down the path, but she heard me, so this time I was as quiet as an autumn leaf released from its branch and she, still clasped to me was like my own silent feet working toward The Hut. It was still a distance and we were getting there when I head a man's laughter. It stopped us dead for a minute or so, and then we were working closer, coming down the path. We branched off on one of those little pathways around The Hut like there is, coming up on it from the rear, pretty much.

And now voices whispering like ours and sounding like shouts ricocheting off clouds like thunder does, rolling back and forth among the clouds. A man and a woman.

"It's Sara," I said quietly in the ear next to me and 'Manda moved against me, rubbing differently from when we walked all wrapped in each other as we were.

"Who's the other one?"

"I can't tell."

"Sh-h-h."

"It doesn't sound like Marty."

"My God!"

"Who is it? Can you tell?"

Whoever it was there was shuffling around. Pretty much as 'Manda and I moved together against each other, getting ourselves sorted into a more comfortable position between the two of us, and listening.

We couldn't see a thing of course. It was dark and we were out back and couldn't have seen anyway, but the sounds to two people in there were like you'd expect from a couple of lovers, an occasional real word or whole series, and the moving of clothes or blankets of people getting themselves settled. And sentences of comforting words one to the other and so it went.

"We've gotta get back."

"Yeah. At least we know they got together."

"Then we're a success."

"We'll know in nine months."

"Maybe four."

I gave her a squeeze.

"I GOTCHA, YOU FORNICATING BASTARDS. I GOTCHA YA. I KNEW I WOULD."

"That's The Dick!"

"Over there on the other side of the chasm. How'd he find us?"

"Not us, them in the Hut."

Both of us, choral speech: "We've gotta get out of here." And she was pressing against me as if herding cattle.

We were moving, slowly and not as quietly as we'd come.

"There you are. I see you, you cussed Anti-Christians, I've got you." And then in a quieter voice as he fought with himself. "Where's my glasses." Then yelling. "I got 'em. I can see in the night with these. I'll have your names and tomorrow the sheriff'll pick you up for breaking God's Laws. YH-h-H-h!" He let out a massive yell.

"Night glasses, 10 by 50s, I bet. I swept 'Manda around in front of me with my back to the other side of the chasm to protect her from sight and identification, and she was falling. There we were, both of us on the ground in a tussle. There amid the bushes, out of sight. She was groping at me and I trying to pull her my way, we were crawling along one of those little paths around The Hut, keeping low amid the brush and moving up the path. He'd come across the rope bridge in a moment and really get us.

"DON'T YOU TRY AND GET AWAY NOW, HEY WHERE YOU NOW, YOU BLASPHEMERS. I'LL GET YOU. I GOT MY CAMERA HERE. YOU'RE HEADED FOR THE GALLOWS. FORNICATORS, HERE I COME."

We could hear the groaning of the ropes on the rope bridge as it does when someone is crossing.

"Christ. He's coming." 'Manda was ahead of me, moving as fast as she could along the path. It came out into the open onto the regular path and I ran into her, for she stopped, unsure whether to run or crawl into the brush at the side. My arms went around her as I heard, we both heard, a new voice.

"Back off, buzzard. I'll chop the bridge and you'll die."

"Whose voice was that?"

"It's her lover. Must be."

"Not Marty."

"Who? But we've gotta go." I was wrapped into her.

"Not Marty. NOT MARTY?" she was too loud.

" Sh-h-h-h."

"Oh my God."

We were peeking out from our set of bushes. Seeing shapes by the end of the bridge and some form scurrying back to the other side, about a third of the way across and going back fast. Then The Dick and the man on this side were yelling back and forth.

"It's Jeff," said 'Manda as she grabbed my clothes and pressed close, her mouth in my ear. "If, no it's –"

"Forget it. We've gotta get out of here while he's arguing with him." And we went fast, crashing through the bushes and up the trail. On the other side The Dick was yelling at someone, whoever it was on this side and starting up the path. Someone else was with him, another form which had to be Sara, the two running to escape him. He didn't know we were also over here. The Dick with his camera and binoculars and whatever else he had moving up the path on the other side, flashing his light and revealing his position. There was a gunshot. Oh! He had a gun, too. The two of them were on our side and he on the other trying to get them to stop. He was standing on the tip of the chasm like he was going to fly over them and take prisoners.

"Stay back you fool," Jeff's voice. "You'll-"

Sara screamed. I had Mandy round the waist, and we watched through the bushes.

We saw the tiniest movement as he tried to fling himself back and up but it was no good. He was losing his gadgets, things falling from him as he grabbed back toward the cliff face, but he was low and slipping fast. The Dick was falling off the chasm wall, some stones falling with him and behind him as he went down.

"GOD!" choral speech again. "God."

'Manda's mouth was opening and she was about to scream too when I got a hand on her face to stifle it. With her free hand over her mouth as she conformed to my tugs, we were as soundless as possible on the little stones along the path and the bushes all over.

And we were running. Back along the path we heard Sara scream again and the man's voice and The Dick gone down, his screams diminishing as he dropped farther then the roar of the chasm's water covering his shouts. We stopped again and looked, the overhang giving us a view, but it was dark and he was gone. The noise from any screams down there covered by splashes, if he screamed. Gone.

Chapter 48
Out and Away

"Oh my God," Mandy said, leaning forward to see better into the chasm. What could one see in this darkness? The moon was out and full, but the chasm was deep and shadowy. There was nothing to see, but she leaned anyway, looking.

I held her, drew her back, too near the edge herself and no need for two deaths this night. She clasped her hands over mine circling her waist and allowed herself to move back, turned to me to speak when another strong scream came from down the path near The Hut. She jumped at its suddenness as did I, and we looked into each other's face. My God. Again?

I tugged at her and we started running up the path again, "They will come," I said. "They will want to get away, too. We must go. Hurry."

Thus we went, her hand in mine being tugged along over the bed rock spots, over the small stones and around the occasional bush, keeping as far from the chasm edge as possible. The roar of the river below flinging itself over the boulders that made it so treacherous for the once-a-decade white water enthusiast that wanted to give it a try. Of those, most gave up before they entered the real narrow and deep part, the rocks too many and too dangerous. In the worst case scenario a few bodies were pulled out, well down stream and away from the gorge where the river becomes tranquil at the small lake there and then weaves on down through the forest to the beach on the ocean where it looked placid and calm and inviting. But we weren't down in the chasm messing in the danger directly, only running along its edge, careful to avoid the fate of its latest victim. We were running up the narrow trail between cliff on one side and the chasm on the other, running as best we could, here up and over a steep section. At the higher spot we stopped, she becoming a drag on my arm pulling her along.

She was panting, as was I, an eighty-year old geezer ain't any better than an ordinary woman at this point. Next to me she turned to look down the trail, then released my hand and took two steps toward the edge and peered over, seeking to see into the gorge, seeking to see The Dick down there, sitting miraculously on a boulder and waiting for the sun to come up and expecting help in getting out.

He wasn't there, naturally, and who could see to the bottom where the dark was darker and all obscure? He'd gone in a little ways up from The Hut and that was hundreds of feet downstream from here. I said all that, explaining to her, and she stepped back and looked at me, shuddering at how a life ends.

I shrugged.

She spoke. "He was a dreadful man, yet still a life is gone from Earth. Our God, his God, the one he prayed to and worked to spread his gospel for, and for that he was important. He's gone." She looked to me. "Does that make sense?"

She never got her answer. There was another scream, a series, and we listened, then turned and started away, becoming frightened of them coming behind us, for that's how it sounded, like they had abandoned The Hut and were escaping the incident as we were.

'Why are we running?" 'Manda asked amid pants behind me, coming along at my tug. "Why – can't– we wait– and meet them, see what– they saw?"

"No way. Everyone– knows –the use of – that place – and do you – want people talking about you – like you – were there for a tryst?"

It took maybe twenty more paces and then her answer. "Oh Trevor, would they think that way?" she had come to a stop and I couldn't tug her into motion. I turned, looking at her in the moonlight and seeing her panting and standing there, her chest working. We only had a little more to go to the road and then the car and we'd be away. She let her head drop and panted. Her chest working and again I was impressed with how much the woman she was. I stepped close, her hand in mine, moved toward her with my arm around her waist we looked back down the trail. We'd see whoever it was, the moon was bright and the gorge side reflected it, it was lighter down there.

"Who was the man with Sara?" I whispered into her ear.

"Do you really think it was Marty, like it was supposed to be?"

"It had to be Marty."

"I'm not sure." I listened carefully, wondering where they were now. There were no screams, nor ever had I heard a man's voice. "In fact, I don't think it was Marty."

She curled around and faced me, "No? Not Marty? Who then? Did you tell anyone but him she'd be here?"

I shook my head. "Of course not. Maybe she said something to her girlfriends. They could have sent someone to meet her."

'Manda was so close. Very close. Of course the trail was narrow, and I certainly didn't want her crossing over to the edge and looking out again. Foolish girl, she could slip, too, just as he had, a loose bit of rock or sand, and she'd be gone. It was too much to think of and I got my arm around her waist again and urged her toward me, pressing us back from the cliff side and looking back there to see how far from the edge we were. Her arms came around me.

"It's close here. Do you think it was an accident?"

"Think it was an accident? Well-l, an accident he did to himself. I didn't see anyone else around. Enough people have said they'd kill him or get even, but he was there all alone. At least as I saw it." I was whispering, trying to listen for sounds of their coming. "We've got to move on, we don't want to get caught here."

"Are you sure? It was shadowy. Someone could have been in the shadows, even he wouldn't see them. Of course he was upset for what he thought was going on, he might not have noticed."

"I don't think so, no one else." We were in each other's arms and whispering. She felt warm. "We need to move on. No one should see us here."

"It's alright. No one's coming. It was so sudden, and he was so noisy, yelling at them."

"Well, he did have it on the mark, they were into making love I imagine. That's what we got them together for, you know."

She pulled tighter against me, "I know. Were we wrong?"

"I don't know, but this isn't the time to be discussing it. We've gone over it enough. We thought we were right." The pressure of her bosom against my chest was delightful and my hands were running up and down her back. Her pajamas under her housecoat felt loose at the waist and, yes,

I liked the feel of her. Experimentally I kissed her hair, and pulled her tighter. This was as close as we could get. She was looking up now and I kissed her on the forehead. I was losing focus. This girl is altogether too distracting, even in a situation like this. We MUST move on.

"Should we be doing this?" and there was a tug and flurry and she was pulling at me and her lips were on mine and I was responding, pulling away from her bosom. Too much. Me! At my age! We should move along before someone appeared. No one but us knew of this tryst of Sara's.

Our kiss had the most wonderful feel to it, so soft, moist, giving, and yet offering, and I was responding, pressing back, feeling the tips of her breasts touching me, and I wanted her.

A sound came from way down at the beginning of the steep climb. The Dick was gone over the side, and someone was coming up the path, escaping as we were doing. We had to move on. We'd be discovered and somehow implicated.

And yes, that was something of a foolish move, I thought later. He goes over the side and that's it for him. We were not directly implicated and certainly had nothing to fear. We knew of his death, and could, should, report it and avoid all the circumstances that were to come, but we didn't. We were two illicit people, afraid of having our late night messing around discovered, afraid of her husband knowing we were together, even though we had nothing to hide, but that was the crux of it. No one would believe we were just friends meeting in the dark. No one would believe that.

I broke our kissing, our feeling, for my hands were upon her nakedness under the pajama top and feeling of her softness. She was pressing against me. We had to stop. For heaven's sake I'm over eighty and she's just a kid. Maybe she is fifty five, but still thirty years younger than me. In forcing myself away, ignoring her sounds of desire I was putting the last caress once and for all done. No more chatting, no more making plans for other couple's pregnancies, no more interfering, that was for our God, or the God of The Dick who he had gone to assist, if his God did guide him and looked upon him with favor. He was an annoying and un-liked man, and had gotten his due.

So I pulled her arm and we were moving along a flat section of the path, the rock cliffs on our right and the gorge, the chasm, on our left, each in our own thoughts about what had happened. Not past tense. Yes, it had happened, but we were thinking not of that past event, but of what was happening now. How we fitted in and what would be said of us, if anyone knew. Our little "do good" experience had come to fruition and we had to move on out to save ourselves. We needed to be free of criticism, be able to look and talk of it impassionately. It had to be.

We went along far enough so that I knew we were out of the danger zone and could take our time, walk to her car, drive to her place, let me out and I'd walk up the hill to home. She'd be there, just coming from the girl's get-together, her story to George. Good.

That didn't fit. She was in pajamas and house coat. She'd not have been out with her girlfriends that way. I stopped. She bumped into me and again we were in eachother's arms.

"Mandy. I called George and he was home. How did you get out put together like that without him knowing, or questioning what you were up to?"

"I went down the back stairs. He's had this fixation on someone sneaking up the back stairs to have an in-house tryst with me. ME! He's had that idea for weeks. He even got his gun out once. I got the idea and tonight, while he was up there sleeping, I sneaked out the back way." She shrugged. "Okay?"

Well, there was no question that she knew her house, but it sounded like a touchy situation to me. "Can you get back?" We were plastered together again. I began worrying for her, trying to think up alternatives to being discovered by George, especially as she was dressed for, well, certainly not running around the chasm or anywhere else outside the home.

Her kiss ended with the words, "Don't worry. I have it worked out. Let's get going."

And we went, but still I kept worrying for her.

She was behind me now, and I felt her reaching around with her arms, pulling me back and turning me to her. "Trevor. We've made it."

And me like a fool, having resolved hardly five minutes ago to act like a gentleman and stop all this messing around found myself reaching around under her pajamas, to her skin, and reaching up her back and drawing her tightly to me, her arms around me and me bending my head to meet her lips. She knew what I was intending and we met, kissing and feeling. She pulled my shirt tail out and caressed me as I her. We were doing exactly what we both knew we shouldn't.

And we were doing it.

And did it, and did it, and did it.

I hadn't realized I was that swayed by her, wanted her that much, needed her that much, and she must have felt the same. She was in my arms, and we were entangled, and she was mine, at least for these brief minutes. Or I was hers. Sensibly we knew it had to stop and we moved on. Not a sound, no talking. Quiet and thoughtful. No doubt castigating ourselves individually.

We got to her car and drove off.

You know where that slight turn is in the road? Where there's that wide spot with a few bushes, enough to hide a car on that old section of road? That's where she stopped. No words were necessary. It served its purpose with me, needing a woman in my life that was more intimate than proper.

Somewhat later she dropped me off at the intersection where she turned toward her house, and without a word we parted. We'd had an hour and a half of intimacy and knew each other like folks deep in love should. I walked up the hill to the house. Marty was asleep in his room. Sara was driving in the yard and I pretended I was asleep.

Chapter 49
Over Between Us

In the morning Sara slept late and Marty went off to work with the usual disgruntled expression on his face. He said little when I asked, mostly grunting about lazy women unable to get their family underway in the morning.

Sara came down about nine-thirty, rested, gay, exuberant. Suddenly after about a half hour she went sullen, quiet and, well, she almost looked scared which held till lunch time. The phone rang and somebody was on the line talking to her, then she was oddly relieved. When the call ended she looked at me across the kitchen table, reaching to put the phone extension back on the shelf behind her.

That was Rachel," she said. "Said it was a great evening."

I nodded and stared into my Shredded Wheat.

Sometime later I found out that neither of them were where they said they were. Rachel was meeting occasionally with a fella from Canyon City. Somehow Sara and she found out about each other and covered for the other, which was a surprise. I never knew, and Marty didn't either, but these things do come out eventually. Not a pleasant surprise, and 'Manda and I felt like fools, but that's more the end of the story than now so let it ride for the moment.

I walked down to the coffee house even though it was late, not expecting 'Manda to be there. We'd pretty much expressed ourselves last night, for right or wrong, and I figured she'd feel the same. It had gone too far and we needed to quit before something happened and the whole town found out and got to talking. That was how I felt, and an honest feeling it was. And like always happens, it was shot out of the sky. Here I come sauntering along the sidewalk and turn onto Grover Cleveland Street to the *Empty Plate* and who should be coming up from a parked car but 'Manda. She was coming too, just in case I happened to be there. She'd thought it through and come to the same conclusion that we had to really stop this business growing between us. Well there she was, it all thought out and closed down forever. Here she was, and there I was, each having the same thoughts. So what do we do? What do any two do in the same circumstances? We walked up to each other, greeted, our eyes never leaving the other, turned as one, she took my arm as she always had when we met outside there at the coffee shop and walked in together, her maybe a little tighter to me than ever before, and me hugging that arm as close as I could and still looking nonchalant as we slid into our table.

She looked at me, and I looked at her, and believe it or not, we kissed right there in the coffee house and anyone wanting to watch could. It was one of those wonderful kisses that said mountains of words. But we didn't need mountains. We just kissed and it said it all.

Then we chatted, even joined by Pastor Dressel for one cup's worth of conversation before he left. Our big decision this day was to continue meeting for a reasonable period to make us look natural, not like we knew something, or anything of importance.

Three days later the whole town was wondering where The Dick was.

Chapter 50
The Investigation's Aftermath

One of the workmen at the high rise building said he'd seen him during a break and looking at the view, in this case over the side down into the gorge, said he'd seen a spot of color down in the gorge that he's never seen before. "So what," others said, and accused him of being an artist-at-heart. Plus he was one of those Mexican workers that were beginning to show up 'round the country. Well, that was two strikes against him so pretty much shut him up and he didn't look no more. But it sure was true that The Dick was missing, or gone, whatever. The new Church people he had gathered up and was preaching to wondered about his whereabouts, and wandered about looking in places. Someone even called the surrounding towns for his fame had spread, but he didn't seem to be anywhere. All the men who had sworn to kill him looked at each other keenly, trying to trick one into an admission. No luck, just a lot of serious suspicion. A little delegation or two was sent to George and 'Manda's house to inquire, but George was off on another business trip which only heightened curiosity. In fact some people reported they'd heard George and The Dick having an argument a week or so ago, and George saying he was fired and then the thought was that since he wouldn't go when paid off and ordered to go, George had taken matters into his own hands, he being the one responsible for him being here, he killed him and dumped his body someplace. That rumor petered out as all the others had. 'Manda was asked about it all, but she knew nothing.

George returned from his trip and was questioned hardly before he was out of his car. Nothing. He was as puzzled as everyone else. 'Manda told me he was secretly glad, because he'd gradually taken on a fright about the guy. So my advice is don't go about hiring private detectives, but no one listens to me. Nevertheless the town was on edge, expecting him to come back and cast new rules around and generally interrupt the smooth running of a helpless little podunk village.

Thursday two couples, muscular looking men and sun-browned semi-clad women, came to town with their gear. They had canoes and kayaks and light weight equipment, and they asked about the gorge stating that finally a team (them) was going to transverse it and break the mystique that it was impossible.

They got sent to lookouts and places like The Hut where you could look down into it and see the rocks and white water and the occasional log that had gotten stuck in it one way or another. Someone suggested going up into the high rise to look down from it, which was a good viewing place, so they did. Being modern and outfitted expensively they had everything, even a GPS which was so unnecessary once they went into it. It was a straight line till it reached that lake out at the end and only a few miles from the ocean where the sound is.

So they went to the third floor to look out, no one paying any attention to them as tourists are all alike, regardless of how outfitted. Shortly came the shouting and yelling and a few screams and dead silence. All that got the workmen's attention, and a clustering around and then men running through the streets calling out about it all.

No work in town the rest of the day, everyone going up to the high rise to see.

That spot of color the Mexican guy had seen was real alright.

Those outdoorsy members of the team claimed it was a body, the shirt of the person's back and mangled things like arms or legs or maybe parts of one while the head was more or less draped over this great rock, the river lapping at it as it went by, but the body so squashed out like by a great spatula such that the somewhat scattered mess was filling every crease and tiny crevasse of the rock and wouldn't be swept off, washed off is more like it, by a bigger than usual sweep of water.

It really was a mess up there in that new building with everyone up there, in there, trying to see and talk about it, who it was and all that. But the river somehow seems to have gotten interested too so it was louder than usual, or so it seemed to the superstitious who claimed it knew about the sacrifice and was pleased, so singing to itself about it. Well, that's the way some people think. Mostly it was too noisy to talk.

'Manda and George went by in his big Bentley. They went up and came down and talked to everyone about it. Someone said the State Police corporal for this district was on his way over to identify and post the death and investigate and all that sort of red tape stuff bureaucrats get themselves involved in. And a few nearby neighbors came over from other towns. It was the thing-of-the-day.

No one could get down to it, 'cept maybe on a line, but no one was that organized yet.

It was The Dick they all said, doing the corporal's work for him before he even got here.

So comes the investigation. Checked his room, checked everyone out who had anything to say so's the cause for the suicide or the murder could be investigated and written up thoroughly. And it turns out that everyone reported everyone else, all those killers we had in our midst, ready to do him in.

Since the chasm was so obvious a danger it could have happened any which way even without someone trying to get rid of him. Too much talk, too much gossip, too much speculation. A good chance to cause trouble for someone you didn't like, so this corporal had to be smarter than Solomon to separate truth from fiction. He took a week of interviews and re-interviews.

'Manda and I looked at each other. It was an accident, we'd seen it. Sara and whoever was with her must have seen it too, they were yelling so. 'Manda and I had realized we weren't needed there and started to leave, saw him go, that slip of earth giving away and him groping for something to hang on by, and going down. We looked at each other and wondered if we should tell. 'Manda the pure wife, and me the old codger, us out there together - people would have us making love out there. Not good. We had to live here and talk would ruin a person's life. 'Manda looked at me and I looked at her. We couldn't destroy our reputations. The corporal would give up trying to pin it on someone and go off and it'd be over, a tale in the history books of the future, folklore, a mystic death, or whatever. Just wait it out, we told each other and again vowed not to see each other anymore.

I could always leave here, go on back to the country I'd come from. Maybe kick it off by taking a back-packing trip or a canoe trip for a week or so. Let things settle down a bit around here. A canoe trip would be better on my not so good body now that I am getting on. It would get me out of people's memories. On the other hand, not being here, they could blame me for The Dick's death and that would be very bad.

Chapter 51
The Provocateur

The trend came to George. Yes, he was out of town that collection of days when the Dick disappeared and came up dead, but think: maybe he'd gone off and sneaked back and killed him, then returned to his job and reappeared at home just as if nothing had happened. He was the one! He had hired the guy, gotten out of him what he wanted, namely that his wife was not fooling around and the Bernice girl was available, going off to college soon, and the B&B was her real local boyfriend or protector, or whatever you wished to call him. George was trying to horn in on B&B but had this Dick reporting every damned misstep by anyone, even him, so now couldn't get rid of him as he'd become the new Christian leader here in town. So the big Dick had found a place to clean up in Christ's name and wouldn't go, doing God's work. So death to the interloper.

That was how it was beginning, just one of many possibilities. It was George.

'Manda called me up. We weren't seeing each other anymore.

We can't tell the truth, because it would reveal our being together and they'd think we were lovers. 'Manda didn't want to give up her husband even though they didn't get along well. I was the factor in her life, but only an amusement, a nice little side interest, which didn't actually make me feel all that good.

Sara and whoever was with her couldn't report, as that would ruin her marriage with Marty. And who knew who the other was? Marty wouldn't put up with that, as evidenced when he poked Jeff in the nose.

So now here is how things stand: the corporal has gone back to his regular duty and some magistrate has come to continue the investigation.

The rumors about George being the culprit were from B&B. Why they centered, or rather why he centered on George, are speculative rather than fact. The fact that George would stop on his walks into town and have overly long conversations with Bernice could have upset B&B. This might have made him jealous, or could be a contributing factor to his opinion which he expressed freely. B&B's big underlying condemnation of George came from the future. Namely if Bernice was living off someplace during her college education, George, always off on business trips, could find easy opportunity to visit her. These things happen. That was B&B's fear, and everyone passed it on. I spoke of it to 'Manda when we passed each other on the street the next day, but she merely scoffed. "Not George" she would say, "He wouldn't have time, and besides, he loves me."

"But is your married bliss tarnished, is this evidence of love growing old?" foolish me asked.

"No." and she laughed and her face got minutely red. "We have a very pleasant sex life, if that's what you're asking." and looked doubly embarrassed as her eyes pierced mine.

Not too smart of me asking right out like that, but the truth of the matter is I still couldn't get that night running up the path from where The Dick went over the side out of my mind.

Chapter 52
To Get Things to Jell

So they used the dance hall, it being the biggest place outside of the church to have a meeting. The church was so split up between the regular parishioners and The Dick's new Everlasting Good Church of the Bible, his name for it even though his "church" was in the middle of Main Street, that it, the church, just wouldn't do for a big, mass community meeting. Anyway they had a big supper, and everyone, just about, came. Set before the dance, it collected a few that wouldn't be seen in a dance hall no matter what. That was where B&B made his statement that gave the go ahead to the motion against George.

B&B is a big blow-hard, but I keep my mouth shut because he's a power in this region and could do an innocent fella harm while not meaning to, like George, for instance. B&B happened to be near the head table, eating a mountain of mashed potato with his mouth open, and what a sight that was. He said it out loud and with no apparent maliciousness, but it pretty much kicked George's goose.

"Now we got this murder on our hands and if'n we don't clear it up right fast the whole state'll know about us and every Tom, Dick and Harry will be down here wanting a piece of the action from our high school girls and we don't want that for our town, do we now?" That was B&B talking.

"Well, no, of course not," a few put in, quietly, not knowing what was coming and how it'd affect them. People pay attention to B&B.

"Now some of you know I been taking care of Bernice, seeing that she has a steady life, being a young girl as she is, seeing that she doesn't get mixed up with the wrong kind of boys or men from outside. You know, looking after her, and doing her good. I've seen some of you men, married and not so married and not even married at all, and you look at her and I don't blame you. She knows how to dress and show herself without being obscene about it. She don't make any effort to get in with the wrong crowd and she and I talk a lot about how life is and how a girl as nice as her has to be careful who she selects as friends, and it's worked for us. It's a lot of work bringing up a young girl like that, but I stick with it. To save a soul from terrible mistakes in life is real work. You folk with children know that and understand. So I look after her.

"So what do I get a few days ago but a letter from her over there a few streets where she lives. She's planning on studying to be a doctor. We talk on the phone every other day or so, and I go down and take her out for errands and socials with her friends on weekends. She's a nice looking young woman and you fellas, and the women too, talk with her and I vouch that not a one of you would dare criticize how I'm doing because she is so well-cared for. Now ain't that right now?" And he looked all around.

Well the whole place had shushed itself by then and everyone in the whole town listening to how Big and Burly was caring for this voluptuous, young girl he had all to himself.

"So we have lots of time to talk about personal matters. But a letter comes, penned by her, and she mentions how one of us town folk stopped by to see her out to supper. They went into Portland proper and some late night place for a wind-up drink, then home to her house. Quite a night. She was appreciative, she said, but wasn't swayed into the road of evil. That's how she put it, because I have taught her about men who showed they wanted her. She is so pleased with her resistance and yet politeness, all that I had talked to her about, and she wanted to thank me, and this was her way of doing it. A letter."

He stopped long enough to look all around and see the faces, faces he'd known since way back before the Bible was written almost, as he had once described it. People were making sounds of shock at this dinner and just like B&B had planned someone said, 'Who was this bastard out to tarnish our Bernice?' and sounds of agreement, and attention. Did he ever have their attention! Every face looked intently at him. If all those looks could levitate a man, he deserved to be six feet about the table. I was dying to hear who it was.

"Why who else? Who do we know that's always out around the country all the time. Who else?" Well he hadn't said who. Didn't need to. So B&B was the agent, the provocateur, the one with the word that accused, but hadn't. He was sitting there scot-free.

Someone yelled it out.

"George."

"George Cunningham. By Christ, it was him!"

The room was swelling with ooh's and ah's.

I knew George was out on one of his trips so wouldn't be here. But 'Manda? I looked over at the table she was at, and there she was. Her mouth open, blinking and swaying somewhat in her chair. My 'Manda. George's 'Manda. All alone over there taking it all in with everyone looking at her and accusing with their eyes. She was married to an unfaithful man and it was her responsibility to know and protect him and stop him from acts like that.

I couldn't go to her. A week ago we'd decided no more visits, chats, or meetings, and we had to stick to it this time. I was tempted, but she's said emphatically "no."

I stood up to go over there, watching her swing around and cover her face with her kerchief. She bolted out of her chair and was gone out the door in a flash, and there was a hand on my belt pulling me back down into my chair. I don't know who that was that stopped me, for I was watching her go. Embarrassed and humiliated probably. And at that moment I was paralyzed. I couldn't go to her. My mind raced and common sense came and took over my emotions. I sank back.

Chapter 53
She Needed Me

The dance went on after the great meeting which B&B had Ipso Facto taken over. Other candidates of the murder fell by the way side as George soared like a giant black falcon over the relieved residents of the town and up and down the local countryside.

I almost went over to George and 'Manda's house on the way home to, well, you know, console her. Maybe even our pact not to see each other could be put aside, but as I walked by the end of the street where she, they lived, I saw an old couple sitting a bit before her house. Minions of B&B's watching the house. They probably wouldn't bother her, or were waiting for George to show up from his business trip.

So I headed on up the hill to Sara and Marty's and went to bed, although I couldn't sleep, my mind just ran that meeting over and over. What could I have done that would have influenced the outcome. Anything? Not much if I were to keep the pact with 'Manda. We had agreed we'd say nothing. This town was so old-fashioned in some ways. The chances are it would poke along as always and this incident would get forgotten. That was our modus operandi. Sit tight and keep quiet. We could step forth and say we'd seen him go over the side, but would they believe us or choose to think he'd discovered us having a little tryst and pushed him? We killed him. Thus known: 'Manda and Trevor were having a love affair behind George's back. We'd agreed we'd keep quiet unless some innocent person was accused and in danger of being found guilty. We couldn't let that happen so at that point would have to take courage, accept that we were lovers in order to save the accused life. Then there was Sara. She'd never said a word one way or the other. She also knew he slipped and fell. She had to, she was there. So she and this boyfriend, whoever it was that met her there instead of Marty, could step forward and vouch for the accused. But not a peep had come out of her either.

Would she stay quiet during a trial? Had she and the boyfriend made the same pact with each other that 'Manda and I had?

I've watched her for days since then, but not a word or sign. Who was it, and had they consummated the very act that 'Manda and I had envisioned for her and her husband?

We'd know in three or four months when the little tyke would start to show. The trial wouldn't wait that long, and what effect would a presumed baby have on the trial?

And then my mind would shift back to 'Manda. How does she feel finding out in such a public way that her husband was having meetings with Bernice? Bernice, the woman of the exquisite shape, the woman every single man in town had thirst after even as B&B carried her off each night.

Pouring over that and shifting around continually in bed made my mind sharper, more active, more open to suggestion.

Here was the suggestion. Maybe B&B was responsible for the death and was thrusting it off on George because he was an easy target. He'd been carrying her off from dances, and who knew what else. No question B&B was big, fat, and sweaty with an uncouth mind and power among the dregs of society around here. He dressed with a pair of suspenders and his shirt front was forever open half way. He had a loud, gravelly voice, pig eyes and rough hair cut.

If people around here were convinced there had to be a killer, then why not improve the world by transferring the blame to B&B? With the exception of a few, everyone was wary if not outright afraid of B&B. Nobody worth knowing would worry if B&B were executed. The applause would shake the trees as far as Skowhegan. God! I wanted to tell 'Manda and reached for my clothes to go down to the phone. If we could solve Sara's problem with some careful plans, we could certainly set B&B up somehow.

So I thought as I lay in bed.

The phone rang and I heard Marty moving to answer it. I didn't realize he was still up.

His voice came up the stairwell. "Trevor. It's for you. Some woman."

My heart flipped. 'Manda. Had to be her.

A shaking voice, intermittent with crying, came over the line. It said stuff but I couldn't make it out. One word came through: Trevor. It had to be 'Manda, and she was in a state, probably like mine, wondering what to do, what was going to happen, all that, and what about us.

I said, "Goodbye, I'll come down." I don't know if she understood me through all her noises, crying and slobbering words into the phone, but had to assume she did.

I looked at Marty. "It was 'Manda Cunningham. Upset. I'm going to walk down and see her. Try to help."

He stared at me, no words, then gestured with his right index finger, gestured to the chair and made a up and down motion.

"Now Dad, don't you wish you'd stayed away from her six months ago?"

I haven't been here six months yet, but that wasn't the point, was it?

When talking seriously to me he always started with "Dad" like Sara called me.

Well, I sat there staring back at him, thinking on what he'd said. It wasn't long. No, I was glad I'd met her. I loved her. She was pleasant company, a woman with ideas and willing to work for them, obviously a wife left out of her husband's business and so with that 'marital loneliness' that effects some people. A beautiful woman in that wonderful combination of features and mind. It called to me when I didn't realize I needed a close companion. If we were younger when we met we'd still be together, that oneness of man and woman that occurs and lasts and lasts, sometimes into marriage, in a way that released another dimension into me.

And now she calls to me, the way I would call to her in a pinch. 'Manda, that body that I imagine in my mind, those words that set a tone within us, for truly, we are that much together. Thirty years earlier and we'd be together and with a parcel of kids.

Stay away from her six months ago? Well, if it had been that way my life would have gone on, but I doubt truly that I'd have found another woman such as her to commit myself to, to stay away from because she was married and therefore her life on a path enough different from mine that we should not violate. I met her and we meshed. I wouldn't change it. So I am not staying away from her, therefore it is incumbent on me to go to her now, accept her lead in how she wishes to respond to this crisis in her life. Play my part, for in this she must be the leader.

I looked back into Marty's steady eyes. "No. She is a good friend and I must play my part as a good friend. I would expect it of her, and she expects it of me. I will go to her and see how I can help, her married life is going topsy-turby on her and I must help her replace herself in this world. Her life is being threatened by others. As a friend I have this responsibility. I must go to her." I didn't tell him that I loved her. In some ways that word 'love' encompasses everything I said.

Sara and Marty's life did not have that level of love, upsetting events had tarnished that once precious feeling. 'Manda and I had strived to rekindle it with this baby scheme and it might work. Time to see it result in fruition was needed. So patience with my step-daughter and her husband.

"You're stepping into someone else's trouble. She a married woman who should go to her husband for aid and consolation. You're an outsider, unless you're planning to be the marriage-buster."

"No, Marty, I'm no marriage buster. She has a husband accused and I am but a band-aid. She and George must work this out. I help, hopefully."

"You've been seeing her ever since you got here. You're not just an old codger who's wife is gone, but a real, live older man who is in need of another wife. Face it.

"Everyone's watching you two, watching to see when she breaks from her husband and runs off with you. Come on. Face it."

"Everyone's watching us? Who? What do they say?"

"Oh come on. You must know everyone's watching you two."

"Well maybe; but why, for heaven's sake?"

"You sit in that *Empty Plate* a couple of hours every morning and then go off, and people see you together later during the day. What'd'ya expect?"

"Well they're all wrong. You tell 'em that."

"Behavior speaks louder than words."

"Baloney! We just talk about art, music, the world situation, politics, authors and their stories. She's got a brilliant mind but no one around this pissing, tiny town to talk with. What's wrong with that?"

"They see you holding hands sometimes, and you go off taking walks around the outside of town. Kissing out there, hugging, holding hands. They've got your number and so now George is trapped and that sets the bird free. You going to move down to her house when he goes off to prison? That's what people'll say, or are saying right now, who knows?"

I was flabbergasted. No doubt we'd been seen, that goes with the activity, but it must be widespread. How much had whosoever seen? And if they'd seen us around The Hut, had someone else seen The Dick go over the side besides us and Sara and whoever? That would be good if someone else had. No need for us to report what we saw, or Sara and whoever. They could report the truth. But would they? If a friend of B&B, probably not. B&B was getting what he wanted, namely Bernice and George split apart. And then I wondered, how much had George and Bernice done. That was a question!

This was eating time when I should be with 'Manda. We could discuss philosophy some other time. I got up and said, "We can talk about this more when I get back, or in the morning. I gotta get down there." And out.

A car was parked at the end of the street, someone watching for George, so I ducked into the brush and hedges and up to Mandy's back porch. She answered the door after a while, saw who it was and in an instant was plastered to me, arms around me, head on my neck, and then squeezing tightly, and then her lips on mine. And then we were down in the basement room where the windows were covered with blackout curtains and things were fitted out very nicely. She drew me to the couch where she cuddled up against me, her head on my chest, and whispered, "What do we do?"

"What any sensible couple would do. I guess we stay apart until this blows over." I was so, so relieved that I really don't know what happened thereafter, or why, except that our affection for each other made a difference, and we went ahead. She had unfastened my shirt down low by my belt and slid her hand in slowly. My arm was around her shoulders and we sat this way talking so naturally. She got up to lower the lights. Eighty-four and getting on and still she felt marvelously good.

We talked about George and the unexpected nature of the whole thing. What we could do, what I should do. I got my sense back and prepared to leave as she helped me dress. She was a beautiful woman and obviously could be mine but it was terribly late. Maybe too late for what was developing between us this night. In the darkness of the upstairs she came to my arms and then I was sliding out the back door into the darkness and in a confused state of euphoria wandered up the way to Sara and Marty's. What had happened that suddenly we were so close and how close would we have become if I had not left and what did this mean for George whenever he got home, and what did it mean to the old codger? Was I that lonely that I would use this miserable situation to sever 'Manda from her marriage? No way, lovely as she was, friendly as she was, sensual and sexy as she was.

Maybe someday, well who knows? But no messing around during a situation like this. Marty met me at the door. I was flattered in a way, that he felt so strongly for my position. He was still fully dressed, although rumpled, as if he'd waited up to talk more about it. We sat down and repeated the same stuff he'd talked to me about before. He was a good man at heart.

I told him 'Manda's funny story that somehow lately George had gotten the idea that she wanted another baby. She laughed about it and noted that just before he left on this last trip he'd said, 'No more babies. That's a foolish idea. No more!' The whole thing was a joke to her. "It's too late, but he didn't seem to realize it. Isn't that a riot?" Marty thought it was unusual and funny too. I didn't tell him that we had tried to get Sara to have a baby, nor our strategy for doing it. He'd have blown his stack, no doubt. Nor did I tell him that I'd thought 'Manda and I should give it a try because he'd think I had really become unhinged. Actually I liked the idea, even just trying it sounded great. I am dumb sometimes. I thanked him for his views on the whole situation and we both went off to our beds, he a lucky guy with his woman to curl up to. Me? My bed was filled with just a dream in an old man's heart.

Chapter 54
Town's Gettin' Worked Up

They were at it in town the next day, everyone talking and taking sides and in a way moving back and forth from group to group, getting the picture straight in their own minds. I went walking, looking at the gorge from its beginning near the ancient glacial lake that had corralled the runoff to the part near the beginning where the highway went over it, then down to the new building going up, then farther down where the rope bridge crossed to The Hut, and again farther down to where you could see it coming out in a wide, shallow river and finally the lake there where the waters waited to go out to the sound at the ocean's edge. It was a long way, and it took a whole day of walking, but it was good for me in this state of mind. I didn't see 'Manda, if she went to the *Empty Plate* for I wasn't there, so people would talk saying we were already breaking up. No need to pry us apart. We were.

The town was still talking about us, George, and the death, but now with a new direction becoming evident. Namely: we don't want no magistrate coming down from the capital or county seat to judge this situation. It's over. George may or may not be to blame, but The Dick is gone and our world here can become serene again. We can play Steal the Flag on a grand scale if we want. We can have little trysts in The Hut, we can have our dances Saturday night, B&B can have his Bernice, and the Christian's can have their differences. Sara can have her baby and all us folk live happily ever after.

Of course, sitting on the big, exposed root of a tree it seemed so simple. But it wasn't that way at all. I resolved to get away, just a few days. Let things settle a bit and then take up residence again. I got the canoe, sleeping bag, light tent and the kit I'd packed anew after the last trip. I'd go to the ocean side of the gorge and put in to go down river into the lake, where the water flowed out the outlet and along all the way to the coast, then across the sound to the barrier island. Hit the road and call Sara to come get me. Maybe in our trip back she'd talk about the baby that was coming. And I could report success to 'Manda. It might be a mite early to expect her to know a baby was coming, but then if she was like some women, she'd have kept perfect data on her fertile period and would know that she'd conceived. Even find out who the father was. Certainly not Marty because he was home all night unless he sent a bottle of liquid containing sperm and a hypodermic to inject it. So!

Chapter 55
The Girl from Frisco

With my wide-brimmed hat protecting me from the gray sky, I made long-reaching strokes to ease the tiring sameness of the paddling. I rounded the corner the river took at this point and ahead on the left bank there appeared to be a lone figure sitting on the sand, head down resting on knees. This person was too far ahead to detect gender.

This person was all alone with nothing around: no tent, no canoe, no boat of any kind, no pans, no food, no back pack. One would guess he, or she, had been left here, either voluntarily or otherwise, to await the return of the rest of the party, or maybe left deliberately. Marooned.

Interesting. It is close to lunch time so one would suppose the rest of the party will be returning soon. Should I wait and eat with them, or continue on around another bend and eat alone?

I remembered the words from one of my bosses on a job at lunchtime. I had walked in toward the end of the group and took the first seat available, one of four empty chairs at a table slightly removed from the others. Someone else took one of the others and the boss appeared in about two minutes. He sat for a moment, greeting his two table companions. He sat quietly, listening and looking around and suddenly said to me. "You're sitting here, away from the others?" The boss sat a few more minutes and then got up and moved to a vacant chair at one of the other tables. The message was not lost. Being a bunch quitter marked you. If you want to be left alone, people will leave you alone. You can be a loner inside yourself so that no one knows. Our society frowns with suspicion on those that won't be part of the team. It makes life easier to stick with the group. So, was this person on the beach marooned because of a foul personality, or just a bunch quitter? Was this person waiting for someone else to come along and get him on her way to wherever headed? Man or woman, it didn't matter. Same problem.

I struck out with the offshore paddle, aiming toward the shore. Between current and a few paddles I'd beach slightly to the side of the person so that his friends could pull up directly in front.

Not a he, but a she. I could see now that it was a woman in jeans, crumpled wool over-shirt, big hiking boots, scraggily hair; rather nondescript. She wasn't aware of my quiet approach until I said, "Morning."

She jumped, surprised. and I was about to apologize when she burst out at me, chastising me for sneaking up on her, for frightening her, what was I up to, who was I, where did I come from, what was going on, who else was with me, where were they hiding, what did I want, ending with, "Don't you dare come near me, go back where you came from, this is my beach."

I noted (who wouldn't) that she was rather vicious, at least in speech. She hadn't unseated herself although she was no longer sitting all wrapped into herself. I pictured her scampering off into the brush at the slightest questionable movement on my part like a wary squirrel, a frightened bunny, or some bewildered, isolated, abandoned, pure bred woman out of her element.

I asked, "Do you work in some computer office in a big city?"

It sounded like she snarled. Maybe it was more hiss-like, a cat making its warning sound. A snake.

"Well, ma'am, being as how this river and its banks be part of the public domain (I wondered if that could be true) I reckon I's got as much right to put in here as the next feller and you got no right to sit there on that sand and upbraid me. I'm a-landing so if'n yer planning to beat it, or smack me with a piece of driftwood, you'll shore be in the wrong." So I nodded, as if satisfied that the problem was solved, looked over at her, thinking that it wasn't wise to be giving her ideas as she seemed so ornery. And what's this got to do with my life anyway? Or the great troubles back in the village. I'm here to get 'Manda out of my system and that whole business thought out.

I pulled the nose of the canoe up on the shore about seven feet and unloaded my primus and the box of food. I set it up and in a jiffy there was hot water. Being of expansive mind I made two cups of cocoa, rather watching the woman out of the corner of my eye from time to time noting that there was no reaction to me. She continued to hold her head between her legs and made no sign of life. It must be terribly terminal, I concluded. Maybe the cocoa would help life return from the otherwise apparently dead. I even got a paper napkin out to accompany the cocoa. Very proper.

Both in hand I walked across the twenty-five feet toward her speaking quietly about the benefits of a nice cup of cocoa when it was totally an uncomfortable day what with the clouds gray and the air making up to have a slight chill and it being getting on toward lunch.

No response.

I bent slightly, offering the cup out toward her and smiled. Everyone needs a smile on a day getting to be lousy. A hand burst out from the clump of person, struck the hand with the cup full center and with noise went flying off, bounding on the sand and coming to a stop fifteen feet away, the cocoa gone in a jiffy into the sands leaving no trace. A face was looking at me briefly, teeth showing in a soundless snarl. It must have held there a whole minute, indicating hostility and then lowered back to the knees and disappeared between the two arms again, all curled up into herself satisfied that I wasn't going to react to the sudden disappearance of my offering.

By God, was my thought. You ain't the wife, nay, the mother, of The Dick, be you? You got all his mannerisms. Are you here to find the body and weep over it?

I studied her a very short period, wondering if I should complain at the small pain where my fingers had almost been ripped away by the exiting cup, or ignore the pain in the name of increased awareness that some people, no matter what, didn't want to be interrupted in their misery.

I moved to retrieve my cup, noting aloud that it was a good day for misery and misery does have its place in this impersonal world. No response, of course. So much for humor.

Back at the primus, the soup was heating nicely and in less time than it takes to say, I had a fried cheese sandwich cooking. It certainly smelled good. And a word came my way from the woman but I was too late to catch a look at her face as she said it.

"You must be a total asshole to –" She didn't finish for her head slid back down.

"My, we certainly do have an unpleasant mouth for such an interesting day." Internally the remark was: Screw you. It certainly is annoying when someone is so impolite, especially out here in the wilderness where man should help man especially when without friends or gear, as far as intents and purposes go.

Why couldn't this have been Mandy and us arguing over being separated by a not-understanding world. Or George gone, accidently caught in an earthquake and buried never to be seen again. Just Mandy and me. I shook my head. This is no way to forget the finest woman in the world.

So I looked over at this more or less piece of white female trash. Where the hell is the rest of her party? Where's her stuff? How'd she get out here and where'd it go to and what's she doing out here anyway so completely, well, what do you say, without clothes, equipment, friends, supplies, whatever. And the day isn't getting any better. I bet it gets to rain by dusk.

The pan-fried grilled cheese was ready.

"I say there, Miss, care for a sandwich? I got more'n one here and would be willing to share. It is time to eat, you know." I sat back on my haunches, slumped to my elbows and relaxed, eating slowly.

She surprised me when she said "Why don't you shut up? No one asked you here. Don't you get the message?"

So I ate in silence and finished half the sandwich. I'd eaten enough and making another attempt to be the Good Samaritan I took a napkin, folded it, and inserted the remaining sandwich inside and walked to her, about four feet in front, rather certain that she was surreptitiously aware of me, put it on the sand and quietly retreated to my cookies, three chocolate Oreos, and an apple.

I had coffee and began talking about canoeing down the river and the quiet of it all, the overcast, the chance of rain, and the blue heron that had flown up river about thirty feet overhead. There was some debris by the river maybe a half-hour's paddling from here. It looked like old stuff, maybe a day old, certainly not today's stuff.

There was movement over there and I pretended not to notice. She scooped up the sandwich and in a jiffy it was gone. That was the start, and in about twenty minutes we were actually talking. It was a shaky conversation and then all of a sudden in the middle of a sentence she stopped dead–quiet. No talk. Nothing. I looked around, studying her again. Her hair looked like a bear had fixed it, and her clothes, as stated, were ratty. Now she spoke in a quiet, steady voice, a rather pleasant voice, actually. She apologized for her previous nastiness and thus it was over. No explanations, just a simple apology.

I said I was headed into the lake at a camp open to anyone and she could put up there if it suited her. "I'm headed back tomorrow so you'll be on your own again."

I left it hanging so she could add her own ending which was nothing but an "Okay, let's see it."

So following one bit of confusion, arguments, considerable grousing and finally cooperation we headed out. She wasn't unfamiliar with canoeing and it actually worked out. We made progress and reached the camp.

We had changed places again and she was in the rear, guiding the canoe. I turned and looked at her. She was hunched down, looking up at the camp situated on the rise of ground well up above the water level, scrunching up her face and peering markedly at its location above the lake, the scattering of short brush between it and the water, and the high pines thrusting up into the sky.

"There's a short beach beyond that big rock. We can pull in there." I turned back to my paddling. Being the front, it was my job to keep the canoe going at maneuvering speed, more a motor than anything else while she was the navigator, steer and paddle some, more an auxiliary motor. We rounded the rock and swung in toward the beach, about twenty-five feet long and maybe ten feet wide and cuddled into a ten foot high stony bank. I rested, looking at the setting, then picked up the paddle and thrust in toward the rocky lined beach. We closed in, I grabbed hold of a rock, and stepped out ashore, holding onto the side of the canoe and steadied it firmly, looking at Miss Congeniality with the "Coming Ashore" look on my face, I hoped, eyebrows up in question.

Her lower face shifted from disapproval to a pout of annoyance which reached her eyes that went to slits. Her nose crinkled. The paddle, pressing, holding the canoe in position until I did what I promised with my eyes.

I stepped into about six inches of water, hauled the nose up and steadied the canoe until she had moved forward and climbed over the nose and ashore. She was pretty agile and apparently capable around a canoe.

"You planning to break in here?"

Oh how nice, the same usual raspy voice and lack of appreciation of others and their possessions. I sat, wondering about the chameleon, so changeable in expression. Which is the real her? Not that it mattered. Still, people are an interesting study. I closed my book on study of her and looked along the shore, the lake, back to the cabin wondering as I had times before how a stranger would see it or feel about it. It wasn't much of a place, looks considered. Almost black shingles, all being old. Nice new sand-colored roof one of the towns-people had put on a year ago. Long screen across the front. From down here on the beach it looked mighty high sitting up on its stone pillars keeping it above the spring high water mark. Actually rather non-descript looking. An ordinary old camp.

I stretched up, rolled my shoulders, enjoying the relief from the hunched-over feeling of the long paddle along the lake, looked along the shore and over the end of the lake stretched out ahead another mile or so, up at the distant sky beyond the close-in hills out there, gray and with that I'm-going-to-rain-on-you look, and pretty soon too. So be it.

It turned out she had a teeny, silly pack with her, on her back and so flat that it couldn't have anything much in it. I hadn't even noticed it at first. So now, the fireplace bright and making its slight roar, the place getting somewhat warmer, she disappeared into the room she had selected, reappearing several minutes later and WOW! She had changed from that raggy-taggy sweater into a blouse, colorful and well-fitting. Wow! She was no longer the crud-of-the-world but a fine looking woman. I must have stared for she stopped on her way to the kitchen and came over to me, stood about six feet off and flicked her hands in front of me to break the obvious spell I had fallen into. Not only that, but she actually smiled. Well, she was quite a dish. Now to see if she had also changed her attitude from the raspy, disgruntle mood of before.

She spoke and it was a pleasant, well modulated voice. It was obvious that I had to clean up my previous reactions to her and get with it. So I did.

So we had a supper from the food I had brought. She was an okay cook and served up a mashed potato with hamburger gravy and peas on the side. Tasty, simple, good flavor, and enough to stave off starvation for another day.

I couldn't get over the change in her and sitting opposite her over coffee I was reminded of Mandy, the very thing I had come on this trip to forget. This one was no slouch, no dummy, no uninformed tramp from the ghetto of some east coast city. I wondered what had happened to her companions, who she was, where from, what sort of occupation did she follow, and what in heavens was she doing out in the canoe wilderness all alone. She gave the impression of class, and my desire to know ate at me. She talked well, good grammar and vocabulary and wide interests. Heavens but she reminded me of Mandy.

"What is your name?" I finally asked, standing it no longer and knowing that the "Flo", for "Florence" she had given earlier when in the canoe could not be right.

She looked at me a long time, her face changing expression several times and I sensed that she was going over old conversations with someone or some group for her eyebrows frowned and her face would harden and this would be swept away, replaced by softer expressions, the trace of a smile, even laughter. She was certainly a complicated individual and she finally said her first name was Katherine, with a "K" which gave rise to many, many nicknames: Kate, Kathy, and so on. We passed on to other topics and gradually I realized I was being questioned about our little town, its tempo of life, its' goals as a community. Goals of a community as if it were a living thing, and as I sat there listening to her and placing answers to her inquiries I realized that was true. A community of people, like an organism, moves forward slowly, but it moves, and this was true of our little town too. This thing I was here trying to forget, this love of Mandy, was part of it, this grander organism. My love, thwarted as it was, would affect how I behaved and thus others would be changed a slight amount too, just as this death of The Dick had created a lot of thinking of one kind or another in how the whole town was going to deal with this so called murder. And a mark would be left for us all to deal with.

She asked about the big game of Steal the Flag, about the lives of the folks running our collection of stores, she asked of the robbery, or was it the crash of the armored car and loss of its contents, of the marriages and births, deaths and sickness, the dance every weekend and of some big man called B&B and his girlfriend, of the man named George who was supposed to be horning in on B&B (that perked me up – how did she know of that?). I waited for her to ask about this George-man's wife, called 'Manda, but that didn't come. How did she know so much of this for I'd never seen her before around our little town. I started to ask how she knew so much when she dropped the real big one.

"Tell me about this murder."

"Murder?"

A hand came out and had my forearm. "Now don't go dumb on me. Tell me about the murder."

The burning oil lamp was producing smoke, so I took this opportunity to remove the chimney and trim the wick, unessential diversionary busy work. A chance to reflect on the question, who she was and why was she here? I sensed this was the one she'd been after through all our conversation.

"The murder?" I echoed.

"Yes. I want to hear about the murder."

"There wasn't any murder." I said. And I knew that to be the truth.

"Don't give me that. There was a murder and you damn well know it. Now spit it out."

So there it was. The way everyone felt and somehow it had gotten to this complete stranger. I could feel my lips pressing together, my body tense. I knew enough of human reactions, of psychology, or whatever the reactions of the body experienced in moments of stress to know I was preparing for battle. Suddenly it struck me funny and I laughed. It was tinny, and not a good laugh. I heard it as if I was completely detached from this sound. It was higher pitched than I speak, or laugh, for that matter. But it was a sign which made me stop and take stock.

This situation was ridiculous and this girl was part and parcel of it. I'd found this young lady abandoned on a sandbar and none too happy, headed for a cold night, maybe in the rain, lost and without help. Why I didn't know, but you can't leave someone stranded like that, despite how obnoxiously she spoke and acted. Not much older than high school age herself, she was here with me in this cabin. Me, way up in my eighties and we were going to spend the night here together. If I were fifty or sixty years younger it'd be a perfect set up for some great sexual moment. Shakespeare would make a masterpiece out of it, great acting and a tense situation, a combat between animal instincts and morality. But this was me, too old for such foolishness in addition to being in love with the murderer's wife. What fun he would have with just the mental conflict there, much less the interplay of body desire versus propriety. This woman was not a bad looking chick at all now that she'd washed her face, fixed her hair, and put on probably the only spare clothes she had.

I heard that laugh again from me. I was laughing at a ridiculous situation. She heard it too, and her look passed to an assessment of me. I was her cabin companion for a night and I could see it in her face, she was on the verge of a laugh, but one of straight out amusement. Her and me in bed together was the height of improbability and she was stirred to laugh. Frankly, I felt foolish. 'Manda and me, by all means yes, but I had rejected that for she was married and loved George. I was just one of the instruments that made her life work. But with this child? Shakespeare would have loved it.

So I finally got myself straightened out. Was there a murder? No, but not a soul knew that but 'Manda and me, and Sara plus her companion in The Hut. And neither us nor they could speak out the truth. We'd be known as breaking the vows of Christianity, according to The Dick, or the moral rules of marriage. We'd be the ones to take the brunt of everyone's ire. It broke in on me, her words, this girl.

"So tell me, old man, who murdered The Dick, isn't that what they called him around here?"

"The Dick?" I echoed. It seemed like I'm always echoing her which was certainly a clue that she was leading this conversation. "Where do you get all this information? You know more about what's going on in my town than I do."

She tossed her head, a cute move, but basically a sneer at me and my reticence in sticking to her topic. "Speak up. The murder. Tell me about it."

"Don't know much. He was out walking at night, he did that a lot. Got out by the chasm and fell in apparently."

"That's not what I heard. People got to dislike him and just about everyone threatened to assassinate him. Let's hear your story again."

Now there was something about her that was different. We don't use words like "assassinate". Her speech was correct and without localisms and everyday low class common words. Plus I've never seen her before, in this town or nearby ones, and I've seen lots of people hereabouts.

"You a lawyer?" I asked.

"Not me, baby. Answer my question."

"There's not much to say. He was out by the chasm, walking alone, apparently. I don't know of anyone who claims to have seen exactly what happened. He was missed but it wasn't until a couple of days later that anyone saw his body. It was on a rock down in the chasm. Only got it out with the greatest of effort. No marks on it that would indicate foul play, or so the authorities said. I don't know how they could tell being as he fell a goodly distance and it must have been swept about as it was and so got all banged up. Still experts in that sort of thing didn't find any gunshot wounds or knife cuts. According to them as I've heard it, he got bruised up by the rocks."

"So why do they say it was this guy George that did it?"

"You want opinion or facts, lady?"

"What d'ya think, you asshole. Come on, spit it out for Christ's sake."

She was getting edgy, slipping back into that low class-speak again.

"I guess that was just B&B's way of getting back at George for trying to steal his girl, accusing someone who wasn't around at the time."

"Tell me about his girl. She some paragon of beauty that no man could resist? Another Helen of Troy?"

There it was again. Helen of Troy? Who around here would make that analogy? Who is this broad?

"Where did you come from?"

"Forget that. Who was she?

"Is she, she's still alive. Present tense."

"Just tell me."

"Bernice is a smart, pretty girl in her last year of high school right now. B&B's pretty much been her boyfriend for a couple of years. Folks hereabouts think of them as a pair. Maybe they'll get married someday, leastwise that's how folks seem to think despite the age difference."

"Which is?"

"Thirty years, maybe more. B&B don't have no wife, so she's maybe his next. He must be close to fifty, and she's his girl. Her folks don't seem to mind, and she sticks by him, I guess. Young girls need someone to look after them, be available if someone bothers 'em, you know. She's no different than anyone else. She needs someone to look after her. It's him. It works for them. He's got a girl for comfort or whatever a man his age gets a hankering for. She's got someone to call on when she's being pestered, or tired, or lonely. What's wrong with that?"

"I'm from the city, Frisco. People don't bother girls out there. This place must be close to the dregs of society from the picture you lay out. So why does this George butt in on B&B? It doesn't sound to me like she's very true to him, that B&B character, if she's taking up with George. And he's married, isn't he? That's what people tell me. Well?"

I felt for 'Manda. If this is the village talk, and she knows, she must feel terrible, the plight of the married woman when her husband gets the urge that calls for satisfaction. And this one must have gotten her information from someone in town, or maybe several, and if this is what the town-folk are saying or thinking, what can I do? She must know and feel terrible. I should do something for I can't let this go on, but neither can I let out the truth. Sure we should, but to say to the world that 'Manda and I were together out on the other side of the chasm is like saying 'Manda and I are having a cute little affair out there and saw him slip. Oh-h. So 'Manda and Trevor are seeing each other while George is away, huh? Those two having a little play behind George's back? Maybe that's why he started seeing Bernice. Maybe them two got caught out there so had to kill The Dick to keep it quiet; wouldn't surprise me a bit. Those two, doing that behind every one's back. That's what they'd say. And then they'd be after me, or her, or both of us.

"A-yeah. Married to 'Manda Cunningham, his wife. Happily married, I'd say."

She looked skeptical and said. "So who's she pal around with when he's out of town on business. He's got that kind of business, so she's alone a lot. Who's she spend time with?"

I knew what was coming next and thought to cut it off at the pass 'fore she said it. "Well there's me. I see her most any day at the coffee shop for a cup of coffee. We chat, maybe an hour or so. I suppose she has other friends maybe up to her house for tea, or whatever friends do. There's an old friend of hers by the name of Frazier. Who have you heard about, anyone?"

"There's you, but you're old enough to be her father. Who's more her age? You must know of someone." She was studying me like under a microscope.

"There used to be Frazier, like I mentioned, who was a friend from Massachusetts where she used to live. Otherwise I don't know. She talks to him, but about everybody does. She knew about everybody in town."

She gave me a look of disgust. "He wouldn't waste time on her. Someone else?"

"Why not him? They're close in age. She's attractive and vivacious. He was a good looking man, and like her, trying to make the world safer and less mean spirited." I thought of The Dick, He probably had had words with her. I spoke it, "There was another man, name of Dick, I think."

"Dick?" She laughed. "Not The Dick. You mean the detective."

"Well, he was brusk and aggressive and she the opposite, quieter and persuasive. They could've meshed, being of different sorts."

"He wouldn't mess with a married woman."

"Why not? He's a man and men go after women and some don't care if they're married or not."

"Not my brother. He wouldn't play that game."

"Your brother?"

"Of course. You think I'd come way off out here from San Francisco to look for some stupid private dick who got himself murdered? No way. Men aren't that valuable. Men are a dime a dozen. Ask any girl. Always hanging around bothering us, trying to get a night's pleasure and leaving their wives home with the babies crying and feeling sorry for themselves. That's all men are good for, right?"

'Your brother? The Dick?"

She turned on me a little bit fiercely I thought. "You deaf or something? He's my brother and I'm here to moan over his remains if I can get them, and find out if the killer owned up to his misdeed and is going to be killed, because he should be!"

I pulled myself out of the shock of her words and thought she was really getting cranked up. Uh-huh. But why not? My God! His sister!

And she wouldn't stop. "And now that you mention it, it could have been a woman, like that one you were describing a few moments ago. That, what's her name?"

"'Manda."

"Yeah. Amanda. She could be one. For instance she's Miss Goody-Goody, and they're usually the types that operate behind the scene in these extramarital affairs, breaking up marriages and all that. She could be. Might not be, but could be. Doing good deeds every day making people feel loved all over the place, sneaking around and starting rumors and gossip. Hiding behind her goody-goodiness. How many boy friends in this village has she made use of already? Go on. Tell me."

"'Manda isn't that way, for heavens sake."

"Like her, don't ya! I've heard you're sweet on her. Seen in the streets walking hand in hand, maybe even kissing behind trees where the street lights don't shine, sitting in that restaurant all morning and then not seen for the rest of the day, out walking with you, always with you. Uh-huh, a couple of teen-aged lovers you two be. Happens all over. A woman gets sick of her husband, for one reason or another can't divorce him, or even worse, kill him, so she –

I interrupted with a blast to "Shut up. If you want a talk then let's –"

But she insisted in a stronger voice, finishing her soliloquy.

" – takes on a steady boyfriend, maybe holding hands is all, maybe they go farther and she survives with that as her crutch. You –"

I was up and leaving, heading for the stairs and the bedrooms up there, just to get away from her.

I didn't fall asleep immediately. For one thing I had broken my routine. I hadn't brushed my teeth, and her talk was disturbing. Could 'Manda be behind this? Was my thinking all screwed up? I finally realized I'd been with her, yes, but we had both seen him slip as the rock face crumbled under his weight and then go down to that mournful crash or splash, whichever described that almost impossible to hear blow as he landed amid the rocks and water.

In the morning we found a half gallon of maple syrup that someone had abandoned after getting this far, and some Betty Crocker pancake mix, so we had a decent breakfast, and no words of reproof.

"How do we get out of here?"

With that we were on our way. Down river between the tall deciduous forest sprinkled with evergreens, beside the sand banks that marked the trip since the end of the chasm at the escarpment that broke from the coastal plain and marked the higher land of a different underlying tectonic plate. We didn't talk until finally we could see the colored dots far ahead that marked the village at the edge of the sound and the ocean waters. This was the end of the trip and the end of my confusion about where 'Manda and I stood. For her, The Dick's sister, I didn't know. For 'Manda, I suspect she'd stick with her husband. We didn't have a real life together, just a few incidents, and I, a man, like men from the time of the caves to our present sophisticated state, still a man is always ready, and I guess I was. I was attached to her and it had to stop. She had her George, and I had no one. It would be time to move on when this debacle was over. However it worked out.

"You'd have been still sitting on that sand bar if'n I hadn't come along."

She was in good spirits for her response was, "If you think I'm for one minute fooled by that half-ass accent like you'd lived here all your life, think again. What were you really, in your work age. Certainly you're not actively working now. You some professor?"

She had fooled me. No jerky, half educated spawn of the ghettos of Frisco but some woman with education and command and experience. So it was my turn. "Me? An underpaid, unappreciated minor college administrator, so you're close. Now a budding author with what I used to think was a good head-start in literature. I get lazy though, and life is leaving me in the dust. But it's your turn, you're on a quest to solve what everyone thinks is a murder. Good luck. It wasn't, but no one listens in this stage of the investigation. Now tell me, that aside, who abandoned you on that sand bar, and why?" I waited, studying her looks, changing as they had yesterday as she thought something through.

"My traveling companions. We came east together, they to go mountain climbing in the east, me for my brother.

They'd heard about the chasm. Apparently it's some unconquered physical feature and they wanted to give it a try. No go, though, too dangerous. But a canoe trip at the end of it sounded good, so off we went." She looked sour. "I was still concerned about my brother and that mess that got him dead, and I talked too much about it. They finally told me to please shut up, then it was shut up or get out. I was just so caught up in it all that I couldn't stop. I got left, which made me angry. They couldn't have been more than twenty minutes ahead when you showed up. I was in a mood. Sorry 'bout that."

I could understand her position. "These things happen. Well, so you can go back there and talk to more people, but it wasn't a murder, just an accident, I'm sure. Try and think of it that way. George or 'Manda aren't involved in anything. It was unfortunate that it took Mr. Dick's life." I didn't want to get involved in this conversation any farther. 'Manda or I'd get caught if we talked too much. Always happens. Inadvertently you let something slip by and it gets picked up and you're caught. Seen it a hundred times.

"I got a lawyer coming in a week. He'll find out." She gave me a sour look from her position at the front of the canoe, but turned around and paddled again. We'd be at the outlet after a few hours, and I'd never see her again. This whole thing would blow over and life could go on. I'd stay out of sight and move on in a couple of months. Maybe take a trip like this on the Susquehanna, visit Delaware and the Chesapeake. Do something like that.

Chapter 56
Thus it Goes

I got back into town on the bus, me and my backpack. I left the canoe at the rental back there on the sound where the river came to an end, a lazy river now where boys fished from branches overhanging that now slow, sluggish bit of water. This water that came down from the escarpment, dropping its grains of sand and small stones and filling up its bed till it got sick of that and overflowed its banks. All the locals, towns folk, and farmers and fishermen, put up a holler over the injustice of flooding and the government back in Augusta and Portland and Bangor and a few other spots stirred and talked of dredging, and setting things right, and appointed committees and study groups and all that busywork that kept them in office. So be it, things would quiet down and some businesses would move over to the new channel that the river makes by itself as they have done since the beginning of time with no need for mankind.

So here I am getting off the bus and there was no one to meet me. I hoisted up the pack and started the two mile walk to Sara's place, my little three day vacation done and here I was entering the world of man. The place was still agog with talk of the murder. The town had even gotten the sheriff's office to send out a signal across the United States to find George and send him back to face charges.

I frowned. Man alive, things had accelerated in the last few days and someone had to stop it. Where were the two that had been in The Hut? They knew the truth. Why didn't they speak up? Well, obviously, for the same reason 'Manda and I hadn't spoken up. Tinkering around with Christian

sanctity and belief about behavior of man and wife and
those back stair affairs pretty much set the pace and
although dunking ponds were no longer in style, the
thought still lived on.

I got a ride half way there. Sara came along in the car
and there we sat talking, she apprising me as to the state of
the village. Pretty close to a lynching, I surmised. Big
meeting tonight, she told me. You should go, she advised
the innocent me, frightened that I'd say something out of
turn and get 'Manda in trouble, and George not even here
yet from wherever his business appointment was.
Apparently 'Manda hadn't told. I studied Sara, thinking
about her time in The Hut and whosoever with her, waiting
for her to breathe that she knew what had happened, but
she made not a sound. Nor did I, uncertain as to how we,
'Manda and I, should handle this.

So I got myself spruced up, shaved, bathed and off to
the meeting and who should I find in the mob outside the
church hall but The Dick's sister, giving everyone a loving
sister's opinion. She'd cleaned herself up just as I had and
looked pretty good. Course she was young, in her twenties
someplace, pretty dress on, hair neat and all in place, and a
show-piece, no question, and influencing everyone into a
mood of settling this thing once and for all. No need for a
deputy from the county seat, or a judge from Bangor or
Portland. And the whole mob went marching off through
town, someone had a drum and it set a pace and that guy
who played the trumpet got gathered up too, so they had a
horn and drum and a good marching beat and it was a
healthy little parade around the three blocks of the center of
town, in and out, a figure eight, and they marched and
started singing some sort of made up words about truth,

and God, and righteous causes and The Dick's truth about mankind's behavior and those that had wanted him out and the living memory that would forever be his, all this to the tune of Marching Through Georgia, no one knowing the original words, but making up their own phrases to the music. The music was enthusiastic, and people who might have been doubtful about this affair felt their bones stir and joined the mob. It was big, but boded ill. George was in deep trouble. And he hadn't even been in town.

I longed to give 'Manda a call, but held true to my decision. Probably a mistake.

So I watched the parade getting gradually bigger. By its fifth time around the figure eight of the three blocks of business section it got more strung out so that the front coming around the corner was almost caught up in the tail just going out of sight. Probably people coming in for the church meeting expecting to see George Cunningham lashed to a deacon's chair on display so everyone could see the guilty party and do whatever chastising to him that they felt was needed.

Who hired him to come here?

What was he supposed to do? Why'd he come?

What did he do here?

What did he say to people?

Did he try and correct people's unchristian behavior?

Who did he focus on and why them?

Let's hear one of them types stand up and tell what they was doing and how he'd stop them and what's it like now for them?

And people would get up and give testimonials? Take Bertram Hillsworth, the town drunk, one of several but he had the guts, or stupidity, to stand up. Heather reached over

and took the pint bottle from his left hand as he swayed, a
hiccup to start and then his story, always drunk, and his
poor wife suffering him all these years. The Dick had come
up to him and took his Jack Daniels and simply dropped it
on his head, broken glass in the street and whiskey down his
back and some on his right shoulder and of course he didn't
know it because he laid in the street there for about an hour,
unconscious. When he awoke he laid there thinking it over,
dreaming of the new man he'd be. He needed that kind of
treatment for years but his poor wife didn't want to hurt
him and now how he could hear them all down the street at
the front of the church where The Dick was honking forth
about the guidance of the bottle. Arthur Bradley poked him
in the other side and said, a bit too loud for everyone to
hear, "It ain't bottle. It's Bible. They were singing about the
Bible." He gave Hillsworth a shove to start him off again.
Yessiree, The Dick was straightening up the town and
anyone who said he wasn't should be shoved over the edge
into the chasm. There were Amens and calls of Right, Right,
Right-on and such.

And Bernice's plight got a review. Her parents were old,
no question, but spotty people here and there shouted out
how they'd done all they could and Bernice had been
slipping into unheard of conduct on the streets and at
dances. We could all see it, we were told, and by gum some
out-of-towner got up and recited the limerick about the lady
riding the tiger and the tiger was the devil in disguise and
Bernice, tender, innocent child that she was (seventeen, five
foot nine and amply endowed with curves all over and a
bosom suitable for a nursing mother of twins) and tending
to too much exposure of skin when she was running
errands for her folks or working in their garden. Well, she

was put on the straight and narrow by our own B&B and straightened right out and was turning into the most beautiful, well dressed young lady and all thanks to B&B taking the time and the money to spruce her up. Some folks thought this wasn't exactly proper for an older man to be involved with her, but she was soon to go off to college to be a physician all thanks to B&B. The Dick watched and even had counseling sessions with Bernice to help her and keep her from the advances of amoral drunks and drug slingers and people like that George Cunningham who was only after her body. Now he's gone, but we understand how much B&B has been doing to help her along too. Some guy from the English Cask bar over this side of Ellsworth near the highway poked me and sneered about B&B "gettin' it". I shushed him 'fore someone heard this sacrilege.

We were in the hall now, people after people pouring in and the place echoing with calls for George Cunningham to come forward, but of course he wasn't here, and his name became a chant that went on for maybe five minutes before the Reverend got folks calmed down and B&B to the floor for a personal experience. He related coming to pick up Bernice one weekend and she had gone with that Cunningham bloke to someplace and didn't get back 'till around eleven and looking a little disheveled and almost in tears. The place positively shook with the calls and yells and pandemonium directed at the real devil amongst us all. I felt terrible for 'Manda over by the door, cowed, then several women taking someone out. 'Manda, I was sure.

It was pandemonium. Yelling, shouting, whistles, bedlam. A few, it looked like, were readying for a fight, after all, this was big stuff for a small isolated village. So what would you expect? It sounded, however, to me that the vigilante committee was going to be called out, resurrected from some far ago time. Prance out amid cheers and exhortations. It was like a good, old-fashioned Western. It gathered everyone up into this great one hundred percent village hysteria.

An old guy was up at the podium, hollering along with the rest. It was the old retired doctor, come here (Sara had told me) like five years ago. He had an aura of respectability and trust, but there he was like the rest, hollering away. I pushed my way through the men, women and children plus a few dogs out for a holiday party and this was it. I hadn't realized that the people were so out of sorts, aching for a change before winter came and locked everyone in. They sure were a rattled bunch. Up on the podium the Doc looked at me. He was saying something with his eyes and gesturing with his head. Amid all the racket and noise I followed the trajectory of his eyes, and there on the wall was this door, pretty much recessed, a glass front and inside a fire hose and valve. I frowned. I hardly knew the guy and looked back to him, raising an arm now and obviously shouting along with everyone else, yet his eyes were on me and now nodding. I may be dumb, but I caught on. He and I were going to control this mob if it got out of hand. My God! What a great idea. I had to protect my love any way possible whether she was here or not. I gave him a down thrust of the head and he returned it with a giant wink that twisted his lip almost up to his ear.

I slid past people caught up in the mood and got the fire hose, it had a control valve on the nozzle so I was in business. I turned on the control valve in the tiny closet which activated the hose at my command the moment I squeezed the nozzle. I dragged it through the people to the edge of the podium, where he and two others were standing and shouting along with everyone. I lifted the nozzle of the fire hose and looked around, studying the situation and where to direct the aim. No one paid any attention to the hose snaking across the floor amid their feet. The enthusiasm for what was about to happen, the trial, in absentia as far as the culprit was concerned was going full bore. If it got any worse, and it would, the walls might vibrate off their foundations. Wow! And all directed at poor Mr. Innocent, George Cunningham.

I was watching the old Doc for any hints, kind-a hoping for my chance to spray down the players in the game, but it didn't come. It was early on in this meeting, but I nevertheless saw the Doc's eyes go wide and then a smile creep across his face. Beyond him two of the supposed community town hall workers, selectmen or mayors, were standing shouting away, also ready to try and run things. We will see. I had paid no attention to these town leaders throughout the time I had been here, just expected the town to run right so paid no attention to them. Their look said they needed me for they were sensing what was going to happen. The old doctor was smiling, almost laughing, and thrusting his clenched fists shoulder high.

I released the trigger and a fountain of spray issued forth into the air wetting down all the people in the first three rows. There was a new sound now, screaming and chair rows being emptied. The trigger closed and the shower stopped, but it had had its effect. The whole place fell silent except for the movement of all these sprinkled people. It was the doctor's moment and he took it.

"Now you people listen here!" he repeated, shouting to his best, and the crowd turned quiet.

"Now this here meeting ain't no meeting 'less you people shut yer mouths and listen up. Jed here is in charge and will tolerate only one speaker at a time. So you others listen up and pay attention so's you can say yer piece." He was backing off the podium and Jed pressing forward calling some man's name. "You want to say something so stand up and say it."

Thus the meeting got to order and thus, I supposed, George's guilt was sealed. That's all they'd think about as Mr. Thibideau stood up to give his ten cents worth. He said it well, very impartial, but that wasn't what they wanted.

So the serious part got started. Jed ran a good meeting, but it was still noisy and boisterous with shouts and stamps and applauses and whistles and people pounding sticks on the floor, and at least once on each other.

There were lots of good things said about The Dick, testimonials you'd call them, exhortations about how he'd cradled the poor and destitute into a religious group with everyone helping everyone else and sharing food and places to stay. Now our town ain't but a little place, but it was a great moment when these people got up and said their pieces. Yes, The Dick was a great man. His loss was manifest.

Then there were lots of bad things said about The Dick. He cleaned up the streets at 10pm and that was annoying. All the crowd out front of the church every day and night were a constant mob to have to walk through each time you went into town or the stores for something. That was a bad thing. The two saloons, the cocktail lounge groaned about the eleven o'clock closing time cutting into profits and folk, at least the cocktail crowd, liked to stay late, no drinks, but good conversation. Then his poking into the construction to make sure code was followed was an annoyance and getting your face beat in because you used the wrong size nails for example, was plumb ignorant. Following certain women home scared some ladies, and his banging on doors and doing interviews with the house owner or renter was un-American, and him filling out documents, and questionnaires had no purpose but his own to see who everyone was. There was a riot at this point because some husband thought he was just trying to get all the girls and women of child bearing age lined up so he could establish a dynasty here on the Maine coast. The movement to change the name of the town that he had started was represented by the group of three old ladies and two old wheel-chaired men. They said it was harmless and others cried that mail would be sent to all the wrong places and another little fracas. Some eighteen men that been beaten up in the middle of Main Street at eleven in the morning, usually on Tuesdays but by no means every Tuesday, insisted on retribution for, according to one, The Dick was playing out his own reenactment of the Okay Corral epic right here in Portage, so named by the early colonial settlers who had come from England before the word-nickers had evolved and given the poor collection of log homes a fancier name. That historical bit sent the young men who hadn't heard that tale before and were standing at the back by the doors, half in and half out, into a noisy realm of remarks and beer until Jed threatened to have the police put 'em in the hoosegow for littering them there beer cans all over the front of the building. Thus it went. However everyone agreed, in a great crashing movement that the town was straight-laced, but a proud town now, not one of those roadside collections of houses like otherwise up and down the state 'cause of the depression, lack of jobs and Democrats what with their colorful tourists blocking the dirt main streets so honest folk couldn't get through. This attack on The Dick was so imbedded into history now that his loss was tantamount to a national calamity.

It went on. Three matrons, big busted types, forced Andrew McCarthy up front to utter his endorsement of a lynching committee to see to the details. He kept toppling left and right and acting loose and falling asleep and needed help staying upright. Everyone gave their greatest of hollers to support his motion, thinking physical, not legislative.

"Tell us what you said," cried out old Theresa Widdafork from up Sara's way who was helping hold the old gent upright and for some reason the whole community seated in the center place full of people fell silent. Martha Janbury wiped his mouth and prodded him. It was noticeable that they were quite familiar with Andrew giving truth to the gossip about what he was up to with these three elderly cases.

"Go on. Tell 'em. We was hollering for The Dick. Tell 'em."

"He straightened up for a moment, looked all around overhead above people's heads and started. "Tet and I —" He stopped, took the handkerchief and wiped his mouth, and coughed once. He went on, "Tet's a cute name, don't ye think?" He stopped to grin at the people.

Martha was pounding on him and he was wobbling. "YOU BASTARD, You never told me you was with her! Why you —" and she pounded him in the face. He went down and then a pin could drop and we'd all hear. He was giggling. She went to kick him but Martha stopped her. "Make him tell his story."

The sounds in the hall started up but then he fell again as Martha and Theresa got him up, held him. Some man nearby handed him what looked suspiciously like a paper bag and muttered at him, not overheard by many as they were not quieting down well. This was going to be a tempestuous revelation. He was holding the open end of the bag to his mouth, leaned his head back, wiped his mouth again on the handkerchief, got his arm around Theresa and spoke his piece.

"We was up there, Martha and me, out fer a walk. Saw The Dick ahead and kinda slipped off the road fer a moment." Coughing, a tilt of the bag and he continued, being held tight at the audience by the two. "We kinda slipped out of the trees where we'd been sitting and looked fer The Dick but he was nowhere to be seen. The coast was clear." He stopped, turned to Martha and said, "You want me ta go and tell all these nice folks?"

She hit him in the stomach, but as he saw it coming and held on tight he stayed upright and Tet whispered loud enough for the first two rows to hear. "Go on tell 'em what we saw?"

"We was hiding, ya know. A voice came out of The Hut across the chasm. Said somethin'."

Tet muttered for him, "You mussel head. We heard a woman talking, I thought it was The Dick, but it was a woman. Tell 'em."

"It was a woman." His legs went and the two grabbed him and straightened him up. "I thought it was The Dick but she said he'd gone up the path. You know the one by the chasm on this side?"

"Oh shut up," spoke Martha. "Tell 'em."

"We was gonna go to The Hut but these—"

The assemblage was astir, mutterings and pointed looks. Someone yelled. "Okay, Andy, who was it. They meeting The Dick? Gonna make love to—"

He got no farther. Someone shut him up, but the words were on the air and everyone was listening and not chattering away. The words, "Who, Spit it out. Speak up, Come on Andrew. Let's hear it all. Martha, you tell it, and soon."

Theresa said. "A woman, he said. Sara Bradmarski."

Andrew got the lead back. "Yeah and it weren't Marty neither, who was with her. It was the guy who got punched in the nose. Remember him?" A sigh went through the hall in the quiet. People held their breaths looking this way and that. They were looking for Sara, and looking for Jeff, the guy with the broken nose. Jeff. It was old stuff by now, part of history but now history was reliving itself. Jeff in The Hut with Sara? That was supposed to be over. What would Marty do now? Sara! Her!

There was a little crush of people over by the left rear door among the crowd and they were wrestling someone forward.

I watched thunderstruck. Sara, my step-daughter. My God! And with Jeff again. In my mind's eye I saw 'Manda and me trying to get Marty and Sara together. And it'd broken down because Marty never left the house. A set up for the two to meet there together, to get Sara pregnant, a baby missing from their lives up 'till that very moment. But Jeff got there first. Had they consummated the act? The wrong man? My God.

And someone tugged on the hose and I looked down into the eyes of 'Manda. She must have been outside for a while, threatened by the whole thing and slipped away. Now she was back and her eyes were speaking to me. Our big, fat idea. And the wrong man got there. Sara still liked him, or loved him? Had she been seeing him? And we didn't know or suspect Jeff!

From somewhere else Jeff was being dragged forward to face the music.

Someone yelled, "So it wasn't George like we thought." And he finished over the yelling and noise and everyone heard. "Jeff killed him! 'Cause he knew The Dick would track him down and make him pay."

More pandemonium.

Jeff was up on the podium with me and Marty backing away from this. What else to do? This was what the meeting was about. It was to get the George man, but here was the real killer.

Sara was out on the floor yelling and people fell quiet, listening. "It wasn't us," she called, siding with Jeff in their untrue love.

"It wasn't us. Yes, we were in there chatting." Groans from the audience. Mistrust. She lies. "And we heard him." She stopped because of all of the hissing. "We heard The Dick yelling at us for being untrue." There was more noise placing retribution on her. Retribution to come.

"Jeff or Marty?"

They were yelling at her and calling for punishment, someone's loud voice calling for the Retribution of God on this woman. Sounded just like The Dick, the new reverend for Portage, our good leader now dead, and he did so much for us, showing where we went wrong. Everyone was quiet while this one yelled on, both hands high overhead and called the True Christ to come and claim the punishment.

Marty was back by the door now, surrounded by supporters and him or the others telling him to renounce her right now. He started to shout, we could see it. You had to shout to be heard at all, but Jed had given me a nod and I did as directed. I hit the trigger of the nozzle of the fire hose and a spray went out over the left side of the hall.

It did quiet the mob down so's Jed could call for quiet and order and it worked.

"So we got a new problem to solve for the good of the community. You think Jeff is the agent of death in this?"

Someone was reciting the Lord's Prayer.

The group tied Jeff's hands behind him, and rapped their fists on him from time to time.

Then we heard Andy. He'd come alive amid all this. He was standing tall and straight and pointing at Jeff and Sara and his words were: "Now that man and that woman were in The Hut together. Lord only knows what they did. But I never saw Jeff go up any path. He started across the rope bridge to us, dragging Sara along with him. And I'd say willingly. No one followed them. Not anyone that I could see." He looked at Theresa. She nodded and called out, "True, true." We all thought she'd said her piece but suddenly she called out with an arm outstretched at Sara, "No one else was in there. Just this woman with another man not her husband, and you know what a man and a woman do together. You know what they did. They did months ago, too. Remember when he got his nose broke." She cackled and pointed, and then danced up and down, so help me, like a chicken.

"Where did The Dick go?"

"He went up this side of the chasm, yelling back at The Hut and who was in it, chastising them."

"Why didn't he cross over to them?"

"He coulda, but didn't. He stayed this side like he was chasing someone else."

"Did you see anyone else?"

" 'Course not. George grew up around here. He'd know all the paths."

"You saw him?"

"No. I said I didn't see no one else. He was yelling, though, The Dick was."

"Why was he yelling?"

"To stop someone I guess. Who knows?"

"You said you saw no one."

"Just them two fucking away the evening, I suppose."

Sara yelled and started forward but Marty there stopped her.

"That's not true," she was screaming.

I looked down at 'Manda at the edge of the podium on the floor, her eyes back to me.

"So when you saw these two, at that point The Dick was going farther upstream?"

"You know it."

"Why do I know it?"

"I just told you so."

Jed looked at Burside, the town's once-in-awhile sheriff's deputy. "Get him outta here."

At the door Arthur McCarthy got turned back, and yelled over the hubbub. "I ain't seen The Dick since. And the kids came back and said there weren't nobody on the trails, either side. You should stop them kids from going 'round there. It's fucking dangerous and someone'll get hurt."

Jed turned to Sara, standing alone, six feet away from Marty with a few men around him. The men were curious and trying to ask him questions.

"So you," she came to attention. "You see or hear anyone around The Hut while you were in there?" He asked the same of Jeff who replied he thought he heard a scraping once but was busy with something else. Laughter from assorted people.

Jeff yelled out, almost like in a panic, "Anyone see any strangers hanging around the town the other night?"

Jed bent over and whispered to Doc. "I don't like this. We all thought it was George Cunningham. Even Bernice came up to me and said something about it, mostly that it was George, but I suspect B&B put her up to it. What'd ya think?"

Someone close by said, "What about B&B. He'd know."

I heard one of 'em on the stage say, "I wouldn't trust B&B with my grandmother. So I suppose he probably coulda set her up. All he's trying to do is see that George hasn't got a chance in the world of stealing his girl away from him. George is married. How could he go after Bernice anyway?"

"I'll call the State and see if any of their leads have found George. You better talk with his wife. That 'Manda always seemed like a level-headed girl to me. Shame for her for not keeping track of what her husband's doing."

"He's off all the time on business. Pretty hard for a wife to keep track of him then, he has to be trusted alone."

"You think she trusts him? Him walking downtown and stopping to visit with Bernice? I don't wonder B&B don't want him around. Maybe it's just talk but when Bernice and George stop and talk who knows what they do other times?

She's getting on to marrying age. George is clean and good looking, he's got a good job, why not George? Besides, he must be ten to fifteen years younger than B&B. A divorce is common and easy these days, could take two weeks to several months. Bernice maybe couldn't wait that long. 'Course Bernice and he could have all the joys of marriage before the divorce is final, after all." He poked Jed in the side to emphasize his remarks. "The first baby only takes even as little as a few hours whereas all the others take nine months. So what'd you think?" And the doctor was grinning at Jed.

I stood there, listening to the two and wondering just how come the town had settled on George Cunningham as the culprit, the murderer. Was it all really B&B's remarks that did it? Where else could they have gotten that idea? Somehow it had to come to an end because he was no murderer. I was pondering this, and if that erroneous idea didn't go away what would 'Manda and me have to do to get the truth out of the box and agreed on. Then grieve for The Dick and his God inspired life. And there was the sister. She had to be convinced.

And as if in direct contact with the almighty, there was The Dick's sister's voice calling out across the hubbub of the meeting hall.

"NOW LISTEN UP YOU ALL. Yes, some of you know I'm his sister. Been here in town a couple of days getting the lay of the land and what I like and I don't like." People were quieting and drawing away leaving her like a lone statue in the middle of the hall, a vast circle around her, all attentive and quiet. Funny how some people have command of a situation, and this was an example. Take B&B for instance. He had command of a lot, but he was quiet, and things got done his way I suppose all the time, but with none of this loud bravado. A man's way is different from a woman's, I think. Look at her. The other day out on the sand bar she was grubby, unkempt, sour as bittersweet berries, foul mouthed and anti-everybody. It's the same woman now but look at her charm a town, a full load of ordinary people including me. There she stands moving her arms up and down and changing her position and direction to face one side and then the other and those in back, and every move is accented with the way she stands, hip up one side, down another. She ain't no dummy, you can tell that, using her femininity as a tool here. George's death assured, that miniskirt tugged tight around her bottom showing off those smooth-looking, tan thighs says tons about what she could offer a man. That part from the waist down was mighty attractive, and no doubt accented by the narrowness of her waist in comparison, and of course that made her upper parts seem all the more daring. And looking around at the crowd listening intently as she postured and called out her message, I had to believe she was no new one to this sort of thing. Yes, she had power. I suppose in the fifteen hundreds Joan d'Arc must have had the same impact on the natives of France although her dress was different, but probably had much the same effect. And the message she extolled was giving that powerful effect. I could look around and see people swaying, nervous and twitchy with growing energy approaching a surge like a wave coming in, engulfing everyone. A whole community paralyzed with inaction but the bursting point growing.

Chapter 57
B&B

From over left came the voice of Big and Burly, B&B himself booming out over her, and his form appeared through the people. Walking out in his stilted bad-knees kind of gait, one arm pointing at her, the other on his cane, held out forward like coming off a tournament field after killing the Red Knight, and his voice yelling that this woman knew what had happened, she had seen it in her booth at the fair in California, the Spirit had come over her and related what was happening as it occurred. She knew. And she came right here following the direction of the Greatest of all Spirits as it spoke.

I crinkled my nose. Hogwash, I said to myself. The Dick fell off the chasm at night. Late at night. And this female bimbo says the great Spirit came and told her during the day? Nuts! Obviously a lie, but they all were eating it up. I found I was squirming and twitching in place, all a-bothered by this travesty.

Now B&B was telling everyone how this is The Dick's sister and their bond so tight that the minute it happened the Spirit brought it to her, melding its great world-wide knowledge that all God's have, knowledge from The Dick's last moments as he fell tumbling into the chasm his screams ringing out echoing over the sides, pushed by that dastardly Cunningham. Calling out for help in his last moments, crying the name of his killer, crunching into a dead mass on the rocks below.

I never knew B&B was such an orator, deep voice echoing out as an amazement to me, and he was carrying them along. The girl still twisting and posturing as if his puppet. The two of them creating a dark mood in the hall. Up on that raised structure that was the podium with the two chairmen and below this lynching mob and I wanted to yell out and argue points, but this was nothing to do with reason. It was all emotional release. And the people were in the midst of this maelstrom of feeling. I shook my head, seething with bolts of power within me ready for the blast off into their false thinking, into their story, killing these false urges and sending all the people home.

The feel of a hand on my calf as I twitched there in place holding onto the nozzle of the hose. I looked down to see 'Manda! She was there at the edge of the podium-stand looking up at me. Terror in her eyes.

Her eyes, fastened on me, and my urge to call out what we knew was the truth. No, those facts are wrong. But I could not yell it out.

The sister was calling out again, commanding the assembly hall, a vast room full of men, women, children even, all staring at this woman in the middle of the place, her arms reaching straight out from her sides, and moving up overhead, calling on an invisible God, it was so apparent to everyone, calling on her Christian God, nay, her brother's Christian God, to reveal himself and affirm her views, her views that he, that Cunningham, having debased his wife for another person, an over-stacked high school girl, and then defying his God and vows to his wife, wanting only this high school girl's body to salve his own passions brought death to her brother, a deed that must be avenged. "It was his voice as he died in the pushing, in the falling, in the crashing of his frail body onto the rocks below, his screams lost under the great noise of the river in the gorge, in the chasm, yet calling across a continent to avenge his death just as the primitive God of the Israelites called for the eye for eye and tooth for tooth, that ethereal voice reaching across the continent to her in California, calling to me, his sister, calling a Knowing that travelled across the continent, a Knowing that called out as he fell in his destruction. 'I am being killed by an impure man debauching this Christian Goodness for the sake of the body of a young girl. I call on you, my sister, to avenge this evil. You must act. Come to the scene. Avenge me.' Those were the words that came to me and brought me here."

Suddenly her calls changed. Now more rough, more deep-voiced and more force also showing in her arms as they held up-reached, allowing the loose sleeves of her blouse to fall away revealing strong muscles arm to shoulder. She gripped the left sleeve and ripped it from its blouse, then the other, one of the rips pulling down the material and ripping more to reveal one of those big, chest encompassing bras of a well-endowed female, an ancient Biblical tactic that called to all mankind to act now in the pursuit of justice. Pure ancient emotion. God calling in its primitive way that her whole being be thrust into revenge. And she stood there, still crying the word she had already uttered, repeating, in a strong, almost masculine voice, now directly in her basic goal, the death of her brother's killer. Death by dismemberment. Death by crucifixion. Death by dismemberment. But death for sure.

And 'Manda, muscles of one hand still clenching into my calf, nails digging, staring at her while with the other, knuckles curled at her mouth, stared at this woman from the Old Testament revealing herself, all but slashing her arms, her face, her breasts, with some obsidian knife as did the women of old when a death, a travesty, an unspeakable deed was committed to her people.

The sister was calling for 'Manda to come out, come forth and stand with her against the cowardice of a people who faced with clear evidence of a foul deed against this family and this community refused to act and complete the circle of life, conceived, born, lived, procreated, life unto death, the circle of life completed, failed to act on this obvious transgression to our ancient gods.

She had them in the palm of her hands. The atmosphere pure emotion, and 'Manda had left my leg, was walking toward the woman, reaching with her arms as she approached, and then against the sister 'Manda embraced her, holding on to her as she had held on to me once, not so long ago, holding her and echoing every word as the sister spoke, called, yelled with her for the end of this man, once her loving husband, father of her children, but now so truly having turned to the way of the Devil's minions. Kill. Stop this evil invading our town. This evil personified by this foul deed. Kill!

This is my 'Manda? She was captivated by this atmosphere, as was the whole mass of a cowed, unthinking mob. Mass hysteria coming, maybe here at this very moment. And 'Manda part of it. She knew the truth. Why couldn't she sever herself from them and proclaim the truth? We knew, she and I. This was the perfect opportunity to proclaim the truth. But she was silent, and then this sister-thing, crying to the heavens for the cleansing of this atmosphere into which we all had fallen, cast away our own pleasures to follow the ways of communities laid out by The Dick, by the Bible, by true believers.

I fingered the trigger on the nozzle, half ready to press and flood the room, maybe in manner of the cleansing waters of John the Baptist, come here to abet this travesty.

'Manda was out there calling for her own husband's death for loving another woman and abandoning her when truth and love and family should be more important. This was the True Way. The sister was leading her, and from somewhere she had gotten a Swiss Army knife, I could see the small red blade flashing in the overhead lights as she slashed her left arm. A red strip appeared and 'Manda was hugging her, gripping her, holding her hand and then the sister was slashing at 'Manda. Caught her on the right side near the waist and as the crowd yelled and hollered and danced and surged toward the two women in the shouting belief and glee, saw her swipe the blade in 'Manda's blouse and up-lift the cloth and reveal something of her underclothes, pink or white and 'Manda sheering away but forced back by the press of people and the two hugging each other as the crowd called "Dick and 'Manda and Sister" to lead the calling for Cunningham to come to his judgment. It was mass hysteria. 'Manda, caught in it, calling with the rest of them.

I looked at Jed and the two Masters of Ceremonies and saw them entrapped too, everyone yelling and hugging and encircling friends and unknowns, and jumping almost to a dance of total cataclysmic mass sacrifice of themselves in this natural mania, unexpected, even unknown, as to what they were doing.

That was when they brought in Cunningham. Disheveled, clasped by three burley men who despite his own height, towered over him. His nose had bled for the dark red-brown of dried blood ran in a slant across his face and down his left side into his neck area.

Dead silence, then all closed in on the man. The man who had been off on one of his business trips and not in attendance that night in which The Dick went over the side.

Accusations came loud and clear from individuals and the whole mood took them up and it became a chant. The kill, truth, retribution, and revenge were its meat, and its focus was Cunningham. Immediate closure.

Death to kill the infection lest we all became infected by the evil of this one man. They were jumping up and down, waving their arms and yelling and 'Manda and the sister, and now Bernice were the center and screaming for the judgment. Who would make the judgment? Who would thus release the group to do the deed and open goodness to enter? They had swiped the knife or something through Bernice's hair and she, shorn, looked completely distant. B&B was somewhere close, grabbing for Bernice and getting only a sleeve as she was whisked away in the mob to be pawed and pitied and farther disrobed ready for some minor punishment. 'Manda was there too, blouse ripped and slacks peeled around the hip, and the sister with more slashes at the shoulder and back where her dress had been ripped away. I thought of a stoning, and was glad we were in the assembly hall, for the mob was in a mood and so had I been. Now somehow, I was seeing us all back in some middle-eastern, old testament village and the mood reflecting a great death wish, if not for a clear sensible trial, which this was becoming. No one was free and no one was in command, except the sister.

Booming voices were shouting a melee of questions at the cowering Cunningham, trying to raise himself to a commanding stance and being bullied down, shoved, prodded, venom spitting people pressing at him.

Someone in the mob with a baritone voice, called out that, "Since he had lured him to the chasm, and then pushed-" It was lost in a great mass of shouting and that was as far as he got. Was the true God intervening? Someone had to stop this descent from civilization.

I hit the trigger releasing the nozzle control which thrust a great column of water toward the ceiling. Was it me that did that? Was it the true God of the Christians that did that? Was it the human spirit that lurks in all men to make a slowly improving world that did it? Who knows. I know not.

A great mist of water descended over the entire hall, blasting off the ceiling and dislocating one of the ceiling lights which crashed down making a noise louder than all the yelling that was going on.

Silence.

They were all looking at the podium. At me.

My mouth opened to call out the truth, a truth that would reveal Mandy and me as a couple of adulterers, even though it was an exaggeration, untrue at this point, when words burst into the damp quiet of this community of people crammed into this Assembly Hall not meant for so many. Words from B&B.

"All ye true believers listen up. This is a trial here in our own town and we must act and act now. It is us that must act. Look aloft all ye good people."

He stood there, revealed as folks moved slowly away from him, and there he was in the middle, damp like the others, one arm around Bernice, hair shorn, holding her blouse over her bosom as best she could where the mob

had ripped her clothes in their frenzies. B&B's other arm
raised with his hand pointing up.

I was frozen, mouth open ready to call out the truth, but
I looked up too, as did everyone. Overhead was a roughly
square gap in the ceiling from where the light fixture had
fallen. With it, the ancient trap door into the ceiling that had
been the light's anchor point was also revealed. A dark
square hole beckoned and B&B was putting it to use. "You
men, go up into the attic and throw a two by four over the
gap. Let the rope fall to us. We down here will place the
rope, hoist, and death to the killer of the finest man that
God ever sent to cleanse our community. Are you with me?
ARE YOU WITH ME!" A question, but now a statement.
"YOU ARE WITH ME!' A call to action.

The response was immediate, seven men separated and
were gone to reappear around the edge of the hole, holding
a heavy beam across, bracing it and all amid the scuffling
and scraping noise of the deed the entire crowd, to a man,
were chanting the great chant that was to be the end of the
evening, the end of the man. "WE ARE WITH YOU!"
Hands were going up into the air, fists were clenched,
voices strong and I was standing there like a dummy, mouth
open and history passing me by. Untrue history. An incident
they painted that was untrue and I stood there like a
voiceless imbecile. Around me all over, the clash of all these
voices screaming the latest chant.

B&B, with the girl on his arm, had somewhere found
one of those four by four pallets and was standing on it, a
big man anyway, tall, he was even taller now and above the
heads of everyone suddenly with an abrupt motion which
dislodged Bernice's arm from her bosom and sounds, gasps,
loud gasps of amazement at B&B and his girl lost in the

shouting of YES, YES, YES. NOW. JUSTICE. JUSTICE
FOR THE DICK. It caught on, whoever had started it, and
the mess of ants, or worker bees blindly following some
devil-leader, began a slow surge to somewhere, a vast
movement of everyone. A vast circling around Cunningham
so that all would see this thing, once man. B&B and Bernice
struggling with her clothes were both on the palette for all
to see and follow, for that was what was happening now,
the mood had changed and the words from B&B flooded
over the masses. He was reciting the crime as the entire
room full began a great slow revolution around the culprit.

"Yes, this man, a minion of the devil, even with a
beautiful and faithful wife, tried to seize this woman…" and
he gave a shake to Bernice, ordinary sized as she was, that
almost cast her off the pallet and into the crowd's arm,
again breaking her futile attempts to make herself decent,
"…as his own, yes tried to take her unto himself as his
concubine. She came to me, yes me, to save her. He is evil
and an infection in the good life of our people, of us. Of
each one of us. He must be destroyed, despite his living
wife who is still attached faithfully to him, and knowing The
Dick had been here to save her."

"Sent by God," came the sister's voice from somewhere
in the crowd. This God fearing disciple working to bring
God's way to us all was lured by this man to the chasm
where others, Jeff and Sara, fornicating in The Hut, saw the
deed. Yes, he pushed The Dick over the side and into the
maelstrom below, to his death.

I couldn't understand his reasoning. He also was caught
up in this thing of his own making.

Cunningham, they had a rope neck-tied around his
throat, no hangman's knot to break a neck and reduce

struggling, this a simple slip knot to hoist and strangle him, a prop to his slinging back and forth as he struggled to stay alive, slowly strangling the body of air, of voice, just pain and suffering slowly to everyone's enjoyment.

How do you stop a scene like this?

I aimed the nozzle at B&B and his girl, being squeezed into his side and unaware, blindly yelling his litany of death of a non-Christian, an adulterer who hadn't come back to his wife nor faithfully followed the ways of his fathers in behavior toward women.

That lying, selfish blob of a smelly, big body with his high school girl attachment was making a travesty of Christian goodness.

I released the trigger and the thin powerful stream struck the two together, further ripping her protective cloth from her grasp as she pressed into B&B's fat carcass for protection and forced his head to turn away and grab her rather than toppling for he had no cane with him on the precarious stage of a pallet. They were turned partially from me and no words escaped, just the splash of the stream next to him.

And the hall was a single mass of silence as they studied what was happening midst their private fantasies over B&B and his girl, her beauties being demonstrated, a fat B&B, fat to the death awaiting him from diabetes. Yes. God had already tapped him as one to die of his excesses.

I called out the truth as they held onto Cunningham, half strangled already from a too-tight rope, eyes bulging, gasping air, face turning red.

"WILL NO ONE TELL THE TRUTH OF THIS INCIDENT?"

I was looking at 'Manda, standing there. The sister and she locked in an embrace. But there was no recognition in her face.

I called out my truth, called over their heads, exerting as powerful a voice as I could, remembering public speaking course in college, remembering as I called out, to lower my voice, yell with the deepest voice I could muster. A deep resonant tone they told me afterwards. A deep voice that no one knew I had, much less myself. I called out the message.

Someone gave a tug to the rope and it straightened taut, stretching Cunningham to his tiptoes and I knew the moment was close. I saw B&B's mouth open to cast his vote for death but that made me one move ahead in this deadly game. My words overpowering his start.

"There is a truth here. Truth about Cunningham. Now listen. Listen you all." The water had silenced them and I silenced them more.

"Sara and Jeff in The Hut together making love, they say. Okay. They heard noises. They heard The Dick coming to the rope bridge. He had discovered them and called them fornicators." That brief bit caught their attention. The partially naked Bernice had whetted their appetites for pornography and here was someone leading them down the path, to let the scene run in their imaginations. They were quiet, internally stimulated, wanting more, like people everywhere.

"He yells and they yell, hiding, yet threatening him if he mounts the bridge. He goes up the trail on that side. There is no path on the other side. He calls out Sara's name, recognizing her voice. He stares across the chasm and Jeff comes out, revealing himself in there with her, making love, they say."

"Liar" comes out of the mob, from Jed's voice on the podium, then Sara's voice somewhere from the floor, denying, trying one last time to cleanse herself.

"Picture this, The Dick on the bridge. Jeff throwing rocks at him. The Dick starts up the path."

"Liar." Again from Jed, and then Sara's voice. "I was there alone. No one else was there. I was reflecting on life. Doing a retreat-like The Dick said. I –"

The mobs call for her to 'SHUT UP' was almost unanimous.

"Sara. Fucking Jeff. That was you." I call over her denials. And it had the desired effect. Everyone went quiet like a blanket had been pulled over them, wanting to hear more in so many words. And I gave it.

"I know it is true for someone was with me. Someone else in this Hall was there and knows it is true. Will that person step up here and repeat the truth?" I waited, tense. Would 'Manda have the courage to stand here with me and acknowledge that what I said was true? Would she?

No. I barely dared look over at her, fearing that some smart ass person would point to her and she'd be exposed. Another fornicator, adulteress, cockolding her husband when he was away on business trips and having an affair with me. Some thought it but weren't sure. If they called that out, because she and I were always together, there was just enough possibility for it to be believed even though it had never happened. No, she stood there clasped to the sister. I caught it in that sweeping glance over the assembly.

"There is another who was there," I yelled.

Someone called out, "But what happened?"

"Stones. Standing on that risky rope bridge was dangerous. And The Dick was no fool."

"The Dick started up the other side where there was no path to cross over at the covered bridge and get those two cheaters." I had let my voice quiet, I was almost whispering, but the silence, supreme, held and my words went forth.

"But two others had been there and were already retreating up The Hut side of the chasm. They were getting away, sneaking off before Sara and Jeff caught them. Before The Dick discovered them. They knew what had happened. They were eye witnesses."

From the silent mob, the whole town of Portage, came a few calls of "who" and died away in the silence. But no one stepped forward.

"Will that person step forth?" And I looked over the mob that stared back expectantly.

"I was one. We saw and heard."

I raised one hand part way, as if listening, reenacting that moment. "And The Dick saw something of these two, or heard a stone skip, a branch snap, something. He called out someone's name, he had seen-" I dared not say her name. It would be a dead giveaway and 'Manda would be incriminated.

But in the mob was a woman's voice, some gossip who had visions of everyone in town being cheaters, some embittered wife, this voice yelled out, "AMANDA CUNNINGHAM?" It was the sudden sound of a voice in a darkened, dead, silent room. "Amanda Cunningham." Two words. But it set the assembly hall alive. Hushed whisperings and lookings around. Where is she?

I saw the sister, grasping 'Manda to her side, leaning away and looking horrified at the woman at her side. Others near recognized 'Manda and slowly moved away making a small isolated circle around the two. The sister now moved away a few steps and 'Manda stood alone as the point, the focus.

All this was the dead giveaway.

'Manda had no choice. It was her. She had been with me, the two of us spying on Sara and Jeff, and The Dick.

The Doctor's distinct voice came into the silence. "So, the two of you."

The voice of the town, the leader tonight, Jed said, "You two saw – what? What happened next?" And of course he was looking about the room, separating the followers from the few leaders who would support him and the Doctor, and me, in this revelation, someone who had integrity and would straighten out this lynching party and give the town such a bad name throughout the state and this nation.

"What happened next" was a Lamb of Peace sound running about among the citizens.

It was me again, standing on the podium, the nozzle of the hose hanging from my hand. "Yes, it was us together. We heard The Dick coming." There was no need to yell, I quieted to a confidential tone and could see some of them, that great mass of typical people, edging forward to catch every word. "We heard the interchange, the arguments back and forth, the accusations of The Dick that those two were doing wrong." A gradual rumble began, mostly women's voice exhibiting onemanship with The Dick, his so often publically calling for the integrity of man and woman to each other, true to the vows of marriage, and everyone's job was to cleanse.

I pressed ahead, raising my voice. "The stone throwing was to force him to leave the site and leave them alone, but by so doing had revealed themselves, two people who had long before started a union, despite her being married and being punished for it by God through the medium of her husband beating Jeff, and this night by one other, The Dick coming to see that The Hut was secure, and discovering those two trying to escape, afraid of his gaze, his knowledge of their wrong-doing, trying to escape his sight, unable, and trying to stone him away from crossing the rope bridge and bringing them to God's justice. Yes, yes, biblical stoning." I hesitated a long time. "The Dick moved off, going up the trackless town-side of the chasm, the more treacherous side, and hearing sounds across the chasm, branches, stones, something, he knew that two others lurked up there, also trying to escape his gaze. Two others watched him stop and peer to where they were hiding, and he stepped closer to see, to see who?" I stretched it at this point. "To see these two others, indistinct in the dark, but there, also at The Hut? Or watching the two at The Hut? He didn't know, but intrigued, he stepped forward for a better look. There were two others watching The Hut, and Sara and Jeff were trying to escape. He stopped, you know how the chasm is so narrow at the point farther up, and he accosted them across the chasm, calling to–?"

A touch on my arm and here was 'Manda at my side, and not a sound from the people against her now. She was standing next to me. My arm wanted to go around her but it was not appropriate and she was interrupting me, facing the crowd, and saying, "It was me. Us. Trevor and me. We were there watching, and why we did that is a long, long story that we cannot tell even now. But yes, The Dick had us, and as we stood there, looking back at him and he gestured in that preacher-way he had, he stepped toward us to emphasize his words, which started as he does with a call to the Lord to listen to this poor pilgrim in this evil world, that's how he started, and he stepped forward to emphasize the truth of God's word, and, and–" She covered her face with her hands as if seeing the deed all over again. It was dramatic and silence covered the room.

Then a crescendo of, "Yes, yes, go on. He–" Everyone was on their toes to hear. "Yes, yes–"

"He slipped. He heard a slight sound, a crack under his feet, a crackling sound and the edge of the chasm, the stone there cracked and fell. He went with it."

Stone silence.

The rope fell from overhead to the floor. The square of the hatch in the ceiling was dark, there was no one there. Someone of those men had sensed what was happening and let loose of the hanging-rope, but to us on the floor it was a sign. The atmosphere among those many had made the decision and released the victim. He was not guilty. It spoke louder than any action the people might take to exonerate this falsely accused man.

Someone said as much into the remaining silence of the room. He spoke quietly into a silence as loud as if broadcast on a great man-made loud speaker amplified a million times, or as if God himself were announcing from the top of that mountain on which Moses had heard him speak.

It was finished. I felt 'Manda's arm go around my waist at that moment, holding onto me. 'Manda, forced by the situation to come forth as she inevitably had to. But now her arm around me was sliding away, as was she. I had been left again, alone there before a crush of people, facing a threatening, noxious crowd. But it too, was disintegrating.

Oh 'Manda, why couldn't you have stepped forth sooner? You held back. Yes you finally came to my side in this terrible situation, but only when forced to. If unforced would you have waited it out until it was over and done and who knows what might have happened? The death of your husband? The lynching mood sweeping you along with it?

Now it was over. Some people leaving the assembly hall already, as there are always a few who want to avoid the crowd and leave when the end is apparent.

Now it was over. 'Manda was reciting her husband's itinerary and how he was in Oregon and it could be proved. She had given the itinerary to that group of men who had come for him, and so, despite the time lag of air travel, they would not listen and said he was here and must be judged. He had been aboard a plane to come home, and she was awaiting his return for they usually went out dining upon return, and she had been true to him throughout despite having friends. Some listened, others started leaving. The loyal doctor, not our old community leader but the new one who came over from Ellsworth once a week to tend to the ills of the town, was there at Cunningham's side, checking the release of his neck from its strangling imprint. Some were tsk-tsking 'Manda about her behavior when her husband was away. The sheep were leaving. The storm of wolves and B&B's minions were off already to the bar down town where they hatched their nefarious plans and thus released that tension with B&B leading them I was sure. Bernice had left with her parents. It was over.

Sara had given me a little smile and left with her husband and I thought of 'Manda and me down at The Hut to check them out, expecting she and her husband to have met for a tryst and it was a failure. The wrong man had reached the female. Would she conceive and what life would the child lead as he or she grew to adulthood and would the town's knowledge of this tryst mark him or her for life?

I was amazed that they had accepted my story. It must have broken the hypnotism that had affected everyone. A terrible incident, a close one for the God of the Christians, for the Devil's God and Devil's minions had barely lost a battle. Truth won out, as it should. Yes, evil lives among us. Those that live among us seeking selfish aims, those who would manipulate us, and in a greater sense upset God's world and all its beauty for their own comfort, they lost a battle. Praise God, as The Dick would say.

So 'Manda got her husband back. I don't know what was said at the kitchen table in their house, but she never again showed up at the *Empty Plate* for early morning English muffin and coffee. I went there a few times but it wasn't the same without her. I loved her, I guess. But somehow it wasn't meant to work out.

Sara thought I shouldn't live with her and Marty any more but get my own place. I can understand that. It took about two weeks watching her and Marty before I really got moving. I got in the old car with the jerk driver from down Clute's way and headed on back, stopping to see friends along the way as I had coming up to stay.

The End

www.ingramcontent.com/pod-product-compliance
Lightning Source LLC
Chambersburg PA
CBHW051440260626
47162CB00001B/179